WHAT GOES AROUND

Michael Wendroff

HEAD
of ZEUS

An Aries Book

First published in the UK in 2024 by Head of Zeus,
part of Bloomsbury Publishing Plc

9 7 5 3 1 2 4 6 8

A catalogue record for this book is available from the British Library.

ISBN (HB): 9781035900084
ISBN (E): 9781035900077

Cover design: Simon Michele

Typeset by Siliconchips Services Ltd UK

Printed and bound in Great Britain by
CPI Group (UK) Ltd, Croydon CR0 4YY

Head of Zeus
First Floor East
5–8 Hardwick Street
London ECIR 4RG

WWW.HEADOFZEUS.COM

For my family, forever with me.

Prelude

I'll remember the day I died for the rest of my life.

Prologue

The sign at the gate read, "Trespassers will be shot. Survivors will be shot again."

It was before dawn, the night sky still dark and the compound silent as a cemetery. The cabin loomed in the distance: a den of crime, a place where the armed drug dealers spent much of their time. The police team approached as quietly as they could, the crunch of twigs beneath their boots the only sound to break the eerie silence. Fear tiptoed through their souls, its icy fingers tracing the contours of their restless thoughts. They took a collective inhalation of breath, not knowing if they were walking toward their death. They knew the property owner, the leader of the group, wasn't kidding with his sign.

What they didn't know was that a baby was crawling on the floor of the cabin they were about to storm.

Jon Eddie considered himself a champion. Now he understood he was in for the fight of his life.

Forty-two years old, with bulging eyes, a bushy beard and Fu Manchu mustache, he'd covered himself in self-righteousness, the way his tattoos covered almost every inch of his bulky body. He was proud of the group he'd brought together. Eddie liked to believe he was simply an entrepreneur, as his annual white power music festival, Nordic Fest, attracted skinheads from across the country. Full of music from "hatecore" bands such as Angry Aryans and No Alibi, supported by shouting speakers spewing their idiotic ideology, it provided a nice source of income—in addition to the dues Eddie charged, and the contributions he asked for. His major source of cash, however, was a raging drug-dealing business, his biggest sellers being meth, molly, and of course opioids.

His girlfriend, Krystal, was yelling at their baby to stop crying. Krystal, no mother of the year, picked the baby girl up and was about to shake her when Eddie noticed movement at the front of his property.

Outside, the thundering silence was deafening. Two police officers accompanying the core team were selected to check the dense tree line that surrounded the compound's fence. They knew there were often guards stationed behind the evergreens—if so, they needed to take them out as quietly and quickly as possible before the main assault could begin.

Everyone was on high alert. Though it was cool, sweat darkened their uniforms. Up ahead, closer to the cabin, they spied a truck with monster-size tires. Through binoculars, a sticker affixed to a large dent on the rear bumper was evident. It was a monstrosity, with a silhouette of crossed AR-15s next to the slogan, "Yours for White Victory."

One cop, Jack—built like a sequoia tree—towered over the policewoman beside him, even though she was above average in height. He pointed his head toward the tree line and looked down with a smug expression. "You ready for this, Jill?" he asked, his voice full of confidence.

She rolled her eyes. Her uniform was pristine. "Shh. You know I can take care of myself," she whispered.

He laughed silently. "Sure you can, Jill." Then, under his breath, said, "Just don't get in my way."

Jill gritted her teeth and ignored his taunts. She'd always been competitive with him, ever since they were in the police academy together; they were like two racehorses heading neck and neck toward the finish line. Jill was determined to prove she was just as good as he was. No, better.

They looked at the team leader, who nodded. The two of them slowly moved forward, their breathing becoming more rapid. As they approached the fence, they heard rustling in the trees.

Krystal had never wanted to be a mother.

She'd really had no ambition to be anything at all. Stuck in a rut of life, like a sailboat without wind, she'd been tending bar when she met Jon Eddie. It wasn't much of a bar; as you pushed open its dilapidated door, you were immediately hit with the pungent smells of bitter beer, cigarette smoke, and salty sweat. A long, sticky bar dominated the dimly lit interior, lined with shaky stools and chipped coasters. The walls were covered in peeling, nicotine-stained wallpaper, and the floor was littered with discarded peanut shells and spilt spirits. Normally, the regulars, their lives littered as well, would sit hunched over their drinks, staring blankly into the distance. Unless Jon Eddie was around.

Eddie often drew a crowd, a mix of people in awe of him and people in fear of him. His mannerless mouth and domineering demeanor attracted Krystal. He clearly thought he was the shit, and just as clearly was a mean son of a bitch. But Krystal thought he was someone who could protect her. At first, she would shrivel from his drivel. Later, not knowing any better, she began believing him, impressed by his purported big ideas that the men around him enthusiastically nodded their heads up and down to. When the bar closed one night, he was in the parking lot, hovering, waiting for her, wanting her.

She went out the back door and saw him.

With an almost imperceptible shrug, she got into his truck. She stayed the night with him, which then became a month of muddling. Once she was pregnant, she was there for good. Or so she thought.

"Grab the guns!" Eddie yelled over the baby's wails.

Krystal looked at him, frozen, as she held the baby.

"Leave the damn kid on the floor. Just grab the guns!"

They could see two guards ahead.

The guards were behind a large oak tree, chatting quietly while looking at a cell phone. One laughed.

Jack motioned to Jill to wait a moment as he silently made his way to the larger of the two guards. Before anything even registered on the guard's face, Jack started in on him.

Jack got him down, using a headlock and fireman's carry maneuver that landed the guy on his head. He was knocked out and would have a concussion, but he'd live. Jack allowed himself a quick smile, then turned to the other man, who was backing away, suddenly preferring flight to fight. Jill had watched momentarily in admiration of Jack's fighting skills but couldn't admire for too long; the other guard was her job, and she had to be just as capable with him. He'd turned to run but had a gun in hand.

Jill moved catlike toward her prey. A tree root tripped her. The guard stopped. His gun hand was shaking.

Fast and agile, Jill quickly recovered, jumped, and landed

a swift kick to his shaved head. Her steel-toed boot landed right in the center of his swastika tattoo; blood immediately gushed onto the soil. All those years of martial-arts training paid off. The gun fell out of the man's hand, and Jill kicked it away before kicking him in the stomach to make sure he stayed down. The man's eyes were wide, and it looked like he'd had enough, so she stopped, not wanting to overdo it. Jack watched her, ready to act, and looked similarly impressed, though he didn't say a word to her after they'd cuffed and muzzled the guards.

Other cops quickly came over and dragged them away.

"Well, that was the easy part," Jack said.

Jill, panting, just stared at him, knowing those words to be true. For a second, she thought of her dad, a former cop, and hoped his fate wouldn't befall her.

The core team warily walked forward, heading into the unknown. Jack followed closely behind. Jill wiped the blood off her boot with some leaves and joined them. Her heart pounding, but with a lot of backbone, she put her best foot forward.

The team leader, Nic, was as determined as a bulldog with a bone. He knew he had to stop the drug dealing, and he hated the group's ideology. But even more, he was given this mission because an informant had told of a plan this group had to blow up a government building. Tomorrow.

As they came closer to the cabin, he scanned the area for any signs of activity. He saw movement within the cabin.

He could feel the sweat dripping down his face, the adrenaline pumping through his veins. While his officers were highly trained, he could see the fear in their eyes. It wasn't a surprise. It was too easy for things to go bad.

He motioned for the team to spread out and be ready, with two officers heading around to the back. He knew they were dealing with very dangerous people but hoped to take them in without bloodshed.

Especially their own.

The smoke bomb exploded on the floor.

Chaos. His vision clouded, an officer yelled, "Police, come out with your hands up!" There was more movement inside; Eddie was fuming. But no one emerged from the thick fog of smoke. The cops moved in, like a tidal wave crashing onto shore.

One of the team members was hit immediately; he was dead before his body hit the floor.

More gunshots rang out. As the men frantically searched the rooms, the team leader headed straight for the source of the gunfire, bullets whizzing by at a dizzying pace. Amidst the mist, Jill saw a woman on the floor, bloodied and unmoving. She then heard a cry, and looking down, saw a baby. *Holy shit*, she thought, and tried to yell to the others, but in the mayhem, she knew no one would hear or understand. A hail of bullets came their way, and Jill got down, covering the baby with her body, like an embryo in the womb.

Another gunshot rang out, and Jill saw blood.

Jon Eddie moved his massive frame as quickly as he could. Low on ammunition, he got halfway out the back door. Jack and the second in command, Sam, had been waiting there to stop anyone who tried to escape. When Eddie burst through, they yelled, "Stop!" but there was no way the man was going to listen. Instead, he raised his gun and pointed it directly at Sam's head.

Sam's heart raced as Eddie's finger tightened around the trigger. He had tunnel vision; all he could do was stare at what looked like the barrel of a loaded cannon. Sam knew that his life was about to end. He thought of his wife and children, and all he'd never said.

The gunshot rang out.

Eddie's head jerked back. Blood spurted from the hole in his forehead. Sam's eyes widened as he watched the man crumple to the floor, his lifeless body twitching on the deck, like an electrical wire downed on the ground.

As he turned, he saw Jack standing a few feet away, his own gun smoking. Sam exhaled sharply. He couldn't stop shaking.

"You saved my life, man," Sam said haltingly, still in shock.

Jack nodded, but knew the danger wasn't over.

"Jesus," Sam said, "you were like a guardian angel swooping down from heaven."

"It ain't over yet," Jack said. "Be ready."

The sound of more gunfire broke out.

It was quickly followed by, "Officer down!"

Jack looked all around, his head spinning like a compass needle gone haywire, desperately seeking north but finding no direction. And no Jill.

His heart skipped a beat. Without a second thought, he turned and sprinted inside, his gun at the ready. He knew he was going to have to act quickly if he was going to save his fellow officer. The inside of the cabin was bedlam as Jack moved further in, searching, seeking.

He could see activity just ahead as he passed through a

ruined room full of felled furniture, and what looked like a baby's cradle crashed on its side.

Then he saw a figure lying motionless on the floor.

"Jill," he yelled.

His heart sank.

Mike, an experienced ambulance driver, was sitting at the base when the emergency call came in. His muscles tightened as he heard the dispatcher's voice.

"Officer down. GSW. Repeat, officer down. Requesting immediate ambulance support. Get that bus here now!"

Mike knew this was his highest priority call. His hands shook as he reached for the keys to the ambulance and raced out of the base. He could feel his heart in his chest as he navigated through the busy streets, siren blaring and lights flashing.

As he drove, Mike's thoughts were focused on the injured officer. He wondered who it was, and how badly they were hurt. He could hear the communications in spurts and was told to proceed with caution upon entering the compound as shooting may be ongoing.

Jack ran over and was astonished at what he saw.

Jill lay motionless, frozen.

But she then moved as if thawed. She turned and slowly sat up. One arm was around a baby, the other arm bloodied. The baby was crying, about to have a meltdown. Jill was obviously shaken, and through a pained smile managed a few words: "Baby's OK!"

"But not that one," Jack replied, looking at the clearly dead woman on the floor.

The gunfire had expired. The baby stopped crying as Jill

shushed her and held her tight. Jill patted the soft blond hairs on the baby's head. "Well, this little one is safe. And saved from a life of hate." The baby looked at Jill, as if understanding. It smiled, making a cooing sound.

An intermittent red glow bounced off the walls of the cabin. The ambulance had arrived, and the EMT quickly patched Jill up. The bullet had just grazed her arm; she would be OK.

Unfortunately, the first officer who had entered the cabin would not be needing the ambulance.

When they were done, Jack slowly approached her. The baby had been taken away, and Jill looked contemplative.

"Hey, you OK?"

Jill shrugged.

Jack continued, "You know after what happened here, me shooting that guy dead, I'll be off for a period of time. Standard protocol: my gun taken away, go through interviews, see the shrink. But just wanted to say, pretty decent work today."

Jill smiled a half-smile, considering how unlikely it was for Jack to say anything nice to her given their history.

Then he added, "Even if you did manage to get yourself in the way of a bullet."

Jill looked back at him, her pupils constricting. "Damn it, Jack, we *lost* one of our own today."

"Hell, we almost lost me!"

Jill's expression was deadpan.

"Well, two degenerates are dead," Jack said. "Good riddance. They probably would have been the death of that baby, anyway. Off to hell they go, never to return."

"One hopes," Jill said. "That would be heavenly."

She looked away, lost in thought for a moment.

Jill's face turned red, and her voice was as loud as could be, given her weakened state. "Goddamn Nordic Fest! We have to fight this shit, Jack. Stand up for the rights of everyone." A drop of blood flew off her arm.

Jack nodded, then stood up. "Well, at least there won't be any concerts here anymore."

"We need to fight them everywhere," Jill said.

The memory of the baby's cry, followed by her small smile, would never leave Jill. She'd looked into her innocent face and felt a renewed sense of purpose, a sense of grace. She vowed never to forget the evil of men like Jon Eddie and their ideology.

And she didn't.

But evil seemed to follow her.

I

Who would have thought killing would be so easy?
I have to admit, it began innocently enough. Just a little target practice on a lonely tree stump. A quiet, secluded area on a hillside, far from examining eyes and eavesdropping ears.

The air was still, the scent of evergreens permeating the area. I took in a deep breath, immediately regretting it, disliking the scent. I definitely prefer the smell of dying deciduous trees, leaves decaying, then gone forever. Death. Not sure though how I feel about the fact that there will be a rebirth, fresh, green leaves sprouting anew in the spring, a perennial cycle.

Better to focus on the rifle. I was surprised that shooting a gun wasn't nearly as hard as I thought it would be, once you got the knack of it.

It's true that at first, I was a bit stumped. But training at BullsEye Firing Range on firearms safety, grips, stances and sighting was a great help. "Hey, it's a dangerous world; we need to be able to defend ourselves," I'd said to the instructor, who enthusiastically responded, "Hell yeah!"

Hell yeah.

The rifle itself wasn't as heavy as I expected; new synthetic materials are surprisingly lightweight. Still, the recoil took a little getting used to, but that came too. The feel of the stock pressed firmly on my cheek was empowering, like becoming one with the gun.

I'll let you in on a secret. Using a scope on the rifle made sighting simple—so much easier and more accurate. The crosshairs provide a perfect targeting mechanism. All you have to do is press the trigger (press, don't pull, I'd learned) using constantly increasing pressure until it, well, basically surprises you by firing.

The tree stump didn't stand a chance.

2

He couldn't believe it.

Jack Ludlum had arrived at the testing center to take the exam to become a detective with the State Bureau of Investigation and in walked Jill Jarred, who he'd worked with occasionally while a cop on the beat the last few years. They'd never gotten along, and after the academy, they'd taken different shifts. Jack liked the night shift—fewer people around the station, less supervision, and no need to be with Jill at roll call. And like Batman, he liked to work in the shadows, so he loved the dark nights.

Now he'd been looking forward to not having anything to do with her at all, hoping to become a detective with the State Bureau of Investigation. But as he stood in the lobby, in walked Jill. *What the hell!* he thought.

"Jack, what are you doing here?" Jill said, a hint of annoyance in her voice.

"I could ask you the same thing," Jack replied. Then recovering, he said, "I didn't think you had the guts to take this test."

"I didn't think you had the intelligence to take it," Jill replied, and turned away.

Jack's eyes followed her as she walked into the testing room. He then brushed past her to get into the room.

"Really, Jack?" she said. She caught up and stood in front of him. "I thought you were perfectly happy being a beat cop for the rest of your life. You know you won't be able to use your fists as much as you like if you actually did, God forbid, become a detective."

"Don't you worry. I've beaten you most ways as a cop. I'll do the same as a detective," Jack said, walking away.

"I don't think so, on either account," Jill said.

The tension between them was palpable as they took their seats and began the test. The exam assessed their knowledge in three areas—criminal investigations, interviewing techniques, and relevant case law—and each section was extremely tough in its own way. The criminal investigations section required both basic knowledge and insight—a bit of art and science. The interview techniques section seemed designed to sink them; it was like navigating a treacherous river, with hidden currents and unexpected obstacles. And the case law section was especially hard to get through, almost requiring a photographic memory.

Once they finally finished the test, they looked exhausted and emotionally drained.

"Well, that was brutal," Jack said, wiping his forehead.

"Was it?" Jill said coolly.

Jack smiled, shaking his head. They walked in silence for a few moments before Jill spoke up.

"You know, I may not like you all that much, but I have to admit, you've been a pretty good cop," she said.

Jack was taken aback. "Thanks, I guess," he said, not quite sure how to respond. Then, after a moment, he added, "Oh, I get it. You're just saying that because you want me to stay a street cop. You don't want the competition as a detective."

"Ha, you caught me!" Jill said. She looked up at him, her amber eyes clear and piercing.

Jack shrugged.

"Hey, I'm OK if you become a detective," Jill said. "I think. Then we can still test each other—but I'll clearly come out on top." A perplexing smile was on her face.

"Beware what you wish for," Jack replied.

3

It wasn't far from where the tree stump was used for target practice that the woman's car broke down.

So much for doing a good deed! she'd thought, having borrowed her boyfriend's clunker to visit an ailing aunt.

It was near dusk when a vehicle approached. She'd been awaiting a tow truck, and squinted into the oncoming headlights, watching warily as the vehicle headed toward her. The air was motionless; the only sound was tires crunching on gravel, gradually coming to a stop. Her face filled with disappointment as she realized it wasn't the tow truck, but a lone man who had slowed his automobile, approaching her disabled car by the side of the littered blacktop.

She stared, holding her breath as the man peered at her, all alone on this deserted road in the middle of nowhere. She felt her pulse race; wished she was anywhere but there. She was twenty-four, and knew that look in his eyes. Sitting beside the rear of her car, she watched him glance quickly at her backside. She wondered if he knew that in these parts, getting a tow truck to come out on a Sunday would be a long, long wait. Certainly long enough for him.

She flinched and her eyes widened as he got out of his car. He was alone. Seeing a large man approach her as it was nearing dark made her nervous. She looked around, up and down the road, her head swiveling like an owl on overdrive.

She then noticed a clerical collar at his neck and exhaled when she saw it, along with the friendly smile on his face. He didn't come right up to her, just talked from a distance. She appreciated the separation he kept; her muscles eased a bit from their hardened state, though she felt drips of perspiration run onto the back of her shirt and could still feel her heart beating quickly.

"Need some help, ma'am?"

"Thanks. But I'm good. Had some car trouble, but the tow truck is on its way. Should be here any minute, in fact."

She wondered if he knew she was lying.

He pointed to his collar. "Well, I was on my way back to my church. To the rectory. I'm a pastor." Her breathing started to return to normal. "You want me to wait with you until the tow comes? I know it's scary here."

She looked up hopefully at his charming and disarming smile. She considered the offer, her thoughts vacillating like tree branches in a storm. A raven cawed in the distance. She breathed in deeply and wiped the palm of her hands on her shorts, taking a second to tug them down a bit in a futile gesture to cover up more of her thighs. She saw him unconsciously lick his lips.

"I'll wait in my car. You wait in yours, with the door locked," he said. She looked into his extremely dark eyes, about to take him up on it. But she still wasn't sure—waffling, wavering, worrying.

"I really appreciate that. Thank you. But I don't want to hold you up. The tow truck will be here real soon. I think I hear it in the distance. Really."

She knew he heard nothing.

"OK, ma'am, whatever you want," he said with a shrug. He started to get back into his car. "Oh, hey, let me at least give you a couple of chocolate bars from the parish drive. It'll make your wait a bit sweeter!" His eyes sparkled, his tone inviting.

Shit, I am hungry as hell, she thought. *Gotta stop skipping meals.* He grabbed the chocolate bars and waved them at her, a sanguine smile upon his face.

"Oh, OK. I guess. Thanks!"

They walked toward each other.

4

She was terrified.

The email subject line was "State Detective Test Results." Jill didn't want to open it. She checked her other mail, then went back to it. Stopped to check her Facebook page; she hadn't posted in quite some time, but enjoyed seeing what her old friends were up to. Thought about posting some more. Decided to check on Instagram. She went back to the email, hovered over it, then decided to check the weather report. She then realized she was more afraid of opening the email than she'd been facing the toughest crooks.

Oh hell, here goes nothing, she thought.

Jack Ludlum didn't think it would happen.

As he waited for the test results, he felt it wasn't so bad being a cop on the street. He tried to convince himself that it all begins on the streets, and that's where he's been so useful, ending it for many. But then he thought of Jill, and how she would have a big smile on her face as she walked by him, surely having passed the exam.

From his perspective, Jill Jarred was a gnat. It had all started when they were at the police academy together. There were only two women in the academy at the time, and he just didn't quite believe they should be there. He was brought up in an old-fashioned household where the thinking was that being a cop was a tough and dangerous job, not something for a woman. While he would learn otherwise, at that point, he'd held a bias from his background.

The other thing he'd learned at home growing up was the use of his fists. Jack had watched the way his father, slurring his words, beat on his mother. She couldn't stop him, couldn't fight back. The screams of, "Please, stop!" still rang in Jack's ears, haunted his heart.

It stopped when Jack was fifteen and grew bigger than his father. It was after one strike too many, his mother falling to the floor, when Jack exploded like a building with a gas leak ignited. He surprised his father and bested him. Jack's dad never hit his mother again. Jack had saved his mother from further aggression, at least physically, which thrilled him. But he also learned that his fists could solve problems.

During his time at the police academy, the most challenging thing of all was that Jill was his toughest competitor. Whether it was firearms training, the obstacle course, or the many classes, they were neck and neck at just about every challenge, at every task. And her neck was lovely, Jack thought, which made it even more disheartening. In his backward way of thinking back then, if there were going to be female cops, at least they shouldn't look like models.

A layer of complexity had definitely been added to Jack's experience with the undeniable allure of Jill's physical presence. During training runs, he saw her rich brown hair with golden glints that the sun made sparkle. Worse, Jack recalled, was watching her on the obstacle course. He couldn't help but notice her figure. And then there were those amber eyes that glistened like gems, but usually left him cold with a piercing gaze. With that package, and at five foot seven—closer in height to him than most ladies—Jack should have found her attractive. But he found the fact that she bested him on almost every test, even though he had always been considered the smart one wherever he was, really pissed him off. And she wasn't bashful in letting him know—especially how the one thing he kept getting wrong was the "Shoot Don't Shoot" drill—Jack was just too aggressive.

Every encounter with Jill turned into a challenging blend of competition and distraction, and sometimes, he just wanted to wring her lovely neck. No matter how often he tried to swat her away, she dodged him, only to be buzzing in his ear, getting into his head. A gnat.

Now he didn't look forward to her beating him out for detective.

5

It was dead.

That tree stump was pretty much gone after all the days of target shooting. *Dead and gone*, I thought. Need to find another one next time. Maybe in another area, for variety. Variety is good. I headed out, walking back to the car I left in a secluded area off the other side of the road. It would be a bit of a hike, but that was OK. Time was no issue. The car would be there, waiting. If anyone actually saw it, which was unlikely, they'd leave it alone. The old Mercury Marauder was on its last legs when bought used a year ago. Now it mostly hobbles. But it was cheap and was perfect for my needs.

The scream was piercing.

It didn't sound all that far away. I decided to check it out and headed in its direction.

6

S he screamed.
Jill read the email three times before she believed it. She shrieked again and jumped out of her chair, throwing her fist up high in the air. She'd passed! She was a detective!

The first thing she thought of after her mini-celebration was her dad. How proud he would have been. She thought back to his final day.

Frank Jarred didn't know that day would be his last.

Jill Jarred was destined to be a cop. Not necessarily the detective she became, but at least a cop.

Her dad Frank was a cop. That day, back when she was a child, was supposed to be routine, a normal day patrolling the streets. That morning, he shined his shoes and put on his pressed blue uniform. Jill, six years old, ran in as he was trying to tie his tie for the third time; it had to be just right. She still had some sleep in her eyes, but they opened wider as she approached her dad. Jill was wearing pajamas with a cowboy print on them; no princess nightgowns for her, she'd insisted to her mother. She jumped on the bed and then jumped onto her father's back. Hugging him, hanging on as he pretended to fall under the weight. They ended up on the floor, laughing at each other, tickling each other. Their morning ritual. A typical day had begun.

Jill scampered off to get dressed while he finished getting set, and then Frank headed downstairs. Jill could smell the aroma of freshly brewed coffee wafting up, a mysterious and enticing scent, and wondered when she would be old enough to sip some. She'd looked down the staircase as she was wont to do, always curious, always investigating what was going on. She spied a smile on her dad's face as he bent down to give her mother a kiss on the cheek. Her mom stiffened.

Her dad had explained to Jill that there were some times that her mother didn't quite feel like herself, and at those times, it was probably best to leave her alone. This looked like one of those times. He'd said when she got like that, it was usually because of a rough night sleeping. Jill once asked her mother if she'd like to sleep with her favorite stuffed animal, a dark-brown pony. She just smiled sadly in response.

Frank put a piece of bread in the toaster. The sounds of silence were severe as he impatiently waited for the toast to pop up. He poured himself a cup of coffee and felt the need to say something. It was in his nature to try to fix situations, and no matter how many times something may not have worked, he never gave up trying.

"Coffee is good. Thanks!"

His wife just looked at him.

"Let me know if you need me to pick up anything after my shift is done. I see we are low on bananas."

"No, I don't need any shit. Don't stop, come right home and clean out the garage. I've been telling you to do that for weeks."

"Sorry, hon, you know how tough it's been, the overtime I had to put in. But at least that's done for now."

"And look at the overflowing garbage," she hissed. "You were supposed to have taken that out last night! Now we missed the collection day."

"Jesus, I'm sorry. I forgot."

"You forgot. What if I forgot to make you dinner? What if I forgot to drive Jill home from karate? What if I forgot to do the wash, clean the house? Goddamn it, Frank, come on! Now just get the hell out!"

She pushed him hard toward the door just as Jill came down the stairs. Jill knew her dad didn't like her to see them fighting. She'd seen the shove and hurried toward them.

"Mommy! Don't hurt Daddy!"

They both looked at her, though her mother made no move. The ticking of the wall clock could be heard.

"It's OK, baby. Mommy and Daddy were just having a talk when I tripped a little. Nothing for you to worry about."

"You need to be careful, Daddy!"

Frank grabbed Jill, got on his knees to be closer to her height, and looked into her eyes with a smile on his face. "I will. I'll be careful. I'll be safe for Daddy's little girl." He gave her a hug.

"I'm not so little anymore, Daddy. And I am a girl... but... I want to be just like you. I want to be a policeman too."

"You'll be a great police*woman*," he said, as he took his police hat and put it on her head. It just about covered her eyes, as she peeked out with a big smile.

"Just like you, Daddy."

Jill's mom looked on with an exasperated expression and motioned for Frank to go. He kissed Jill and headed out. "Love you," he said to his wife, who simply turned away.

"You be a good girl for Mommy now."

"And Daddy," Jill said. She watched him leave. The door closed firmly behind Patrolman Frank Jarred.

7

The chocolate was never tasted.

Instead of the chocolate bars the "pastor" offered, she tasted blood. Blood from where his hand enclosing the bars, instead of handing them to her, reared back and smacked her in the face. The thwack thundered in her ears and bolted down her spine.

She staggered and screamed, knowing what might be in store for her from this predatory pastor. She had her keys in hand, and managed to deeply scratch his arm, small, crimson beads of blood appearing. He roared, but kept a grip on her, the keys falling.

She poked at his eyes with her long nails, barely missing as he quickly jerked his head back, his crooked collar coming off. Breathing heavily, she twisted and tried to knee him in the groin. He blocked it and maintained control. She fought back bravely, but he was just too big.

He now had his hand over her mouth, suppressing subsequent screams. He pushed her down to the ground.

I looked down the hill and could see a man on top of a woman, tugging at her shirt while she struggled. Though certainly not close enough to see her face, it was very clear what was going on. I took a few deep breaths, uncertain what to do.

Uncertain if anything at all should be done.

He grabbed at her again, ripping the fabric of her shirt, of her soul. Panting, he grunted that he had a knife, and if she continued to struggle, he wouldn't hesitate to use it. The wild look in his eyes told her she'd better listen. Her body went limp, the fight finally out of her, like a wrestler after the count. She closed her tear-filled eyes and prayed.

8

Though it was years earlier, Jill never forgot that night, waiting for her father Frank to get home. He was over an hour late. And he was never late.

"Goddamn. I told him to come straight home. I'm going to kill him," her mother shouted.

There was a knock on the door.

Jill's mother looked out. There were two men on the doorstep. She must have known they were detectives, must have known what was happening as she held the doorknob, but did nothing. They gently knocked again. She slowly turned the knob and opened the door just a bit. She looked at their faces, and her whole body seemed to sag as if under a heavy weight.

"May we come in, please?"

"Nooooo! Nooooo!"

She tried for a moment to push the door closed, but one of them put a foot in front of it, saying, "I'm so sorry." She let out a shriek, and he grabbed her, held her gently in the foyer as she sobbed, until she slid down to the floor, with one last shout of, "Frank!!"

Amidst the sound and the fury, a little head could be seen peeking down from the upstairs landing. The little girl was confused, though on another level, she understood. And cried.

*

The funeral had been unbearable for her mother, but little Jill managed to stand strong. They were told Frank was killed doing what he did best: helping people. In this case, helping a victim of domestic violence. The woman had clearly been beaten by her husband, who had then put her in a choke hold, a knife to her neck. Neighbors heard the commotion and called the police. Frank and his partner were the first to arrive, his partner saying they should wait for backup. But it got noisier so Frank got closer. His partner said Frank saw the look in the woman's eyes, as well as the look in the man's, and was ready for action. When it looked like the man might actually kill her, Frank stormed forward. In the fray, Frank ended up getting knifed in the heart.

His death was like a knife to Jill's heart as well.

It was overcast and gray, no sky to be seen, as she stood still and quiet, watching the funeral procession; it looked like the entire city had come to a standstill for it. There were hundreds of police officers in attendance from across the country, their badges shrouded. The lengthy procession of the flag-draped coffin passed in front of her and her mother. There was a last radio call, ending in "Gone, but not forgotten." At the cemetery, there was a color guard and a twenty-one bells ceremony.

The eerie sound of bagpipes playing "Amazing Grace" mesmerized Jill. For the rest of her life, she couldn't listen to that song without crying.

They took the flag off the casket, folded it, and handed it to her and her mother. Rain fell lightly, like tears from heaven. Jill was wearing her father's police hat; she refused to part with it. As the casket was lowered into the ground, she saluted her father, her two little fingers placed stiffly across her forehead.

It was many years before the police academy, and even more before getting the news she'd passed the detective exam. But Jill would never forget that day, the day she knew she'd reincarnate herself from a little girl to a policewoman—to make her dad proud.

9

I made a decision.

I lined up the shot, though it was farther than I'd ever practiced. The rifle wasn't staying steady. There hadn't been any jitters while shooting at a stump. Shooting a live human being was proving to be something altogether different.

The first shot was about ten feet off, hitting the side of the car. *Damn!*

My second shot was closer, pricking the dirt a few feet away from them, but close enough to the woman to cause earth and rocks to skid onto her. Sweat poured down my back, and my finger felt slippery on the trigger.

By the time I was ready to fire the third bullet, the rapist was looking around frantically. He stood up, almost tripping as he became entangled in her shorts while attempting to shove his penis back in his pants and run. He wasn't successful; the bullet tore into his chest. He was dead before he landed with a thud upon her, his blood ejaculating all over her body.

I heard the woman's screaming as she struggled to push his body off of her. I'm sure the blood made it slick, and his weight must have felt as if she was being crushed by a boulder. I watched through the scope, fascinated, as she frantically moved about beneath him. Finally, she managed to slide out from under him and rolled to her side, where she promptly vomited.

I'd seen enough and knew it was time to disappear. I still couldn't believe the shot had actually hit the guy. Seemed like a miracle. It was a strange feeling, though: a mix of surprise and exhilaration. And something else.

I ran off and headed back to my car. It was quite a bit away, but my steps felt fast and light; I was in high spirits and got there quickly. Perhaps this was a sign.

My destiny?

10

She was bloody and broken but breathing.

The gunshots were quieted, though her internal screams were as loud as ever. She was shaking out of control; wherever she touched her body, she found blood, causing her to shake her hands off each spot in a frenzy. The source of the blood—the would-be rapist—lay beside her. She tried to inch herself further from him but her body wouldn't cooperate. Her clothing shredded and her face covered in blood, she looked like Stephen King's Carrie at the prom.

A wrapper from a chocolate bar blew by.

It took a long time for her to calm down enough to slowly drag herself back to her car, away from the body. She sat slumped on the ground when she got to the vehicle, not enough energy left to even open the door. She kept looking around, still shaking, not comprehending what had happened. She'd never been attacked before, and the attack was worse than she'd ever thought one would be. She'd been scared to death, and her heart was still racing as fast as her skittering thoughts. She wasn't even sure it was over.

She didn't notice her shirt was shredded, and began muttering beneath her breath, bowing her head and shoulders back and forth, her upper back smashing into the side of the car with each sway back. It made a dull thud each time. She didn't hear the noise or feel the pain.

She saw another vehicle approach. She crunched into a ball, trying to make herself small.

A man came out of the vehicle and walked toward her. He seemed huge.

She screamed.

"Jesus Christ, what the hell happened here? Are you OK?" the tow-truck driver exclaimed.

She cowered by the car, trying to open the door, not able to say a word.

"Don't worry, lady, I'm not going to hurt you." He looked over at the dead body beside the road, grimacing. In a whisper, he added, "You're safe now."

He tossed his jacket over to her and called 911.

They were no strangers to blood. Though they had little experience with dead bodies.

The police got there quickly, not having much else to do in town. One cop checked on the man, and shook his head to the other, then hurriedly looked around to double-check that there weren't any weapons or other assailants nearby. The second cop, a female, was with the victim, eyes fixed on her blood-stained clothing, or what remained of it, quietly asking questions, trying to calm her down.

The first cop called for an ambulance and the medical examiner, then cordoned off the area with yellow crime scene tape. The cop interrogated the tow-truck driver, who they knew well from town—known to be a hard-working and decent man—and then ordered him to stay in his vehicle. The female cop was about to clean the woman up when the first officer stopped her.

"Hey, wait, you know we need pictures taken of everything."

"Right. We shouldn't touch her until the medical examiner gets here. We'll need to collect any evidence, and then her clothing, or what's left of it, gets bagged."

"Yeah, though it's pretty clear. We have a dead guy here, and the woman who killed him, and she's not going anywhere."

The woman made a sound, and the female cop looked at her pitifully. "We'll get you cleaned up, honey. Soon." She turned to her partner. "Get a blanket from the trunk; she could be in shock." He looked at the shaking woman and headed to his patrol car.

"Now please, tell us what happened. He was assaulting you?"

She haltingly explained what happened, in bits and pieces, out of order, that at first made little sense. The female police officer eventually got a vague picture of what had occurred: the car breaking down, a pastor, an attempted rape, bullets flying from somewhere, and blood: lots of it.

The cops had a surprised expression as they looked at each other.

"Another shooter?"

"Hmm. We haven't found a gun she could've used. So maybe. Let me look around again."

"Carefully, please."

After a few minutes, he came back. "Nope, nothing." Then they both looked at the surrounding hills.

The female police officer said, "Could it be that a hunter was up in those hills? Not supposed to be now but wouldn't be the first time."

Her partner said, "Maybe. Could be a Good Samaritan had been in the woods, saw what was happening, and got a lucky shot in. Probably wanted nothing to do with the whole thing and took off."

The woman on the ground just looked confused.

"Can you tell us anything more about the shots that were fired? What did you see?"

"I have... have no idea," she stammered. "Saw nothing." She looked off in the direction of the hills.

"Please try to remember something. Anything. Anything at all could help."

She looked at them, then looked away, concentrating, holding her hands to each side of her head. "I remember."

They looked at her, eyebrows raised.

"I remember I prayed."

She looked up at the cops, her eyes brightening, "I prayed... maybe he was heaven sent."

The female cop stared up into the hills, a thoughtful expression on her face.

The male cop covered a smirk, thought about it, then muttered, "A killer? Hopefully not from hell."

II

She never smiled anymore.

So Jill's first thought was to call her mom with the news she was a detective; maybe that would make her happy. She remembered the last time she saw her smile: at her graduation from the police academy. She remembered it well.

Graduation Day couldn't come fast enough. The academy was tough, both in the training, and in Jack, perhaps her biggest obstacle.

Jill was glad her mother was coming—her mother who Jill knew never forgave herself for that final morning. She'd pretty much been in mourning since.

She'd regretted not saying that last goodbye, not saying "I love you" when she had the chance—a chance she'd never have again in this lifetime. She now said it, and much more, in her frequent visits to the cemetery, but there was no answer from Frank—just the chill of an ill wind, and a whisper from the leaves in the trees.

Jill also thought about how hard her mother had worked to raise her; she never remarried, worked two jobs, but always managed to be there for Jill when needed. She'd without fail take time off to attend the many ceremonies where Jill received awards. And though she had discouraged Jill's career choice, sometimes vehemently, she proudly watched Jill graduate the police academy, first in her class.

That day, her mother walked up to her when the ceremony concluded. From behind her back, she pulled out her husband's police hat. They looked into each other's eyes and cried. It was the first time since her dad's death that Jill had cried in public. She prided herself on being tough, and certainly wouldn't show emotion in front of her peers. But this time, she couldn't help it.

Her mother then put her late husband's police hat on Jill's head. This time, it didn't fall over Jill's eyes. In fact, it fit perfectly.

12

Most of the local authorities had no clue, though they had some physical clues. Sheriff's Deputy Tracy Dixon was concerned.

They had three bullets recovered from the crime scene and body, which were pretty beat up. Given the distance they must have traveled, what seemed to be their trajectory, and the report that they came in quick succession, they were believed to be from an automatic rifle up in the hills. The detectives were able to identify the would-be rapist; that was easy: his I.D. was real and was confirmed by fingerprints. He was no pastor; he was a prisoner—only recently let out of jail after a prior rape charge was overturned.

The victim hadn't seen the shooter, and probably wouldn't describe him even if she could; after all, he'd saved her life. The woods were checked by the three sheriff's deputies and a couple of reserves, using a strip method: heading in a straight line for a distance, then reversing themselves. But the foliage was heavy, and there had been a downpour soon after the shooting, so no evidence was recovered. Overall though, they didn't really search very far, or very hard.

Tracy Dixon's boss, Sheriff Earl Klamp, was a large man, though hadn't dealt with any large cases during his tenure. There had been no murders in his quiet little town during his twenty-plus years on the force, and he appeared unsure of himself dealing with this. To make up for it, he just spoke loudly, barking orders that didn't always make sense.

"Had to ah been a hunta," he said when it was clear there wasn't any other evidence. He had heard that theory from the patrol officer and figured it was as good as any. "You knaw, a stray bullet from eh automatic weapon can travel two miles." He looked proud of himself for stating that fact.

Sheriff's Deputy Tracy Dixon looked at him archly. She knew him better than anyone else, having been on the force just about as long. Tracy also knew better than him about most everything. She thought he was quite a dolt of an adult.

A brunette whose mid-length hair was just starting to show some gray, she was slightly overweight, obsessively neat, often sarcastic, and had good street smarts—not that she had to use them much in her quiet town. Besides some speeding, selective shoplifting, daft drunks, and the periodic peeping Peter, it was a pretty placid gig. Drugs, particularly opioids, had started to become a problem, but they seemed to have a handle on it. At least they thought so.

"A hunter? With three stray bullets that happened to have ended up in the same area, including one in the body? I don't think so."

Sheriff Klamp appeared flummoxed. Then Tracy saw the light bulb come on over his head. It was dim, but it was there.

"I didn't mean a damn stray, girl. I meant the hunta saw what was happenin'. Saw it from afar and did his job. Bagged him a good one."

Deputy Tracy thought about it. "Right place at the right time, I guess." Her voice had more sarcasm than support in it.

"Yeah, but wrong for our dead man." He chuckled, probably thinking himself smart. He then coughed and spit into a dirty handkerchief.

"Good for us too, I guess," she said.

"You betcha. No need ta spend too much time trying ta identify the hunta. That guy did us a fava. Let's finish up the basics and not spend our good citizens' tax dollas on anythin' more than that. We don't want to get any of our good ole boys in trouble now, do we? Especially with an election comin' up. Unless ya wanna find that shoota ta give him a medal." He guffawed.

Tracy considered his direction but wasn't sure she agreed they shouldn't investigate further. She knew only about half of all murders are solved, down from ninety percent in the 1960s, but didn't think this was a premeditated murder. Still, she was concerned about anyone who could kill someone and simply stand down, disappear. It didn't quite sit well with her.

But she finally said, "I guess so," though her expression said anything but that. And she knew it was but a guess.

13

The shooting of the would-be rapist had been big news in their small town. They dubbed him "The Pretend Pastor." From book clubs to church groups, after the initial shock, everyone marveled at how this could have happened, and wondered who'd shot him. The gossip was non-stop. Every guy in town known to hunt in those woods—legally or illegally— was looked at with curiosity… and newfound respect. Even the tow-truck driver suddenly found himself extremely popular.

A fund was set up to help the poor woman involved, though as soon as she could, she swiftly left town, never to set foot there, let alone drive through, again. She did, though, use a consider-able amount of her savings, and a loan, to buy a brand-new car.

It was just a few weeks later that a rare twister swept through the town. A few old barns collapsed, the awning above the Texaco station fell onto the pumps, and tree limbs were down all around town. Some old trees that had been in town forever were uprooted, changing the complexion of Main Street. The local paper did a big story on the unexpected storm and damage, and people talked about what they should do to protect themselves from the next one. Many argued with their insurance company on claims, and some residents even talked of moving. "The Pretend Pastor" was no longer news, replaced by the reeling of townsfolk from the storm.

But at least one person did not forget the killing. In fact, it got the person thinking.

The couple walked out of the Ponderosa Steakhouse, stuffed.

They walked hand in hand to their car in the parking lot, laughing, his brown hand squeezing her pale-white hand. She teased him about eating all the German chocolate fudge brownie with vanilla ice cream—after downing a sixteen-ounce T-bone sizzling steak, garlic dinner rolls, a scoop of extra cheesy mac and cheese, a massive mountain of mashed potatoes, and a hill of beans. He patted his belly contently, saying at least he was still in decent shape. He flexed his arm muscle at her and gave her an affectionate peck on the cheek.

I watched through my Bushnell Holographic sight.

I steadied it, targeting the man in the Ponderosa Steakhouse parking lot. It was so clear. I could even just about make out what they were saying.

The man turned to the woman. "Damn, left my glasses in the restaurant." He started back.

She looked back at him sweetly. "No, you didn't!"

"I didn't?"

She whipped them out of her purse. "I picked them up for you when you were in the bathroom. You've left them behind too many times! Almost as much as your credit card."

"Well, that's because my credit card is the same damn brown color as the check holder! But thank you."

He turned back to her. "Where would you be without me?" she said and reached up to stroke his cheek.

As her fingers touched his face, it exploded about her.

14

*D*amn! Jill thought.

She was in the bustling headquarters of the State Bureau of Investigation, excited to start her new job. Then Jack walked into the room where the new detectives were to assemble. They stopped and stared at each other for a moment.

"Well, well, well, if it isn't Jill Jarred," Jack said with a smirk.

"Jack," Jill responded, her tone cordial but cool.

"So they found a way to get you kicked off the streets, I see," Jack said, trying to hide his irritation.

Jill rolled her eyes. "I passed my detective exam just like I guess you did—somehow, Jack."

"Well," Jack responded, "I knew for sure I would. Wasn't too sure about you, though."

"Yeah, right. Tell me about it," Jill said, turning away.

"Well, let's see who solves their first case," Jack said, puffing out his chest a bit.

Jill couldn't help but feel a twinge of annoyance. She just wanted to become the best detective possible, not to waste time on him.

"Sure, Jack," she said, her tone clipped. "I'm just here to do my job."

They then received a briefing and were paired up with

senior detectives. Jill looked forward to the challenge. She knew the job was dangerous; that was ingrained in her by her dad, Patrolman Frank Jarred, like a deep scar that never goes away. She understood detective work could be just as hazardous.

Extremely so.

15

"Think it was a hunter again?" Sheriff's Deputy Tracy Dixon asked, her voice dripping with sarcasm.

Sheriff Earl Klamp had been first at the scene of the Ponderosa Steakhouse killing, even though it was just over the county line. He'd been in the area, searching in the bigger town's Walmart for some fishing lures, when the call came in over the radio.

Later, after some heated negotiations with that town's police chief, they agreed to at least use the same medical examiner from the first killing, and jointly investigate what was going on. "Maybe even have ah task force," Earl suggested, not that either county had much in the way of investigative resources. They considered bringing in state resources but decided they didn't need to—didn't want anyone else being a hero in their backyard.

"No need for others buddin' inta our affairs. Ain't nothin' we can't handle," Earl had said.

Now, back in his office, he was discussing the shooting with Tracy Dixon. He stood in front of her desk, one button missing from his shirt right where it stretched over his bloated belly.

"Well, maybe it was a hunta."

Tracy peered at him with an incredulous look on her face. "What?"

"Well, ah, maybe our shoota was a hunta, took care of the first guy, got a taste for justice, and went huntin' for some more bad guys."

Tracy's eyes widened even more. "Are you friggin' crazy? Just because the Black vic was dating a white woman?!"

"Cuss not. Though some people round here may disagree. But it does turn out he had a record, ya know."

Tracy's eyes widened. "What?"

"Drugs." Earl smiled.

"Shit," Tracy said, shaking her head.

"Did some prison time."

Tracy thought for a moment. "What kind of drugs?"

"Marijuana," Earl said sheepishly, looking away.

"Oh, give me a break. For that, he went to jail?"

"Well, times have a changed. Things were different back then."

"That's such bullshit." Tracy stood up, waving one hand in the air. "Hey, the Jones brothers, you well know, are growing it in their backyard right now."

"I know, I know, but they're good boys."

Tracy gave Earl a sharp glance. "But back to the vic, that certainly doesn't make him a bad guy. Certainly not worth being shot over!"

"Very true. Very true. But who knows what goes through the minds of people."

"Well, we got a killer here; let's get to work." Tracy sat back down behind her steel desk, the wheels of the ripped faux leather chair slowly sliding.

"We don't know if they are really connected, really the same killer."

Tracy's head snapped back, and she looked at Earl like he was nuts. "First you say it's the same 'hunta,' now you say they may not be connected. Make up your mind!"

Earl shrugged. He looked like he'd had about enough of her for one day. "Well, there's a lot we don't know. Like ya said, let's git to work."

If Earl and Tracy weren't sure about it, this time around, the news people certainly connected the two killings. It quickly became a huge story, almost as big as if a flying saucer had landed in the center of town. People couldn't stop talking about it, at the barbershop, at the luncheonette, all over the county. The media, which loves to name things for their headlines, didn't neglect to mention the second dead man had done prison time, and they, along with other people around town, mostly men, started calling the shooter "The Avenging Angel." Other newspapers, noting it was a Black man killed in both shootings, started calling the shooter "The KKK Killer."

While some in town didn't think either moniker made much sense, most people started forming opinions along this divide, becoming almost as hostile as Republican versus Democratic viewpoints had become. None of this was making the investigation—which wasn't going anywhere—any easier.

The last thing this town needs, Tracy thought, *is for there to be another killing. Ugh.* She looked out her window on the placid town green. *Not on my watch.*

16

It was unfortunate.

To their dismay, they now bumped into each other all the time. Back when they were cops, it was more unusual. But now there was a string of robberies in town and two sets of detectives were working the case. Jill and her partner were doing all the routine things, checking off the boxes. Jack decided to follow one lead by himself.

Two thieves skulked about like skunks in the night.

So far, the robberies had been easy, and they were eager to get on with the next one. It was like an addiction, or a game, and they found in this sleepy town a way to make some easy money, maybe even some fame. They knew they couldn't stay around much longer, though; they'd need to find just one more good place for their next heist, then head out in haste.

Jack Ludlum just didn't like the look of the car, an old and dented vehicle moving slowly, almost aimlessly, in the better part of town. He'd watched it circle around. Jack was in his own car: in reality, not that different from their car. He saw two guys, thin, probably in their late twenties. He followed them.

He'd stayed back quite a distance, almost lost them at one point, then glimpsed their car entering a driveway. Jack got out of his car a block away and hurried to the residence they'd gone to. He silently went up the long, tree-lined driveway, crept to their car as he got close, cursing the gravel, and slowly peered inside.

Empty.

He'd headed around to the back of the house and spied a door ajar. Jack saw two men sneaking around, wearing gloves and masks. He saw them picking up a TV and rushed in. Within milliseconds, he was on them, kicking one in the guts as the TV slammed to the ground.

"What the hell!" screamed the thief, in obvious pain. The other one got a kick to the nuts and instantly fell down like a building detonated. His accomplice reached for a knife, swung wildly, and cut Jack's new shirt at the shoulder, making him even madder. Jack kicked the knife out of his hand, snapping his wrist with the action. He then picked him up by his metal-band T-shirt, gave him a roundhouse punch to the nose, and heard it break between his knuckles, blood raining on his partner in pain. Jack threw him like a bag of dirty laundry against the wall; he landed on top of his accomplice.

"Enough," they'd both shouted hoarsely in unison, panting and raising their hands.

"We'll leave your house, calm down!"

"Ha. First, it's not my house, I'm with the police!" Jack yelled, while handcuffing them together. "And second, you're not going anywhere. Now where's your stash?"

"Huh?"

The response was a punch in the eye, which swelled almost immediately.

"There's been a string of robberies. I know you're responsible. Where did you hide everything?"

"Hey, no way, man. This is the first time. Please believe me!"

Jack likewise met his response with a punch to the eye. "Now you look like your buddy here. Think carefully before I ask again, assholes!"

One of them started crying, the other was mumbling "please God" over and over under his breath.

"Where? I don't want to waste my time tracking this shit down!" Jack roared, as he decided whether to punch or kick this time. Maybe one of each.

Their eyes widened, watching Jack rear back.

Just then, the sounds of sirens broke the silence. The sound intensified as the cars rapidly approached the house. Jack took a deep breath in as he heard the screech of tires outside and reached for something in his back pocket. The cops busted through the door like the bulls of Pamplona, and the burglars looked at each other in relief. The first police officer in had a quizzical expression and exclaimed, "Wow, these crooks actually seem happy to see the police!"

Jack took his notes out of his pocket and started reading them their Miranda rights.

"What happened here, Jack?"

"Had a good lead. Caught these scum here trying to rob this nice house. Just reading them their rights before taking them in for questioning. Glad you guys got here."

"Right, just reading them their rights," the cop said, looking at the cuts, blood and swollen faces of the criminals, as well as Jack's condition. The crooks looked like a mob had trampled them underfoot.

"Just doing my job," Jack said. "Go ahead and do yours."

"I see they just won't give it up. Let me go in and talk to them."

"Listen, Jack," his partner said. "You're a detective now.

I'm not having any more of that cowboy shit. Or ex-Special Ops, if I got that right. Look, it's great we can lock them up for the robberies—looks like that case is closed—but we can get into some big trouble with the condition you left them in. Good thing we have a lot of friends here."

Jack looked unperturbed. "That's right, case closed."

"Are you looking for trouble?" his partner asked.

"Trouble seems to find me," Jack said.

17

All they did was yell past each other.

Sheriff Earl Klamp and the county law enforcement officials weren't getting anywhere. The small room was hot, the air was dead, and it smelled like socks after a 10K race. They couldn't agree if it was one killer, or just two random shootings in their little geography, let alone if the motivation was to take out bad guys, or if they were racially motivated, or something else.

"We don't haf no damn serial killer here, man," Klamp shouted, his face the color of a tomato.

"FBI says two related killings done separately is a serial killer," Sheriff's Deputy Tracy Dixon said.

"Whoa, listen to you. Screw da FBI. And we don't have proof they are related, just a bunch of slapdash theories. Let's not go crazy here and get everybody in town all upset."

"The newspapers have done that for you," the county chief, Gil Gulim, interjected.

Earl looked at him and softly said, "Things'll quiet down. Ahm sure of it."

Tracy suppressed a laugh.

"I think we need some help from the state. They have a lot more resources for the investigation than we do," Gil Gulim said.

"I will not call in the state!!" Sheriff Klamp bellowed. Gil took a step back. "They'd just love to get into our business. We can handle it! And besides, I think whatever there was, it's over. Moved on. Or there wasn't any damn connection in the first place. Mark my words, there'll be nothin' more."

Gil and Tracy exchanged fearful glances but said nothing.

18

No way!
Some time had passed since they'd become detectives, and each of them had learned a lot from their respective partners. Then Jack's partner was asked to move over to the narcotics squad because of a major opioid outbreak. Jack looked thrilled, likely thinking he could really show off his skills as the lone ranger. Jill was still shaken from the past week's massive heart attack her partner had experienced.

They both stood in front of the chief's desk, trying to conceal their disappointment. They'd been looking forward to their next case, but they hadn't expected to be paired up with each other. No way, Jill thought again.

They exchanged glances, both looking like they were feeling a sense of dread. The chief noticed it.

"Listen, we are short-handed. But it's only temporary. You two have got to learn to work together sometime, you know. We're not a very big department even when fully staffed!" he said. "And, Jack, you can learn from each other. I know Jill is a skilled listener and has a nice way of talking to people, making them believe her. I'm sure she'll help you with the reports too, since most guys around here deliver reports that suck."

Jack looked unconvinced.

The chief continued, "And I hope she'll keep you from being

like some other meatballs in this department who just kick in doors and end up with problems with the state attorney."

The chief made a face when saying "state attorney." At the same time, Jill gave Jack a knowing look.

Turning to Jill, he said, "And, Jill, I'm sure in a life-or-death situation—and undoubtedly there will be some—you'll be happy to have Jack at your side."

"He might be happy to have me at his side," Jill said.

"Right," Jack snickered.

"OK, you two, get to work."

"Great, just great," Jack muttered under his breath as they walked out of the office. "This is like two toddlers learning to walk, trying to hold each other up."

Jill groaned. "Thanks for the vote of confidence, Jack. But I'm no baby; I'm ready."

"Well, if you're ready, I'm more than ready," Jack said, but this time with a smile.

They soon realized they'd need to set aside any differences and work together, though it wouldn't be easy. They began poring over the details of the case they were assigned, which involved cybercrimes and identity theft.

As they worked the case, they kept second-guessing each other, and their competitive nature made it hard to agree on anything. It was slowing them down, though at the same time provided more options to explore. Jill would never give up but felt like they were two inexperienced climbers trying to scale a mountain with no ropes or safety gear.

After a week with little progress, they talked and brainstormed deep into the night, and something shifted. It appeared they began to truly see each other's strengths and realized they could complement each other. Jill was contemplative, with a high emotional IQ. She was great at reading people. Jack had a real go-getter attitude, never backed down, and was superb at analytics. Together, they could cover more ground, find more leads, and generate more hypotheses.

Slowly, but surely, they made progress. They put in long hours, worked tirelessly. And they cracked the case. Jack gave Jill a high five, and after a pause, their fingers intertwined. They both stood breathless for a moment.

They looked into each other's eyes. Then looked away.

They quickly disengaged, and Jill started putting papers into her briefcase. Jack cleared his throat and hit his knee on a desk with a thwack as he quickly spun away.

Later, the chief congratulated them on the good work. "You know, maybe two relative neophytes working together isn't so bad after all. You two actually make a good team. I think I'll keep you together. That young blood brings some good energy to the investigations."

Jack audibly groaned, while Jill looked unfazed.

"Yeah, you two, let's keep you as a team," the chief said with a big grin. "There's been a couple of strange shootings in a small town. May need you to look into it soon."

They walked out of the office, both with expressions of grim acceptance on their faces.

Jill wondered if it would really turn out all right, not sure what type of team they would actually be longer term.

Then Jack said, "Oh, no!"

"What is it now?" Jill said.

"Now that we've been teamed up..."

"Yes, what?" Jill asked.

"We are friggin' 'Jack and Jill.'"

19

I wasn't happy.

Never really had been. So many things had gone wrong. Life wasn't fair. I had to work hard for everything I got, while others, not nearly as worthy as I, got things handed to them.

As I got older, learned more, experienced more, something ignited within. The fire in my belly burned brighter. The truth became clearer. All those people around me getting ahead in life, while I remained stuck in the same damn place. I watched these less-deserving people get the breaks I should have. *Made me want to break things, break people, perhaps.*

One day, I guess I'd had enough. I was tired of playing by the rules and getting nowhere. I had nothing left to lose. Time to take matters into my own hands.

The fantasies were taking over. And I liked them.

I've been consumed by some very dark thoughts that I can't shake off. I'd often sit in my room for hours, lost in my own mind, imagining violent scenarios that I could carry out. Maybe deep down, I knew it was wrong. Maybe not. Maybe they deserved it. But I couldn't help myself. The fantasies were the only thing that made me feel alive.

I could imagine fulfilling my darkest desires. In fact, in my dreams, it felt amazing; the world was my playground, and I'd be king.

I knew I had to be careful or I'd become fully consumed by my fantasies. Though at first, they were idle fantasies. Now they seemed more like reality.

Or at least, perhaps it was time to make them reality.

20

"You gotta change!"

Jill had intercepted Jack in the hallway. "I'm actually serious, Jack. You know you really gotta change if this partnership is gonna work!"

Jack scoffed and started to walk away. Jill grabbed him by the shoulder. "Hey, I'm trying to help you!"

His natural reaction was to stiffen up at the contact, but he didn't; he liked the touch. He was confused.

"Listen," Jill said. "We've known each other for quite some time, and now we have to work together." She wrinkled her nose. "We need to do things right. People are still to this day whispering about what happened to the robbery suspects you apprehended." Jill looked away, before continuing. "You have to realize you're no longer doing your old job, terrorizing terrorists. I've heard those rumors, how you were like the reincarnation of Attila the Hun while in the military. As detectives, we need to dig harder, not fight harder."

"Yeah, yeah, I get it," Jack said, upset and with a tinge of regret. "It's just that this detective business can be so hard." He looked at Jill, now uncertain if he'd said too much to her, unsure of her reaction. Surprising himself, he then continued, "Hard to know where to draw the line, where to seek help, where the puzzle pieces fit." Jack exhaled. He often felt like he was circling a rotary and didn't know where to exit.

"I know. I often feel the same way," Jill said. She looked at him, her eyes large. "But I know you are a smart guy. You can do it."

Jack looked down at her, shocked, but said nothing. Didn't know what to say.

"Just tone down the physicality. Hey, I get it, sometimes the job requires it. But rarely." Jill looked at him, obviously thinking, then continued, "Why are you like that, anyway?"

Jack stared at her, and took in a deep breath, his eyes turning to slits. It looked like Jill immediately regretted having asked that.

"Sorry, stupid question. Forget it."

"We all didn't have great fathers, like the famous Frank Jarred," Jack spat out. "And we all don't go chasing ghosts, either."

He looked at her and immediately regretted the remark. Jill looked as if she'd been slapped and turned away in a hurry.

"Wait," he said, grabbing her arm, which she brushed away. "I'm sorry. My father was no superdad. After foster care, I was thrilled to finally have someone I could call a father. But I was wrong. Don't even remember the last time I celebrated Father's Day, if ever. The problem was how he treated my new mother. And to keep him from hurting my mom, I had to learn to use my fists."

Jill turned back to him and looked into his eyes, not sure what to say or do, her thoughts tangled as a ball of yarn. She then nodded slowly. "I guess..." She paused, then gradually continued, "But you're a man now. You don't want to be like him."

Jack stood there, not sure if he was mad as hell or interested in her interest. He took in a few deep breaths. Then he made a decision.

"Let's have coffee down the street after work. I'll tell you a story. But it doesn't have a happy ending."

21

The Marauder was at least good for something.

The old Mercury Marauder had an immense trunk. Huge and empty. I decided to experiment and got into it. It was roomier than I'd imagined. Much roomier. With a few modifications, it could actually make a nice rolling sniper's nest. Take out the back seat, allow access from there to the trunk, and provide some room to lie prone. Create a hole near the license plate for the barrel and sight to stick through.

Then do what has to be done and drive away.

It was uncomfortable.

They each sat looking down at their coffees, knees almost touching in the small booth of the coffee shop. For Jack, at six foot six, most places were uncomfortable. But he was not just physically uncomfortable, but emotionally too. Jill looked the same. They'd never been this close together.

"You mentioned my time in the military—Special Ops, actually," Jack started. "I think I learned a lot from being in the military: learning about how critical teamwork and cooperation is, learning to persevere and be resilient—Jesus, with everything that would happen, if you weren't resilient, you'd never make it. And certainly learning discipline and self-control were key in the military."

"Self-control?"

"Listen, Jill. Lots of things happened over there, none of it pretty. Let me tell you a story about one incident that still keeps me up at night."

Jill nodded her head, obviously steeling herself, and looked directly into his eyes.

"I was leading my team on a mission to take down a dangerous enemy stronghold in the heart of their territory. I crouched behind the rubble of a destroyed building as I surveyed the battlefield. Gunfire echoed through the narrow streets, and smoke billowed up from the ruins of bombed-out buildings. As we approached the enemy compound, we came under heavy fire. I ordered my men to take cover and return fire."

"Despite overwhelming odds, our team fought bravely, taking out enemy after enemy. We were outnumbered and outgunned but refused to give up. We had a great team, a guy named Doug was especially courageous, and a young guy named Dmytro ended up saving everyone's asses."

Jack stopped for a minute. He looked away, then gulped before finally continuing.

"But in the chaos of battle, I screwed up. I'd come face to face with the enemy, about to kill him, when I realized he was just a boy, probably no more than sixteen years old. I could've easily killed him. Or I could have beaten him and taken him prisoner—but that's no picnic for the enemy. We were alone, and something in the boy's eyes made me hesitate. I let him go. 'Run, kid. As fast and as far as you can. Go back to your momma,' I said. And just like that, the kid was gone."

"That night, after thinking the fight was over, the enemy ambushed us. Just a few of them came in quietly, stealthily. I looked over to Dmytro's bedroll and could see he was bleeding. It looked like he was stabbed in the heart."

"Running out was the boy I'd let go earlier."

"I rushed over to Dmytro, and I could see there was nothing that could be done; he was dying."

"Dmytro was actually just a kid himself. Just turned nineteen a few days before. I kneeled next to him. He was gasping but managed to whisper toward me. 'Daddy?'"

"'Yes,' I said."

"'Help me… Please.'"

"'Yes, I'm here, Daddy's here,' I said, squeezing his arm. 'You're going to be OK.'"

"'I see you, Daddy,' he said, looking upwards, a smile forming."

"Then his eyes stared out, fixed; he was no longer seeing anything."

Jill's eyes were wet as she looked back at Jack.

"I learned my lesson. Sometimes, you need to use your fists—or more—and take care of problems, finish it, or you'll get screwed in the end."

Jill took in a deep breath. "I get it. I understand."

She then took a minute, as Jack looked away. Her mouth was slowly opening and closing. She took in another deep breath, and began, "I do understand. But while it often feels like we are at war out on these streets, we're not at war, Jack. Jack, reach out with your mind, not your fists, as the first instinct. Jack, reach deep into yourself. You can do it."

Jack looked disturbed. He stared back at Jill, stared back into the unknown.

"There can be a happy ending, Jack. I can help," Jill said, taking his hand.

22

Tracy was surprised.

The sheriff's deputy had heard from her good friend Jill that she may be called into her area to look into recent murders. Nothing was official yet. Tracy invited her over to her place to talk about it, but mostly to catch up; Jill and Tracy had met at a training seminar and had become fast friends.

Tracy was making her special tacos and had her favorite bottle of red wine to share with Jill. Tracy was a divorcee who happily lived alone with her cat, named Nine, who was dozing peacefully on a corner chair. They sat on the couch in Tracy's cozy living room as she poured the wine into two glasses and placed them on the coffee table. The scent of the wine mingled with the aroma of spicy tacos, which were neatly arranged on a platter beside them.

Tracy was surprised at who Jill said she was now paired up with as a detective. "Jack! Isn't he the guy you told me was a Neanderthal?"

Jill's face reddened a bit. "He's not that bad."

Tracy looked at her funny. "Not bad-looking maybe. He's a big guy, right?"

"Yeah, real big."

"You must feel protected with him around."

"I don't need any protecting."

Tracy looked at her and smiled. "Course not. Nor do I." She smiled and continued, "But I think you did once say, after a few tequilas, that he was good-looking—in a rough-and-tumble kind of way."

"Well, definitely rough around the edges," Jill said, laughing.

"And I distinctly remember the description you told me. I knew you were a good cop because it was pretty detailed. Broad forehead, cleft chin, a face that looked stubbled even after he'd just shaved. Oh, and a small scar on the side of his cheek. Think you even said his uniform could barely contain his frame, let alone his massive muscles." Tracy smiled, while Jill's face turned as red as a radish.

"Jesus, you have a good memory. Too good. But the truth is when we first met, I couldn't stand the sight of him," Jill said.

"Yeah, I remember those stories you told about the police academy."

"That's right. Oh, those days were something. I remember how proud I was to put on the uniform with 'Recruit' emblazoned on my shoulder; happy to be embarking on my new life. It almost made me feel like I was born again."

"I kinda felt the same way. I was so energized! Watching all the shows on TV about law enforcement, it looked so exhilarating. Had to choose that as a career! So that first day was exciting for me too!"

"Still excited?" Jill asked.

"Well, as you know, movies and TV it ain't! You know, my father could never understand my decision, my original excitement. His first reaction was 'WTF? Are you nuts?' But he appreciates what I do now."

Jill looked back at her with a sad smile, thinking of her father, Patrolman Frank Jarred.

Tracy continued, "And my father understands me now. He understands I like getting the bad guy. Getting him off the streets. You know, sometimes, it's almost like a game to me."

Jill nodded her head, and said, "But first we had to get through the academy! I thought I'd prepared myself well physically for the academy. Running, sit-ups, push-ups, weights and more were part of my daily routine back home."

"Shit, I didn't do any of that." Tracy laughed. Then she pinched a small roll line by her waist. "Maybe I should."

"Don't be silly. You're perfect," Jill said.

"I don't know. One of my friends is bugging me to take SoulCycle classes with her."

"Well, anyway, I guess that part of why I killed myself getting in shape was because I felt that being a woman, I'd have to prove myself a bit more."

"Know the feeling," Tracy said. "Know it well."

"And then I met Jack, which just proved it. He did some stuff at the academy that I don't think he'd be proud of now."

"And he's going to look for our killer with you? Now you're OK with him?" Tracy asked.

"Maybe. The jury is still out. We'll see."

23

I aimed from the trunk of the Mercury Marauder.
     It was slightly awkward: cramped and somewhat incon-
venient. But looking down at the convenience store below, it
seemed it would work. *A convenient spot indeed.*

I watched as a woman left a packed car and went into the
store. Some stray receipts and food wrappers blew in the wind
about her, like dry fall leaves near death. She looked to be in
her late thirties, with a tired gait, exhausted face, and dubious
fate. Must be the mother.

There were a few gas pumps beside the store, and the father
took a minute to decide which type of gas to get, his hand
wavering between two octane levels. I watched him check the
price, then decide on the cheapest unleaded. He clicked on
the automatic setting and relaxed, looking like he was enjoying the sweet smell of benzine in the gasoline.

I set my automatic weapon. Everything was so clear; even
the expression on his fucking face was easy to read.

He looked around at the others pumping gas and seemed
happy for a moment's respite from the three little girls in
the back seat. Surely they were tired and cranky. I thought the
father probably hoped they could be put to sleep now, though
the long journey was almost over.

The father turned his gaze to his wife walking back to the

car, three ice cream sandwiches in hand. From the telltale residue of chocolate wafer on one side of her lip, it looked like she had eaten one before heading back out. The father seemed to stare at the ice cream, then shook his head in disgust and put the handle back on the pump with a bang. Maybe he was thinking of all the sugar that would make the kids too lively.

As I watched her approach, I moved the gun target from the father to the mother. Then back. Then back again.

That dad has a nice family. But he looks like a jerk. Doesn't deserve it.

And that mom. Looks like she can't be trusted. Probably just spoiling those kids. Kids can't be spoiled, dammit!

Unsure.

I knew I had little time.

I looked again at the three little heads in the back seat. I felt my teeth clenching. Never had much of a childhood myself.

I moved the barrel from the father to the mother and settled on the little girls.

Three shots would happen so quickly with this gun.

24

B am!
"That was the sound of the door hitting him in the ass," Tracy responded to Jill, who had said, picking up a taco, "Your turn, tell me more about your ex-husband."

Tracy sighed. "My ex-husband was a real bum, you know? He never appreciated how hard a policewoman has to work, just complained constantly about my long hours. And it's not like he ever really wanted to be with me, to do anything with me. All the ass wanted was to be *in* me. Sex, sex, sex, that's all he desired. Jesus, just leave me alone! Well finally, he did. And good riddance."

Jill shook her head sympathetically. "I'm so sorry, Tracy. You deserve so much better than that."

Tracy nodded and took a sip of her wine before continuing. "Yeah, maybe someday. I tell you, I think about my parents and how different it was. Married over fifty years, and so in love. They had this beautiful connection that I always admired."

"Wow, fifty years," Jill said, looking almost incredulous.

"Yup. Fifty years. Hell, with my ex, I knew it was over in fifty days!"

Jill laughed and Tracy joined in. They lifted their wine glasses, then savored a sip. Then two.

Jill, intrigued, leaned forward and said, "Tell me more about them."

"Well, they met while in college. My dad saw my mom struggling with all her new books and offered to help. They started talking and just clicked, like two puzzle pieces fitting together."

"And they managed to keep it going all those years!"

"They did. They really had a fairy-tale life together. In fact, my dad said before my mom, he'd felt like he was living in black and white his whole life, and suddenly, he was seeing the world in color."

"That's so sweet," Jill remarked.

Tracy clinked her glass against Jill's. "Cheers to true love. It's so rare these days."

After a sip, they both looked away, lost in thought for a few moments.

"So how about you, Jill? What's going on with your love life?"

"Love life! Ha. Who has time for that? You know how it is. Work, deadlines, endless to-do lists. It's a never-ending cycle."

Tracy studied Jill's face, sensing something beneath her casual response. She waited to see if Jill would say anything else.

"You know, Tracy, I've been so focused on my career and other responsibilities that I haven't made time for romance."

"I understand, Jill. Life gets busy, and it's easy to let certain things slide. But remember, you deserve happiness. Maybe it's time to make room for love in your life, even if it means adjusting your priorities a bit."

Tracy looked at Jill, seeing vulnerability in her eyes. Jill softly responded, "Well, Tracy, the truth is, I have been feeling... lonely, lately. The days blur together, and it's hard not to notice the absence of someone special. Someone to share moments with, to laugh with, to simply be there."

Tracy reached out and placed her hand gently on Jill's. "I know, Jill. Loneliness can be tough. But remember, you're not alone in this; I'm here for you. And who knows? Maybe when you least expect it, love will find its way to you."

Jill half-smiled and gave it a moment's thought. "You're right, Tracy. I'll open myself up to new possibilities. Definitely."

"That's the spirit, Jill. And I'll be right by your side, cheering you on every step of the way." Tracy squeezed Jill's hand gently, then they both shared a smile, and quietly contemplated the future.

Tracy broke the silence, pouring them both some more wine, and saying: "But at least I have Nine."

The cat looked at them, a Cheshire grin on its face.

"How'd you get that cat? You both look smitten."

"Oh, that's a long story. But I will tell you when he was a kitten, he was actually stuck in a tree! Never believed those stories till I saw it myself; he probably could have gotten down by himself, but a little kid was crying. I happened to be there, and I certainly wasn't going to call the fire department."

"Well, I certainly know you're no damsel in distress," Jill interjected.

"Good thing I wasn't wearing a dress! The poor child was yelling that the kitten was going to fall, going to die. So I shimmied up the tree—me, believe it or not—with some jerks below who came by hooting and hollering. But I got that kitten down. Then it jumped out of my hands and disappeared."

"Wow, I didn't think that tree stuff really happened! And good for you! But how'd you end up with it, if it ran away?" Jill took a bite of her taco. Juice dripped off the side of her mouth and she wiped it off with her napkin. "By the way, these are yummy!"

Tracy put another taco on Jill's plate.

"I shouldn't but I will." Jill laughed. "I've had a yen for them for a while!"

"Hey, you can afford it; are you still doing fifty push-ups a day?"

"Fifty-one, but who's counting," Jill said and laughed again.

Tracy put down her own taco and pushed it aside. "Wow!"

After a moment, she continued, "But to answer your question, it's amazing. That cat has nine lives, I tell ya! A year later, I was called out to this location, not far from the tree incident, where a cat was stuck down a drainpipe."

"Yikes," Jill uttered.

"Yup, it was him." Tracy nodded to her cat, smiling. "Same markings, same devilish face. And the other stuff in that drain... ... ugh, you don't want to know."

"Yuck."

"I had to get some help that time, but we got him out."

"Yippee!"

"And *this* time, I held on tight to him. No one claimed him. I kind of was yearning for some company. So eventually, I took him home."

"Yay for you!"

"Yeah. And Nine has been sitting in that chair ever since."

Nine looked back at Tracy and purred.

"Well, it's nice that you have him," Jill said.

"And now you have Jack?"

"Well, just partnered up," Jill said, looking away.

"For better or for worse," Tracy said.

"Till death do us part."

25

The little girls squealed.

They'd seen their mom approaching with ice cream from the convenience store. I tried to stretch out a bit more in the car's trunk, repositioning my feet on the rear seat. The crosshairs stayed on the back of the little girl's head as she sat in the middle of the car's back seat.

The rear door of the car opened; the mother passed the ice cream in. The girls squealed again.

I wasn't quite sure about the kids.

I moved my sight to the mother, her smiling face now in the crosshairs. Smiling face. My mother never smiled.

She bent down low into the car to give out the last ice cream, just as the father screamed.

"What the hell?"

I moved the sight to him. *How simple this is.*

"That ice cream is gonna keep them up the rest of the drive!"

Now I couldn't help but smile.

I carefully lowered the gun. Then, I put it away.

Nah. Nothing to do here today.

But it sure was good getting some practice into how all this might work.

"Goddamn it, why can't anything go right?!" the father muttered to himself, slamming the door.

He put the car in drive and roared off as the girls squealed in delight once more.

26

It became increasingly clear they were good together.
Good at what they did.

They now actually enjoyed seeing each other, working cases together, solving some of them. They would even occasionally spend the little time they had off talking together, usually at O'Reilly's Bar. Somehow, against all odds, they'd become friends. Or at least, not quite enemies anymore.

"We've done pretty well together," Jill ventured. "But things are heating up, as you well know. Do you think the chief is going to assign us new partners?"

"What, and break up Jack and Jill?" he said with a half-smile.

"Ha," Jill laughed. "Jack and Jill. There's only a Jack and Jill in your mind."

While they wouldn't fully admit it to each other, or even to themselves, they *did* like the idea of being Jack *and* Jill.

"To tell you the truth, I've been wondering the same thing," Jack said. "Who knows? Half the time, the asses in charge do a half-assed job."

Jill laughed half-heartedly.

"Well, maybe someday we'll be in charge—open *our* own shop. Private eyes! Someday. But of course, you'll still be taking orders from me," Jill said, laughing more fully now.

"Yes, boss," Jack replied, smiling. "We can be like a regular Sherlock Holmes and Watson," he continued, with a wink.

"That's right, but I'm Sherlock," Jill replied, a twinkle in her eyes.

Jack laughed. "Someday. But first, we've got work to do now."

"Yup, let's figure it out," Jill said.

She took his hand and gave it a squeeze. Jack looked at her hand on his, slim fingers belying her strength. She felt a change in his gaze, and he didn't move his hand away.

"Sure, partner," he said.

27

It was the last thing they expected.

Jill was working cases with Jack but continued with her unofficial night work: keeping tabs on white supremacist activity in the area. She'd always wondered what became of the baby girl they'd saved years ago at the compound and kept her vow to do what she could to, at minimum, uncover supremacist illegal activity—as well as get a heads-up on anything big going on. She did so by tracking online conversations and forums, often on the dark web, and keeping tabs on rumors of local meetings and activity in the area. It took on a new urgency with some of what Tracy had told her, newspapers blasting their theories about a "KKK Killer" on the loose.

Jill had contacts throughout the state, and acting on one of their tips, took a road trip to investigate. On a not very good Friday, she got in her car and started driving across the state. It was evening, rapidly getting dark, when the sound of a shot rang out.

Normally unflappable, its unexpectedness surprised her. Jill's car immediately began shaking violently, and pulled to the right, before a louder sound, like a locomotive slowly clanking down its tracks, assaulted her ears. A puff of black smoke came from her exhaust, and she smelled gas. The car lost all power as it slowly slid to the side of the road, then stalled.

Shit! she thought. *Why did I ignore that "check engine" light this week? That's not like me. Gotta stop being so wrapped up in the job, damn it.*

She was on a lonely stretch of state road on the outskirts of an even lonelier town: a town long past its prime, laced liberally with crime. Jill knew the area was renowned for its gang violence.

Clouds covered the sky, gearing up for an impending storm. There was very little light as Jill looked around, wide-eyed. The few buildings on the sides of the road were long since abandoned, standing about her like jack-o'-lanterns grinning with evil intent.

The road was littered with debris for as far as her eyes could see. Broken glass, decomposing garbage serving as a habitat for rats, neglected nails—which in combination with the perennial potholes that squatted in the middle of the street presented an obstacle course without remorse. She now felt like a prisoner in her car: its quiet captive.

Her options were few, and she quickly discarded the less viable. She knew a thing or two about cars, thought she may have had an engine misfiring problem, but really didn't know what to do now. She usually kept her gun within reach but had packed it in her overnight case when changing earlier in haste—a case closed in the trunk. *How stupid!* she thought. *I'm supposed to be a pro, goddamn it!* But the idea of exiting the car at this point to get the gun seemed silly. *Why should I?* she reasoned, since she could just phone for help. She double-checked the door locks.

The cell phone was of course her best recourse. She simultaneously praised her decision to keep it in her purse on the front seat and cursed a prior decision not to join AAA for roadside assistance. Who to call? The police? *No*, she thought, *what good is that? The only crime here is the stupidity of driving through this stretch alone so late at night—and they'd laugh once they found out I was a detective.* Then she thought of Jack. *Shit, he'd laugh more. I'd never live down his damsel-in-distress comments.*

Jill then figured, *What the hell, I'm not only a grown woman, but also a detective. Let's get real.* She decided to get the gun from the trunk just to feel more comfortable, and then she'd try to reach a tow-truck service. She unlocked the doors.

From her peripheral vision, she saw two figures quickly approaching the car. They didn't look at all like Good Samaritans.

28

M e and my Marauder were just over the state line when I
got lucky. Very lucky.

The man had been feeling very good about himself. He'd
bought a new car, decided to fully test it out on some wide-
open, lonely roads, and it had performed perfectly. But now
he found himself at a dimly lit Gulf gas station. Pumps open,
but otherwise deserted. He'd looked down and seen the tank
was just about empty, so he had to stop—though his instincts
told him not to get out of the car, to just get home on fumes.

But since the car was new, he couldn't calibrate whether
he'd have enough gas to make it. He knew he shouldn't take
any chances. Last thing he needed was to run out of gas on the
dark stretch of road ahead. So he stopped.

He started pumping the gas, but kept looking around,
as he couldn't shake the feeling of being watched. The hairs
on the back of his neck were standing up, his throat felt tight,
and he had goose bumps forming on his arms even though it
wasn't cold out. He thought to himself, *This is crazy. Gotta
stop watching those horror films.*

He finished filling the tank and bent over to pull the handle
out of the gas tank opening. As he did that, he felt the barrel

of a gun pressed to his head. He stopped with the handle half in and half out of the fuel hole.

It was a large man, holding an even larger gun.

"Easy now. I just need the car."

His hand was shaking as he held the gas hose trigger, while he stammered, "Keys in the ig-ig-ignition. Just take it. Pl-please, don't shoot. I have a family."

He looked at the man's massive, mahogany-shaded finger on the trigger of the gun. It wasn't shaking at all.

I felt my finger trembling on the trigger.

I hadn't expected to come across the robbery scene at the gas station below. I'd just wanted to practice some more since I'd made further adjustments to my car's trunk. Practice makes perfect, I'd been told.

But I certainly wasn't unhappy that there could be some real practice below. Much better practice.

"Put the damn gas handle back on the pump, and slowly reach in your pocket and give me your wallet."

"Wa-wal-wallet is in the ca-ca-car-."

The carjacker stared at him, exasperated. He lifted his hand high, butt of the gun extended, preparing to smash it over the man's head. The man's eyes widened.

My eyes widened. It was immediately clear to me what was happening. I saw who was attacking, which fueled my rage.

Happy to be of service.

I pulled the trigger.

29

Damn it!
There were two men—though they looked more like nocturnal animals to Jill as they'd peered in at her, pressing their dirty and distorted faces to the windshield.

Damn it! she thought.

One of the men, a burly figure with a menacing look, banged on the driver's side window. "Open up, lady, we just want to talk."

She knew this was trouble but stayed calm. Her first instinct was to grab for her cell phone. She swiftly glanced at the last number listed. Jack's. She pushed redial, not really thinking it through. It was just the quickest thing she could do.

After the fifth ring, it went to voicemail. She noticed her battery was running low. The men were pounding on the windows, then one of them went to look for a large rock beside the road. Jill's breathing came quicker. She pushed the numbers on the phone to call the police, but as she was doing so, one of the men, the huge one, jumped on the hood of the car. It caused the entire car to rock down, then upwards, and Jill's phone slipped from her sweaty palms.

Jill took some deep breaths, keeping her eyes fixed on the creatures outside. She knew she had to stay calm and not panic. Jill had been trained. She needed to quickly come up with some

options, as she had in the past. Jill had been through many
tough experiences before and knew how to handle herself. She
knew a few tricks and would fight the good fight, she thought.
But it was two against one, if it came to that. She tried to think
of a way out of it. Perhaps simply talking with determination
and reasonableness would work. But as she got a closer look
at them, she knew she'd better start with shouting.

"I'M A COP!" she yelled.

They laughed.

One replied, "And I'm Little Bo Peep, and you look like my
lost sheep."

They pulled on the door handles, as she grabbed for the
phone again to dial 911. Nothing. The last of the battery's
juice was gone.

Just then a piece of concrete came flying through the side
window.

One animal started to paw his way in, sticking his hand
through the smashed window and reaching for the unlock
button. Jill dove over to that side of the car, and pressed
her fingers over the mechanism, but they were immediately
met with a pounding fist and a loud growl. Her fingers felt
as if they were crushed, and her hand instinctively flew back
from the source of the pain, allowing the man access to the
lock again.

With her last ounce of willpower, she jumped back toward
the man's hand as it was about to open the door, ready to bite
down hard on it. She opened her mouth, and just as she was
about to chomp down, the sight of filth and open sores weakened her resolve. She just couldn't do it. The door flew open.

They didn't say a word to Jill.

The one who had opened the door just laughed uncontrol-
lably, the yellow and black of his few remaining teeth showing
as spittle dribbled down his chin. He reached in and down,

grabbed the keys, and threw them into the woods on the side of the road.

Shit, so much for getting my gun out of the locked trunk, Jill thought.

Then his fat and hairy arm grabbed the cell phone and handed it back to the other one. This other animal was as thin as Woody from Toy Story, and simply stared intently, in complete silence—probably had a thin brain. His wide eyes looked at the phone as if he'd never seen one before, and then he hurled it into the woods as well, mirroring his partner's actions. It shattered Jill's last hopes.

She grabbed her purse and extended it toward the fat one, saying she had fifty bucks in it. This caused another fit of laughter, though he grabbed the money out of it, and stuck it in his pants. "Woody" saw this and ran over, then began jabbing him with a bony finger. The fat one ripped a chain off Jill's neck, causing a cut on its way off that bled. He handed it over to Woody, then pushed him away. That seemed to satisfy him, as he departed in dance from the car, flashing the chain back and forth in front of his face like a child with a shiny new toy. Jill gasped at the small gash on her throat, hoping that they were now satisfied. But instead, the big one stopped laughing and pushed his bulk into the car, smashing against her side.

She pushed back and began punching.

"Oh, a feisty one," he said, as he slapped her across the face with the back of his hand, her head swinging to the side violently.

Jill changed her tactics.

"Please, please, please," she murmured repeatedly. In response, there was laughter once more. His aroma permeated the car, smelling like a dead animal left out to rot.

"What are you begging me for?" he said. "You want something?"

He grabbed her roughly, then tugged at her shirt.

Jill spotted headlights in the side mirror, hoping for help, but dying a bit inside when the car just sped by, no interest at all in investigating anything that was amiss in this area.

A noise on the hood distracted him. Woody was back again, the chain hanging from one ear as he sat on the hood of the car facing them, leering like a loon.

She knew screaming would do no good in this desolate place and steeled herself. She still had enough resolve to know that one more move and she would fight to the end.

The goon suddenly lumbered out of the car, headed over to Woody, who with "mine", was saying his first word. He shoved him hard, sending him slipping off the hood and onto the ground. He shrieked in pain, then grabbed a bottle from the side of the road and threw it at the big one, missing by much. He then ran off like a scared deer, tail up.

Jill watched this curious episode, thinking the two mentally ill, not sure if that bettered or worsened her chances. Not wanting to stick around to find out, she slid out the door while the two were occupied with each other. She ran down the road in the opposite direction.

She almost made it. It was her bad luck that tripped her up.

The big guy was immediately back on her, no longer laughing.

He pressed her to the ground, and she could taste the oil that stained the road. She felt gravel scraping her chin and tried to butt her head back into his nose. But he put his hand on her neck, and knee on her back.

30

The trigger was pulled.

The trigger of the gas pump handle was squeezed as he tried to use it to fight off the carjacker. The gas started spilling out as the first bullet ricocheted around them.

Shit, missed.

I squeezed the trigger of my gun again.

The second bullet hit the carjacker in the back, looking like it severed the spinal cord, as he crumpled to the ground and didn't move at all. At all. He had to have been immediately paralyzed below that spot. He went down as if in slow motion, his gun falling from his hand and skidding to a stop by the gas pump. At the same time, the ricocheting bullet hit the pump, sparks flying onto the puddle of gas, igniting it with the sound of "whoosh."

I watched as the car owner stared at the paralyzed carjacker on the ground, and saw the flames filling up the area, getting higher, getting closer. Wow, I was so lucky with that fire! Full service!

The man's eyes widened as the flames approached his car's gas tank. He must have felt the heat on his skin. It looked like his hair was singed as he turned to run.

Through the gun's sight, I could see the attacker on the ground mouthing the words "Please… please."

The man said something in response, looking back, as he ran.

Within minutes, the entire station was engulfed. The dimly lit Gulf station was now as bright as a downtown Las Vegas street. Man, I was pumped!

By the time fire and police vehicles got there, not much was left of the car, or the carjacker.

31

A shot rang out.
It wasn't a backfire. It wasn't a flat tire. Jill couldn't believe it, but it was Jack speeding toward them, Glock pistol in one hand pointed out the window while the other hand held the wheel. The big lug saw the gun, jumped off Jill, and ran. Jack sideswiped him, taking him down, and skidded to a stop, just in time to jump on the guy's back. Jack took a hard look at Jill's face, then smacked the man on the side of the head with his Glock.

"Woody" was back, and ran over to Jack, putting his fists up and moving them back and forth, feigning a fighter in the ring. Jack took one step forward and clocked him; he immediately collapsed. Jack then rolled him over to Jill. "Your turn."

Jill looked Jack in the eyes, reared back, and slammed her foot into the crook's balls as hard as she could. Her eyes never left Jack's, and he stared back intensely. They were laser-focused, as if they were seeing each other for the first time.

Both guys were done, crumpled on the road.

"Those guys deserved it," Jill said, shaking slightly.

"Well, well, let's not get too violent, Ms. Jarred," Jack said, managing a wink, though still panting.

Jill offered a weak smile in response. Jack dragged the two

bodies to the side of the road, giving each a kick in the head for good measure. They barely moved. Certainly not dead, but down and out.

Jill began trembling violently now that the incident was over. Jack went over to her and held her. "Deep breaths, honey, deep breaths." Neither of them noticed the word "honey" had slipped out.

Jill looked up at him, and Jack softly ran a finger along the area of her neck that was cut by the chain. Neither said a word, though Jill then placed her head for a moment on his broad shoulder.

Jack called the police, who came quickly. It was easy enough for the police officer to gather up the two and take them away. "Not the first time these guys have caused trouble," the local cop moaned. "Just wish the system would put them away longer—or at all."

Jill didn't want to spend more time in the area but looked over to the dark and heavily wooded side of the road. "I guess we'll have to search for my keys in the morning."

Jack conferred with the local cops, who said it should be OK. They'd make some extra rounds on the road that night, and even help them look in the morning. Jack clapped the lead cop on the back, while Jill managed a feeble smile.

Jack gently helped her into his car. She wasn't shaking anymore but was still obviously rattled. Jack got in, said, "Let's roll," and drove on, his brow furrowed in deep concentration. It was hard to see what lay ahead.

Jack seemed hypnotized by the yellow stripe running down the road. Jill stared intently out the side window, not daring to look at Jack. She seemed in a trance, but at the same time, her eyes were opened wider than they'd ever been before.

They still hadn't said a word until they were a respectable distance from the incident, and in front of a respectable-enough-looking motel. She touched his arm as he got out of the car. It wasn't incidental.

Jack roused the hotel clerk while Jill waited in the car. She locked the doors.

When he came back, Jill got out of the car; she was much more composed. She finally asked, "How the hell did you get there? Not that I'm complaining."

"I'm a detective."

"Come on, really. I called you but didn't think it went through. And you came so fast!"

"I'll confess, as long as you don't get mad."

Jill looked at him quizzically and grabbed his arm. "Don't think there's much you can say now that would get me mad."

"I was following you."

"What! What the hell? I take it back, I am mad." Jill suddenly felt like a bull about to charge the matador.

"Wow. Glad to see you're back to your old self."

"Why the hell were you following me?"

"Why were you out there?"

"I'm afraid that's none of your business, Jack."

"You almost got yourself in big trouble. Why?"

"OK, I was following a lead about white supremacists."

"Ugh, your hobby."

"It's not a damn hobby, Jack. We were both at that cabin!"

"OK, OK."

"And it *is* my job! Tracy, my friend and a sheriff's deputy, told me about the killings in her area. Said Black men may have been targeted, that it could be nazis. At least some of the media thinks so. But she's really concerned, even if her boss just pooh-poohs it. Obviously, we've got to stop this guy."

"What?! What the F! We haven't been assigned that case yet."

"Yeah, yeah, yeah. I believe in taking initiative."

"Goddamn it, Jill. I thought we were a team."

They stood there looking at each other, breathing heavily, cold stares through eyes of ice. Then their breathing slowed, and their eyes softened, like a glacier melting in the sunlight.

"I'm sorry. We are a team, Jack."

Jack nodded. There was no sound, both holding their breaths, the world momentarily no longer spinning on its axis.

"A team," Jack said. He wasn't sure what to do. Had never quite felt this way before. "Jill, I followed you for a reason. Not a business reason. Believe it or not, I do care for you," Jack said, first looking away but then clutching her hands. "I understand that you've done some investigating on your own time. I felt I'd better see what you were up to. Just to be safe. We are partners, after all."

"I don't know, Jack. I usually can take care of myself. I should be able to have my privacy." Jill pulled her hands away.

Jack grabbed her hands again. "Listen to me. Please. I was just trailing loosely, just in case. It's not like I have a lot going on in my life to occupy my time." Jack looked so different, like a little lost boy. "But really," he said. "You may not think so, but I've cared for you... for so long. Even back at the academy, and then our days on the beat; looking back, I think I always have."

"Well, you've had a strange way of showing it."

Jill's eyes felt moist and as large as they could be.

Jack took a deep breath and continued, "Dammit, I've cared *a lot* for you. *Care* for you. And tonight, I didn't want your obsession getting you in trouble. I saw the missed call from you—was actually out of my car getting coffee when you called. But I knew you wouldn't be calling me at this hour unless there was a real problem. I know these parts have some mean streets, some desolate areas, especially for a beautiful woman all alone."

Goose bumps appeared on Jill's skin when Jack said, "beautiful woman." He'd never commented on her looks before. She'd hated when guys made comments about her looks. This time, though, it felt damn good.

"Well, Jack," Jill said haltingly. "I still don't like you following me, but I guess I can forgive you, given the circumstances." Jill grabbed his hands. "And I guess if we are to remain partners, we have to be honest with each other, so I won't sneak around without you. Ever. Promise." She looked up at him, putting her hand on her heart.

"Yeah, partners," Jack said, looking somewhat glum and confused. For the first time in a long time, if ever, he seemed completely unsure of himself. "Yes," Jack continued, "I agree. Honesty. Always." He sighed. "Now, let's get you cleaned up. The room is just down that way."

They walked together. Jill tentatively reached out her hand. "I'm still a little shaky. Take my hand, please. This lot is so uneven," Jill said.

Jack smiled, and responded, their hands coming together in a comforting clasp, intertwining fingers, the way their lives had become intertwined, but both completely unsure of the future.

They approached the rooms, Jack having gotten two side by side.

"Don't you worry," Jack said, "I'm right next door if you need anything."

"Thanks, partner," Jill whispered. "Thanks for being by my side."

32

The cop was waiting for them.

After a quick phone call, they met with the local police back by Jill's car. The police officer was standing there with keys in hand, a smile on his face. "There's nothing like having a good metal detector around," he said.

Jill smiled. "Hey, did you..."

Before she finished, the cop pulled a phone out of his back pocket. "Yours, I presume."

"Oh God, thank you so much! I'd be lost without my phone!"

"Don't I know it," the cop said. "Hey, your car is pretty banged up—and you don't really want to drive with that shattered window. My brother-in-law owns a body shop. I can have him go get the car. He'll get it looking like new in no time. No more than a couple of days. Of course, with a professional courtesy discount."

Jill hesitated a moment, thinking about a return visit here. *What the hell*, she thought. "Wow, you're great," she replied.

They answered a few more questions, then spent the rest of the day following up on the white supremacist lead Jill had wanted to pursue, in a town called Pleasant Falls.

It took a while, but a local cop finally agreed to talk to

them over a beer. After what turned out to be a three-beer discussion, which followed a long day of looking around and talking to locals, they really had nothing much to go on. There were the typical bad guys in town, and talk of worse stuff, but nothing that could be pinpointed.

He did tell them about a weird group of men that call themselves Incels—thought they were harmless, but hateful and should be kept an eye on. Jill said she certainly would.

The cop told them if anything came up, he'd call them, though Jack knew nothing would. To Jack's considerable relief, Jill was ready to go. It had been a somewhat awkward, but strictly professional day.

It was late. "Another night at the motel?" Jack asked.

"No, it's been a long day." She gave him a slight squeeze on the arm. "We best get back."

Jack's eyes saddened, but he could see the weariness in hers, along with the frustration in her slumped posture. "You OK?"

"I'm fine. I just want to get out of here. Don't like the vibe in this Pleasant Falls." Jack could see Jill's resolve melt like a frozen pond at the approach of spring. "And I guess you were right; I probably should do things a bit more by the book. Even so, I'm glad we tried." She grabbed his hand, gave it a pat, and said, "But, yeah, I'm OK. Thanks."

They drove back, Jack immersed in his own thoughts, Jill apparently as well—a myriad of meditations twirling about their brains, like mini twisters across the open plains.

The drive was near its end. They passed Jack's house on the way to Jill's. Jill noticed another car in his driveway. "Didn't know you had a second car; what are you doing with what looks like such an old boat of a car?"

"There's a lot you still don't know about me."

Jill slanted her head to one side, looking up at Jack, her eyes narrowing. After a moment's hesitation though, she smiled. "Happy to learn."

33

"We really need help!"

Sheriff's Deputy Tracy slammed the door behind her as she charged into Sheriff Earl Klamp's office. He looked more disheveled than ever. "That's three murders now!" she said.

Klamp looked up, his face instantly red. "Now calm the F down, missy!"

"Don't tell me to calm down," Tracy said, putting both hands on his desk.

He looked at her wide-eyed, but remained calm, almost laconic. He then started speaking to her as if she were a child. "Ya haf to understand, this third shooting wasn't in *our* town. Wasn't in *our* county, or the next one over. Wasn't in *our* state. So it's none of *our* business."

"Don't be ridiculous; it was just over the line!"

"Not our state."

Tracy straightened up and crossed her arms. She couldn't shake the feeling that something big was looming on the horizon. Tracy was now concerned there could be a serial killer out there. She presented her theory to Klamp.

He rolled his eyes and moved his chair back, his fat jiggling.

"Come on, Tracy, you're always so dramatic. It's just a few unrelated homicides. The perps will be caught, eventually."

Tracy knew better. She was smarter than Klamp and had a gut feeling that something terrible was going to happen if they didn't act fast. Tracy couldn't just sit back and do nothing while innocent people were being murdered. She felt her blood boil. *How could he be so dismissive of a potential serial killer?*

"Remember the last time you brushed off a case as 'unrelated'?" Tracy asked, her voice shaking with anger. "It turned out to be a string of robberies, and if I hadn't convinced the others to take it seriously—shit, my own father would have been a victim!"

Klamp looked like he had no clue what she was talking about. Tracy thought back to the case, where the last robbery victim had been hurt badly. She remembered that oh so well. She'd stood in the break room, surrounded by her fellow law enforcement personnel. They'd just received news of another robbery, and tensions were running high.

"Listen up, everyone," Tracy had said, her voice firm and commanding. "We've got a string of robberies happening here, and we need to step up our efforts to catch the person responsible. We can't afford to let this continue."

One of the other deputies, a burly man named Joe, had grunted in agreement. "Yeah, but what are we supposed to do? We've been chasing leads for weeks now, and we have gotten nowhere. And Sheriff Klamp doesn't seem concerned. If he's not, then maybe I'm not."

Tracy had held up a hand to silence him. "I know it's frustrating, Joe, but we can't give up. And I'm in charge of stopping these robberies, understand? We need to stay focused and work together to catch this guy."

Another deputy, a young woman named Diane, had spoken up. "What if he strikes again before we catch him? Someone could get seriously hurt."

Tracy had nodded grimly. "That's exactly why we have to

redouble our efforts. We can't let this criminal continue to victimize innocent people in our community. You all know we have a duty to protect them."

She had turned to Joe. "I know you've been leading the efforts so far, but we need fresh eyes on this. I want you to team up with Diane and start going over the evidence again. Look for anything we may have missed."

Joe's face had turned pink. He'd grumbled something. But he'd eventually nodded, slowly, then averted his eyes. Diane had looked grateful for the opportunity.

Tracy had turned to the others. "The rest of us will hit the streets, talking to witnesses, and keeping an eye out for anything suspicious. We need to be vigilant and work together if we're gonna catch this guy."

There was a moment of silence as everyone processed what Tracy had said. Then they'd nodded in agreement.

"OK then, let's get to work," Tracy had said.

They'd eventually apprehended a suspect right before another robbery was about to happen. To the surprise of all, especially Tracy, the potential victim turned out to be her father!

Now, every year on the anniversary of that failed robbery attempt, her dad took her out to the fanciest restaurant in the area. Having just had that dinner last week, the memory was fresh, and she briefly thought of it, savored it.

She'd looked forward to the tradition, and as she'd stepped into the restaurant, she'd immediately felt the weight of the day slowly melt away. The scent of freshly baked bread serenaded her senses, calling her in. The hostess had recognized her and gave her a smile, then pointed the way. Tracy walked over the faux Brazilian cherrywood floor, passing tables with soft linen tablecloths and overstuffed, upholstered chairs, and modern art on the walls.

She'd spotted her father sitting at their usual table. He was wearing his best suit and had a big smile on his face.

"Tracy!" he'd exclaimed as she'd approached the table. "You look beautiful tonight." Then he looked a little concerned. "Am I allowed to say that these days?"

Tracy had smiled and hugged her father. "Yes! You're my dad! And thanks! You look pretty sharp yourself."

They'd sat down and ordered a couple of beers—imported, given it was a special occasion—and they'd both asked for steaks: well done for him, medium-rare for her. As they'd waited for their food, her father had reached below the table and pulled out a small bouquet of flowers.

"Happy anniversary," he'd said, handing the flowers to her.

Tracy had smiled and smelled the sweet fragrance of the flowers. "Aw, thanks, Dad. You always know how to make me feel special."

Her father's eyes had twinkled with pride. "You are special, *Sheriff's Deputy* Tracy. You saved this town from a lot of heartache."

Tracy's heart had swelled with pride as she'd recalled the string of robberies she'd solved.

"You're the reason I'm here today," her father had said, reaching across the table to take her hand. "I'm so proud of you. I love you."

Tears had welled up in Tracy's eyes as she'd looked back at her father. She knew how much he loved her, but it was nice to hear him say it. She'd squeezed his hand.

"I love you too, Dad."

Her dad had looked away a moment, seeming choked up. "Well, just continue to keep this town clean."

"You know I'll do that, Dad. For you and for everyone who lives here. Always. I promise."

Thinking of that night brought her back to reality. Tracy

took a step closer, her frustration rising. "Sheriff, we can't just ignore it and hope it goes away."

Klamp chuckled, taking a sip of his coffee. "You're getting all worked up over nothing, Tracy. I tell ya, it's just a coincidence."

Tracy felt her blood boil. *How could he be so ignorant?* "Sheriff, this isn't a joke! People are dying. We need to do something about it!"

Tracy clenched her fists, feeling the anger building up inside her. She couldn't sit back and do nothing. She had to take matters into her own hands. But first, she tried one other tactic and took a moment to calm down before she started.

"Listen, Earl, think about yourself. You can't ignore this because you won't get re-elected if there is a serial killer around and you pretend your town is as safe as ever. The people are concerned. Believe me, you are gonna want them to see you as a man of action."

Sheriff Klamp looked at her as if slapped; Tracy could see the concern in his eyes.

"Plus the media has quieted down, but you know they are going to go nuts now. Another guy shot, burned to death at a gas station. I can see the headlines now: ': The Avenging Angel Strikes Again!' And the dead man was Black! I can see competing headlines screaming 'KKK Killer Still On The Loose!'"

"Well, maybe, just maybe ya right. Let me talk to the county. But as for now, don't you damn go blabbering to the press. They haven't made the connection. Don't ya talk ta anyone else for that matter!"

Tracy didn't trust him. She knew it was time to make it official and knew exactly who she was going to talk to.

34

His name was Saint.

And he was an easy mark.

Jill was following up on the tip regarding the group called Incels, and what she learned shocked her—and she'd seen and heard a lot.

At the same time, Saint was learning about them too. In a dimly lit room, with posters of bands adorning the walls, Saint clutched a photograph of his father, who'd passed on before Saint was even born. Tears welled up in his eyes as he gazed at the image, feeling the immense absence of his father's love and guidance.

In a voice so low, he could only hear it in his mind, he said, "Dad, I wish you were here. I feel so lost and alone... I don't know what to do." He felt a stirring within, but no answers.

Saint wiped away his tears and glanced at the nearby mirror. He saw a reflection of a boy who didn't quite fit in, with perpetual sadness etched on his face. The memories of being bullied at school flooded his mind, like a rising river about to drown him.

Then there were those murders.

Jill received a call from Tracy, who wanted to talk further about the murders in her area.

"Sure we can get together, unofficially," Jill said. "But first, let me ask you something else."

"Shoot."

"You ever hear about a group of guys known as Incels?"

"Sounds vaguely familiar. What's up?"

"Just doing some investigating. Seem kind of nuts. A weird combination of lovelorn misogynists. Can't quite figure them out."

"Dangerous?"

"Don't know. Who isn't? But if they are a crazy hate group, perhaps there is an association to other crazy hate groups."

"Well, you better be careful. Don't know what I'd do if you were gone; who can I talk to besides my cat?"

"The lovely Nine! I'll be careful... as much as I can. Don't think I have as many lives to lose as Nine."

It never ends.

The next day at school, the cafeteria buzzed with students chatting and laughing, while Saint sat alone at a table, his lunch untouched. He watched as a group of girls giggled and whispered, casting occasional glances his way. He got up quickly, grabbed his lunch tray, and threw it in the garbage.

He hurriedly walked out of the cafeteria, but on his way noticed a couple sitting nearby, holding hands and sharing long looks and affectionate smiles. Saint yearned for that connection, for someone to see him and accept him for who he is. He shook his head and dragged his feet. *I'm just destined to be alone.*

His mother, Deja, tried and tried to cheer him up. But it just wasn't the same. And her work kept her out of the house most of the time. The house Saint came home to was usually dead quiet. Too quiet. But he accepted it as part of his fate.

That evening, in his darkened bedroom, Saint scrolled through his social media feeds filled with pictures of seemingly perfect lives. Each image amplified his sense of inadequacy, deepening the loneliness that enveloped him like a suffocating shroud.

It's scary.

They were at a small office in another town when Jill told Jack about some of what she'd found online regarding Incels.

"I asked Tracy about them, but she didn't know much," Jill said. "She's really preoccupied with the possibility of a serial killer."

"Well, shouldn't that be our priority?" Jack said.

"We haven't been called in on that, Jack. You know that. But I'm scared; some guys in this group sound like they can be very dangerous too."

"How so?"

"Lots of language against women; some actually talking about violence. Some of it I'm sure is just bluster, but I need to check it out."

"Well, if you are concerned, so am I. You always have great insights."

"Really, Jack?"

"Really."

"Well thank you," Jill said, staring into his eyes and rubbing her hand up and down his arm.

Jack felt a tingling sensation that traveled from his arm through the rest of his body. It felt like a soft breeze of anticipation danced across his skin.

*

Saint really had no choice.

He spent his days and nights in his own world, his online world, where he didn't need any friends—and in fact where acting unfriendly was more the norm.

He'd always hated the name Saint; it just gave the kids at school another reason to make fun of him, to shun him. So he escaped to the web, became entangled in it. It was there where he finally embraced his red hair, eschewing the name Saint for the screen name "El Diablo."

Naïve and alone in his room, alone with his thoughts, he was quite impressionable, fascinated by the opinions of other friendless phantoms online. The sites he lingered on were full of guys broadly blaming everyone else but themselves for the problems they had. Seesawing from one tilted perspective to another, he started to become narrow-minded.

He became more bitter at never having had a girlfriend. Or a best friend. Or even one friend. Now he usually rushed home from school to feel safe: secure but seething. Back to his room he would flee; eventually, he just stopped going to school most days, unbeknownst to his mother Deja, who was at work. The school really didn't seem to care. So he spent his time alternating between online gaming sites and chats that were more like jousts.

Saint, now seventeen, happened upon a group online calling themselves "Incels," which he learned stood for "involuntary celibates." These were males who would rail about their state of affairs—or non-affairs. Mostly in their twenties, they were angry with women for not wanting to date them, let alone have sex with them. Saint found comfort in the fact that he wasn't alone, that there were other guys feeling just as lonely and upset.

It pleased him to hear that when it came to women, he

wasn't the problem. It surprised him to be told it was instead, the females of today that were the issue. While he wasn't sure about how he felt about that, it gave his ego a bit of a boost; perhaps he wasn't all bad. He chatted it up with this new group of friends, his first friends, and took counsel on what strategies might someday work to nab a lady; he may have been named Saint, but he didn't want to live like a priest.

A typical chat:

ElDiablo: Any tips?
ScottB20: Girls are bitches.
ElDiablo: Whoa! Hold on. They can't all be—I'd at least like to be able to talk to them.
ScottB20: Don't bother. It doesn't matter what you do. It's not you, it's them that's the problem.
ElDiablo: I'm gonna try a new haircut.
ScottB20: If you insist. But I still wouldn't open myself up to more rejection. Hey, how about your clothes? You make sure they're neat and clean.
ElDiablo: Thanks!

A conversation the following week:

ElDiablo: Well that didn't work.
ScottB20: Told ya. Not your fault. Women are cruel.
ElDiablo: No, it's me. I'm a loser.
ScottB20: Not you, bro! Never you.
ElDiablo: Any other suggestions?
ScottB20: Well, if you still want to start with a Stacy, maybe keep working on looksmaxing. Hit the gym. I have a contact for some great steroids.
ElDiablo: Maybe.
ScottB20: On second thought, Stacys will only follow the

money. You can be dumb and fat, but if you have the dough, a Stacy will do you. Do you have dough?
ElDiablo: No.
ScottB20: Then go for a Becky. But hit the gym first.
El Diablo: Thanks, coach!

Saint wasn't in a position to hit the gym, but he started working out in his basement with simple weights, push-ups, and pull-ups. It's not that he was in horrible shape, but he was kind of scrawny, and definitely could use some filling out. He didn't take ScottB20 up on the steroid offer but did down protein shakes and bars whenever he could, and often asked for steak for dinner, though mostly got burgers instead. He saw some improvement, so he kept at it every day, breaking up his time between being online and offline physical training.

Sometime later, he went back to the Incel chat room:

ElDiablo: So besides being a dating coach, what do you do?
ScottB20: Dating coach! That's a laugh. Last two times a girl agreed to see me, she never showed. They just make you suffer. I found out where one works and just tried to talk to her, and the bitch called the cops! I didn't do nothing. Just wanted to talk to her, that's all!
ElDiablo: Wow. Sorry, man.
ScottB20: Treacherous. Lying treacherous women. You are better off staying love-shy.
ElDiablo: You're probably right.
ElDiablo: Hey, so what do you do??
ScottB20: Don't start sounding like my mother. I hear enough of her shit daily.
ElDiablo: OK, OK, it's all good.
ScottB20: Like most of the guys here, I'm a NEET.

ElDiablo: NEET? Hmm. I know what a Stacy and a Becky are, but what's a NEET?
ScottB20: Man, you've got a lot to learn! Good thing you've finally found a friend who can teach you a few things.
ElDiablo: Yeah, man. Appreciate it.
ScottB20: A NEET is "not in education, employment, or training." For you dummies—not in school or working.
ElDiablo: Sweet. Sounds like a good place to be. I guess.

There was a girl in his neighborhood that Saint was really interested in, from a distance. She appeared shy, was pretty in a plain kind of way, and seemed super smart the couple of times he'd overheard her talk in town. She hadn't gone to his school, so he thought she'd be a good trial case for him: someone he could finally approach and say a few words to, someone that would be a fresh start.

The sun peeked through the clouds, sending a gentle kiss of warmth to the earth. Saint took that as a good sign. There were no other boys around when he spied her in front of the drugstore. *Well, it's now or never*, he thought. *New haircut, new clothes, new body, worth a shot.* For a second, he almost turned back. But then he gulped, straightened himself up, and got up the nerve to head toward her. As he got closer, he saw her smile. His stride quickened, hands perspiring, and now with an ounce of encouragement, he began to say hi. Just as he opened his mouth, she started laughing, looking at him and saying something under her breath to the girl beside her. Saint realized she was laughing at him. His face turned as red as his hair, and he turned around, walked away quickly, then tripped as he rapidly ran. He picked himself up, looked at the tear in his shirt, and headed back home, head down, shoulders hunched, a tear in his eye.

It wasn't long before he was isolated in his bedroom, and back in the chat room.

ElDiablo: I hate them!

ScottB20: Told ya!

ElDiablo: I'm never gonna have a girl.

ScottB20: There's always hookers.

ElDiablo: Nasty.

ScottB20: Men like us are entitled to sex.

ElDiablo: I think so.

ScottB20: Females can't deprive us of sex. It just ain't right.

ElDiablo: I guess.

ScottB20: WHAT'S THIS I GUESS SHIT!!!! Women can't deny us our rights, we deserve sex. The skirts better understand that, or there will be retribution.

ElDiablo: What do you mean?

ScottB20: We can only take so much. If they don't give us sex, then we'll take it.

ElDiablo: Huh? Take it? You don't mean forcing yourself on them?

ScottB20: You know what I'm saying.

ElDiablo: Gotta go.

Saint was shocked and was sure that would be the last chat he'd have with ScottB20. He looked down and saw a spider about to crawl up the leg of the desk. He stood up and tore a piece of cardboard off the back of a pad. Saint corralled the spider onto the piece of cardboard on the third try, then opened his window, laid the cardboard on the sill and closed the window again. "You're free, little buddy. Just stay out."

It was a while before Saint returned to the chat room. When he did, he tried avoiding ScottB20. Not that the other guys online were much better. One guy, RodgerDodger, started up with him.

RodgerDodger: You a man or not?

ElDiablo: What's your problem?

RodgerDodger: My bro ScottyB says you're avoiding him. I know you're an unfuckable, but are you a man??

ElDiablo: Yeah, I'm both.

RodgerDodger: Forget about Scotty, I'm just messing with you. ScottyB isn't really where it's at. If you want to be a man, then you're gonna want to hang out with this group of guys I know. Real men. You should hear what they say. I'll give you the skinny on how you can talk to those guys if you'd like.

ElDiablo: I talk to plenty of guys here.

RodgerDodger: These guys are in the real world. Can be your real friends. Like brothers. They have rousing events you can go to, actions to take. Like an exclusive club.

ElDiablo: Sounds interesting... I don't know.

RodgerDodger: You don't know? What the hell else you got going on in your life?

ElDiablo: Ugh. Right. Well... maybe.

RodgerDodger: Hey, some of these guys even have tradwives. And sisters. Meet some cute chicks.

ElDiablo: Sick. Hmmm. Got nothin' else to do. OK, I guess.

Saint didn't know what a tradwife was, but "cute chicks" sounded all right by him. He started talking with a guy from the group RodgerDodger suggested. The guy was vague when they talked but invited him to a get-together. Just prior to that, a last chat with ScottB20 cemented his thought that it was time to leave the Incel group, time to move on:

ScottB20: I know you're there, Devil Dog. Answer me!

ElDiablo: What's up?

ScottB20: That's a good boy. Why you been avoidin' me?

ElDiablo: I haven't. Just been busy.

ScottB20: Hope you didn't say nothin' to nobody on what we last conversed on.

ElDiablo: Course not.

ScottB20: Well forget what I said, anyway. But just don't you forget women are hateful. Need to be punished for making us suffer.

ScottB20: You still there, pinprick penis?

ElDiablo: Still here.

ScottB20: You can help me with somethin'. Prove you're a man. Prove you've learned your lessons right. There's somethin' called a hot yoga studio not far from me. Women in their yoga pants, showing off their asses and you know what else. Enticing all the guys but keeping their legs closed, laughing at us. As usual.

ElDiablo: Seen that. Those outfits do kind of drive me nuts.

ScottB20: Well, it's time we got some revenge. Time to teach them a lesson. They want hot yoga, we can make it real hot!

ElDiablo: Umm... I'm not so sure about that.

ScottB20: Goddamn wimp! Maybe you have a pussy. Maybe I should take care of you after I take care of them!

ElDiablo: See ya.

Saint thought about calling the police, but then figured ScottB20 must be all talk. Lots of guys in the chat rooms just made shit up.

ScottB20 took a gas can and lighter to the hot yoga studio that night, a Glock 17 in his belt behind his back—just in case any tried to get away.

35

What does it mean?
Jack couldn't stop thinking of Jill. Every time he'd pick up a case file, his thoughts wandered off. Every lead he'd start to follow just led to Jill. He was perpetually lost in thought, unable to focus, in a daydream from which he couldn't escape. He'd admitted he cared for her but didn't get much in return. He kept thinking of every touch, and began recalling every one of her offhand comments, dissecting each for a hidden meaning. Every song he heard reminded him of Jill; every text notification received he hoped it was from her. *This is crazy.* We are colleagues, nothing more, nothing less.
What should I do?

What does it mean?
Jill was focused on following her leads. She'd managed to get some information about a possible planned hate attack by an Incel on a yoga studio, and she was hot on its trail.
But every now and then, her thoughts would turn to Jack, interrupting her work. Last night, she woke up and couldn't get back to sleep as she traced the contours of his face in her mind, down to his small scar. *Crazy*, she thought. *We are professionals doing a job. A job that is key to focus on. Nothing*

more, nothing less. Must be the case making her mind go back to him. She texted him on the latest Incel information she'd found, and where she was going. But even after that, his image kept interrupting her thoughts, like an intrusive wave continually crashing onto the shores of her mind.

What should I do?

What does it mean?

I'm loving this. Found some guys who think like me. Feel like I belong. No, feel like I could lead. Should lead. Love to hate. The power. Feeding on each other. Feeling it get stronger. There's plenty of ways to accomplish what I want. What I need. That's all I can think of, all I can focus on now. Crazy. Yet, it's all very clear—nothing more, nothing less. But where to go next?

What should I do?

36

An instinct told him not to meet with the guy.

Saint thought about the invite—about checking out the other group RodgerDodger had recommended, meeting the new guy he spoke with on the phone.

Based on his instincts, he wasn't going to do it; it was like he knew deep inside of himself that this would just be another kind of trouble. But he felt more alone than ever, having looked for support from the Incel group but finding nothing but disappointment and crazies there. Now, he had no one. Alone again, unnaturally. The thought of meeting up with some new guys, maybe making some friends, was more than enticing, like a lifebuoy thrown to one floundering at sea.

The meeting spot wasn't far from his town, and now that at eighteen he could drive, he asked his mother Deja to borrow the car: an old, used car they'd had for several years. He knew she was concerned about his driving skills, and when he asked, she hesitated.

"Come on, Mom, you keep saying you want me out of my room. I can meet some other guys!"

"Well, you're right, I certainly don't want you always holed away in that dark room, like... like a Ted Kaczynski."

"And besides, some more driving practice would be good for me, especially now that I'm an adult."

"Sort of an adult," Deja said with a smile. "OK."

With transportation finalized, Saint now had no reason not to go. So off he went. Not without some trepidation, but at least with something to look forward to.

"Could this be right?" Saint wondered.

He had scribbled the directions on a stained piece of paper. This quest was not on any map; no GPS would locate it. Getting off the highway and following the road through town was easy enough—though he heard cars beeping at him more than once but didn't know why. The town was quite ramshackle, looking like it fell into a deep sleep fifty years ago and never woke up. But that didn't bother him. It was finding the turnoff, which was not well marked, and only discovered on the third try, followed by another turnoff down a dirt road that had him perplexed.

He headed down the road, a trail with mini-craters dotting the path and slowing him to a crawl. He heard the brush scratching against the paint on both sides of the car, and prayed there'd be no obvious marks that Deja would see. If so, he'd be without wheels for quite some time.

After about a mile, he saw a handmade sign with the words "Very Fine Men" etched in black on a weathered plank and followed the pointing arrow until the road dead-ended into a clearing. There looked to be about a dozen men hanging out, beer bottles in hand, scowls on their faces. The men looked at him as if he didn't belong; Saint felt the same way.

Tricked out in tattoos, jean jackets with skull patches, unshaven—except for some with shaved heads—cigarettes dangling from their mouths, studded leather wristbands, brass on some knuckles, they watched as Saint got out of his car. Not a single greeting, just staring eyes with ill will, making

Saint feel sick. A couple of the men walked toward him, bats in hand.

Saint tried to get back into his car, thinking these men weren't very fine for him.

Rough hands grabbed him before he could. A gigantic man—huge muscles and an earring—got in his face, shouting, "What the fuck, Prom Boy!"

37

The girls in their yoga pants were enticing.

ScottB20 watched from his car as they entered the studio, many with long, flowing, blond hair—his favorite shade—so they'd be the ones to go first, he thought. They came in with their rolled-up mats, water bottles, and knowing smiles. He gazed at them through the plate glass studio window as they greeted each other, a few with hugs, a few with shrugs.

Scott was simmering, and unconsciously clicked his lighter's spark wheel continuously. The neon sign in the window flashed "Hot Yoga," casting a pinkish purple haze along the walls of the dark strip mall and the closed luncheonette nearby.

He spent a few minutes thinking of all the women he believed had wronged him, starting with his mother. Seething more with each recollection, he reached boiling point. He screamed out as he exited his car.

"Treacherous bitches! It's retribution time! Karma, baby! What goes around comes around! And it's coming-around time!"

ScottB20 raced toward the yoga studio, gas spilling out of the overflowing can as he ran. The women had started their class, backs toward the window, focusing on their movements. Scott moved closer. He started splashing the gas on the door and the entire front of the studio.

He knocked the can into the window as he finished spreading the gas, and some women turned around. Their mouths opened wide as the gas can, smell, and lighter in his hand registered.

Saint backed away from the big, bald, brawny man yelling at him, seriously regretting that he'd come.

He felt like he was about to pee in his pants. Then a very slender man with torn jeans and a white muscle shirt came sprinting up.

"Hey calm down, big guy! This must be the kid I invited. Listen," he said, looking at the others who had gathered around. "I spoke to this guy; he may be useful. May not look like much, but he's got a brain, unlike some of you."

Saint stared at the man, relief on his face. Thin but appearing strong and wiry, he looked like he could hold his own against the big, brawny guy, though that was a fight Saint hoped he'd never see. This man, seemingly the leader, appeared to be in his late twenties, his nose curved to one side looking like it had been broken multiple times. His small, dark eyes seemed to dart from place to place, before landing again on Saint. He clapped him on the back, Saint feeling the thud of more weight than intended.

"Hey, you need a beer. Let's grab one and I'll introduce you to the rest of the men," he said, then with a wink, added, "And while my name is James Dylan, as I said on the phone, I prefer to be called The Exterminator."

Saint dutifully complied, and just about downed the entire beer before saying his first hello. "So whatsya name?" a guy with a long, brown beard asked him, motioning him to sit on a tree stump next to him.

"Sa... I mean Diablo."

"Diablo! Now you're talkin'. You can call me Sarge."

"Yes, sir!"

Sarge laughed, slapping him on the thigh. "Good to meetcha. We's just a bunch of guys who look out for each other, look out for our little community, and our country. No offense, but you looks like you can use some looking after too. Now git yourself anotha brewski, and then head over to the barbecue pit. We'll talk more later. You knows, we make the best damn ribs you'll ever have. Can't you smell them smokin'? Delish!"

Just then a large, black dog came bounding toward Saint, snarling, spittle spewing from side to side, dripping off its enormous jaw. Dirt kicked up as the dog powered forward, a ferocious bark pounding Saint's ears. Saint's eyes were now one hundred percent focused on the sizable incisors protruding from its enormous mouth, which looked like they would cut him in two. The Rottweiler leapt, all 125 pounds of pure muscle and open jaws heading toward Saint.

It was like a battering ram barreling into him.

He went down like a prizefighter knocked out in the first round.

The lighter slid out of his hand and skidded into the parking lot. ScottB20 crawled toward it when a heavy foot landed on his hand, crushing it. He shrieked but got to his knees, just in time for Jack's kick to hit him flush in the face. Blood gushed from his nose and mouth, though his crazed eyes looked like he wasn't ready to quit. Jack saw him reach behind his back with his one good hand and a split second later, he was staring down the barrel of a Glock.

Jack spun around, hoping for help. He saw the women from class crowded in front of the window, staring out at him in horror. Jack thought of Jill and all the things he wished he'd said to her.

ScottB20 yelled out, "You ruined my plans, asshole!" His hand was trembling, but with his finger firmly placed on the trigger, he pointed the gun up at Jack's head. Jack knew he didn't have time to reach for his own gun.

38

S aint yelled and jumped back.

Just as the Rottweiler was upon him, it stopped in mid-air and fell down to the ground. A heavy steel linked chain affixed to his collar was now fully taut, a man on the other end of it holding tight.

"Just wanted you to meet 'Rotten'," he said. "This dog is always ripe and ready to help out people like us."

Saint blinked his eyes and unconsciously put his hand on his chest, then exhaled loudly. By then, everyone had gathered around, laughing, one of them laughing so hard, he looked like he was going to have an asthma attack. Saint looked down, his face first red from fear and now red from embarrassment. The dog, at present docile and whimpering, sat at the end of the rusty chain, its enraged eyes morphed into a sad state. The other men were still tittering. Saint didn't know whether to laugh too, but certainly knew he couldn't dare show any signs of weakness, even though his eyes felt a tad wet, and he prayed his pants didn't show the same. Feeling relief and embarrassment, he peered back at the man holding the dog and just gave a nod.

"I'm Viktor. Just wanted to see if you'd piss your pants. You passed the test. So maybe we'll let you come back here again." The guys applauded, and then slowly dispersed.

Saint thought that coming back was the last thing he'd do.

Just then a hand reached out to him. "Here, give Rotten these and he'll be your friend forever." He looked down at the hand and saw a couple of meaty ribs in a paper towel. He grabbed them and walked slowly to Rotten. "Good boy, here you go."

Rotten stood up quickly, and Viktor yelled, "Down!"

Saint wasn't sure if Viktor meant him or the dog.

Saint stopped for a second, but then got to within a couple of feet of Rotten. He tossed the food in front of the dog, who rapidly devoured the meat, and then sat wagging his tail at Saint. His sad eyes looked expectant now. Saint tentatively put his hand out, fist closed, and Rotten took a sniff, and then a lick. Saint let a small smile escape his face, but quickly stepped back. Quit while I'm ahead, he thought. And intact.

Saint gazed back at the hand that had provided the meat and did a double take. Had the Rottweiler torn his throat open and sent him to heaven? Scrutinizing him with a sympathetic smile was a well-put-together woman. Blonde hair in a bouffant style, large pearl earrings, ruby-red lipstick, a flouncy, polka-dot dress. She smelled like peaches and cream. She grinned at him, saying, "Welcome to our community, sir. Hope you stay with us."

Saint's wide eyes and open mouth no doubt made him look like the "Surprised Patrick" character. She looked like she was from another era... but looked just fine to him. Just then The Exterminator came by.

"What's the matter, never seen a real woman before? This is Sarah, my beautiful tradwife. Stick with us and maybe you'll get yourself one too."

Saint still wasn't sure what a tradwife was, but perked up when Sarah said, "I've got a sister just around your age. Come by our gathering next weekend, and maybe she'll be here. She's a real cute lady. May be just right for a cute boy like you."

Saint didn't know what to say, so said nothing, just nodded as the incongruous sight he was beholding mesmerized him. But he didn't stop smiling.

Soon, he had met the rest of the guys—none all that friendly. They acted as if he were a peculiar animal that escaped from a zoo. They played some poker, had arm-wrestling contests (which Saint stayed away from), and drank more beer (which Saint didn't stay away from). Many of the guys didn't say more than two words all night, while others grumbled about how their jobs were being taken away, replaced by immigrants for close to no pay. One guy walked by, kicking dirt into the circle, saying, "Stop griping. I've no desire to do anything more than what's necessary to get by. Working sucks." The others nodded their heads in agreement.

Several guys were playing what looked like a form of darts. The board was hanging from a tree limb as if from a noose. It had concentric circles, differing shades of brown in the rings, with black in the center. Instead of darts though, they used cold steel knives. Saint was told they made these seven-inch knives with carbon steel blades and a black finish, that they had excellent balance, and were perfect for throwing, cutting and carving. He heard the swoosh sound of the knife rotating in the air and the thunk sound as it hit the target. Swoosh Thunk. Swoosh Thunk. Swoosh Thunk. Three knives straight into the black heart of the target.

It impressed Saint. The Exterminator told him their group had frequent skills training events and group exercises. "Believe me, with the physical activity we do, there's no need to join a gym. We'll have you stronger than you ever thought, in no time."

"Wow, sounds great. What's it all for, though?"

"Men have to be able to defend themselves and their women. We'll teach you how to handle a knife, how to fight right—all sorts of practical skills." Saint thought that made sense. He'd certainly want to protect a woman like Sarah.

"Understand that. Especially since Sarah sure is pretty." Saint stopped himself for a minute, afraid he may have overstepped his bounds. But The Exterminator smiled and looked proud, so Saint went on. "You said she was your 'tradwife'. Sorry for my ignorance, but can I ask you what exactly that is?"

"A traditional wife, of course. One who knows how to dress like a female should, stay home and take care of her man, know her place, and—of course—submit to male leadership."

Saint was quite surprised, but his look just registered a bit of confusion. "So you mean kinda like the way it was back in the fifties?"

"Yeah, kind of like that, I guess. But this is the way it's gonna be. Doing it and bearing a lot of children that look like us, that's key. In fact, I'm proud of Sarah. She started up a challenge: 'The White Baby Challenge.'"

Saint's eyebrows lifted and his eyes opened wide.

"Yeah, Sarah has a following, and she has a slogan: 'Procreate with your white mate.' Catchy, isn't it? Even better than the fourteen words."

"Ugh, yeah," Saint said, though he thought it was pretty cheesy and just plain wrong. And he had no clue what fourteen words he was talking about.

"You bet it is! The goal is six kids—meet it or beat it." He pushed his elbow into Saint's ribs. "And the trying sure is fun!"

Saint had a fleeting vision of him and Sarah's sister rising to the occasion. He laughed, and gave The Exterminator a high five, his soft palm meeting a calloused hand with a thwack.

Soon after this, Saint realized it was way later than he'd planned to stay out and told The Exterminator he had to go. He thanked him for the invite, and promised him he'd be back, though sincerely doubted he would keep that promise. He liked the camaraderie, at least after a few beers, thought he could learn some useful things, and certainly hoped to meet Sarah's sister. But the whole situation was too weird and scary for him, the guys not only rough around the edges but rough through and through. And he was concerned about the comments regarding immigrants.

Saint peed behind a tree and then headed back, stumbling to his car in the pitch-black. He got behind the wheel, fumbled twice with the ignition before he got the key in the right spot, hit the gas pedal too hard and lurched toward a tree. He jammed on the brakes, the car doing a jump back and forth before calming down. Saint slowly backed away, straightening the car out. He wasn't sure if he'd make it, having long ago lost count of the beers he'd downed. He felt like a wreck.

39

The gunshot was loud and a direct hit in front of the hot yoga studio.

Blood spurted out; brain matter splattered his shirt. The top of his head was gone, though his eyes remained, forever frozen. He slowly crumpled down to the dirty pavement.

Jill stood, stared at Jack and then the man missing most of his head, and dropped her gun. She stepped toward Jack, who looked like he'd just seen a miracle occur.

"Jack, what the hell?" Jill said in a trembling voice, rubbing the tight muscles in her neck with one hand.

"I don't know. I got your text. But thank God you got here in time."

"Somehow, you beat me. I've just been a little unfocused recently." Jill looked at him, her face turned to the side.

Jack went over to hug her.

"No way, not with all that blood on you," Jill said, putting her hands up in front of her. "I heard that crazy freak yelling shit about women. I ran as fast as I could."

Jack looked at the crumpled body and said, "Don't think you did much to improve his perspective on women."

"Yeah, well, he can hate all he wants in hell."

"True," Jack said, looking at the dead body. "Don't think he's coming back."

Sirens could be heard approaching, their sound getting louder and louder. A car skidded to a stop in the lot, almost crashing into another one parked in its way.

"It was really weird," Jill said, her breathing and voice returning to some semblance of normality. "When I saw the guy pointing the gun, it was like that's all I could see. Not you, not the building, just the guy. And when I moved, it felt like I was in slow motion. I really didn't think I was going to make it in time."

Jack smiled. "I for one am happy you did, or that would have been me missing half my head."

"Weirdest of all, when I shot him, I almost felt like I was out of my body, like I was hovering over the scene."

"Well, thank God for hovering! But you're trembling. It's going to be all right. I'll take care of you," Jack said, tentatively putting an arm around her shoulder.

Four police cars entered the parking lot, all at about the same time, sirens screaming and lights ablaze. The women had left their yoga mats on the floor as they ran for the door, some crying, some crying out, some in a bit of a daze, others thanking the Lord they didn't meet him that day. They tried to rush out but were stopped, first by the narrow doorway, then by an officer. A fire truck came into the driveway; a symphony of flashing lights lit up the lot like a discotheque in hell.

The cops, guns drawn, approached Jack and Jill, who had put their hands up as soon as they saw the cops open their car doors. Jack shouted he was a cop and yelled to them which pocket his I.D. was in. The yoga instructor shouted out that they had saved them. They frisked Jack and grabbed the I.D. and did the same to Jill, while one of them carefully picked up her gun.

Jack grunted to Jill, "It's gonna be a long night, and after that the whole review, the critique."

"I know. We can do nothing right according to that process! But hey, at least we'll be together," she said, looking him in the eye. "Thought I lost you for a minute there."

Jack looked like he'd be lost without Jill. Then turning back to the scene, said, "Jesus, wonder what the hell this was all about."

Jill looked around, and then back at him, shaking her head. "So much damn violence in this world, in this place. So much evil." She thought back to the violence that affected her life. She thought of her dad, Frank. "Something's got to be done. This is one crazy shit show. One of too many."

"Well, not much we can do now," Jack said.

"Guess all we can do is take it one situation at a time," Jill said. "I tell ya though, I'm going to get to the bottom of this one. I'm not gonna end till I find answers. Find out who else this Incel jerk was communicating with. Gotta stop what else may be about to happen. Obviously, it hit way too close to home. Way too close."

"Literally," Jack said, shaking his head.

The ambulance came into the strip mall last but backed out soon after assessing the situation. There was no one to revive, and the firefighters were spreading sand; the hot scene was under control. The coroner was on his way to take the dead body, as usual.

Thankfully, just one body this time.

40

"Are ya stupid?"

"Don't you talk to me that way, Earl!" Tracy Dixon said, her face completely red. She thought no one was stupider than Sheriff Earl Klamp. She stepped right up to him. "That guy, ScottB whatever, is a killer!"

Klamp recoiled a bit, his puffed-up chest deflating. "Yeah, but there's nothin' in that killin' that was like the others. Christ, he was just a crazy!"

"We are nowhere with the other shootings. Three of them! You were supposed to talk to the county about getting help from the state. What the hell is going on? At least I have a theory!"

Klamp started to object, but then stopped. Tracy continued, "Think about it. Maybe this guy was the shooter, but now wanted something bigger. Wanted to make a name for himself, maybe even go down in a blaze of glory. I mean, all this violence all of a sudden in this area. There must be some kind of connection!"

Klamp looked like he was considering it, then shook his head. "Well, there almost was a blaze, I give ya that much," Klamp said with a harrumph. "But why would he do that? Makes no sense to me. He ain't the guy. Totally different situation. Open-and-shut case." He clapped his hands back and forth for emphasis.

Tracy looked down, took a few deep breaths, and knew she wouldn't get anywhere with Klamp. She had as much patience with him as she had waiting in her car for a drawbridge to come back down. She stared at the overflowing ashtray on Klamp's desk. *Asshole isn't supposed to be smoking in here,* she thought.

"Well, I'm gonna look deeper into this Scott's background—certainly a lot more than the little that has been done so far," she continued. She knew she needed to further enlist Jill's help, even if it meant ignoring protocol and going above Klamp's thick head.

"Tracy, we've done a most thorough investigation, talked to everyone at the scene. There is nothin' further ta investigate. Like ah said, the perp is dead. Shut and open. Let's move on."

Tracy sighed. *The damn idiot can never think out of the box. Shit, with him in charge, we'd never close cases and keep order in this town.*

Klamp smiled. "Everything is just A-OK. Don't ya worry ya pretty little head."

One of these days, I swear. One of these days, Tracy thought.

41

It wasn't planned.

Just a few days after the hot yoga mess, Jack and Jill were working late.

"Well, time to go," Jack said.

"You don't want to miss your date!" Jill teased.

"Ha! Date! What date?"

Jill locked eyes with him.

Jack exhaled. "Come on, you know," he said.

"Know what?"

"You're the only woman in my life."

Jill looked back, surprised, but at the same time as she looked into his eyes, she knew it to be true.

"I think... honestly, I think you're the only woman I'd want in my life."

"Jack..."

"I know. I'm sorry. I understand we're just colleagues. But you're amazing. Truly. So smart, so determined. And you really know me—know me better than myself. Maybe we are a bit Jekyll and Hyde, but maybe we complete each other."

"Wow, I know I saved your life, Jack. I appreciate all you said, I really do, but you sound like you have survivor's gratitude."

"I do have gratitude. But I think I've felt this way for a long time. It just took a shot to wake me up."

That woke Jill up as well.

As they stood in the dimly lit room, their eyes locked in a heated gaze. There was a palpable tension between them. They both knew what was about to happen.

Jack leaned forward, first reaching out to gently brush her hair back from her face. She leaned in to his touch, her heart racing with anticipation.

Their lips met in a soft, tentative kiss at first, but it quickly deepened as their passion ignited.

He pulled her closer, his hands tracing the curves of her body as they kissed with a hunger that was impossible to ignore.

For a moment, they were lost in each other, oblivious to everything else around them. It was as if the world had faded away, leaving only the two of them in their own private universe.

As they finally pulled away, gasping for breath, they looked into each other's eyes, both wondering if this was the beginning of something that could change their lives forever.

"Wow," Jack said.

"I know," Jill said.

"But we'd better stop now, before I can't stop at all."

Jill felt disappointed. *That's different from most guys*, she thought. *Surprising. I guess that's good. Or maybe he doesn't really want me that badly?*

"OK, sure. Tomorrow's another day," she said.

"Thank God for tomorrows," Jack said.

42

The fire trucks were long gone.

Tracy headed over to meet Jack and Jill in a small office, in a location near where the conflagration had almost erupted. Tracy looked around the unimpressive space but didn't comment on it. Jack served tepid black coffee and sat after the introductions were made. While they didn't have a second cup from the carafe, they did have a nice back-and-forth discussion.

Tracy became more comfortable with Jack, though she did pick up on some tension between Jack and Jill. After a while, she began gossiping about the people in her department, particularly regarding the poor response to the shootings. She described their approach as like waiting forever at a broken stoplight for the green to come—which of course it never would. Jack and Jill both appeared fascinated by that; they said they'd certainly heard some of the basics of what had happened, seen some news reports, but hadn't realized the lethargic response involved. Dereliction of duty in Tracy's mind.

Tracy then got down to business. "So, the reason I've come to you is that our department thinks what happened at the yoga studio was a completely separate incident from the shootings, totally unrelated," Tracy said.

"And you don't?" Jill countered.

"Well, you know this guy, with the screen name ScottB20?"

"Uh, yeah," Jack said sarcastically. Jill shot him a look.

"Sorry, of course you do. What I meant was, there's not a lot of info as to who he actually was. Seems to be a shadowy figure, someone who had hidden his tracks well. I want to learn more. Why don't we start with you retelling what happened that night."

Jack and Jill recounted it detail by detail, though Tracy learned nothing new.

"So why the questions again?" Jack asked. "We've been through all this before."

"Well, I just thought there has been a hell of a lot going on for a relatively small area. I thought there might be a connection. Thought maybe this guy could've been the shooter, the killer of those others."

Both Jack and Jill had deadpan expressions, so Tracy continued, "And the guys in my department, they don't care. They said it's one less dirtbag on the streets; he's dead and gone. Said they have enough trouble with a killer on the loose and can't be bothered with it. They also said we don't have that many resources and need to keep our eye on the prize, not get distracted."

"Well, that does kind of make sense to me," Jack said.

"And the way he was going about his attempt at the yoga studio was so different," Jill said. "I'm afraid the people in your department may be right this time."

"But the violence just seems like too much of a coincidence. Shootings, deaths, and now this ScottB event that could have resulted in dozens of deaths. Hey, we're just a small town! Maybe it was this guy," Tracy reiterated.

Jack said he didn't know, doubted it, and anyway, the state really couldn't get involved unless called in by the local authorities. Tracy slumped, knowing how reluctant Klamp had been.

"We can always do some work on the down-low," Jill said. "In fact, I've already been looking into this ScottB20 and the Incels on my own. I'm happy to have us help each other on this. In fact, I've tapped into a computer forensics guy to see who ScottB was communicating with. I'm sure this guy will quietly help locate them."

Tracy looked relieved. Jack looked aggrieved.

"Well, that's all fine, I guess—as long as we are handling our current caseload," Jack said. "And—"—

"We are," Jill quickly interrupted.

"What I was going to say," Jack said, a slight edge to his voice, "is let's not have any blinders on. You've had multiple shootings, all Black victims. Who knows, we may have a serial killer here. If ScottB was the one, great, our work is done. But..."

"You're right," Jill said. "We'll start with this Incel hate group, and who knows, maybe there are connections to other hate groups. Maybe we'll find our killer there."

"Oh boy," Tracy said. "Hate and killings. What a wonderful world."

"That's the world we signed up for," Jack said. "We need to stop this guy, whoever he is." He thought for a minute. "Gotta make sure the killer doesn't become as big as Little."

"Huh?"

"Samuel Little. Killed ninety-three women. Strangled them soon after meeting them in chance encounters. When he was caught, his only explanation was: 'It was like drugs. I came to like it.'"

"Shit, how does someone get away with ninety-three murders?"

"Well, lots of people not doing their job, I'd say. But while he did kill all sorts of people, this lunatic often went after victims who no longer had contact with their families. Often dirt-poor, good people, some struggled with addiction, some resorted to prostitution. Unfortunately, their deaths got little attention, sparked little outrage."

"That's pitiful," Tracy said, looking down.

"Well, let's hope our killer doesn't become another Little," Jack said. "And as we pursue our investigations," he continued, "let's not forget how dangerous this wonderful world is. Ladies, we have to be careful. Very, very careful."

43

I have to be careful. Very, very careful.
  I cleaned my AR-15 lovingly.
  Big plans ahead.

"Got a dollar?"

Jose Alvarez carefully passed the same dark and narrow alley on the way to work every day. It smelled like old piss and lives amiss. The hiss of his rubber-soled shoes quickened with his pace. He heard the voice ask a second time, and was about to further speed up his stride, when the plaintive quality of it stopped him. He looked in the alley and saw an elderly white man, very dirty but with a certain dignity, holding a ragged coat closed, buttons missing, a thin face with sunken eyes peering out.

"No, *señor*, no money."

The man looked down, his face a sad frown, and turned back into the alley. Jose put a hand up, motioning to him to wait.

"*Un minuto.*" He fished in his pocket and found a few coins and gave them to the man.

"God bless."

Jose entered the restaurant a few doors down. His job as

a dishwasher and busboy paid little, but he hoped one day to be a waiter. He dreamed of it, and studied English at home whenever he could, though he found watching American TV and listening to English songs was the best teacher—and one he could afford.

Jose spent the next six hours moving dirty dishes and nasty napkins from the tables into the bussing tote, stealing a glance at the servers in action. He scoured pots when there were no tables to clean. The slop often ended up on his clothing, but he didn't mind, and could usually be found smiling and singing in a low voice, thinking of Juanito, his four-year-old pride and joy. When his shift was over, he was delighted to often be given some of the leftover buffet table food, which he would bring home to his wife Rosa, who was grateful for it after working long hours at the Value Inn, making beds, cleaning bathrooms, and emptying garbage.

That night as he left the restaurant in the dark, he passed the alley again, and heard a sound.

"Hungry."

It was just a whisper. But Jose looked in and saw the homeless man again. This time, he was sitting on the cracked cement path, frail and frightened. Jose looked down at the brown paper bag in his hand, thought of his wife Rosa and son Juanito, looked skyward, and then softly laid it by the man's side. "*Buenas noches.*" He sighed, and headed home, empty-handed.

Jose entered his one-bedroom basement apartment. It was small and neat, decorated in cheery colors of red, orange and yellow. He gave Rosa a big hug and kiss, and Juanito jumped in his arms for his hug. He explained to Rosa what happened to the food. She nodded her head in understanding. Her large, brown eyes looked into his as she told him he was a good man. She looked away, as she often did when thinking and unsure, clasping and unclasping her hands. Then she hesitantly said that maybe they should give him a little money to survive, a little charity. Juanito overheard this, and a minute later came back into the room, piggybank in hand.

"*Para el hombre*," he said.

From that day forward, half of the leftovers that Jose left with, and sometimes all when there wasn't much, were given to the nameless man, along with a few dollars on payday.

Unfortunately, The Exterminator's favorite bar was across from the restaurant Jose worked at, and he didn't like what he saw. Not one bit.

The Exterminator grew up angry. Angry that when he was a boy, his father lost his job and ended up a part-time dish-washer. Angry that his father was an alcoholic who beat him every night until he fled when he was fifteen years old. Angry that the first girl he really liked left him for a Jewish man. Angry that the military didn't understand him and gave him a dishonorable discharge. Angry with all the women who had left him after one strike too many—or after the first one.

But now he was less troubled, if not less angry, having found his tribe—along with a woman who shared his philosophy. He had a purpose. His goal was to expand his crew to fulfill all he wanted to do. He wasn't sure about the new kid, Diablo. The boy didn't seem angry enough. Sure he could talk him into belonging, becoming blood brothers as part of a family of real men. But he wasn't sure he could get him to feel it viscerally and be a man of action, which was vital to make the changes The Exterminator thought necessary.

I need to test him, he thought. *We'll see if he's the Devil or not.*

44

It was a long time coming.

Jack and Jill continued to do their jobs professionally but had barely spoken since that singular kiss. When they did, there was tension in the air. Jill felt unsure of what to do, unsure of what her heart was saying. Sure, they'd had a great evening, albeit short. Really just a moment. She wondered if that night was simply a reaction to the life-or-death situation they'd faced. In truth, she hadn't thought they'd ever have a romantic relationship after all this time. They were so different, in so many ways.

Jill sat in her living room, swirling a glass of red wine and contemplating the stillness and empty space around her, feeling as alone as someone on a desert island. She was lost in thought, pondering the possibility of a relationship with Jack and what that would mean. They'd worked together for years, and she'd always admired his intelligence and work ethic, but was also bugged by his less desirable traits. But now, she felt herself drawn to him in a way she couldn't ignore.

As she thought about him, her mind raced with questions. How much would pursuing a relationship complicate their work dynamic? Was it worth risking that for a shot at something more? Should they run with the romance before they'd walked? If they continued, would they ever get across the finish line? Jill knew she needed to talk to Jack about it but wasn't sure if she should take that step now. After some hesitation, she finally made up her mind. She picked up her phone and dialed Jack's number. As the phone rang, she felt her nerves fray. What if he really doesn't feel the same way? What if I'm making a big mistake?

After a few rings, Jack picked up.

"Hey Jack, it's Jill," she said, her voice a little unsteady.

"What's up?"

"Can you come over? I think we need to talk."

There was a moment of silence on the other end of the line, and Jill felt a knot form in her stomach.

"Talk about what? The case? There's nothing new."

Jill sighed audibly. "No, not the case. You know what," she said, a bit more stridently than she'd planned.

"Yeah, I guess I do." Jack's voice sounded to Jill like this was the last thing he wanted to hear.

"Sometimes, you gotta talk things out," Jill said. "Otherwise we're wasting time. I don't think we have time to waste."

Silence. Jill wondered if he'd hung up; she didn't breathe.

Jack finally said, "Uh, OK. OK, you're right. I guess. Be there as soon as I can."

Jill exhaled. After hanging up the phone, she took a few more deep breaths. She knew that this conversation was going to be difficult, but she also knew that it was something she needed to do. As she waited for Jack to arrive, she tried to organize her thoughts. She knew she needed to be honest with him, to tell him how she felt and to listen to his response. She just hoped they would come to an understanding, whatever that might be.

"You're not doing it!"

"Not after last week, coming home so late, drunk!"

"Mom, they're just a bunch of guys. Like a fraternity."

Deja recoiled at the fraternity description as it brought back terrible memories. She left the room, yelling, "No!" like someone watching the killer approach in a horror film.

Saint almost felt relieved, having been indecisive all week. He was almost glad his mother was deciding for him. Those guys were just off. But with the relief, a sense of melancholy returned, like a sunny day suddenly turning cold and dark. He went to his room, slumped down into his chair, and got on his computer, skimming from one thing to another without being able to focus. He quickly lost interest. Saint shut off his lights and lay in his bed, though it was early. He stared at the ceiling but found no answers there. A couple of hours later, his mother knocked on his door.

"Go away."

"You have to eat. I made your favorite. Meatloaf and mashed potatoes with gravy."

"Go away."

Deja pushed the unlocked door partly open and saw Saint on his bed in the dark. She took a few steps in and got a closer look.

"Is that a tear?"

"No!" Saint shouted, turning over. "Now go away!"

"Baby, it can't be that bad. Like they say, 'The sun will come out tomorrow.'"

"The sun never comes out for me!" Saint fiercely exclaimed. "My whole life. Eclipsed. Some days, I wish I was eclipsed."

Deja, a look of shock and concern on her face, grabbed his arm. "Saint, don't talk that way. I love you. Nana Gloria loves you. And one day soon, I promise you, you will find a love of your own."

"Not if you force me to stay home all the time!" Saint

shouted, with a vehemence he'd never used with his mother before.

"Honey, I've never done that. I've always encouraged you to get out. It's just this thing you want to go to again, it doesn't seem right for you."

Saint didn't answer.

"I know nothing about these people," Deja continued. "All I know is you came back reeking of beer and cigarette smoke, and you could have been killed driving on those dark roads. Do you want that for yourself?"

"Maybe I do."

Deja grabbed him and shook him. "Stop it! Stop it! There'll be no such talk in this house. I lost one man; I will not lose another!"

Saint looked at the horror in her eyes; he'd never seen her so upset. He took a step back, holding his breath, wide-eyed. He took a moment to recover, then said, "Mom, of course not. I was just being dramatic. I'm sorry."

Deja hugged him; they both had tears running down their cheeks, though Saint tried very hard to hide his.

"OK, you can go."

"What?"

"You can go this weekend."

"You sure?"

"Just promise me no drinking. Go hang out with your new friends. Perhaps it'll be good for you." She kissed him on the top of his head, then said, "Come on, let's have that meatloaf before it gets cold."

Saint managed a smile, but almost wished his mother hadn't granted him the permission.

He then thought of meeting Sarah's sister, and his smile broadened. Deja saw it. "Wow, you got happy quickly! Hope you'll always be this happy."

45

The Exterminator was not happy.

He left the bar that night at the same time Jose Alvarez was leaving work at the restaurant. A heavy cloud cover obscured the sky, and a light rain was falling. Jose's shoes were making their squeaking noise against the pavement. The Exterminator followed him into the rain-streaked alley and saw him give a rolled-up paper bag with oil stains to a ragged man.

"What the fuck are you doing?"

Jose turned around, obviously startled and scared. "Nothing, *señor*."

"Don't nothin' me, wetback!"

The Exterminator grabbed the rumpled bag and opened it, seeing the food. It smelled pretty good to him, and the bag felt warm. "Why you giving this to a white man? You think you're better than him?" The Exterminator spit the words out. "He'd have a job and be able to feed himself if not for the invasion from your kind!"

"*Ay, Dios mio!* I'm only a dishwasher."

An image of his father the dishwasher danced in front of The Exterminator's eyes. His father, as broken as the plates often ended up, rearing up and taking it out on him, the belt snapping across his rear. The Exterminator held the bag of food up high and smashed it down on Jose's head. The bag ripped open and hot spaghetti sauce dripped down Jose's hair and into his eyes. The homeless man backed away further, smelling the spicy sauce, smelling fear in the air.

"We don't accept charity from their kind!"

The Exterminator glared at the homeless man cowering against the wall, who started trembling. He then turned his attention back to Jose, taking a penknife from his pocket. Jose's eyes widened as The Exterminator opened the blade.

"I'll bet you stole that food."

The Exterminator glanced at the dirty blade's pointy end and smiled. "Now get lost, before I really get mad." Jose started to move, and The Exterminator made a motion to throw it at him, before pocketing it.

Jose made a dodging move, then wiped the food from his face, and scampered around The Exterminator. Jose looked back as he hurried out. The Exterminator kicked the remains of the bag down the alley, shouting, "And don't let me catch you accepting anything from goddamn border jumpers! Keep to your own kind. Go to the fucking Salvation Army!"

It was just a few nights later, on his way home, that Jose heard "Hungry!" in a soft and sickly voice.

He hesitated a moment, then started back home. He thought about Juanito and Rosa and staying safe for them. But he also thought about the people who'd helped him navigate his way in a new and overwhelming country, a country far from home—where he didn't know his fate, where he felt like a man in a maze with no direction known.

He frowned, then looked around. He dismissed his concerns for the moment and couldn't resist leaving the bag of leftovers at the alley entrance, before quickly sneaking away, his heart pounding.

He hadn't seen The Exterminator watching the whole thing from across the street.

He didn't hear him mutter, "Fucking unbelievable."

Nor did he know The Exterminator followed him home.

46

Jack walked nervously up to Jill's front door, heart pounding in his chest.

He thought about how unusual it was for him to be going to see her outside of work—unofficially, in her own home. While they had been co-workers for years, he now realized he'd always harbored a secret infatuation for her—though he wasn't sure it was now safe, not sure if that ship had sailed. But now here he was, a bit winded, standing on the doorstep.

Jill answered the door with a smile that made Jack's heart skip a beat. She looked stunning in a simple white blouse and jeans, bare feet with pink polished nails, her long hair falling in soft waves around her shoulders. She tossed her hair a bit as she greeted him.

"Hey," she said, her amber eyes sparkling with excitement. Or was it uncertainty? "Come on in."

Jack followed her inside, taking in the inviting living room with its plush couches, multiple pillows, and warm lighting. Abstract paintings were on the walls, in vibrant yet soothing colors. On an end table was a copy of Mitch Albom's *the five people you meet in Heaven*, a bookmark sticking up around halfway through. A bookcase filled the far wall, lined with a combination of professional texts, non-fiction books, and what looked like a slew of mystery novels.

Jill saw his eyes hover about, taking it all in like a vacuum cleaner.

She looked at the bookcase. A copy of *Audrey Rose* lay on its side.

"Always like a good thriller," she said, mischievously.

Jack smiled, but then became contemplative. He had always known that she was special, but now he was realizing just how much he had been missing out on all these years.

"You know," he said, "after the other night, I was so confused. Happy but confused. I wasn't sure if it all was just a reaction to what we, especially you, went through that night." Jack stopped, feeling as if his throat had constricted. After a few moments, he continued, "We've been professionals for so long..."

Jill's eyes widened and seemed to be wet.

Jack felt the tension building between them, the unspoken attraction hanging in the air, vibrating like a tuning fork, the uncertainty surrounding them like an orchestra without a conductor. It seemed they were both very much aware of the possibility of something more, but neither one knew for sure if it was right.

Jack mumbled a few things that made little sense to Jill.

Jill leaned in close to Jack, her breath hot on his cheek. She put two fingers over his lips to shush him. "I was wrong. Enough talk. Life is too short to mess around. I think we understand each other, what's happened, maybe what has always been. Maybe what will always be." Jill stopped a second, looking at Jack, afraid to look at Jack.

"We seem to have missed the clues, but we don't have to miss anything anymore. As detectives, we always follow logic. Now, let's follow our hearts."

Jack looked deeply into her eyes, knowing she was right. He closed the distance between them and pressed his lips to hers.

At first, it was a gentle kiss, but as they continued, the passion between them grew. The kisses became electric; Jack felt his heart racing as Jill responded eagerly to his touch.

He pulled Jill closer to him, savoring the feel of her body pressed against his. He could feel shivers going down her spine. They kissed deeply, hungrily, exploring each other's mouths with an urgency that had been building for years. They came together with an enormous embrace, pressing so tightly, Jack felt they'd become one just by the sheer force of hugging.

As they finally broke apart, gasping for air, grasping to get together again, Jack knew that this was just the beginning. Jill had always fascinated him. He admired her, even if he wouldn't admit it before, but now he realized that he'd fallen for her, hard. Completely. Now he was willing to admit that to himself, and to her. And as he looked deep into her eyes, he knew she felt the same way.

Jill's eyes were wet, tears slowly dropping. Jack wiped them, saying, "I've wanted this for so long. Even if I didn't know it, I have." His voice was hoarse and barely a whisper. "What a fool I've been. It's so clear to me now that you make me whole. Without you, I'm like a body without a soul."

"I know," Jill said, "I know," as the kisses resumed, all over faces, necks, shoulders.

Soon, they were tearing each other's clothes off.

They left a trail of clothing on the way to the bedroom. Once there, she ran her hands over Jack's rippling muscles, then grabbed his butt. Jack put his arms on her shoulders and gently pushed her back. He stood still and looked at her, mesmerized, taking in the totality of her, the totality of her body.

Jill watched him drink her in, feeling that his thirst for her was unquenchable.

He moved his mouth to her breasts. She gasped. And then he

couldn't help himself; he entered her quickly, and they moved together, still holding each other tight enough to leave marks.

The second time was much slower, on the bed, Jack taking his time investigating every inch. She shuddered, then cuddled up in his arms, their sweaty bodies satiated.

Later on, when the third time came around, they could only attribute it to years of holding in their feelings, a burning, pent-up demand exploding like a fireworks factory on fire.

Jill stroked his chest.

"Wow, after those tumbles, I guess we are Jack and Jill, for real." Jack laughed.

Jill groaned, then replied, "And I've certainly fallen for you," as she playfully threw a pillow at him.

47

It's fun to reminisce. I couldn't quite believe what happened at the Gulf station. The whole thing went up so quickly. That fireball was like a North Star, calling to me, guiding me.

Damn I'm a good shot! Maybe it's fate. Must be.

What perfect practice! And that guy sure deserved it. He had a gun. He would've taken that poor guy's car—probably even killed him if I didn't step in. The fool! *You can't trust that kind.*

But man that felt good! What a rush! And what a feeling of power. Just goes to show, you gotta take matters into your own hands. Yeah, the world is a cruel and unjust place. *That's why you have to get control.*

I remember my daddy, what he said once. I was so young. Saw an alligator come right out of a pond and attack a fawn feeding by the shore. Ate it right up. I started to cry. That's when my daddy shook me, and told me that's the way of the world, the natural order of things. To survive, you gotta kill what's weaker. My daddy was a good teacher.

I need more. Life is unfair, but I'm going to make sure I come out on top.

I started whistling.

Time to make new memories.

48

His heart almost stopped.

The disappointment of Sarah's sister not being there was like a blow to Saint's chest. The Exterminator told him to come early on Saturday, as there would be skills training and some guests from a different chapter. When he got there and asked about her, The Exterminator told him there would be no women there today; this was all about discussing future priorities. "Men's work," he said.

Saint looked over and saw some new guys talking together in a circle. The Exterminator called one over.

"Hey, Spencer, meet the newbie: Diablo."

Saint greeted the large, pudgy man in front of him. Hair as black and spindly as a black widow spider, a cherubic face covered by close-trimmed facial hair, thick glasses with blocky black frames, Spencer Heilbach was dressed quite differently from The Exterminator's men, in a white polo shirt and khaki pants. The other guys who came with him were dressed similarly, though with different brown boots underneath their pants legs. Saint thought, OK, *these guys look normal. Maybe I made the right choice coming back.*

"Newbie, Diablo—you been initiated yet?"

The Exterminator stepped in before Saint could answer. "Not yet."

Saint felt confused and concerned. "Initiated?" He had no desire to get hurt.

The Exterminator gazed back angrily at Spencer. "Just some pranks. Maybe head to the Jewish cemetery and spray-paint swastikas on the tombstones."

Saint turned away, concerned they'd see his look of disgust.

Spencer laughed, and rolling his eyes, said, "Kid stuff."

He was about to say something else when The Exterminator cut in. "Anyway, discussion time." He whistled loudly and motioned for everyone to get together.

The group sat in a circle, the hot sun beating on them, the still air providing no relief from the heat. A raven could be heard cawing in the distance as The Exterminator cleared his throat and started talking.

He told them there was strength in numbers, and the two groups could be better together. The guys looked around at each other, not sure if they agreed or where this was heading. The Exterminator explained what he thought were the pluses of coming together, and when he stopped for a minute, Spencer Heilbach's group looked at Spencer. Heilbach stood up, hitched up his pants, and stared across the group, eyeing each man individually without saying anything. One guy coughed, another sniffed loudly.

"Not so fast," he said. "We need to be sure we're all on the same page."

The guys looked at him expectantly. "Things have changed over the years. We need to be certain you get it. We need to do things, and say things, a bit differently than before. For example, I know you like Nazi symbols. Hey, I do too. But to the outside world, we can't be Nazis; we are just *pro-white*."

One guy from his group shouted out, "Yeah, what do poor white guys have? Nothin'. Nobody ever helped a hick but a hick himself!" All the men nodded strongly in agreement, looking disgusted.

Heilbach continued, "That's right. The big problem this country has is being politically correct." He spit on the ground. "If this country gets any kinder or gentler, it will cease to exist!"

"Fuck 'politically correct'!" a man named Slayer shouted out.

"You bet," Heilbach responded, pointing to Slayer. "Immigrants aren't our friends. The masses arriving from foreign places threaten our culture, our way of life, our Christian traditions!"

Shouts of "Yeah!" and "Fuckin' A!" rang out, fists thrust into the air. Saint didn't join in, just listened with concern.

"A government based on natural law must not cater to the false notion of equality! White America has to push back or be pushed out!"

The Exterminator looked on as his guys joined in the chorus of approval, hypnotized by Heilbach, eyes glowing with admiration. He was feeling uneasy, concerned he was losing control to this new guy.

"We can't allow ourselves to become minorities in our own country!" a man named Roof shouted out, pounding his fist on a tree stump.

Saint's mouth was agape. He discreetly moved his way toward the back of the crowd.

"What do we do?"

"Our goal is simple," Heilbach said in a low voice. The group leaned in. "We need to defend our country from cultural and ethnic replacement brought on by the immigrant invasion. We can join together, if we have similar strategies. Let's start with seeing how many ideas we can come up with to help regain our country. Now who's with me?"

"I am!" and "We are!" rained upon Heilbach as he finished to raucous applause. The Exterminator wasn't applauding but gave Heilbach a thumbs-up.

Saint was concerned about what the other guys looking at him would think, and tentatively raised his hand with the pack, like a schoolchild unsure of himself, ready to take the hand back.

Saint then thought better of the raised hand. He stood amidst the sea of people at the rally, feeling a mix of anxiety and disgust. He had come here to see for himself what this group was all about, to make some friends, but now that he was here, he wished he hadn't come. His shirt's armpits were stained wet with sweat, and beads dripped off his brow; his breathing quickened.

There was no denying there was excitement in the air and a sense of belonging, but the speakers were spouting what Saint knew deep inside to be repulsive rhetoric. There was talk of "cleaning up the streets" and "getting rid of the undesirables" in voices filled with vitriol and hate.

He considered leaving right then but couldn't help wondering what the people around him would do if they knew he didn't agree with what was being said. Would they turn on him? Would they see him as one of the undesirables that needed to be "cleaned up"?

He decided for now he was better off just blending in, occasionally nodding his head though inside, he was screaming. He couldn't believe in this, no matter how much they tried to make a cohesive argument. It just wasn't in his nature. Saint looked around, hoping to find someone who may have felt more like he did, but saw only faces filled with resentment and revulsion. Usually, Saint spent all his time alone. Now he felt alone in a crowd of dozens.

The rest of the day—what felt to Saint like the longest day

of his life—was filled with even more of the strangest and scariest discussions Saint had ever heard. Some merriment broke it up so the guys could blow off steam in between the sessions discussing their dreams—dreams of restoring a new world order.

There were some loud arguments, many heated moments. At one point, there was shouting back and forth, fights about to break out. The heat of the day matched the heat of the moment, a shimmering haze rising around them. The Exterminator grabbed a beer bottle and broke it on a rock, glass and foam spewing angrily about. Staring down the bickering bunch, jagged edges pointing out, he quieted them down without a punch. He reminded them why they were there; reminded them there was a greater goal to hold dear.

The long day was done. The shadows lengthened then converged upon everyone. They were tired and beat, but at least not beat up. They tentatively agreed when it broke up that the two groups were a decent match, or at least worth giving it a shot. Saint thought Heilbach probably looked down on The Exterminator's men but didn't let it show, likely thinking that the more bodies under his control, the better.

The Exterminator looked content enough, likely thinking the combined group would have more resources and better planning. Of course, Saint could tell he wanted to make sure he was still in charge. And Saint knew to be wary of Heilbach, to not trust him. He figured beneath that polo shirt could lie the reincarnation of Hitler.

Saint had the worst headache ever. After hearing all that was said, he was truly fearful of what the group might do. He was so disappointed, having thought he'd found a group of guys he could finally fit in with. *I guess I'm hopeless*, he thought. He looked down, his hands on his head, and went home with a feeling of dread.

49

The previous night, The Exterminator had followed Jose home from the restaurant.

The Exterminator kept enough distance so that he wasn't detected, and watched Jose enter his basement apartment. The apartment had hopper windows, enabling The Exterminator to peer past the grime, while still staying in the shadows much of the time.

He stared with disgust at what he saw. *One big fuckin' happy family*, he thought, watching the effusive greetings of a wife and child, thinking that outside of TV, he'd experienced nothing like that growing up.

Why should they?

Saint spent most of the next week on the internet, trying to understand what those crazies were talking about. He read rants about suicide and drug use being rampant among young white males, and after days of reading the same things, thought perhaps there was a real problem in the USA today. He listened to the laments of losers, the blame game being spread about by guys who were down and out. Saint often thought that it sounded like they were looking for someone else to hold responsible, instead of being accountable to themselves. He heard hate, lots of it, with distress and unrest that immigrants—legal and illegal—were taking away what these white men thought were their rightful jobs, even their career prospects.

As Saint scoured their dark web pages, day in and day out, he started to become indoctrinated with their plight; against his better judgment, began thinking his new brothers might possibly be right. It was hard for him to maintain his balance, to let his innate nature stay true, given he was only reading their demented diatribes, one hundred percent of his time spent on the dark side.

He shared their frustration with the world today and began to understand their wishes for a mythical past of many riches. He thought that these days, when having financial security, or even paying the monthly power bill, was an increasing challenge for so many, there was motivation for these guys to bring the past back. Saint saw that the frustration was building and was concerned it would explode, like steam from a geyser, burning all in its path.

He saw a spider crawl toward his desk.

He squashed it beneath his foot.

50

"Got him!" Jill exclaimed.

Computer forensics was a great help, uncovering several people ScottB20 had been communicating with. Further pursuing the electronic trails, one looked especially interesting based on the conversations that were going on right before the assault: someone with the screen name of "El Diablo." There had been talk between the two about hot yoga getting hotter.

Jill had seen enough young people in bad situations. She could often help them, get them on the right path. Now she was determined to follow the lead and get as many of the miscreants as possible put away before more damage was done. She was like a dog playing fetch; she didn't want to stop. Wouldn't let go, wouldn't cease.

As her contact learned more from the IP address, she saw "El Diablo" was living in the same general area.

"That's great, Jill," Jack said. "Attaboy!"

Jill gave him a sour look.

"Just joking, Jill. Lighten up. You know I love you." He saw her still-cold stare. "And respect you."

"Let me tell Tracy and we'll go pay a call on this 'Diablo' man," Jill said.

"Whoa, hold on. We don't have anything yet on the

killer—serial or not. Right now, it's still about these crazy people and what they may have planned. So let's just the two of us go. If it turns out we find information from this Diablo that may lead us to the killer, or killers, then we'll involve her and her department. For now, remember, our participation in searching for the killer is still very much unofficial."

"We said we'd include her. And I still need to get a real name and address." Jill thought for a moment. "But yeah, it's probably premature. I guess you're right, Jack. Now and then," she said with a laugh.

He had a plan, involving the Alvarez family and an initiation for Saint.

The Exterminator knew he had to do something quickly to show the new group—as well as his own guys—that he was a man of action. That he was a leader. He smiled to himself by the basement window. "Later," he mumbled under his breath, smacking his lips in a kiss as he looked at the Alvarez woman one more time.

51

S aint was ready.

He closed his computer. He felt he still had a lot to learn but was ready to trade the written word for actual life experience. He concluded he would officially join the Very Fine Men if they'd let him in, to see if he really did fit in. And of course, he still held out hope of meeting some ladies through their events, if not the mythical sister of Sarah.

He'd heard talk of there being a large rally coming up with both men and women from surrounding states, and from what he'd gleaned, it wasn't something to be missed. "Party with your own kind, be unkind to others," he'd been told. It was the party part that intrigued him.

He called The Exterminator, who picked up after six rings, and Saint told him he was all in.

"You ain't all in unless I say so. On a scale of one to ten, with ten being ready, you are a two. And that's being charitable."

"Yeah, but I know I belong in the group. With your help, I'll keep learning."

"Are you ready to prove it?"

"Yes. Anything. What do I have to do?"

"There's a bad dude in the neighborhood. A fence-hopper. But not just a no-paper Mexican, a real bad one."

"OK... tell me more."

"This guy works in a restaurant. Cleaning crap, of course. But people have been getting sick there. White people. The word is he hates whites and has been spitting in their meals. He's probably even been making them sick—putting shit in their food or something," The Exterminator lied. "He needs to be taught a lesson, and that's your initiation. To teach him a lesson."

"Can't we just go to the cops?"

The Exterminator laughed. "Don't be a goddamn fool. You want in or not?"

"Yes, of course. But what do you want me to do?"

"I'll show you where the guy lives. Alone in a ratty basement apartment, like the rat he is. You'll smoke him out. That should scare him off, along with a warning I'll provide."

"What do you mean smoke him out? You have smoke bombs?"

"Believe it or not, you can actually buy them at regular big stores, along with your bread and insect repellent! With a perfect name: 'Revenge Smoke Bomb'."

"A smoke bomb in his apartment? Isn't that dangerous? I don't want anyone to get hurt badly."

"It's just smoke, man. Cops use them all the time, right?"

"I guess. OK. Let me know where and when, and I'll do my part."

"Will do. You're on your way, kid."

Saint smiled faintly, while The Exterminator hung up without another word.

The Exterminator hadn't told Saint the smoke bombs clearly stated not to set them off indoors; indoors, they were toxic, and a fire hazard. Which is exactly what he wanted.

A real scare, a proper punishment, he thought.

52

"I didn't bring you up this way! What's wrong with you?!"
Deja looked across the small kitchen table at Saint, an
incredulous expression on her face, fire in her voice. She stared
at Saint as if a strange entity had invaded his body.

"Immigrants taking our jobs? Teach them a lesson? What is
this nonsense you are spewing?"

Deja always insisted on having dinner with Saint. He spent
so much time in his room that she made sure he came up for
air and had a real conversation. Normally, he had little to
say, but their mealtime was pleasant, and they never fought.
This evening was different. Over spaghetti and meatballs,
when Deja asked what was new, he haltingly started talking
about white men not having jobs, not having a future, committing suicide. Deja listened, her forehead creasing, her eyes
narrowing.

Saint stumbled a bit, apparently trying to remember the
arguments he had heard and read about, mumbled some. Then
he said, "We have to protect ourselves from an immigrant
invasion." Suddenly, this discussion became harrowing.

Deja was having no part of it. "All Americans are immigrants. Unless you're Native American, at some point you are
from somewhere else!"

"But..."... Saint started, his face as red as his hair now.

"No buts!"

"But it's different. We are... we are white!" Saint yelled, pounding his fist on the kitchen table. A Coke can jumped and fell to the floor, the fizzing liquid erupting just as he had.

They both looked at the can spiraling out of control but neither went to grab it. Deja cried out, her heart beating faster, her face turning a shade of rose. "White! We are all people. It's what is inside you that counts." She took a deep breath and quietly asked, "Do you think your spirit has a color?"

"Oh, please. Get real." Saint's eyes narrowed. "Enough! Listen, I'm an adult now. I'm eighteen, for Christ's sake! I can think for myself." Saint got up abruptly, his legs hitting the table's skirt.

"Sit down! You are under my roof, and you will not talk that way! Oh my God. I always thought you had your dad, Skyler, in you. Now I fear you don't."

Saint sat down begrudgingly. "Stop with this Skyler nonsense all the time! I never even knew my father!! But it's like he's a ghost, following me around. Well, he's not here. I'm here. I'm real, and an adult, so start treating me like one!"

Deja's head involuntarily snapped back. With a tremble in her voice, she said, "You are far, far from an adult; you're nothing but an immature baby!"

Saint got up fully and forcefully, bumping the table; Deja's plate of food fell onto her.

"Fuck you!" Saint yelled, the words hitting Deja like a blow from a boxer.

Deja got up, food falling to the floor, and slapped his face hard.

This was the first time in their lives she had hit him. She saw the mark on his cheek imprinted by her fingers, red lines reminiscent of a scarlet letter. Saint was frozen in place, the slap imprinted even more on his psyche than his cheek. Deja was about to reach out to him, when he went running out the front door, slamming it behind him, further rattling the room.

Tonight was their night to teach some immigrants a lesson.

The plan was to meet up at midnight. The Exterminator filled the black backpack with the smoke grenades and lighter, along with a rusty sledgehammer to smash the window. He had told Saint it was his job to smash it and throw two or three bombs in, and to then immediately take off. The Exterminator said he'd be around the other side, by the door, while Jose was disoriented inside. He'd then barge in and give him a few slaps to the head. "Diablo, this should scare him good so he stops his shit. Get him to leave town. Better yet, run back to Mexico."

The Exterminator had no such plan to rush in. He was going to put a board against the door to barricade them in, and let the toxic smoke do its job.

If a fire erupted, so much the better, he thought.

53

Ever since she got out of prison, she'd been there for them. Gloria had been a presence since the day Saint was born, a true present since Saint's father was gone. Gloria was an enigma. Deja had once told Saint that his father Skyler called her "Mom," though Deja didn't believe Gloria was actually Skyler's mother. Skyler had never been totally clear about the relationship when he had spoken of her. There was something strange there, but Deja could always tell by the look in Skyler's eye and the tone of his voice that she shouldn't push it. And he certainly never talked about how she had come to be imprisoned. But Skyler clearly loved Gloria, so Deja accepted it all. Skyler always believed in redemption, in second chances, in showing you can learn from your mistakes and become a better person. And when Skyler was gone, all Deja had left was Gloria to help her. Her prison release was quite the relief. So Deja accepted her fully—even had Saint call her Nana.

Saint and Deja hadn't spoken since their dinner disaster. She knew she couldn't imprison him at home, couldn't incarcerate his mind, so she simply gave him the silent treatment. She could tell that actually ended up being a very tough sentence.

★

Saint felt incredibly guilty. He didn't blame his mother for the slap, though still felt he was entitled to his opinion, even if she disagreed. Saint wanted to be an adult, to be treated like an adult. He didn't have anywhere to turn to talk it out.

So he went to see Gloria. He could tell she knew there was a problem as soon as she saw him. He knew he looked disheveled and lost, like a little boy who couldn't find his mom. Gloria gave him a hug, which he returned; he didn't want to let go. She asked what was wrong, and Saint confessed to her all he'd done: the fight, cursing his mother, acting like a bum.

"She'll get over it. People have gotten over much worse things that I've done," she said with a wry smile. "But you have to respect her. She loves you and tries to do what's best for you. Now tell me more about how this whole thing started."

Saint haltingly went through the story from the beginning, including the Very Fine Men, not leaving out any details— other than about the tradwives and his carnal interest. And of course, not one iota was said about the upcoming initiation The Exterminator had planned. Gloria raised an eyebrow a few times, shifted uncomfortably in her chair now and then, but remained silent until he finished.

"Do you think these men really have your best interests in mind?"

"Nana, they act like my friends. The only friends I've really ever had. You know how alone I've been," Saint said, looking pitifully sad.

"You have to understand," Gloria said, "some people, lowlifes, can only feel good about themselves, can only uplift themselves, by bringing others down. Do you really want to be with such people?"

"Yeah, but Nana, I'm finally able to feel like I'm something, that there's a group of guys who accept me for who I am."

Gloria considered him, returning the sad look while pursing her lips, and leading with a sigh. "Let me tell you a story."

Saint sat up straighter. "Go ahead."

"I was only a few years older than you when I had a son. Sawyer. There was an accident. He died."

Saint reacted with surprise, his eyes moistened, and he took her arm. "I never knew," he said.

Gloria took in a deep breath. "It was an accident. But it left me reeling. It made me a little crazy. No, a lot crazy. But one day, your father came into my life. Skyler. A beautiful little boy, red hair just like my son had."

Saint looked down, unconsciously felt his own red hair, nodded his head just a touch. Gloria grabbed his hand, and he raised his gaze. She had an intense look on her face. "That little boy, your father Skyler, had a happy life, though also much too short." Gloria gulped, then composed herself. "His life was made happy by having good friends, being surrounded by love. The early years were tough for him. He was in a new town, knew no one. What helped him was meeting a boy named Carlos. 'Little Carlos' we called him. He lived with his mother Maria in an apartment in the same building. He and your dad Skyler would spend as much time as they could together. Laughing, crying, learning, surviving, thriving."

"They grew up together. They loved each other. Unfortunately, horribly, right before your father went off to college, Carlos disappeared. I honestly didn't think Skyler would ever get over that. But somehow, he pulled himself together. He was doing great at college: academically, with soccer, and of course finding the love of his life in your mother, in Deja. I think what kept him going was the memory of Carlos, Carlos who was much more of a brother than any of those fraternity ones your father knew. I believe Skyler felt

he needed to continue on, to be a success for him, for Carlos."
Gloria grabbed Saint's hand.

"Maria and Carlos were immigrants. Same as the people you've been talking about. We all loved each other. We all helped each other. It's in that spirit that you have to live. If your father came back to earth, what would he say about your behavior? I always thought you had Skyler in you; I want to still believe that. Honor your dead father by being honorable. Then you will be grown up."

Saint slumped down in his chair. He had thought he was on the right path, but now he knew it was a rocky road ahead. He shook his head, looking down, feeling he was at a crossroads. Saint wondered if there was any direction that would provide a bit of happiness in his life.

"I don't think I can ever live up to him. To Skyler. To my father."

"He wasn't perfect. I'm sure if he was pushed, if he became enraged, he could do something bad. Nobody's perfect. But he tried. He was a good soul."

Saint bit his lower lip.

Gloria smiled. "God, you remind me so much of him! He used to do that with his lip. It's almost like you're the same person. Almost like you're his reincarnation."

Saint became more upset. "Yeah, right! I keep hearing that. I damn well hope he's resting in peace, cause I sure as hell ain't."

Gloria frowned.

He looked away, his emotions in turmoil—the Saint and the Diablo in a battle for his soul.

54

It was midnight in the garden-less apartment. Good and evil were still at odds.

A cold wind whipped by, rustling the leaves while Saint was wrestling with his thoughts. He hadn't slept at all the prior night and couldn't think straight now. He didn't want to be there but ended up going along—mostly to make sure things didn't get out of hand.

He and The Exterminator had watched Jose enter the apartment a few minutes earlier. They checked their supplies one more time under the moonless sky. They peered at each other, dressed in black, faces covered in charcoal powder, the whites of their eyes the most evident part of their visages. A cat screeched in the distance. An owl fled to the heavens. The Exterminator nodded to Saint, grabbed his shoulder, gave it a squeeze, and headed off. Saint watched him silently go and waited a couple of minutes for him to get around to the door on the other side.

Saint took out his hammer, and with one loud crash, he smashed through the window, pieces of glass exploding around him.

At the same moment, The Exterminator picked up the 4x4 beam he had left behind the bushes, wedged it tightly in front of the door, pounding it in with a brick. For extra measure, he had pre-drilled a hole in each end, and now beat a stake through the beam into the doorframe. With a malevolent laugh of glee, he dropped the brick from his gloved hand, turned around to flee, and never looked back.

The window now in pieces, Saint grabbed a smoke bomb and began to light it. The lighter didn't take the first time, and Saint started sweating. On the third attempt, he got it going, and threw it through the opening, jagged shards of glass cutting through his thin glove. He quickly threw a second in, as instructed. As the first one landed on a colorful sarape blanket, Saint saw Jose in the apartment staring in horror at the canister, which went off with a sound like a sonic boom. After a moment's shock, he ran to it, attempting to pick it up.

Saint looked at the third smoke bomb in the bag and seeing the scene inside, couldn't throw it in. He tossed the hammer in the backpack and turned to lay a board over the broken window as The Exterminator had directed. Just as he was hurriedly doing so, he glimpsed a small figure crying out "Momma!" and then saw a woman coughing and screaming.

Saint started trembling. What the hell! He thought.

Jose was struggling with the door, which surprised Saint. The smoke was getting denser and had a horrid smell. Inside, it looked hard to see, and the little boy was stumbling into the furniture, falling, and calling out for help. Jose was choking as he pushed frantically at the door, which wouldn't budge.

Saint knew something was terribly wrong. Rather than rush away, he moved the board from the window, grabbed the backpack and ran to the other side of the building to help get the door open. He expected to find The Exterminator there, but he was gone!

Saint heard the thump of a body ramming against the door from the other side and was incredulous at what he saw: a beam wedged across the front! The pound of body against the door was becoming fainter with each attempt, though the cries and screams could still be heard from inside.

Saint grabbed the sledgehammer from the backpack. His heart racing, and hammer in one hand, he pounded on the beam, but it barely moved. He smashed it three times in quick succession, the hammer slipping in his sweaty grip, almost sliding out of his grasp, his wrist weakening from the effort.

The beam wobbled with the last wallop. He grabbed the sledgehammer with both hands, held it high above his head, and chopped down like a madman. It broke apart. The door burst open, three bodies falling through the opening, gasping for air. They saw in front of them a figure of black, thinking the angel of death had come for them. Saint turned to run, but not before Jose's eyes had locked on his.

55

What a wonderful world it could be.

The tune stuck in Jill's mind after her previous meeting with Tracy. But while she would like to think that, she was becoming world-weary. While she was happy she had a lead on the Incel connection, perhaps the killer, she was sick of listening in on the hate group chats. After hours of that, she poured herself a scotch, and Jack came over and rubbed her neck and shoulders. She talked about how every day seemed to be filled with darkness and despair.

"You know, I became a cop to do some good, to better people's lives. Like my dad, Frank. I knew I'd have to deal with some terrible individuals, but Jesus, I never expected it to be quite like this. One awful event after another. Day by day, it wears on ya." Jill took a sip of her scotch.

"Don't I know it. It's the grind, the fact you have to deal with bad people, some downright evil, just about every friggin' day. Guess that's why we have this," Jack said, clinking his glass of scotch next to Jill's.

"Yeah, but in truth, there is a lot of good we do," Jack continued. "Listen, you know me. I'm no Mr. Ray of Sunshine, but hey, there definitely are good times, good people. Some pretty uplifting moments. We gotta just focus on that."

Jill cocked her head, like a Jack Russell terrier trying to understand.

"Like what?"

Jack smiled as he recounted a story from a few years back. "Remember that time we caught the guy who was robbing all those jewelry stores, coming through the back entrances in the middle of the night?"

Jill nodded. "Yeah, I remember. 'Diamond Dave,' we called him. Some damn good police work."

"Well, do you remember what happened after we arrested him?" Jack asked.

Jill thought for a moment before her eyes lit up with recognition. "Oh yeah, his daughter came to thank us."

Jack leaned forward in his seat, eyes gleaming with pride. "That's right. Years later. She was so grateful that we caught her dad. She said he'd been struggling with addiction and didn't know how else to get money. But when he got arrested, he finally got the help he needed to turn his life around."

"That's right; Dave got rehabbed and even a degree while in prison. Today, he runs a drug clinic, helping so many others get their lives together."

"Yup. Even got to walk his daughter down the aisle."

"That second chance was all he needed. It was like he was reborn, had learned his lessons and began making it a more wonderful world."

Jill smiled at the memories. "Those were some good days."

"Sure were," Jack agreed. "And it's moments like that, where we can make a real difference in someone's life, that make the darkness worth it."

"I guess. And now that I think of it, there *were* plenty of others. How about that ring of car thieves? Got that break in the case and took the ringleader down! Even recovered most of the cars, amazingly intact!"

Jack nodded. "Yup, got those cars back to their rightful owners. And the look on their faces—priceless!"

"Yeah, remember that young couple who had just bought their first sedan?"? Jill said.

"I sure do," Jack said, "getting ready for a baby on the way."

"Well," Jill continued, "they were just devastated when it was stolen. But when we were able to recover it with no real damage done, they were so relieved, so thrilled!"

"Yup. I bought them a nice car seat for the baby. Pink," Jack said, turning red. "Little sheep pattern too."

Jill looked at Jack in wonder. "Did ya, now?" she said, a twinkle in her eye.

They sat in silence for a moment, both lost in thought about the good they had done for the community. Jill felt much lighter and energized.

She said, "You know, it really is moments like those that make all the long hours and hard work worth it. Knowing that we can bring some peace and happiness to people... it's a good feeling."

Jack stood up. "Well, enough of this. And don't tell anyone that I know about this conversation." He laughed. "But let's go do some good."

Jill stood up as well, touching Jack on his arm. "Let's make some people happy."

Serendipitously, they both at the same time said, "Let's make it the wonderful world it could be." They looked at each other and laughed.

56

"What the hell was that?!"

Saint was livid when he met up with The Exterminator the next day. He shouted that he'd seen others besides Jose in the apartment. He didn't admit, though, that it was he who'd set them free.

"I didn't know there'd be others. I thought the asshole lived alone," The Exterminator lied. "Maybe he had a prostitute with him. I decided to slow his exit, put a simple obstacle in front of the door."

"That wasn't the plan!"

"I thought it was too dangerous for me to hang around there. I figured a bit of smoke. Make him choke. That would teach him enough of a lesson, then he'd get out."

"Prostitute—bullshit! A wife, a kid! Come on! I didn't sign up for that!"

"Relax. Looks like he broke out easily, just as I thought."

At that point, The Exterminator stared at Saint with squinty eyes, but said nothing more. Saint returned the stare but didn't admit to a thing. After a few moments, Saint hoped The Exterminator concluded it must have been a rotten piece of wood, or perhaps faulty nails, that derailed his scheme for good.

The Exterminator pointed to him and said, "You signed up

for an initiation. Now it's done. You fuckin' made it in." Then, with a sneer, he added, "Congratu-fucking-lations."

Saint shook his head from side to side, and quietly said, "I don't know."

"What do you mean you don't fuckin' know?" he blurted in a low growl. Then he composed himself and smiled. "Hey, don't sweat the details. Everyone is safe. And now you have some brothers. And don't forget the sisters."

Saint took in a deep breath and turned the other cheek. "I guess."

"In fact, we'll have a little party for you, a celebration. The girls will be there. I'm sure there will be at least one who'll be happy to initiate you in other things," The Exterminator said with a wink.

57

He was out for revenge.

He trudged through the desolate streets, the only sounds being his heavy footsteps and the distant hum of a lone streetlamp. The air was thick with the stench of garbage, making his nostrils flare in disgust. He felt the dampness of the night seep into his skin.

Fuckin' world, he thought.

As he walked, he couldn't help but feel like he was sinking deeper into a hole he couldn't climb out of. The surrounding buildings loomed like dark, ominous shadows, heightening his sense of unease.

He stopped in his tracks and looked up at the sky, where thick clouds obscured the stars. In that moment, he felt like a prisoner in his own life, unable to escape the darkness that surrounded him. They are to blame. Tall and white, he'd thought everything should've turned out all right. But it hadn't. He shook his head and resumed his slow slog down the street.

Always a solitary figure, he'd had few friends. But there was one guy he trusted, one guy who always had his back, and now that one guy was behind bars. He was sure he'd been wrongly convicted of the crime; he was incensed that a Black judge had sentenced his buddy to a long prison term. He seethed with anger as he thought about the injustice he believed had occurred. That bastard!

As he walked, his mind raced with thoughts of revenge. He imagined himself taking down the judge, making him pay for what he had done.

He thought of the headlines he loved seeing: KKK Killer Strikes Again!

58

The sex was unsatisfying.

Jill rolled over. "You're done; don't worry about me." The bed creaked as she pulled up the light-blue, satin sheet and covered her bared breast. She touched his arm. "Don't worry, you still pass my test," she said playfully.

Jack was frustrated. "You sure?"

"I'm sure. And it's not you."

"Got that right!" he said with a swagger, overcompensating for his bruised ego. Then he frowned. "If it's not me, what is it? I almost feel like I'm having sex with someone occupied with reading the news at the same time!"

Jill furrowed her brow. "Not quite, mister. But sorry. Preoccupied, I guess. I got the additional pieces of information I was waiting for late last night. Went to tell you and you were dead asleep. And this morning... Well, we know about that. But I found out a lot."

"I'm all ears."

Jill looked at his crotch and smiled. Then got serious.

"This guy Diablo not only associated with the hot yoga nut but has been going in secret to white supremacist meetings. And the chatter says something big is brewing. Something big and violent. I have a bad feeling about this."

"Your feelings. Hmmm."

"Jack, this is alarming. And there's more. Listen! We know him. Kind of. El Diablo has been associating with a felon."

Now Jack was interested. "OK, Sherlock, tell me more."

"Diablo's real name is Saint, believe it or not. And apparently, he ain't."

Jack looked back.

"Just got his address. And somehow, he's related to Gloria."

Jack looked back quizzically, but now more interested.

"You know Gloria! The one we helped put in prison. That whole bit with Skyler."

"Gloria. Yes, of course I remember her. Could never forget her. But how does this kid, Diablo, or Saint as you say, relate to her? What's the connection?"

"Well, from what I can tell, she's been helping him for quite some time. Helping his mother too," Jill said.

"Oh, shit... Gloria. We can't escape her! I wouldn't be surprised if she was teaching him to be a criminal."

Jill looked at Jack with a cold stare, her lips pressed together.

"Yeah, well, now Saint calls himself 'El Diablo.' Maybe he helped plan the hot yoga mess. Who knows what he's planning now."

"Now that you got an address, let's pay him a visit, ASAP!" Jack replied.

The sex was supremely satisfying.

Saint thought he was in heaven. Heaven on earth, for sure. He had actually still been a virgin, so The Exterminator wasn't kidding when he talked about his second initiation.

The evening celebration had started with Jägermeister shots, as all the guys toasted their new recruit. There were several women there this time, all good-looking to Saint, and a bunch of campers and vans littering the lot when Saint marched in. The Exterminator earned some respect for setting up the basement attack, and there was an ebullient atmosphere throughout the night, as if their team had just won the world championship.

But the night really began when Sarah introduced him to her sister, Elizabeth. Dressed conservatively but appealingly, like Sarah, Elizabeth had light-brown hair softly cascading down her back, large, brown eyes sparkling with a mischievous look, super glossy, brick-red lipstick on thin lips. His knees weakened when her opening line was, "Hello, Diablo. I've heard a lot about you. I'm feeling a little devilish myself."

He smiled, turning crimson, while she laughed—the sweetest sound he'd ever heard. He stuttered a bit, as various responses flew through his mind, but he couldn't get one out. She stepped in, "Don't worry, I'm just kidding."

Saint exhaled, while Sarah said, "I'll leave you two alone to get to know each other. Diablo is usually quiet, but not this quiet. Good thing you like the strong, silent type," she added with a laugh.

"We'll be fine," Saint said, not sure if he believed that, but trying to regain some manhood.

A million questions danced wildly in his brain; he fumbled to ask one. After several awkward exchanges, Saint and Elizabeth finally got into a bit of a groove in their conversation, lubricated by the red jug wine they were drinking, and the winking flames of the campfire in front of them. They tuned out the guys in the background whining about anyone who wasn't them, and Saint ended up telling her about things growing up he'd never told anyone. Her brown eyes grew bigger with sympathy and empathy. Saint wanted to dive right into them.

As the night wore on, she edged closer to him, their arms touching, Saint feeling as if electric currents were running up and down his skin. His heart beat faster when he saw the top button of her blouse had come undone, the crest of her full breast bulging out of her bra. He'd surreptitiously executed a side glance—though not as subtle as he thought, as Elizabeth smiled sweetly. Then, her shoes off, she rubbed her toes against his leg. He almost jumped out of his seat.

They went for a walk, Saint scared, wondering if his kiss would be remiss. He kicked up some dirt, almost tripping. She grasped his hand, which he knew was sweaty; no matter how often he wiped it on his pants leg, it would be sweaty again, like trick candles on a birthday cake that kept relighting. But she didn't seem to care, entwining her fingers in his.

Dark had descended on the park. They walked on, Saint breathing more heavily with each step, until they stopped in front of a barren pine tree, charred with the remnants of a lightning strike. His thoughts were like a tapestry, woven with threads of curiosity, and stitched with the dreams of possibilities.

Elizabeth looked up at him. He tentatively grabbed her by the waist, his trembling arm bringing her closer to him. She responded by getting even closer, closing her eyes, and planting a kiss on his lips. He returned it, a bit too vigorously, and she laughed, causing him to pull back. But she pulled him toward her again, and with a smile, kissed him softly. He followed suit. Soon, he needed no more lessons, and they kissed deeply for what seemed like hours, but was only minutes. Saint reveled in the sweetness of new sensations.

Rotten ran by, the rambunctious Rottweiler interrupting the scene. He stopped between them, looked at them quizzically, and then took off again, tail up. Apart from that, the area was eerily quiet, and they followed the dog back, passing the parking lot, noting most of the cars had left. Elizabeth stopped, squeezed his hand, gazed at him intently, and quietly steered him to her van.

Inside, he took her shirt off quickly, but fumbled with her bra.

"Do you need help?"

He didn't answer, feeling foolish, and tried again, unsuccessfully. She grabbed his hands and put them at his sides. She undid the bra, her breasts tumbling free, coffee-colored nipples erect with the cool of the night and the heat of the moment. He felt their fullness, firm and soft in symphony. Saint felt like he was back in heaven. She put her hand behind his head, encouraging it closer.

They stripped off the rest of their clothes in seconds. Elizabeth had nothing on but her lipstick. For a split second, he was unsure, but she guided him in. Her red nails dug into his back, and she moved with him, in harmony. His release was like a beast, shuddering and groaning. When he was done, he looked at her, uncertain. She hushed him, and simply said, "Mmmm. Thank you. You are a devil, aren't you?"

59

Sheriff's Deputy Tracy argued vehemently.

Jill had confided in her that they believed they knew who ScottB's accomplice, El Diablo, was, but Jack thought it was premature to have her involved in the initial discussion with him. Tracy clearly wanted to be part of the action, but finally acquiesced. She fully expected to be in on the next step, hopefully taking the killer down.

Tracy settled into her apartment. She took off her shoes, gun and gun belt, and got into sweats. This was often the most pleasurable part of her day—especially taking her shoes off. A glass of cabernet and some mindless TV would enable her to relax in her favorite way. She didn't even mind the Lean Cuisine frozen dinner. It didn't help her lose weight, but it was easy—and she felt better about the slice of cheesecake she'd eat later.

Just then, she got a call from a friend who worked for the campus police department. Tracy didn't have time for a lot of friends, but after dealing with especially disturbing events, she'd have a drink, and often visit with a friend. Talk always helped.

"Good to hear from you. I have a slow evening, thankfully. Was actually thinking about watching *Ghost* again, for like the nineteenth time!"

"*Ghost!* That's my favorite. Oh my God, that scene at the end when Patrick Swayze kisses Demi and then heads back to heaven—I cry every time."

"I know," Tracy said. "Takes my breath away. When they both say, 'See ya,' it's to die for."

"Well, speaking of entertainment," her friend said, "are you done with the latest Colleen Hoover book you said you were reading last time? This campus work can be so quiet."

"Wish I could say the same. But yes, I'm done. And you're in luck; I'll be on special patrol nearby around noon. Easy enough to drop it off; it's pretty damn good."

"Thanks, Tracy. I'll meet you at the campus coffee shop. Right by the main building, near where your favorite judge, Judge Frazier, has been giving his guest lectures."

"Piece of cake," Tracy said. She hung up, and thinking of that, grabbed the last piece of cheesecake.

60

S aint was scared.

Scared that his first and only girl hadn't been back to the gatherings in over two weeks, was totally incommunicado. Scared he'd done it all wrong, messed up his only shot. Scared he'd never get a girl like her again. He spent his days moping around or sitting alone in his room without a sound. Finally, he asked The Exterminator if he knew what was going on.

"Cool your jets. And your dick. She's been busy, helping with the march."

"What march?"

"You know, the United We Stand march, dumbass."

"Oh shit, forgot about that."

The Exterminator put his hand to his head. "Jesus, maybe you weren't ready to be one of us! It's only the biggest fucking gathering we've ever had. People from all different states converging for a weekend. We'll show the world we mean business, that we're strong. Heilbach's group combining with ours is nothing compared to uniting groups from all over!"

"Is that why those guys are here now?" Saint asked, pointing to the larger group of men downfield from them.

The Exterminator looked down on him with an expression of disdain. "You catch on quickly. Now, let's join the others."

They headed over to the crowd composed of no women,

just a cacophonous cluster of loud men. Spencer Heilbach eyed them sauntering in, as they were the last to join. The Exterminator stood tall, erect and proud, while Saint beside him, with slumped shoulders, looked like a before-and-after comparison.

"Guess we can get started now that everyone has deigned to join us," Heilbach said.

"Got that right. Leader should be last to arrive," was The Exterminator's retort, with a snort. Heilbach, obviously annoyed, chose to ignore the remark, and turned away to address the group.

He looked the group over and began with a proud and excited voice. "We are now only a couple of weeks away from our biggest show of power yet. United We Stand will put this country on notice, and pave the way for the changes we demand, the changes so desperately needed."

Everyone was cheering as he continued. "I know you've been putting a lot of time into your training. I like what I've seen. Let's give Slayer a big thanks for the techniques he's taught us with sticks—love the flagpole maneuvers!"

The cheers came up again, and a shout of "Slayer's the man!" rang out.

"As your leader, I'll be coordinating with the other groups when we get there, and—"

The Exterminator interrupted him, "I'll be doing that."

Heilbach ignored that too, and continued, "And let's remember why we're doing this. We're doing the Lord's work! These others that surround us will not replace us."

Saint gulped and stared at his feet.

"We have a big mission," Heilbach continued, expanding his arms out wide. "All those people need to be put away, sent back to where they came from."

"Put them away for fuckin' good," shouted The Exterminator.

"If we get rid of enough of them, our way of life will be sustained. And we will be glorified!" Heilbach shouted, to crazed cheers.

"I'm the God of Hellfire!" The Exterminator yelled to the raucous crowd.

"And we will send them all to hell!" Heilbach finished. "But one last thing. I've heard some asshole groups may have gotten wind of this. So we have to be prepared for counter-protestors. But that will be their funeral. So let's agree on how we'll be armed, what strategies we'll use, and then we'll get on with the next set of drills."

Most of the group started chanting "Heilbach, Heilbach," raising their fists in the air with each ear-splitting cheer. A few of The Exterminator's men started yelling "The Exterminator" in response, returning the fist gesture with one like a tomahawk chop.

Heilbach stood back up and gestured with his hands for them to settle down. "United men, united. United we stand." The men slowly started nodding. The Exterminator stared at Heilbach, an inscrutable look upon his face.

Saint was scared. Scared that his worst fears were coming to pass. Scared that he was now hooked up with people who were completely nuts. And scared because he didn't have a clue what to do.

61

Elizabeth seemed to have disappeared from the face of the earth.

Saint was doubly depressed, both at no word from her and the words he heard at the last meeting. He thought physical training for defensive purposes made sense, but this big rally coming up was something else. His sixth sense said it could be major trouble. He had put up with one terrible incident at initiation and didn't want to be played the fool again. He thought of Gloria's words, thought of his father's best friend Carlos, and thought of making his father—Skyler—proud, wherever he was.

He didn't sleep for days. His mom, Deja, continually asked him what was wrong but never got a response. He finally decided he couldn't continue with the group, even if it meant being alone. Now he just had to figure out how to get out, which could be tough with all that he now knew.

Oh screw it. I can't get anything right. Maybe I'm not cut out for this time on earth, he thought, flopping on his bed, turning the lights out.

Deja was horrified.

It was so unexpected. *Why didn't I see any signs of this?* She thought. They tried to comfort her, but it was for naught. It was so unlike him. Deja believed she knew him, but obviously not.

"When will he be home?" Jill asked.

"Any minute," she stammered.

Jill had done all the talking since they'd arrived, unannounced, at Deja's house: El Diablo's location that had been uncovered. Jack hung in the background. Deja was extremely nervous when they showed their I.D.s and was reluctant at first to let them in, though she knew she had no real choice. At least Jill had a calming way about her, almost like a mother with a lullaby soothing her baby. After assuring Deja that she herself was not in any trouble, they spoke quietly about Saint, sitting in the small living room, Deja rubbing her fingers back and forth over her knuckles. Jill told her how she knew teenagers these days are so difficult and didn't know how as a single mother Deja was able to do it all these years.

Jill then changed from a sympathetic to a serious tone, her face hardening. She told Deja who Saint was associating with and what Saint used as a screen name. Deja grimaced. The fact that he had been chatting with a man who'd tried to burn down a yoga studio shocked her to the core.

"Not that we believe your son was involved in that incident," she said.

"At least not heavily," Jack interrupted, Jill giving him a nasty look.

"But we are concerned about the new people he's befriended. Concerned about what they might be planning, what influence they may have over your son. It could get violent. You know, there's been some shootings, killings, not far from here."

Deja was horrified, and by her reaction, it was obvious to Jack and Jill that she had no clue. Deja then broke down, crying.

"Someone Saint spoke with wanted to kill people? Kill women in a yoga studio?" Deja could barely get the words out.

Jill took her hand, which was wet with perspiration. "We have no hard evidence he actually planned or helped in the execution of that."

"But he's been hanging out with some badasses," Jack interjected. Jill gave him another look and he backed off.

"We just want to talk with him, Deja. Protect him. Make sure he doesn't do something in the future that he may regret," Jill said, looking into her wide eyes.

Jack added, "Make sure he has a future."

At that, Deja cried out, "Oh, God, my baby!"

Right then, Saint walked in.

Everyone stood up, staring at Saint. His first inclination was to run. But then he stared at his mother and composed himself— was even able to play it nonchalantly.

"Mom, what's up? What's going on here?"

She couldn't find the words, so Jill stepped in. "Don't worry, we just need to ask you a few questions."

A huge figure moved toward him, looking to Saint like Hulk Hogan in his prime. Saint backed away. "Have a seat, young man," he commanded.

The male detective, Jack, took control from there. It took a while. Most of the time, Saint's arms were folded across his chest, but after much squirming, Saint knew it was a lost cause. He finally admitted to knowing the people Jack identified. He claimed though they were just friends, really just acquaintances, and he had done nothing wrong. Wouldn't do anything wrong.

"Some friends. I suggest you find new ones," Jack bellowed.

Saint jumped back in his chair, then inhaled deeply and stared at his shoes. "I wish I could."

"There's stuff we know about you, about what you've been doing lately," Jack said, in a menacing tone. Deja looked up, alarmed. "Stuff that will get you into a shitload of trouble. Unless you cooperate."

"He'll cooperate," Deja wailed, looking at Jill.

Saint opened his arms. "Look, the truth is, I was planning to leave the group. They're called Very Fine Men. But they aren't." He looked down. "They aren't."

"We know their name," Jack said.

Jill interrupted him and said, "That's good, Saint. We heard you were a smart boy." She glanced at Deja, giving her an encouraging smile. "We'll straighten this all out." Then she added, looking at Saint, "We don't want you to leave the group. Not at all. But we do need you to feed us some information. Do you think you can do that, Saint?"

Deja looked at him, nodding her head vigorously up and down. Saint's heart was racing, his breathing sped up. He barely got the words out. "You mean, like an informant?"

"Just think of it as helping the good guys," Jill said.

"Something your dad would have liked," Deja said meekly.

Saint nodded his head slowly, feeling like a man just condemned to death.

"What do I have to do?"

"What do I have to do?" Saint asked The Exterminator.

They'd met by a ramshackle shed in the backwoods of his property. The surrounding land was strewn about with dead items, making it look more like a garbage dump than someone's homely homestead. A rusted-out washing machine, a car on blocks that appeared not to have been driven in a decade, and empty beer bottles and whiskey handles decorated the dead zone. A bit of *Deliverance* meets *Misery*. It was dusk, and the smell of decaying detritus perfumed the air.

"Start loading the pickup truck." The truck, a faded-brown Dodge Ram with rusted rocker panels and bald tires—tires almost as big as a monster truck's—sat in the driveway, like a Humvee from a lost war. Covering the rear window fully was a decal of the Confederate flag. "Get the flags out of the shed and start loading them in. Then the shields."

"Shields?" Saint said, looking confused.

"In case we have to defend ourselves. This will be a big march. You never know how douchebags may react."

Saint grabbed the flags, a mixture of American flags and Confederate flags. What they both had in common was that the poles were topped with a sharp finial, as sharp as any spear, potentially deadly to those who drew near. He threw them into the pickup, where they landed with a thud. Then he started moving the shields onto the dirty truck bed. Some were decorated with a black eagle; others had a white background with a black X, reminiscent of a St. Andrew's cross. Still others were decorated with what Saint later learned was called an Othala rune, a symbol from an ancient alphabet representing a rightful inheritance from a mythic Aryan past. He started dumping them in the back as well.

"Hey, better neaten them up."

"Why? And why are there so many?" Saint asked.

"First, they're not just for our group."

"Oh, you mean we are taking stuff for Heilbach too?"

"No, he can carry his own damn shit. And second, we need to pick up more cargo from another group."

"Another group? Who?"

"Don't know much about them. Just that they share our mission. Call themselves the Boogaloo Boys. Crazy name. We are to meet up tomorrow with their leader, a guy named Dirk, and haul some of their stuff too."

"Gotcha," Saint said, a serious look on his face.

"Hey, why so glum? These next few days will be a party. Now, make sure you're dressed right, like I told ya. Hope you've been to Walmart. All black. Boots, pants, shirt—all black. And the black cap I gave you. If you are a good boy, I may give you one of our black helmets too."

Saint didn't look any happier.

"You gotta look good; I hear Elizabeth will be there."

At that, Saint stopped loading and perked up. "Really? Where's she been?"

"Don't you worry about that. And one last thing—to complete your attire, I've got this." He reached into his boot and took out a knife—same kind used in their throwing drills. Saint stared at it and was caught between the optimism of seeing Elizabeth and the pessimism of what that knife meant.

62

Judge Ernie Frazier, a prominent Black judge, was respected by most people.

Most.

The judge had made a name for himself in the legal community for his fair decisions, often communicated with flair. He was also known for his love of family, with a wife and five beautiful children, and his service on the board of directors of a food charity organization named Food Rescue. After particularly tough days on the bench, he blew off steam at the YMCA by swimming one hundred laps. He found himself at the Y often.

He'd just finished a lecture on an insider's perspective on what goes into judicial decision making. The students had seemed captivated by his words, leaning in intently and taking notes on their iPads. He'd said, "As a judge, one of the most important things I do is make decisions that impact the lives of people who appear before me in court." He went on, explaining that meant the need to maintain impartiality, the need to weigh evidence carefully, and the responsibility that comes with making decisions that can affect the course of someone's life.

The lecture ended and the students filed out of the building, buzzing with new insights they'd been given. It was nearing noon as the judge exited. He stopped to chat on the steps of the building with some lingering students who'd stayed behind to ask him some final questions.

The tall stranger looked on from a distance.

Everyone loves the professor judge, he thought, touching the gun in the folds of his trench coat.

Time to teach him a lesson.

63

Deja screamed.

"Kill me now!"

Jack and Jill had paid Deja a visit, looking to get a progress report from Saint, but he was nowhere in sight. They thought they'd wait for him, and in the meantime, Jill used the time to further her relationship with Deja.

"Deja is a beautiful name. And so is Saint. How did you decide to name him Saint?"

Deja looked down, then just shrugged. Jill put her arm around her. "Don't you worry about him. It's all going to work out."

Deja sniffled. "He was a beautiful baby. I named him at birth. Do you really want to hear why?"

Jill looked encouragingly at Deja. Jack looked bored.

"Labor was nearing twenty-four hours and I actually wondered whether I was going to make it. Sweat dripped out of every pore. My hair was plastered to my forehead; then I started vomiting. I was trembling when my lower back seized up."

"I then felt as if I was being stabbed in the stomach. I just wanted to be put out of my misery; I remember yelling 'Kill me now!'"

Jill looked at her with wide eyes. "Oh my God, that's terrible!"

"Wait, it gets worse. I was retreating from reality, the walls of the delivery room seeming to fade further away, while the buzzing, fluorescent lighting above looked like it was about to come crashing down on me. I yelled out for my husband, Skyler. But of course, he was dead. The halos from the bright light were the only response."

"And as long as my labor was, in the end, my baby suddenly slipped out. I guess he finally decided it was time and couldn't delay his appearance back on earth one second longer. With my last ounce of energy, it took one big push and his head popped out, wide-eyed and looking surprised. I was happy it was a boy, and immediately smiled at the wisp of reddish-brown hair, thinking of Skyler's red hair. 'He's here,' I remember whispering. 'Thank God.'"

"Wow. I'm certainly glad I'll never have to go through something like that," Jack said.

"That's because you're not as tough as me," Jill responded. Then looking at Deja with a smile, said, "Well, you went from the lowest of lows to the highest of highs, a crazy roller coaster of a ride... So the naming?"

"Well, I remember he had the sweetest smile on his face when he was put on my chest. Like... kind of like a yogi in the midst of meditation." Deja laughed. "And it was kind of crazy, my first words to him were: 'Nice to see you again.'"

"Nice to see you again? That's odd," Jack said.

Jill shushed him, and smiled at Deja, who went on. "He was perfect. I didn't notice the slight birthmark on the left side of his head then. He actually still has that, under his mop of red hair. But that's all right. I've always told him it was a kiss from an angel."

"Then I said to him, 'Oh my Lord, it's a miracle I made it through this—you little devil!' I actually remember then closing my eyes, making sure it wasn't a dream, and opened them to see my baby still there, reigning supreme. 'And your red hair. You are a devil!'"

"I tell you, his birth immediately ended my death—if you know what I mean."

Jill nodded her head slowly up and down. Jack looked unsure.

"Then I looked deeply into my baby's eyes. You know, I was actually taken aback for a moment. I recognized something. It was so weird."

Jack looked over at Jill, lifting an eyebrow and cocking his head.

"Then I smiled for the first time in days. Actually, I believe it may have been for the first time since before Skyler's death. I think I even giggled."

Jill smiled.

"As I looked at my sweet little redhead, I said, 'You're so beautiful! You're no devil! I know what I'll call you. Saint. You're my angel come back to me, my Saint!'"

Jill took her hand. Deja smiled, then her eyes widened.

"You know, as soon as I'd said that, Saint looked back at me. I was sure I saw a little smile in return."

Deja had to get started on dinner, and Jack suggested to her that they wait upstairs for Saint. Once in his room, Jack scratched his jaw and said, "That one's a little crazy, isn't she?"

"Everyone's a little crazy," Jill said.

"Well, yeah, but saying, 'Nice to see you again?' Recognizing something in the baby's eyes? Doo-doo-doo-doo."

"Oh, please, you belong in The Twilight Zone. She'd just given birth, after excruciating labor. Cut her some slack."

"Fine. I'll just put her story in my X-files."

64

He sat in the corner of the room, in the dark, waiting.
"Late night?" Jack asked.

Saint jumped back, dropping his backpack on the floor, as Jack switched a desk lamp on. "Jesus! You scared the shit out of me!"

"Just conserving electricity," Jack said, with a bit of a snort.

"Sorry about that," Jill said, coming out of the shadows from the other end of the room. "Your mother let us in, and we had a nice little talk before she had to start on dinner. She seemed happy to have us wait up here—don't think she really likes Jack."

Jack motioned with his hands, pantomiming "me?"

Saint collected his backpack from the floor, and hurriedly put items that had come out back in. Then he threw it in his closet. His hair was sweaty, his clothes dirty. "What do you want?"

"You know why we're here," Jack said roughly. "We know you met again with James Dylan: the so-called 'Exterminator.' What's going on? What's the latest?"

"There's going to be a major rally, marching through some town to show off what a big movement they have."

"We know about that," Jack said archly. "These marches have been done before. Just a ragtag bunch of losers, imagining they're a big deal. They yell and drink, pretend to be tough asses, and that's about it, according to our sources."

"Well, maybe," Saint said. "Hopefully. But I think this could be different. They certainly talk a good game. And they've been training to fight... Some will have knives."

"Thanks for the info, Deep Throat, but I doubt it will get violent. Other than a lot of violent puking." Jack stood up. "Now we need names. Names beyond the very few you've given us. What else have you learned?"

Deja stuck her head around the door, saying dinner would be ready soon.

"I haven't really learned anything more," Saint said, shaking his head slowly. He walked back and forth between Jack and Jill for a minute. "Wait, there is someone. A guy we're meeting. In charge of a weird group: the boogies, or something like that. I think his name is Dirk."

Jack looked up. "Dirk? Dirk who?"

Deja's face turned white.

"I don't know. Just Dirk."

Jack and Jill exchanged glances. Jack got closer and hovered over Saint. "What else?"

"That's it! I swear!" Saint said, backing away. "Why are you on me? I didn't do anything."

"And it's going to stay that way," Jill answered. "It's too easy to get caught up with the wrong people, get caught up in problems not of your making. Life is too short. Sometimes, you have to learn the hard way. But not this time, Saint."

Jack just gave him an icy stare. They left the house, telling him to keep his eyes open, both for what more he could glimpse and glean, and for his own safety.

After they left, Jack said to Jill, "Do you think this Dirk and his group are dangerous? Maybe more extreme?"

Jill thought about it. "Could be... but who knows? Sometimes, I think we're a magnet for malevolence."

"Fancy word for shitheads," Jack said. "Well, it's the nature of the job. But we'll just have to keep an eye on Saint at this rally and see for ourselves."

65

Deja just couldn't keep it in anymore.

She met with her friend Gloria. Gloria had helped so much with Saint when he was born. Saint wasn't easy. He was especially hard at bath time, kicking his little legs and crying ferociously.

Saint just hated the water.

Outside, the sky was draped in a velvety cloak of darkness. The soft patter of rain could be heard against the windows. The muted sound of droplets created a symphony that added an intimate layer to the atmosphere.

Deja paced back and forth. She told Gloria that she was still very concerned about Saint, and that she was thankful for the help Gloria had always given them.

"Thanks so much for talking to Saint the other day. I don't know what had happened to him; that certainly wasn't the boy I know."

"He was confused. Lonely. I think he'll do the right thing now."

"God, I hope so. But I have to tell you, I'm terrified." Gloria moved closer to Deja, leaning in to listen. "These detectives came to my house. A big guy named Jack Ludlum and a nice woman named Jill Jarred."

Gloria stiffened at the news. "Jesus. Those two! What did you tell them?"

"They wanted to know about things from the start, so I told them a little about that. Even told them about Saint's birth."

Gloria looked thoughtful for a moment. "Listen, I'm sure everything will be OK. They'll watch out for Saint. Don't be so upset."

"I know, but I heard Saint mention a guy named Dirk. That name brought back such terrible memories from college."

"Tell me."

Deja started crying. "I'm sorry, it seems like all I do is cry lately."

Gloria put her arm around her. "It's OK. You can tell me."

"I've never told anyone."

"You're safe with me."

"Umm. OK. Well, back then, I met some really terrific people. Was learning a lot and having a lot of fun. And of course, Skyler—such a kind and generous man—and I became involved. It was pure heaven." Deja's eyes sparkled. She looked away, took in a deep breath, and her chin began to quiver. "Then that asshole Dirk ruined it all. He delighted in being mean at every turn—to Skylar, to me. I always thought he might have had something to do with Skyler's eventual death. Never met someone like him before. More than mean."

Deja stopped for a moment, feeling like she couldn't go on. "Then there was that night. That horrible night. The party. The basement. I'm sure he roofied me." Deja let out a small cry. She sniffled and wiped at her nose. Her voice breaking, she said, "I've never been quite the same."

Gloria grabbed her arms at these words.

"Thank God Dirk didn't get me pregnant." Deja exhaled.

"My poor baby!" Gloria exclaimed, cradling Deja, trying to create an oasis in a stormy night.

Deja looked away. "You know, I used to giggle. A lot," she said. "Made me sound foolish, I used to think, like a little girl. But I couldn't stop. Well, I haven't giggled once since that day. Maybe a second when Saint was born, but that's it."

Gloria looked back at Deja. Deja could see her entire complexion change—a look of sadness changing into something else.

"That bastard! I've learned things in my time in prison," Gloria exclaimed, as Deja looked back in alarm. "And there's more I can learn. I've always been a good student."

Deja stared at her, wide-eyed.

"Forget Jack and Jill," Gloria said. "If I find that Dirk, I'll kill him. I swear, I'll kill him."

66

It was hate at first sight.

The Exterminator drove the pickup truck over the dry, rocky terrain to the rendezvous spot with the Boogaloo Boys. As they slowed, they saw a group of scruffy-looking men in army fatigues. On a rock overlook above them loomed a lone figure, arms crossed. They were all heavily armed, with all-black AK-47 assault rifles, weighing ten pounds, hanging from their shoulders, their magazines loaded with thirty rounds.

The Exterminator looked admiringly at their weapons, capable of shooting 600 rounds per minute, able to penetrate walls or metal used as shields by opponents. Simple to clean and fire, these guns rarely jammed.

The apparent head of the group jumped down upon their arrival, a black Bushmaster XM-15 semi-automatic rifle jangling by his side. Known for its accuracy, especially at long ranges, it had an average effective range of 600 yards but could hit a target up to 3,800 yards away. It was a somewhat unusual choice for a guy who preferred fighting face to face, but the man had his boot knife—a Gerber Ghoststrike fixed blade—hidden away for that.

As he hit the ground, a cloud of black dust from his black boots flew up into the air.

He proclaimed, "I'm Dirk."

"Exterminator here. And this is my boy, Diablo."

Saint stared at Dirk, his breathing getting heavier, though he didn't know why. His eyes narrowed to slits. He was seething inside, as if this man in front of him had horribly wronged him. He couldn't hide the venomous look from Dirk.

"What the fuck is your problem?" Dirk asked.

"He's practicing his stare for the march," The Exterminator remarked with a laugh. "Easy, boy," he said, as he clapped Saint on the back, "we need to load up some ammo in the truck."

Saint looked around, his eyes darting from the guns to the armed men to the boxes of ammunition and back. The Exterminator saw his look of concern and said, under his breath but heard by all, "Just for defense man. Just in case."

Dirk came over to Saint, getting right in his face, spitting out his words. "You some kinda fuckin' wimp? What... is... your... problem, snowflake?"

Saint stepped back a few steps, sweat beading on his forehead, a wild look in his eyes, like a cornered animal taken by surprise.

"No, sir," he managed to get out, a tremor in his voice. "Just want to make sure I load it up right." He moved swiftly to put the duffel bags full of guns in the truck.

"Good." Dirk relaxed, even gave a hint of a smile. "You just do as I say, and we'll be fine."

Saint looked back, a wave of unease washing over him as if a long-forgotten memory had resurfaced. His instincts were tingling, warning him to stay away from this man. It was as if his very core recognized him, although they'd never crossed paths before.

Then Dirk spread his arms out wide and addressed them all. "Welcome to the race war, gentlemen. Welcome to the Big Luau!"

Saint stared at him but rapidly realized what he was doing and immediately glanced away. Dirk said, "So, devil boy, stop looking at me like that! And be careful with those boxes of ammo. They're very special to me. Take a look."

Dirk opened a box with his dirty fingers and pulled out a bullet. He held it in front of Saint's face. It was etched with the number 88. Saint eyed the bullets, gazing from Dirk to The Exterminator, a look of confusion clearly on his countenance.

The Exterminator quickly explained that 88 is the numerical code for "Heil Hitler," as H is the eighth letter of the alphabet.

"How fucking stupid are you?" Dirk yelled out at Saint. "And don't you teach these knuckleheads anything?" he shouted at The Exterminator.

"He's green, but he's learning. He's no dummy, though. Claims both his parents went to State."

"Big deal. So did I," said Dirk. The others looked at him in surprise. "I'm no moron like the rest of you." He turned back to Saint.

"What were their names?" Dirk asked.

"Whose names?" Saint said.

"Your damn parents. What are you, an idiot? I knew a lot of people there. Believe it or not, I was the hot shit in the fraternity, not that that crap matters."

The Exterminator stared at him. "What? You were in a fraternity? Come on."

"Hey, best way to get the girls. They loved frat parties."

"Still..."

"Not only that, the pledging process provided plenty of opportunities for fun. Especially when I was in charge. Love that it was perfectly OK to spread some terror, do some interesting shit."

"Whatever," The Exterminator said.

"Diablo. I asked you a question!" Dirk shouted.

"OK... OK," Saint stammered. "My dad is Skyler... was Skyler. My mother's name is Deja."

Dirk looked over at Saint, his brow furrowed, looking like he was concentrating, thinking back. "Deja is a damn unusual name, man. Not your good old American name. Don't think someone with that name would make it past high school. Or grade school." He then laughed, joined by the other men. "All right, get back to work."

Dirk scrutinized Saint even more closely as he worked. He noted his red hair, now vividly remembering his own days at State. Remembering Deja. Unable to forget Skyler.

Dirk actually smiled to himself as he thought back to that last night of fraternity hell week. He'd been the pledge master, and the long process had given him much delight.

He remembered how Skyler couldn't breathe.

Sitting in the back of the car, blindfolded, it looked like Skyler could barely breathe—not surprising given the cold; he was only in his underwear, and undoubtedly extremely concerned about where Dirk was taking him. After around thirty minutes, the last few on a rutted road, the car stopped. Dirk pulled Skyler out, making sure he hit his head on the way.

"You bastard," Skyler said through clenched teeth. He then pulled his blindfold off and looked around. He was in a heavily wooded area. And there was only pure blackness.

"So now you leave? And I have to find my way back?"

"Yes," Dirk said, giving him a bit of a push. Skyler fell back but still managed to hold his ground. "But first I wanted to tell you a little story. It's about your bitch, Deja. Stupid fucking name."

Skyler shivered. "What?" he spit out.

"I screwed her."

"What? She would never!" Skyler yelled, a look of disbelief on his face.

"Yeah, she liked it so much, she was crying for more. Begging me." Dirk laughed. "You should thank me; I got her ready for you. Just too bad you couldn't be her first."

"You must've fucking raped her! I'll kill you! I swear I'll kill you!" Skylar charged forward, screaming. His head hit Dirk right in the stomach, something Dirk was not expecting, and he went down. While on the ground, Skyler got the first punch off, though it just missed the mark. Dirk recovered and threw a few quick punches that did not miss. Skyler got a solid punch into Dirk's gut, which felt as if a pendulum had swung and landed in the pit of his stomach; Dirk screamed out. But he was soon back on Skyler. Then, on his back, Skyler thrust his legs forward into Dirk's chest with all his might, pushing Dirk off of him. They went at it again, rolling down an embankment, ending up at the edge of a very large pond. Dirk was on top.

"OK, man, have you had enough now?"

Skyler spit in his eye in response. Dirk reached for a solid tree branch nearby. Skyler was getting back up just as Dirk grasped it. Dirk swung it hard and hit Skyler on the left side of his head. Dazed, Skyler staggered back, falling into the water. Dirk stared at him.

"Done now?" he growled.

The cold water must have been shocking to Skyler. Chest-high in the water, he softly gasped, "Enough." He looked dizzy and disoriented and headed in the wrong direction. Soon he was in neck-high water, feet in the muck that was like quick-sand, water lapping toward his mouth. Dirk laughed as he saw Skyler struggling. "You got a problem, big man?"

Skyler gasped. "Can't swim."

"Poor boy. Don't like water. Mommy never taught you to swim?"

Skyler was struggling more now, finding it harder to keep his head above water, harder to breathe.

Dirk started walking toward him. He was about to head into the water to help.

Then he stopped. He stared at Skyler struggling. He smiled. Then turned around and headed back up the embankment to the car. As he started up, he saw the branch he'd hit Skyler on the side of the head with and flung it far out into the deep water. He continued to see Skyler struggling, his last moments upon him. "See you in your next life, sucker!" Dirk said with a sneer.

Skyler's head sank below the water. The last thing he heard was the car's ignition starting. He tried to hold his breath but was turning blue, then took in a mouthful of water. He sank lower. His eyes darted around frantically but all he saw was darkness. He kept thinking, *I'm going to kill him. I have to kill the asshole.* Beneath the surface, he moved his hands frantically through the water, but soon the movement became slower and slower.

In his mind, he screamed, "Deja!" as his last bit of consciousness left him.

It was late at night. In her college dorm room, Deja woke up with a start. She sat up, holding her small baby bump, eyes wide open, yelling a mournful, "Skyler!"

★

Back at the meeting place, Dirk, surrounded by his Boogaloo Boys, stared hard at Saint. Saint looked back; a taste of bitterness filled his mouth, as if echoes of a past encounter reverberated in his very being.

Dirk held the stare. He now knew exactly who Saint was. And what he had to do.

67

Jack knew exactly who he was. And what he had to do.

He adjusted focus, looking at Dirk through the Nikon Monarch binoculars to the outcropping below, a thousand yards away. The air was thick, the sounds still.

"That must be our man," Jack whispered to Jill. "Dirk. I can tell he's a badass; he'll be trouble."

He handed the binoculars to Jill. She adjusted them and looked, moving an errant piece of brown hair from in front of her eyes.

"Yeah, he's got that look. A lot of them do, but this guy seems to radiate evil. Better keep Saint away from him. Looks like a badass through and through." Jill stood up, wiping the dust from her blue jeans, then suddenly slapping her thigh hard. "So many assholes in this world!"

"Well, that's one asshole I'm going to keep tabs on," Jack said. He got up, inhaled deeply, his fists clenching, the binoculars now dangling from a strap around his neck. They stepped behind prickly bushes.

"Wait, we need to be careful. Even more of a reason now to follow Saint. Not only see what he's up to—protect him if necessary," Jill said.

"You do that; I'll follow Dirk."

"But what about all those guns?" Jill asked, pointing back

to where the men were congregated. "This is obviously not a simple march like the past ones."

"Well, the cops have guns too. But I really think their guns and shit are mostly for show. And if I get into a tough one-on-one situation, there's always this." Jack pulled his pant leg up and pointed to the gun in his ankle holster.

"Yeah right. You've never used that on the job." Jill pulled his pants leg back over the gun.

"But if needed, I'm protected. And don't you worry—I've never lost a fight with my fists either."

"I've told you a million times, violence is not the answer," Jill responded. "You'll never get to heaven that way!"

"Heaven can wait. And by the way, I'm not sure Saint is so innocent. When he was loading up the truck, I saw him stick a few boxes of bullets into his backpack, on the sly. So be careful following him as well. Be careful with everyone. You should have your gun at the ready. Just in case—who knows, one of these nazi marchers could be the killer Tracy is after."

The fires were burning.

At first, Jack and Jill saw it from afar. The torches were lit, their flames glowing and dancing about as the groups assembled at dusk like a coven of witches. There was a combination of thrill, and some fear, in the air, growing stronger and stronger as the rally hour grew near. The smell of kerosene permeated the atmosphere, as the dark smoke of the torches rose upward, obscuring the sky. The air was scorching.

Fires were burning within the hardened hearts of the marchers as well. A myriad of malicious men, an army of arsonists converged, all uniformed in their individual group's garb. Boogaloo Boys in fatigues, Very Fine Men in black, and

Heilbach's crew in khaki pants and white polo shirts. Different attires, but all sharing their tired ideas of hate.

The groups entered a sea of camaraderie, merging together, a cacophonous chorus of crazies. They began marching through the center of town. The sound of their boots in a uniform gait thundered down the streets, echoing 1930s Germany. Saint marched in with them. The excitement in the air was palpable, the beating of the men's hearts out of control. From above, the glowing torches that united the groups looked like a slithering serpent about to strike. With loud and deep voices, their chants reverberated through the dark streets:

"You will not replace us!"

"*Sieg Heil!*"

"Blood and Soil!"

"America for Americans!"

The faces of the men chanting bore a strange combination of glee and fury. Their angry ecstasy glowed as fiercely as the torches, a primordial and primeval display of determination.

The local police stood to the side as they marched by, under strict orders to let people express their First Amendment rights. Most had their arms folded over their crisp blue shirts, some had their hands clasped behind their backs. If things were to get out of hand, they had pepper spray affixed to their duty belts, tasers secured in holsters.

Their eyes darted all over the crowd. They gazed at men passing them with their hands taped, ready for punching, others with brass knuckles. The police watched warily as the shields pushed forward; they were up on their toes, ready to respond. But they were totally unprepared for crowds of the magnitude before them, and hoped there weren't more lethal weapons hidden about. The local denizens continued to stare, mouths agape—though some subtly smiling. The brotherhood of bigots continued their march from hell, Dante's Inferno brought to infernal life on earth.

The first rocks thrown started it off.

A group of counter-protesters from out of town charged toward the white supremacists, matching their fury with their own frenzy, stridently shouting and screaming. Then the fights broke out. First in isolated places, then where the groups converged, like the front line of a civil war. The result was a mélange of misery.

Dirk punched a blond woman. Blood immediately poured out of her mouth and nose and ran down her face, making her look like a refugee from a horror film. A twenty-year-old man with a peace symbol on his shirt was battered by Heilbach's group with lead pipes, then was kicked in the head from behind: a flying dropkick that he never saw coming dropping him to the ground. A seventy-year-old man was beaten with an American flag. One teenager with a white flower in her hair fell to the ground and was trampled underfoot by the heavy boots passing over her, the flower petals ground to dust. The outmanned police force tried to keep order but soon realized trying to stop the fighting frenzy was futile, like trying to swim upstream against a raging river. Too many fights for too few cops.

Dirk kicked a middle-aged man in the nuts. He then ran after a bearded man who had hit him from behind with a protest sign. He raced down the road after him as fast as he could. The man ran randomly, then scooted down an empty side street, stumbling on a trash can, which went rolling around, his rimless eyeglasses falling to the ground. He recovered his balance, leaving his glasses behind. Up ahead was a tall picket fence, white paint peeling off it, the tops of the pickets in a sharp inverted chevron shape. The man had a bad knee, but jumped up, grasping for the top, gasping for more oxygen. His fingers dug into splinters jaggedly sticking up from the top of the fence. He managed to make it over, tearing his pants by his butt, but getting him into a clearing. Dirk was fast on his heels, close behind. The sound of vicious dogs barking with brio assaulted their ears. Dirk was about to catch him.

Just then, from around the fence, a hand grabbed Dirk from behind. Jack!

They both fell to the ground in a bear hug, Jack like a WWE wrestler smashing onto his opponent, pinning him down. "What the hell?" Dirk shouted. They were both gulping in air, trying to catch their breath, all of their muscles tensed and at the ready.

"I'm a cop. Fun time is over, asshole," Jack said, as they watched the other man disappear in the distance. Jack had a feeling about him. "We're gonna talk. We're gonna talk not just about this, but some other stuff too."

"Fuck that. I'm here for important shit!" Dirk growled, as he spit in Jack's face. He pushed him away while Jack was wiping the spit from his eye and he scrambled back up. Jack now felt a thunder and fury, ready to play judge and jury.

Jack lunged at him, grabbed onto the front of Dirk's shirt, and then reared back and punched him squarely in the mouth. Dirk staggered, spit out blood along with a yellowed tooth, but managed to just barely evade Jack's next punch. He spun around and swiftly got off a one-two punch of his own to Jack's kidneys. While Jack was off balance, Dirk landed a kick in the balls with his steel-toe Doc Marten boot. Luckily for Jack, it was a glancing blow, as he moved his body mostly out of the way at the last instant, though the blow caused him to sway back and feel nauseous.

Jack's strength didn't fail him and like a prizefighter finding that last wellspring of energy in the twelfth round, he sprung back into action. He grabbed Dirk by the belt, and with all his might swung him in the air, throwing him toward a spindly tree. Dirk's head hit the tree, dead leaves giving up their last tentative hold raining on Dirk as he slumped down.

"Have you had enough?"

Dirk just stared at him, his eyes glazed over but trying to refocus. Jack thought the fight was out of both of them, like a tire running over a spike and immediately deflating.

"I just want to talk to you! Answer some damn questions and then you're free to go."

"Bullshit... OK, OK," Dirk said. It looked like his head was clearing and his breathing slowly getting back to normal. "Just give me a second."

Jack nodded and slowly walked over to the tree. He knelt down on one leg. "What I really want to know is..."

"Fuck you!" Dirk yelled as he swiftly removed a knife from his boot and plunged it into Jack.

68

The man on campus towered over those around him.

Tracy thought he looked out of place. Dirty and scowling, no books, nothing in hand, and a trench coat on during a beautiful day. Her instincts told her there was something wrong with the way he held his hand in his pocket.

She followed him.

69

S heriff Klamp was drunk.

He'd tripped on the way back from the restroom, urine dribble stains on his tan uniform pants, his zipper half up. He sat at a table surrounded by his bottle buddies. The bar had a jukebox, but the music wouldn't play. Didn't matter, there weren't many patrons that night—or most nights. Perhaps it was the dirt and detritus that kept them away. Perhaps it was the decay.

The dark bar was lit mostly by the reflecting neon blinking *Bud* sign, on and off, off and on, like an SOS signal back in the day. The bar had been there for at least as long as Klamp was alive; he'd had to ask for his dad there from the time he was nine, collect him like refuse before the garbage trucks would arrive.

Klamp was off duty—officially this time, though he was often off duty even when he was on. His "friends" were shooting the breeze, looking for some gossip to inspire their vapid lives of unease. They were all divorced; Klamp had never married. They usually spent the first hour of the evening complaining about their ex-wives, the balance of the time complaining about their lives. Klamp loved these nights, getting to feel superior, getting accolades in spades.

One guy, Johnny Boy, the more rambunctious one of the

group, with a handlebar mustache and oversized alpaca belt buckle, was the dissenter. Toward the end of the night, he entered the conversation, needling Klamp about the shootings.

"So that shooter was never caught, Earl, was he?"

"What shoota, man?"

"You know, a little while ago. Guy up on the mountain road, other guy at the steakhouse? I haven't gone to Ponderosa since then. Kind of miss it. Loved the hill of beans." Somehow, Johnny Boy let one go at that very moment.

Klamp turned red, which was just a slightly deeper shade of the pink his blotchy skin had from drinking. "That was nothin'. Media tried to make it somethin'. Selling thar damn paypers, wantin' thar darn ray-tins. Even Tracy tried to make it somethin'. But it ain't. Ain't nothin'. And it's over."

"I like Tracy. She's a pugnacious one."

"Pugnacious?" Sheriff Klamp choked on his beer, spit some out, then opened the other bottle just brought to him. His bloodshot eyes stared at the loquacious friend who'd made that comment. "Shit, I just think she's trying to take my job. Pugnacious. Hell, don't trust her! Even tried to get me to contact the darn state over the shootins. What a laugh! As if I'd a listen to her."

"I don't know, Earl, she seems smart to me. Cute too."

"Smart? Hell," Klamp said, after swigging down another half bottle, "Thought that yoga studio business was connected. Even thinks tha latest shootin', tha one at the gas station, was connected."

They all stared at Klamp, suddenly sober.

"Another killing? What other killing?"

Klamp suddenly awoke from his somnambulant state, saying under his breath, "Shit."

"Something else happen?"

Klamp thought fast, or at least fast for him. He grabbed his hat off the table and got up to go, the chair screeching as he moved back. "Not really. Nothin' ta worry about: a killing in anotha state, not even ours. You know how many people get killed a day in a state?"

"How many?" Johnny Boy asked.

Klamp squeezed his face in a knot, thinking hard; you could almost see the computer buffering circle endlessly cycling. "Ugh, not a... Ugh, well, a lot."

"OK, Earl, OK, we get the point. I'm sure you're right," a man named Jason said. "Look out for Tracy, though; she probably is looking forward to the next election."

"Oh I will, I will. Believe you me. Right now ahm just crossing my v's and dottin' my y's to help the guys close out that there killin'. Lendin' my expertise. Ya know, it was in a gas station across the state line. Whole darn thing exploded. But nothin' to do with the otha guys. Nothin'. Otha than maybe in crazy Tracy's mind. That girl better shape up, or I'm shippin' her ass out."

70

He didn't want to hurt anyone; it wasn't in his nature. But he felt he had to do something.

Saint stood in the middle of the fracas, as stuck in place as the Tin Man. He was afraid this was going to happen and scared to death now. Saint looked all around him, the sounds coming at him like surround-sound speakers blasting about his head. He didn't know what to do. He had a shield, and mostly tried to hide behind it, concealed from view. Saint was trembling, trying to think, confused thoughts crashing into each other in his mind. He knew many people would certainly see him, and if other Very Fine Men, or God forbid the crazy Dirk, found him standing still and not helping his brothers, he'd be in big, big trouble.

He also knew he had to make it look right, make it look like he was part of the fight, so he could continue to provide intel to Jack and to Jill. The only thing he was now sure of was that he needed to do what he could for the greater good. If he could do anything at all.

Dirk had plunged the knife, aiming for the heart, but hit Jack in the thigh, blood spurting out, narrowly missing the femoral artery. Dirk got up and ran, yelling over his back, "Don't ever fuck with Dirk."

Jack tried to get up and go after him. But he dropped back down, like an infant trying to walk for the first time. The blood was now saturating his pants, leaving a trail as he desperately crawled forward. He reached for the gun in his ankle holster, screamed in pain as he grabbed it and brought it forward. Lying on the ground in a prone position, like a marksman in a shooting competition, he pointed the gun toward Dirk's back. He fixated on how Dirk had just tried to kill him. He knew in his heart, Dirk would kill others. Probably had already.

Dirk at this point hadn't gotten very far. Jack steadied his hand. Dirk's back loomed large enough in his vision. He had a clear, open shot.

There was a gathering of a very different kind on the other side of town.

Karmen looked in the mirror and couldn't believe what she saw. She no longer looked like a fifteen-year-old girl. A young lady, a princess, looked back at her. Her puffy, red gown with ruffles down to her ankles swung about her legs, light as air, while her curled, dark hair bounced upon her bare shoulders. She eyed the tiara on her dresser.

"Your quinceañera!" her mother Yolanda gushed. "My little baby is coming of age."

"Mama, don't cry now! You promised."

"OK, my beautiful girl. Your papa has made such a party for you! Now let's finish getting ready." Yolanda put her arm around her daughter, looking at the two of them in the mirror, marveling. "You look like such a princess. No, a queen."

Karmen laughed, her laughter like a symphony of bubbles,

floating joyfully through the air. Yolanda was transfixed, not wanting to let go.

"I know, Mama. I'll remember this day for the rest of my life," Karmen said, her eyes shining with delight, her mom's tinged with tears.

Amid the chaos, there was Elizabeth.

Saint was pushing forward with his shield, just bumping people, pretending to be in the fray, hoping to save a life. He was not hurting anyone, just shoving people away. Then he saw her, Elizabeth, his first and only love, if only for a day.

Wearing a dress, no less, she was slapping people in her way. She strode next to Heilbach, hand in hand. They found a hole through a bunch of counter-protesters, and jumped through, laughing together as if they were at a party, and rushed on to the next group.

Saint stood incredulous as he watched them momentarily stop and kiss.

Dirk escaped!

Jack hadn't taken the open shot. Instead, he dropped the gun and reached for his phone. He didn't quite know why he did that. *Getting soft*, he thought. *That Jill is a bad influence, always trying to rehabilitate me. Shit.*

Dirk circled around and found his way back to the melee, where he could blend in with the crowd; even his spilt blood helped him fit in. His face red, he was panting hard as he scoured the scene. Some trash cans were on fire, and he jumped on the hood of a car to get a look around the still-simmering site. He found his men in their dirtied fatigues and told them it was time to head out of town, mission accomplished. While fatigued, they resisted, having too much fun, but he insisted, and got most of them to follow him out.

No one really noticed them taking off, as they were caught up in their own battles. But the Boogaloo Boys weren't done fighting.

Jill couldn't believe it.

Not only had she lost Saint in the crowded chaos, but Jack's voice was very low and halting on the cell phone. At first Jill thought it was a poor connection, and the sound of sirens and the clamorous crowd made it near impossible to hear. But she eventually figured out that Jack was hurt and wanted her to go after Dirk.

"Are you crazy? Forget Dirk; if you're hurt, tell me where the hell you are!"

In due course, Jack relented. He managed to tell her roughly where he was. Jack sounded like he was losing strength with each passing moment, and she raced off, rushing through the streets that were like an obstacle course. Of course, she had no clear idea of exactly where to go, or just how bad a shape Jack was in. She could only pray, as she swiftly ran away.

The round tables set outdoors under the white-ribboned trees were gorgeous. White tablecloths with gold lace runners, red silk roses surrounding flickering votive candles, Karmen loved everything about it—the patchy brown grass ignored. She eyed the cake on the corner table, just like a wedding cake: three layers, buttercream icing, decorated with sugary red roses. She went over to it and inhaled its delicious scent, her mouth watering.

"Not yet, my baby," Yolanda kidded her. "Now let's meet your guests. They've already started arriving." Yolanda went to put the music on, as Karmen grabbed her bouquet of white silk flowers with red and gold adornment and happily skipped off. Then remembering she was a woman now, smoothed her dress and walked slowly ahead, beaming.

They heard music.

Dirk's Boogaloo Boys were jogging, sweat pouring down the ruffian's faces adorned with wild, exhilarated smiles. They'd made it to the outskirts of town and just had a small stretch further to go before they'd be at their vehicles.

In the distance, they could hear music playing. It sounded Spanish. They stopped for a moment and looked at each other. Then smiled.

They changed direction.

71

Bastard, he thought.

The huge man had been striding across the bustling college campus, his eyes scanning the crowd for the one person he hated more than anyone else in the world. His nemesis was near, and his pulse had quickened with venomous anticipation.

He saw the judge surrounded by students who obviously liked and respected him; it made his blood boil. His sense of sight sharpened as he fixated on his enemy, taking in every detail of his appearance with seething rage. Disgusted by the sight, he walked toward him, taking his gun out of his pocket.

Tracy dropped the book and started running.

"*Judge* Frazier," the man snarled. "You're going to pay for what you did to my buddy! And for being a Black man who thinks he can sit on the bench and judge white men."

Tracy was gasping for breath as she tried to get near. She was within a foot as he was pulling the trigger.

With fury in his ears, he never heard Tracy coming. She tackled him, aiming low with her shoulder hitting the back of his knees as she'd been trained.

The judge fell to the ground about the same time the big guy did.

The big guy's forehead cracked down on the pavement, stunning him.

The campus policewoman had seen the whole situation come to life in front of her, and had sprung into action. Once the guy was down, she kicked his gun away and sat on him, her own gun pressed against his earring. He grunted and cursed as Tracy got handcuffs on him. Bystanders had called for more police as the action unfolded, and they arrived within minutes. An ambulance had also arrived for the fallen judge.

Tracy, breathing heavily, watched as the judge was taken on a stretcher to the ambulance. The bullet had nicked his arm. With the hand on his other arm, he signaled a thumbs-up. Tracy finally smiled.

Her friend, the campus policewoman, hugged her.

"Jesus, you OK?" they asked each other simultaneously, with a nervous half-laugh.

"I don't know," Tracy said, wiping dirt off her shirt.

"Unreal," her friend said. "Crazy guy trying to kill a judge!"

"A Black judge," Tracy said. "Attacked by a guy full of Nazi tattoos."

A student walked over and handed Tracy the book she'd dropped. Her friend looked down and smiled at the title: *It Ends With Us.*

Tracy smiled more broadly. "You know, I think we got our man."

72

The music was loud.

Loud, joyous, and sometimes sentimental. A Julio Iglesias song was playing at the quinceañera celebration, a song named "De Niña a Mujer." The guests noisily circled around to watch the traditional ceremonies. With Karmen sitting on a chair in the middle of the gathering, her mother applied lipstick to her lips for the first time. It was a shade called Dusty Rose, and her mother's hand trembled as she tried to apply it without smudging. She was only partially successful, and used a tissue to clean around Karmen's mouth, and then dabbed at her own eyes.

Her mother then put the tiara on Karmen's head, the silver, iridescent crystal twinkling as it caught the light from the bulbs above. Karmen straightened up her hair and stepped back as a little girl in a white dress approached. The girl smiled a nervous smile, a front tooth missing. It was time for the exchange of the doll. Karmen reached under the chair for what had been her favorite doll growing up. It was made of porcelain, had wavy, brown hair and tan-colored skin, and was attired in a small gown. The little girl stood in front of Karmen, looking solemn, and tentatively reached out her slight hands. Karmen handed the doll over to her, a symbolic handing over of the torch as Karmen moved on to her next phase of existence.

Behind the little girl stood Karmen's father, in a black suit, fidgeting with his red tie. His black hair was slicked back, his eyes looking down as he walked forward, all choked up, desperately trying not to cry. His was the last symbolic ceremony. He bent down, a pair of high-heeled shoes in hand, and then took off Karmen's flat shoes and put the high heels on her. He patted her feet, giving her a wan smile. Clearing his throat, he looked over to his wife, who came to his side and helped him up.

And then they all heard the sounds of people running and shouting, heading toward them.

Jill was shocked.

She'd never seen Jack on the losing end of a fight, let alone with a pants leg stained with blood. She needed something relatively clean to put on the wound and staunch the blood, as well as something to use as a tourniquet. Jill knew belts don't really work well as tourniquets. She looked around quickly, then tore her own shirt off, buttons popping. Jill was left with just her camisole, light beige with white lace on top.

Jack looked at her, and managed to whisper, "Not now, lover." She took that as a good sign, smiled slightly, and got to work. She rolled a good-sized rock over to where he lay and placed it carefully under his leg, elevating the wound above his heart. Prior to applying the tourniquet, Jill kept pressure on the wound for ten minutes, enough time to let the blood coagulate. While waiting, Jack told her not to call for an ambulance, preferring to have this event undocumented. She looked at him, skin pale, and felt it turning clammy. It was obvious he could not crawl to her car, and while she kept herself in great shape and was very strong, she certainly couldn't carry him.

However, he insisted she at least try to help him walk to the center of town, which was a few blocks from there—and where by now there were many ambulances wailing away. That way, he could more easily blend in as just another casualty of a very rough day. Jill relented, but first—with the blood no longer flowing freely—she started on a tourniquet. She grabbed the shirt, wrapped it above the wound, and knotted it. Jill then grabbed his gun to use as a windlass, tying both ends of the shirt around it, and turned the gun in a circular motion to tighten the tourniquet, Jack grunting with each rotation. She then slipped the gun off, making sure the tourniquet maintained its extremely tight position, while she knotted it one more time. That was the tricky part, and she breathed a sigh of relief when it was done.

Jill then took the gun and ankle holster, hid them away, and slowly tried to get him up. Jack used his one good leg, and both hands, as leverage, while Jill pushed with all her strength. The first two attempts just resulted in gritted teeth and silent screams by Jack. The third attempt finally got Jack up enough to get his arm around Jill's shoulders.

They walked slowly back, finding an alternate path in place of the fence, panting every step of the way. The trail of blood from his pants leg had stopped—another good sign—by the time they got to town.

They made it over to an ambulance idling by, a stretcher being placed inside with a young man on it, his bloody head bandaged, his shirt, emblazoned with an iron cross, ripped apart. "Got room for one more?" Jill asked. They took one look at Jack and helped get him in. Then looking at Jill—Jack's blood upon her, weak from the walk—they asked if she needed to be checked out too. She told them no, and leaned in to Jack, who simply whispered, "Go!"

Jill headed out, while Jack finally put his head back, and was soon unconscious.

★

Karmen stumbled on her high heels as she quickly stood up.

The Boogaloo Boys were running across the lawn, still high from their fights and happy to find more. They looked at the scared people milling about. They ran through the party, over-turning tables, the three-layer cake landing upside down on the ground.

Skinny teenage boys, in suits a size too big, looked like they didn't know what to do, some fleeing with the women, others holding their ground. That's when the punches started, the Boogaloo Boys hitting whoever stood in their way, kicking them when down.

Dirk saw Karmen, who was apparently the star of this cel-ebration. He headed toward her, yelling, "I'm going to rip that fuckin' tiara off your goddamn head!"

Karmen's father ran to shield her and was greeted with a roundhouse punch from Dirk. He staggered back, Karmen yelling, "*Papi!*" He lurched forward at Dirk, getting his hands around his neck. Dirk reached for his knife, grabbing it in his sweaty palm. His hand lunged forward, just as Karmen was running to them to help her dad.

The knife plunged into her heart.

Karmen fell to the ground, and as her father went down to help her, Dirk kicked him in the head with a heavy boot, knocking him out.

Dirk whistled to his boys, and they all fled, leaving the place looking like the battlefield at Gettysburg.

Blood darker than her red dress flowed from Karmen's heart onto the dusty ground. As she drew her last breath, a whispering wind extinguished the flickering flames from the votive candles. The last words from Marc Anthony's rendition of "Vivir Mi Vida" could be heard, then the music wouldn't play anymore.

73

At least one thing had gone well.

Jill had gotten Jack back to their room. He was lying on the bed, bandaged but not too bad off, all things considered. Mostly a flesh wound that was millimeters away from something really bad, but luck was on his side. He had even gotten lucky in the ER, where the intravenous fluids got him going again, the painkillers took effect, and he was stitched up and bandaged. The most difficult thing, in fact, was taking off the tourniquet.

The ER had been packed and chaotic, everyone running around like they had a minute before a bomb was to go off. No one was looking too closely at what people were doing as they rushed to help whomever they could. Like the local police, the small hospital was woefully unprepared for the mass of people: some screaming, some crying, with cuts, concussions, and contusions. There were bites, burns, broken bones, bruises and banged-up knees. People with scrapes and sprains stood outside, knowing it would be a while before they could be seen. The chaos enabled Jack to discreetly make his way out—or as discreetly as a man as large as him could.

Once Jack was back in the motel room, Jill gave him some food. He ate half of it, then fell asleep, not awakening for eleven hours, which was about six hours more than he normally needed. When he finally woke up, Jill told him what had happened: the news of the quinceañera killing was all over the media, and the police were searching for the perps, but had no leads. The whole day was one mass confusion, and all they knew was that men who looked like soldiers had run through the celebration.

"Jesus Christ! That had to be Dirk and his crew. Goddamn it," Jack yelled, punching his fist on the bed, the mattress bouncing up half a foot.

"Easy, easy. You'll pull the stitches out."

"I should have killed him. I should have pulled the goddamn trigger. That girl's blood is on my hands."

Jill grabbed him by his T-shirt and looked him straight in the eyes. She said loudly and slowly, "Look, you are not responsible. He killed her. Not you." She calmed down and softly said, "And you didn't shoot because you are better than him."

"It doesn't take much to be better than him. Next time I see him, there'll be a different outcome. And there will be a next time," Jack said, raising his voice, before putting his head in his hands, shaking it back and forth.

Jill sat on the edge of the bed, putting her arm around his shoulders. "I understand completely. But you did the right thing in the moment. God, this past twenty-four hours have just been a nightmare. I can't believe people could be so evil."

"Don't be naïve. Evil has existed since the beginning of time."

"Whatever happened to the evil ones being sent to hell? Do they just keep coming back?" Jill said. "I mean, ugh, I don't know what I mean. Jesus, why can't people just get along? When will people smarten up? How many lessons do they have to learn in their lifetimes in order to do the right thing?"

Jack looked at her, shaking his head again. "These people. I don't think ever. Certainly not in just one lifetime."

Jill looked back, frustrated and sad. "Don't you think if only people would interact with human beings who differ from them, get to know them, one on one, then they wouldn't hate each other? Couldn't hate each other?"

"I don't know… perhaps so." Then he thought for a minute, before saying, "But maybe there is a reason birds of a feather flock together."

Jill's mouth made a small 'o' shape, and her eyebrows arched. "You don't believe that, Jack!"

"No, no, I guess I really don't. In fact, you know I don't. But these people just believe the craziest things!"

"Repeat a lie often enough and it begins to sound as if it must be so," Jill said.

"Naïve and stupid is a terrible combination," Jack said.

"Or maybe they are just plain evil, Jack. Maybe these evil people keep coming back, not allowed into heaven after they die." Jill looked up, thoughtful. "Do you believe in reincarnation?"

Jack smiled but was careful not to laugh. "No, no, I can't say I do." He grabbed Jill by the arms. "Though the idea of being with you for many lives is appealing!"

Jill nuzzled his shoulder. "Well, we just have to keep fighting the good fight, together. For as long as it takes."

74

"I tracked you down!"

Jack and Jill had made a stop at their office to check on things. Jack was still recovering but feeling much better. He'd grabbed a cup of coffee while Jill was sitting at her desk, scanning through emails and a few snail mails, mostly junk. "How do so many emails accumulate in just a day?!" she said.

Suddenly, the unlocked door burst open.

"What the hell?" Jack said, rushing over.

A blond girl, who looked around twelve, stood before them. She stared at them, her eyes filled with a potent mix of excitement and nerves. The air seemed to crackle with an unexplainable energy.

"I'm Zoe... You saved me."

Both Jack and Jill stood there, looking stunned, their breaths catching in their throats. They stared at the sight of the determined girl standing before them.

"When I was a baby," she said, her voice quivering with emotion.

Zoe locked eyes with them, seeing the flicker of recognition, and tears welled up in her own. They remembered her, even after all these years. Zoe cried as she realized the two people integral to her life were so near, standing right there. And they remembered. Jack's jaw dropped, while goose bumps appeared on Jill's arms.

Zoe had always wondered about the two people who had saved her life. Through dogged research, she'd finally found them.

"Oh my God," Jill exclaimed, rushing over to hug her. "I've often thought about you, honey. I'm so happy you're OK!"

"I'd uncovered bits and pieces of what happened," Zoe said. "I know there was a shootout. My parents, not good people, died. I could have. But you saved me. Then I was lucky enough to grow up in a loving home. I'm here to thank you."

Jack smiled warmly at her. "I can't believe it." He shook his head. After a moment, he looked away. "You say we saved you, but hey, we did what any police officer would do." Then, clearing his throat, said, "But we are sure happy we were able to keep you safe that day!"

They hugged. For Jack and Jill, the reunion appeared to be like finding a long-lost treasure buried beneath the weight of time. It was a fragile moment, filled with unspoken gratitude, overwhelming emotions, and the realization that their actions had rippled far beyond that fateful day.

Zoe's eyes were still filled with tears as she thanked them again for their bravery. She'd always felt a deep sense of debt to the officers who'd rescued her, but finally meeting them in person was overwhelming.

As the hours passed, they shared stories and caught up on each other's lives. Laughter mingled with tears, and the weight of the past began to lift. Zoe revealed the extent of her journey since that pivotal moment. Her courage and determination had blossomed into an unyielding passion for justice and equality. She talked about her school's anti-prejudice group that she'd founded, and the thousands of dollars they had raised to help fight discrimination. She had helped organize events, sold

T-shirts and buttons, and started a walkathon. Her achievements were awe inspiring.

"Quite a lot for a young girl!" Jill said.

"You are amazing!" Jack said.

Zoe smiled broadly.

Then, incredibly, she showed them a picture of herself with the Pope, taken when she delivered a letter to him asking him to advocate for equality for all in the United States. It was a testament to her audacity and the heights she had reached. "No one can believe this actually happened. But you can look it up! My proudest moment," she said.

"Wow," Jack and Jill said in unison, looking amazed at how far Zoe had come, and clearly proud to have played a small part in her life. "You are something else!"

"Well, you kind of inspired me," Zoe said, her voice breaking with emotion.

Jack and Jill looked at each other, Jill with tears in her eyes, Jack trying his best not to cry. It was clear that what was once a vulnerable infant had grown into an adolescent with a voice that could make a difference.

As they continued to talk, Zoe felt like she had finally found her missing puzzle pieces.

When the visit came to an end, Zoe hugged Jack and Jill tightly. "Thank you for giving me a chance at life," she whispered, her words carrying the weight of a thousand unspoken sentiments.

They hugged her back, and it seemed all three felt a sense of peace wash over them.

Zoe had found closure, and she thanked them once again as she left.

Jill reluctantly closed the door, her eyes lingering on the space Zoe had occupied.

"Wow," she said. "That shootout almost took that girl's life, but ultimately led her to a place of purpose. It's like she was born again after we spirited her out of there!"

"Unreal," Jack replied, his voice tinged with wonder. "Good things can come out of bad situations. Guess people can grow up good coming from anywhere."

"Right," Jill said, giving Jack a big hug.

In that moment, as darkness embraced the world outside, a glimmer of hope flickered within their hearts. They knew, without a doubt, that their paths had intertwined for a reason, forever binding them in a bond that transcended time and circumstance.

75

He was petrified.

The Exterminator wanted Saint to attend a hastily convened meeting of the Very Fine Men. They'd all rapidly left the rally that evening, driving all night to get out of town, out of state. They hadn't heard about the killing by the Boogaloo Boys until the next day, once they were safely back home, ensconced in their day jobs, with apparently no one the wiser.

The Exterminator was excited and said they needed to act quickly, have a second act to keep their movement in the news, and make it great. He said it appeared everyone from Heilbach's group made it back safely—cuts, bumps and bruises notwithstanding—and Heilbach still wanted to collaborate ("under my leadership, of course"). A select few of them were getting together to talk about what they should do next; they didn't want to take the risk of a big gathering while people's antennae were up.

"And I've chosen you, my friend, to be one of three Very Fine Men to meet with Heilbach and me," The Exterminator said, pointing to Saint.

Saint thought, *Oh shit. All I want to do is get out of here. Discreetly and completely.*

"Me? Why me? You told me I 'don't know shit,' in your own words."

"True. But I can tell you're smarter than the average dolt. Diablo, I think you'd be a good planner. We have plenty of boneheads to execute the plans."

"Who else is going to be there? Dirk?"

"No way. He and the rest of the Boogaloos are long gone. I suspect they'll be lying low for some time. Something we may have to do too after our next achievement."

Saint looked back, his face filled with uncertainty. "Who's coming with Heilbach? Is Elizabeth?"

"Forget about that girl!" The Exterminator said in disgust. "She's taken. And there are a lot more important things for you to do. You're gonna be a star! Let's keep our friggin' eyes on the real prize, dammit!" The spit from his diatribe showered on Saint.

Saint gave him a half-salute and wiped his face with his shirtsleeve. "I'll do what I have to do."

They held the meeting in the middle of the night by the town dump. It was dark, no stars to be seen. When the breeze blew a certain way, it didn't smell like roses. More like maggot-infested food and mildewed mattresses. Heilbach matched The Exterminator, bringing three of his own men. He came over to Saint right away, saying with a shit-eating grin he was glad to see him again, both knowing he didn't mean it. The other guys congratulated each other on a job well done, bumping scarred fists. Slayer opened a bottle of Four Roses whiskey and everyone took a generous slug of it, before getting down to business.

"Reason I called this meeting..." The Exterminator began.

"I thought I called it," Heilbach responded, a look like "here we go again" on his face.

The Exterminator ignored the comment and went on. "Is

because we've got momentum now, and we need to build on it. So we need to agree on what our next move will be."

Heilbach immediately interjected. "We need to seriously up our game, men." He looked at each of them with a steely-eyed expression, as if challenging them to disagree. "Other than those Boogaloos, we just caused some boo-boos." Someone laughed, and he shot him a look, shutting him down. "Sure, our message got across. But the powers that be need to really take us seriously; we need to spark this race war big time! We need to continue to step off the internet. And not just with marches!"

"On that, we agree," The Exterminator exclaimed loudly. Then, in a more serious tone, said, "Remember, we are losing our young men to suicide. Losing them because their livelihoods are being taken away by immigrants." Then, his voice getting louder, trembling, he finished up with, "It's kill or be killed!"

"Well, then let's go get these people!" Heilbach shouted. All the men vociferously agreed. Saint felt like he was going to puke but nodded his head up and down so as not to get in trouble, though inside, it was nodding in a different direction.

"What's the plan?" Slayer asked.

"Random shootings. One here, one there. From a distance. No one will know what hit them," Heilbach answered.

"Beautiful!" another of Heilbach's men said. "They'll be constantly looking over their shoulders, not knowing when that bullet is coming for them! I fuckin' love it!"

"Not big enough!" The Exterminator shouted. "We need something that will make a big splash right away."

"What did you have in mind, boss?" Viktor asked.

"There's a Hispanic community right in my own town. Those people are always going to church for one thing or another. They crowd around the priest outside. Let's drive a big old car right into them, let them meet their maker right there under the cross."

"That's just stupid," Heilbach said. "You'll never get away."

The Exterminator rushed up, got in his face, and was about to hit him. "Don't you ever call me stupid!"

The two sides quickly separated the men. "Listen, asshole," Heilbach said, "I'm looking out for your welfare. We need every soldier we have. Why lose some to jail?"

"He's got a point there," Sarge said.

"Look, maybe we don't need to collaborate at all. This was probably a bad idea to get together to begin with," The Exterminator said.

"Yeah, you do your thing, and we'll do ours." The men split, Heilbach spit, and not another word was spoken—just grim faces heading out to their own places.

When they were alone, Saint turned to The Exterminator.

"Now what? He did have a point, you know."

The Exterminator gave him a look as if he'd committed treason. But then he shrugged, and said, "Fuck it, that wasn't my real plan. There was a reason I said that. I didn't want them to know what we're really up to."

"Smart," Saint said, playing along. "So what's the real deal?"

"Well, it still involves that Hispanic church."

"La Iglesia de la Resurreccion?"

"I don't know its goddamn name! It's the only church in town they go to!"

"Yup, that would be it. What are you thinking?"

"We wait for a nice big event there. Like Easter. Still use a car, but just don't drive it. Park the motherfucker. Car bomb. Placed in the right spot, it will blow them all the way to hell!"

76

J ack and Jill hadn't answered.

Tracy wanted to celebrate but couldn't reach them. Where are they? It's not every day someone solves the mystery of serial killings, she thought. Even Klamp was thrilled with me—or thrilled to have it all behind him.

So Tracy ended up alone at a small, dark bar in the next town over, called The Midnight Library, needing to drink, needing to think. She was still feeling the unsettling effects of her encounter with that man who tried to kill the judge. She also felt she needed to be one hundred percent sure he was the one who did the other shootings, so really wished Jill had called her back to talk.

A stranger walked into the bar, approached her, and sat down on the round bar stool next to her, even though the place was nearly empty.

Oh Jesus, she thought. This, I don't need.

She was about to say something snarky to him when a feeling came over her. "I'm not using a trite pickup line," the man said. "But don't I know you? Haven't we met somewhere before?"

Tracy stared at him, then smiled. She felt something familiar. "You know, I think we may have." The song "Spirit in the

Sky" was playing on the jukebox; the words wafted toward them.

They exchanged questions about background, travel, friends, but couldn't come up with anything, a dead end. He was making a short stop on a business trip and had never been in the town, or anywhere else Tracy had been.

"Well, sorry to have bothered you," the man said. "I've got to run. But nice seeing you."

Tracy took his hand in hers and gave it a shake. "Nice to have seen you too," she said, both of their eyes boring into each other.

Once he'd left, she shook her head, as if trying to wake herself from a dream. After a few moments of reflection, she went back to thinking about the situation she was in, working for Klamp. Maybe she should be in charge, she thought. Maybe she should run for sheriff; she might get elected given how she took down the killer. Hell, Klamp hadn't moved on seeking further help. Apparently, he didn't believe, or want to believe, that the Gulf station inferno had anything to do with his town. He's useless, she concluded.

"We need to get a move on."

"We sure do… and I'm really concerned about Saint," Jill said.

"As well you should be. We were supposed to keep tabs on him," Jack said, shaking his head. "That boy is so naïve and helpless, we got to make sure he's OK."

"Jack, I think we gave that poor boy too big a job."

"We had no choice. Just like we have no choice now to make sure he's OK. His job is now done with us, anyway. We know who we have to get."

They locked eyes, and both said, "Dirk."

"Before we do anything else, though, let's talk to Tracy. We're due to fill her in. Plus there's probably lots of things that are connected. Maybe she can help uncover Dirk's full background, see if that leads us anywhere productive so we can find him. Get him, maybe get a killer."

"I actually have some missed calls from her," Jill said, feeling a little guilty. "Let's call her. See if anything is new."

"Let's not celebrate yet."

Tracy told Jill all that had happened. She wanted to go out for a celebratory dinner with her and Jack now that the attacker was locked up.

Jill was thrilled for what Tracy had done, but reluctantly told her, "Can't go to dinner just now. Sorry. Too much to do."

"Aww, well I know a breakfast place that has mimosas; let's at least go there!"

"While on duty?"

"I won't tell," Tracy said.

Over mimosas and mini-donuts, and pressed for time, Jack spoke up. "I'm happy for you; you stopped that potential killer. You're a hero."

Tracy smiled.

"But you can't celebrate yet. Where's the proof?"

"Come on, I'm sure he did it; he was a white supremacist trying to kill a Black man. The other dead guys were all Black. How many nazi killers do you think we have running around this town?"

"Listen," Jack said. "You may very well be right. We certainly hope so. But let's see where the evidence leads. And make sure your Sheriff Klamp keeps his mouth shut too, especially with the media. Anyway, I know we'll keep looking, keep pursuing."

"Hey, maybe I wasn't right on ScottB20 being a serial killer, but everything points to this guy."

"Well," Jill said, "even if it turns out you're right and you've got the killer you were after, I'm still going to try to stop any more of these crazy fringe groups from harming others," Jill said. "There are very dangerous people out there."

"We're going to stay vigilant, and I suggest you do the same too until all the evidence is in. And chief of all, we need to find this guy Dirk," Jack said, subconsciously touching his thigh. "I'm sure he and his group were responsible for that poor girl getting murdered on her fifteenth birthday. And who knows what else he's done."

Tracy shifted uncomfortably in her chair.

"Tracy, were you able to get any information on him?" Jack asked.

"Actually, that was the other reason I wanted to talk to you. In all the craziness yesterday, the information came in that Dirk was originally from a town called Pleasant Falls."

"Pleasant Falls," Jill said. "We know that place."

Jack concurred. "Well, let's get out there and talk to the local police. Maybe they can clue us in to some information that will lead to where he is. Hell, maybe he went back there to hide out!"

Jack jumped up, Tracy's mimosa spilling on the table, while his coffee cup crashed to the floor.

"Let's go!" he shouted to Jill.

Jill was already halfway out the door.

77

The origins of a monster.

Jack and Jill were on the trail.

They didn't find Dirk back in Pleasant Falls, but gained insight into who he was, right from early in his life. And lowlife didn't even begin to describe it.

They'd been to Pleasant Falls before and knew a local cop there. They paid their "three-beer friend" a visit.

They brought a twelve-pack.

After a friendly hello, they got right into it; the cop in Pleasant Falls had been very familiar with Dirk and was more than willing to tell them everything he knew—and suspected.

"I tell ya, it was a happy day when Dirk left town. Can't believe he actually went to college. Though I guess he wasn't dumb. Just a mean son of a bitch. Evil if you ask me—or ask any of the dozens of other people who told me stories about him. Never could pin anything on him though—guess he was too smart for that. Anyway, glad he's gone and not my problem anymore." He looked at Jill. "Sorry though if he's yours."

"Let's just get on with it, pal," Jack said.

Jill's eyes narrowed, then she said, "Yes, please," to the cop.

"Anyway, where was I? Oh yes, evil. He must've been born evil. Some say maybe he was the reincarnation of Charles

Manson. Others say he was the Devil himself." The cop shook his head, looking down.

"Sounds like him," Jack said. "But not quite the reincarnation of Charles Manson; he just died, buddy."

"You know what he means," Jill said. She looked back to the cop. "But please, continue. Right from the beginning."

"Sure," he said, eyeing the beer. "From the beginning. Everything I know."

Jill leaned forward and smiled. Jack just stared.

"Pleasant Falls does have a somewhat upscale area—certainly not rich. It's on the outskirts near the river. The people who live there live comfortably; the men are shop owners, the women work too, taking care of the house and kids."

"Dirk was born and raised there, though as I've indicated, mostly raised hell all his life. Again, he wasn't stupid; on the contrary, I learned he had a high IQ. That went along with apparently an even higher set of street smarts. He skated by at school with little studying or work. It seems his parents largely ignored him. They certainly never attended any parent-teacher conferences. You know what it's like: his father worked long hours, and in this case, his mother was home, but only physically. She had been smart as a whip, a strong lady who was the one really behind her husband's business getting going. But according to the gossips, something happened. She became, what do you call it... oh yes, emotionally detached. They say she'd been curiously quiet ever since Dirk was born. Some people said something about postpartum. Anyway, Dirk was usually alone. His father certainly wasn't home. Which apparently suited Dirk just fine."

"Well, so far, I don't think that's so unusual," Jill said.

"Well, there's more," the cop said. "I was told on the rare occasions his father was home, there would be nothing but fighting—usually with Dirk's dad getting on his mother, and Dirk unable to intervene. We had a couple of calls on that."

Jack thought back to his own childhood. His muscles tightened, his eyes squeezed shut for a moment while his mouth twisted.

"The neighbors often heard loud slapping noises. While it was a nicer area of town, those houses still weren't very far apart. Sounded like the mother got slapped frequently. If they caught a glimpse of her the next day, they'd note a swollen lip. They tried to talk to her, but she would just run back inside."

"That shitass," Jack said.

"Once, when Dirk was young, they heard him start to cry, and heard his father immediately on him. They'd heard the father shout, 'What are you, a girl? I didn't raise a girl! Stop that crying now, or you'll be next!'"

"According to the neighbors, it had sounded like it took Dirk a minute too long to wipe away his tears, and his father slapped him twice, once on each side of the face. 'Don't you ever cry again. Men don't cry! Toughen up, or I'll roughen you up!'"

"Oh my God!" Jill said. "Some men! Jesus."

"Well," the cop said, "can't disagree. I'll bet Dirk never cried again. Though he often made others cry, the bastard."

Jack was still thinking of his own childhood.

"Well, he's not the only kid who had trouble with a father. I don't think that made him a bad guy."

Jill looked at Jack with a sympathetic face. The cop took another swig of beer. "Well, looks like that one is dead. Let me grab another can; there's a lot more to tell."

"Sure, we have plenty," Jack said.

The cop burped, then looked at Jill, sheepishly. Jack chuckled lightly.

"'Scuse me. Anyway, his childhood was what you might call a litany of trouble. From what I'd been able to learn, Dirk did make friends easily enough, though never quite kept them. These friends, temporary as they were, or sometimes even their mothers, told us of some interesting experiences involving him."

Jack steeled himself, awaiting the worst.

"At eight, he loved taking a magnifying glass out on his walkway and using it with the bright summer sun to fry ants. He would cackle as he watched them crackle, turning from black to a reddish hue before popping. Then he'd take a deep breath in through his nostrils. He seemed to love the smell, the sensation of cremation."

Jack looked away a moment but said nothing.

"He lost one friend over that but found another interesting thing to do soon after: he'd take a bug and disable it—pull a leg or wing off—and stick the bug in a spider's web. Dirk seemed fascinated by how the spider went to work on it. He'd watched with delight as the spider took a bite, then took its time, wrapping the bug in silk, waiting for it to die. Dirk seemed to especially like the waiting time. Then the spider sucked on the bug, would have its fill, and retire to the side. 'Not a bad life,' Dirk apparently commented to his friend."

"I don't know, kind of like kid stuff," Jack said.

The cop took another swig of beer, shaking his head. "At ten, he would walk by the river to play 'find the snails' with a new friend, but then take out a hammer from his backpack and instead play 'smash the snails.' I'm told he loved when they would first warily stick their heads out, tentacles growing straight out of it like Martians, beady eyes surveying the scene. 'That's the last thing he'll ever see,' Dirk would exclaim with glee. The other boy would just flee."

"Yuck," Jill said, shaking her head.

"At twelve, he went to another boy's house. They say this boy had a really cool model racetrack in his basement. I always wanted one of those," the cop said, remembering with a smile. Then he continued, the smile gone. "Little red Ferraris, one-inch-long blue Bugattis, the cars and track were the boy's pride and joy, a setup that took a few years to set up. When the boy was called upstairs by his mother, Dirk took some glue and piled it on cars and model trees. He lit a match. By the way, I'm told he always carried matches, along with cigarettes his parents knew nothing about."

"OK, go on," Jill prompted.

"He started multiple little fires on the track. Smelling burning plastic and metal, the boy and his mother came running back down. Dirk looked at them, and said he just wanted to make it realistic, so improved it with car crashes and explosions. The model racetrack was ruined, and the friendship blew up along with it."

"Hmm," Jack said. "I once thought about doing that."

"At fourteen, there were the rumors about many cats who disappeared."

"Well, that's not kid stuff," Jill said, eyeing Jack.

"At fifteen, there was that boy in school, a bit different, everyone knew, but with a sweet soul. Skinny as a scarecrow. Apparently, he always looked straight down at the ground, fear fixed on his face. I'm told he faced each day thinking only bad things were in place."

"Oh, no. Were they?" Jill asked.

The cop exhaled. "They were. On a daily basis, Dirk would follow him on his walk home, and every day would grab his books and throw them down an embankment." The cop shook his head slowly back and forth. "You know, someone described the papers scattering like confused birds in flight, and Dirk screeching like a vulture. You've seen that reaction when birds hear a gunshot, right?"

Jack nodded his head. "Right."

"That poor boy," Jill said. "He must have been so scared."

"Well, I'm sure it made Dirk feel powerful," Jack said.

"Ugh, that Sisyphean ritual would kill your spirit for sure," Jill said, frowning, lips pouted.

"Well, I don't know of any sissy ritual," the cop said, finishing off another beer. Jill laughed for a moment. The cop looked confused. "But Dirk did eventually find other ways to terrorize the poor boy. And others. In fact, at sixteen, a girl found her birthday to be not at all sweet."

"Oh no," Jill cried out.

"Oh yeah. And something tells me she wasn't the only girl he bothered."

Jack was clenching and unclenching his fists. "I can't wait to grind his face under my boot."

"Jack!" Jill exclaimed.

The cop went on. "He left at seventeen or eighteen, thankfully. But I tell ya, it was a wonder that we didn't get him on anything back then," the cop said, looking disappointed. "And I always wondered what Dirk would do next."

Jack and Jill looked at each other, exchanging knowing glances. There was always something. Dirk's life in Pleasant Falls read like a ruinous rap sheet: no rapture in store for him.

"You sure you don't want a beer?" the cop offered from the stash between his feet.

"We'll definitely have one now," Jack responded.

"But only one," Jill said. "Because we also wonder what he's going to do next."

78

Tracy needed a sanity check after her latest meeting with Sheriff Klamp—and her experience at the bar. Klamp wanted to hold a press conference announcing that *he'd* solved the local murders and all was back to normal. She thought she'd finally convinced him to tone it down but didn't trust him. She definitely needed a drink after that meeting, and luckily Jill was back in town.

They met at a bar—but different from the last. This one was quite lively, and the sound of laughter was in the air. They took a table toward the back.

"This place is never dead; that's what I like about it," Tracy said as they ordered scotch. "That damn Klamp. Had to spend too long a time with him. Actually, two minutes is too long."

Jill laughed.

"After dealing with him and everything going on, feel my neck, how tense it is."

Jill obliged. "Jesus, hard as a rock."

"Yeah, I need a massage, bad," Tracy said.

"Massage! I envy you."

"You bet. Try it sometime; ask for Jessica, she's the best. Heavenly!"

"I will!" Jill said. The drinks arrived, and as they sipped

their spirits, Tracy leaned in close to Jill and told her about the strange encounter she'd had with the guy at the other bar.

"You know, Jill, I've been thinking about something lately," she said, swirling her drink absentmindedly. "It's strange how sometimes you can have an immediate reaction to someone, without even knowing them. Like love at first sight."

"Wait, are you…"

"No, no, no. Hold on."

"Well, what do you mean?"

"I suspect something like an instinct, a sixth sense maybe?" Tracy said.

"I guess I've experienced some hate at first sight," Jill said, thinking of some criminals she's put away. "Though Jack and I, that certainly was not love at first sight!"

"You and Jack are so funny as a couple." Tracy saw the awkward expression on Jill's face. "So different is what I mean. But you know, I guess it's like… like peanut butter and jelly. Two things that are so different from each other, but when put together are perfect!"

Jill blushed.

"But what I'm talking about is a little different," Tracy continued. "What I mean is you know how sometimes you meet someone and you immediately feel that they're a nice person?"

"Well yeah, I do sometimes get a good feel for a person right away, a kindred spirit," Jill said.

"Right. But I'm thinking of something even more, like you feel an instant connection, kind of like you've known them before?"

"Yeah, I guess so. Maybe once or twice in my life. Or as I said, some people you can take an immediate dislike to. Even the non-criminals! It's just a feeling. But tell me more of what you are getting at. What brought this up?"

Tracy elaborated on the story of the guy in the bar, and

how strange—yet strangely comforting—it had all been. She looked at Jill, hesitated, and said, "Maybe things somehow do continue on, never die."

Jill looked skeptical. "Whoa! What do you mean? Like the collective unconscious? Or what? Did you have a few of those before I got here?" she said, arching her eyebrows toward the scotch.

"No, no. Of course not. I don't really know what I'm saying. Or thinking. I'm sorry."

"Nothing to be sorry about. There certainly are things I wish were indelible."

"But not Klamp," Tracy said. "Inconsequential maybe, but hopefully not indelible."

They both laughed, their spirits lightened.

79

"Easter is coming!" Rosa said to her four-year-old son, Juanito.

Jose, her husband, was stubborn. The smoke-bomb attack on his home had scared his family half to death but didn't scare him into leaving town. At 5 ft 6 in and 127 pounds, he was a lot tougher than he looked. Plus, he had just been told he'd be getting a step up in the restaurant he worked at; the dream of becoming a waiter was that much closer at hand. Still, Rosa often begged him to leave.

"We don't belong here. They don't want us here. *Vamanos!*"

Jose saw the anguish in her eyes, the lines forming on her face. He looked at Rosa with a mixture of understanding and pity. "*Lo sé, mi amado.* But we didn't come this far, just to turn around and run. *Lo siento.*"

Rosa looked exasperated. "Think of your son. Think of Juanito!"

"*Dios mio*, that's exactly who I'm thinking of! I don't want him to learn to run away from problems. Life isn't ever going to be easy for him, so he needs to learn, even at this young age, to be strong. *Fuerte!* And to have courage. *Coraje!*"

Rosa looked back, shaking her head, apparently unconvinced.

"And I'm doing well in the restaurant."

"So? That won't help if you're dead!"

"Stop. I want him to be proud of his father. I want him to see what I can be. To be his *héroe*." Jose thought about the slop he cleared from tables, the days that started so early and ended so late, the people who treated him like he didn't exist, and hesitated. But then he thought there was a chance, some opportunity—if not for him, then for his son. He smiled. "Maybe someday, I'll own the restaurant—live the American Dream." Jose's chest puffed up.

"And you don't think I think of Juanito? All the hours cleaning the motel rooms, brushing the dirty toilet bowls, emptying the overflowing garbage bins, surrounded by used toilet tissues thrown on the floor; I do this for him, I think of him. Back home, I had a degree. But now this is all I can get. For now. I believe in a future—if you allow us to have one!" Rosa's whole body seemed to deflate, and tears rolled down her cheeks. "So I hope to God that you are right. I don't want our life to become an American nightmare!"

With that, she left the room. Jose could see her take a minute, compose herself, and go to talk to Juanito.

Rosa put on a positive face, mustered up as much excitement in her voice as she could, and told Juanito that Easter was coming.

"*Sí*, Easter!"

"Easter Bunny? Eggs? Chocolate?"

"Yes, sweets for my sweet bebé!"

"Not a baby!"

"No. Eres un chico grande!" Rosa looked at him, full of love, and thought for a moment. "So you should also know that there is more to Easter than that. It's the day our Lord Jesus rose from the dead."

Juanito, with eyes wide open, said, "Ghost?"

Rosa laughed and hugged him. "No, mi hijo. Not exactly. He did die, and did come back to life. Para nosotros. For us."

Juanito looked back at her, brow furrowed, eyes narrowed in a mystified expression.

"I see it's a little complicado for you right now, cariño. But all good Cristianos will be, lo que llamamos, resurrected—will be brought back to life. So you be good!"

"Back to life? After death? Jesus." Juanito looked scared and grabbed her by the skirt.

"Yes, but not to worry. Jesus is friendly."

"Casper?"

"Yes, like Casper." Rosa laughed. "We'll talk more when you are a little older." Rosa gave him a big hug, mussed his hair, and let him run to his cartoons in the other room.

Rosa still worried. About him, about living there. At least she'd have some peace Easter Day in their sanctuary, their church, La Iglesia de la Resurreccion.

80

The Exterminator was thrilled as he learned how easy it was to make a car bomb.

The internet was full of information, with basics even on the government's Department of Homeland Security website. Pipe bombs. A cell phone with a timer to initiate the device. Pack them with some enhancements—like nails. Explosive substances like fertilizer and gunpowder. Many options to choose from! Happily, he thought, vehicle bombs can carry a significant amount of explosive material, for maximum damage. Maximum carnage.

He planned to get on dark websites to get more help from the Vets with some experience in this area. Beyond that on his to-do list was to steal a van from out of state, hide it in his shed for a while, outfit it, and then move it into place. A white van, of course.

81

"Oh no!"

While Jill had met with her socially the other night, now she and Jack met with Sheriff's Deputy Tracy Dixon to fully fill her in on what they found in Dirk's hometown.

Tracy's reaction to the stories of Dirk growing up was pure disgust, and an "Oh No!" that became louder with each description of his deeds.

Tracy knew Dirk had to be stopped, but she also wanted to see if they still felt the same way about not shutting down the investigation into the recent killings even though the big guy she arrested was in custody. In her mind, recent killings included the one that was just over the state line. She herself didn't know that much about that one. She'd talked with Klamp, who was uninterested, and details had been sketchy. Really all she knew was there'd been a big fire, a dead Black man, and another guy fleeing the scene claiming the dead man had been trying to steal his car—and was shot by someone else from a distance. Locals over the line thought it was a simple but brutal carjacking case, and then the gas somehow ignited. None of it was very clear and the crime scene had been obliterated.

The only thing they had to go on was a report by a couple of people in the general vicinity that they'd seen a brown pickup truck in the area, possibly a big Dodge Ram; they remembered it because of the big Confederate flag decal covering most of the rear window.

"Well, Tracy, what's the latest with the killer, ahem, or rather attempted killer, you caught?" Jack asked.

Tracy looked down at her feet. "Nothing further yet to connect him to the other dead men." Then she looked up at Jill. "But I'm sure the evidence is coming. I did tell Klamp not to broadcast anything yet, but you know him; he doesn't listen."

Jack stood up. "I have to say, Tracy, and I'm sorry, but I think chances are he's not the guy. And the more I think about this killing just over the state line, the more it's my belief that there is a connection, and it isn't the guy you caught. In fact, in my mind, this third killing changes everything." Jack had spread his hands out wide while saying that.

"And I sure hope that Klamp keeps his mouth shut. Because it's not over. We have killings in two adjacent states, with certain commonalities in the three shootings. Sounds like all shootings were of strangers. Shot from a distance too. Every vic is a Black man." Jack looked over to Jill, who was nodding her head, then back to Tracy. "While Jill and I have been doing what we can to investigate unofficially, I think it's time to get a much bigger investigation going."

"Shit!" Tracy said, having hoped the spree was now over. She sat still for a few moments, her brow furrowed. "Well, I guess it's possible there's someone else out there. But maybe not. I just really hope the dope I got did do all three. But you're right, it's not one hundred percent certain. And I certainly won't be telling the press that it's over." She exhaled, and looked as frustrated as someone who is trying to unlock a door with a key that doesn't quite fit: jiggling and wiggling. "Tell me what you think I should do."

"Well, we certainly need to have the State Bureau of

Investigation involved *officially*. Just to be sure," Jill said, looking plaintively at Tracy.

"Hell, I'm talking FBI," Jack said, slapping his hand on his good thigh. "Killings have crossed state lines. If it's not the guy you got, Tracy, I'm serious that it could very well be a serial killer—still out there. Still looking. And beyond that, it's possible the FBI may get wind of this by themselves and start poking around. To be safe, I think I should make a phone call to an old buddy of mine who works there, just to get some insight. But I warn you though, the FBI can't come in on their own. They have to be called in by the local law enforcement."

"Damn, I don't think Earl will ever agree to that, especially since he thinks it's case closed. He'd surely think I'm nuts by even suggesting it. And he didn't even want the state involved, let alone the feds. But let me figure out how to deal with him."

"You're usually pretty good at that," Jill said with a smile.

"Listen," Jack said. "I have a powerful feeling in my gut; chances are we haven't seen the end of this and Klamp is going to need specialized help, especially if there is a serial killer on the loose. The FBI has an entire unit focused on that called Behavioral Science Services. That's where my buddy works. He's quite the mindhunter."

"Isn't that the group that helped get Ted Bundy?" Jill interjected.

"You bet. Their profiling helped. But serial killers have been around a long time. Way longer than this unit."

"Yeah, like Jack the Ripper!" Tracy said, her breath quickening.

"Hey, I once heard that legends such as wolves and vampires were inspired by medieval serial killers," Jill said.

Tracy shivered a bit. "The real deal is scary enough," she said. "Well, I'd really appreciate it if you can contact your FBI friend on the down-low, and I'll try to grease the skids to get them called in. Somehow. God. I slept so well last night. Now, I'm not gonna sleep at all."

"Don't think they'll be much sleep in our future either," Jill said.

"Agree," Jack said. "Lots to do."

"Jack Ludlum. Well, how the hell are ya!"

"Just fine, Doug. Great to hear that unmistakable, booming, bass voice of yours. How's the FBI treating you?"

"It's been a long, long time. Why the hell haven't you been in touch? After all we went through abroad!"

"You know how it is, Doug. Things happen. Always busy. But still love you, bro."

"Bro? Hey, if we're brothers, it's definitely brothers from a different mother, paleface!"

"Yeah, Ebony and Ivory." Jack laughed, but then got serious. "At least blood brothers," he said, thinking about the blood they'd shed together in Special Ops. Sometimes his blood on Doug, sometimes Doug's on him. But they'd survived. Which is more than they could say for over half their unit.

"So true. So true, bro. Now tell me, what can I do for you? I know this isn't a call to reminisce."

"Well, I'd be remiss if I didn't get your advice on something."

"Shoot."

Jack filled him in and knew if there was anything there to be sniffed out, Doug would know. If he was wasting his time, Doug would tell him that straight out too. He was a straight shooter, for sure. And he was the smartest guy Jack had ever known. In Special Ops, he and Jack were rivals for who was the biggest, strongest, and scariest dude. But when it came to smarts, while Jack was certainly no dummy, Doug Russler's mind was first rate. He rated number one in his class when he went to Howard University in DC on the government's dime after he left Special Ops. While there, he studied criminology and psychology. Then he got a graduate degree from Harvard. He respected Jack's decision to enter the police academy after Special Ops, telling him the criminals didn't have a chance with Jack Ludlum on the job. Little did he know how right he'd be.

After grilling him on every detail, Doug took a couple of minutes, and Jack could hear him rapping on the table as he thought. Doug then broke the silence and told him something serious was definitely going on, and it needed to be dealt with ASAP.

"Serial murders are less than one percent of all murders committed in a year. While most murderers know their victims, serial killers generally don't. Their victims are simply murdered to be murdered. Victims are selected based on availability, vulnerability, and desirability. Serial murders usually happen in a defined geographic area—like what's going on there. They occur in the killer's comfort zone. You need to get the killer before he becomes more adept at it."

"I certainly don't want another killing. But if there is another try, maybe the killer will become overconfident, get sloppy. Perhaps take more chances—and hopefully leave some clues," Jack interjected.

"You're right, that happens sometimes. But I'm sure the investigators down there don't have any experience with serial killers. That's why they'd better ask for our help. The killer won't stop. Serial killing is an addiction. A lot of them have their desire enlarged after a killing, in an ever-increasing need to commit the perfect murder, the one that truly fulfills their fantasy."

"So they are never satisfied?"

"No. It's a quixotic quest—with increased frustration,

repeating their killing in an unending, psychotic cycle. So let's get on it. And I promise you, you get those people down there to request our help, and guaranteed, I'll come down and oversee it myself. Of course, there is protocol; I'll have to get the local office involved."

"Wow, you're sounding quite like the Harvard grad, aren't you? Quixotic quest my ass! But seriously, thanks for the offer; that would be some reunion."

"Hey, getting the two of us together again—the unbeatable team is back!"

Jack smiled to himself, but wondered if they could keep the unbeatable streak alive.

82

J ack and Jill got more than they bargained for.

The next stop in their pursuit of Dirk was to get together with Saint for any further information he might've found, including from the march. Plus Jill just wanted to make sure he was doing OK after all the violence at play. They stopped at his house, and luckily both he and Deja were there. Jack mentioned they learned Dirk was from Pleasant Falls, and asked where he was now.

"I don't know where that asshole went!" Saint said. "I've tried to stay as far away from him as possible!"

Deja's head had swiveled around when she heard the name Dirk. "Dirk—did you say this Dirk you are looking for was from Pleasant Falls, the town where Skyler grew up?"

"Yes, Dirk was. Why?" Jill asked.

Deja became ghostly pale at the confirmation that this was the same Dirk she knew. She tried to say something, but no words came out.

At that same instant, Saint, who looked very upset himself, interrupted. "I told you I don't know anything else about Dirk. Honest! I didn't want nothing to do with him. He chills me to the bone. But listen! You need to deal with something else right away. I was about to contact you when you walked in."

"Huh?"

"It's life or death."

83

It was so easy.

Stealing the van was as easy as pushing the starter button on your own car. The white Ford Econoline cargo van was perfect. No windows on the sides other than the driver and shotgun windows, and the rear had solid doors. Perfectly private. It now stood waiting in the shed, like Stephen King's Christine on steroids. The Exterminator's new-found buddy was on his way to help prepare it with aplomb.

Easter morning was sunny and temperate.

The dogwoods were flowering, the pink buds opening heavenward. Scarlet passion flowers adorned planted beds, lawns finally green after a gray winter. Easter lilies in pure white surrounded the church, their sweet scent sending squirrels scurrying in circles. The resurrection ferns had survived, fully dark green again after their gray-brown desiccated duration. The swallows had returned, chirping their everlasting love while looking down from above.

Rosa, standing at the foot of his bed, looked down lovingly at Juanito. She waited another moment before waking him, thinking he looked like a little angel.

The smell of Café Bustelo was in the air, and she could hear Jose singing in the shower. Singing poorly, she thought.

"Juanito, time to wake up," she said, tugging on his foot. "We have a big day ahead. Time to see Jesus!"

Meanwhile, a white van, with a full tank of gas, slowly rumbled its way down the street to the church.

84

They were shocked.

Jill cried out she'd never thought The Exterminator would take it that far. Never thought that perhaps he was a serial killer, now on to even bigger things. Jack yelled they had to act fast; he made some calls while running out the door, Jill matching him stride for stride. He told Saint to stay far away from the church. Saint seemed to have no problem at all with that.

Deja was doubly shocked at what she'd heard. She still hadn't fully recovered from the recent mentions of Dirk, of Dirk coming back into her life like a zombie; she'd thought that part of her life was safely dead and buried. But for now, the news of what yet another person Saint knew was about to do overwhelmed everything.

Deja hugged Saint. "All we can do now is pray," she said.

They got down on their knees, hand in hand.

The parishioners flocked around the entrance to the church.

Dressed in their Sunday best, they crowded around the stairs and spilled out onto the lawn, hordes of them extending all the way to the street. Talking, laughing, even showing off a bit, they ignored the driverless van parked at the curb.

★

Jack and Jill raced out, jumped into their car and peeled out of the driveway. As they sped toward the church, Jill's heart was pounding with an adrenaline rush. They weren't far from the church and knew they were the only ones standing between life and death for the unsuspecting churchgoers.

"Jack, we can't let that bomb go off!" Jill shouted, pressing down hard on the accelerator and gripping the wheel tightly.

"Calm down, we'll get there in time," Jack replied, his voice steady and reassuring.

When they arrived at the church, they saw a white van in front of it. "That must be it!" Jill shouted. As she approached it, Jack saw a man nearby with his finger on what looked like a detonator. They were the first on the scene, and there was no time to do anything but try to stop him.

Jack tried to sneak behind him. Jill distracted him, yelling, "Stop right there!" She drew her gun. "Put it down. Now!" she shouted, eyes focused on what was in his hand. "Slowly."

The Exterminator glared at her. She could see the hatred in his eyes. "You can't stop me! I'll make them pay for what they've done!" He spat toward her, and yelled, "And you too!"

Dust and noise swirled about.

The Exterminator activated the timer; he smiled, about to enjoy his handiwork. He was ready to detonate the bomb with the cell phone remote control in hand.

His finger pressed on the first number of the code.

Jill yelled at the parishioners to move back behind the church but she was too far away and they were somehow oblivious, caught up in their candid conversations. Before The Exterminator could act, a blur of movement caught his eye. At that moment, Jack hit him from behind, the cell phone falling out of his grasp, landing softly on the grass. The Exterminator never knew what got him as Jack dove on him with all his two-hundred-plus pounds, knocking his chin into the pavement, blood pouring out of his mouth. He lay helpless as Jill ran over and put cuffs on. The Exterminator was extinguished.

A whirl of sirens screamed toward them, screeching to a stop. The police and State Bureau of Investigation took control.

"That was too close," Jack said, his voice hoarse with emotion.

Jill nodded, her own heart still pounding in her chest.

"Thank God," Jill said, looking over at the church.

"Well, actually, let's go thank Saint. Without his information, without him agreeing to work with us, that church full of people would no longer exist."

"Yeah, and we almost just ceased to exist."

85

The FBI wanted him too.

Jack and Jill went to see Saint and thanked him for what he did. They also told him the authorities, probably including the FBI, would soon come around to talk to him. Saint was scared, his eyes darting from place to place, even though Jack told him he'd be fine; he'd done his job as an informant, saving many lives. A hero even. Jill said to trust them. "Hey, we can protect you."

But Saint had heard plenty of stories and didn't trust what might happen to him in interrogation. He feared what type of case they may try to fabricate against him. After all, he was in contact not only with The Exterminator, but also with a man who tried to burn down a hot yoga studio. Plus, he was in the United We Stand march the same day a girl was murdered nearby. In his mind, it wasn't looking very good. Saint decided he needed to disappear. But where?

He knew he shouldn't go near the rest of the remaining Very Fine Men. Saint didn't know where to turn. His lonely existence left him no options. He had no other friends. Never had any friends. Random thoughts would pop into his head; fear paralyzed his thinking.

Then Elizabeth came to mind; maybe she could help him hide for a while. He wrestled with the thought, since he'd seen her with Heilbach. She certainly had several contacts. And he had nowhere else to turn. In his naivete, he thought, *She was close to me once. She sure seemed to really like me. Maybe the rally was just a heat-of-the-moment thing. If I could just talk to her......*

86

"I know that evil man."
Immediately after she'd heard The Exterminator was taken away, Deja felt a bit better about Saint's situation; Saint though was still fearful. Deja contacted Jack and Jill, telling them she had some important information. They'd rushed over. Saint wasn't home, but Deja was eager to talk. For the first time, she was actually happy to see Jack.

She told them that as soon as Saint came back home, she'd let them know. She did, though, want to make them aware of something. "Last time you were here, you mentioned a man named Dirk. From the same town Saint's father Skyler grew up in: from Pleasant Falls. I knew that man. He's evil. He and Skyler never got along. Not in the town they grew up in, not when they somehow ended up in the same college."

"So Dirk and Saint's father had a history?" Jack asked, eager to learn more.

"Yes, though I never said anything to Saint. I didn't want to scare him any more than he already is."

"So you met both Dirk and your husband Skyler at college?" Jill asked.

"Yes, at State. One blessing. One curse. My poor Skyler," Deja said, looking away wistfully.

Jill squeezed her hand. "How did you meet?"

"Randomly, actually. In front of the cafeteria. Skyler was kind of shy at first. I felt him staring at me from afar; I could tell he was trying to get up enough courage to approach me. He finally walked up and introduced himself. I told him I was Deja Jones. Everyone asks me if I was given an unusual first name because my last name is so common, but I remember his response: 'Deja Jones. Nice to meet you. But I feel like we've met before. It feels like déjà vu all over again.'"

"I replied, 'Yogi Berra. Like I haven't heard that one five thousand times before.'"

"'Ugh, maybe we should start over again?'"

"'Next time, come up with a better line,' I'd said with a giggle. I used to hate that damn girlish giggle—couldn't help it though." Deja looked away for a moment, then said, "I haven't laughed much since his death. And I doubt I'll ever giggle again."

Jill's eyes were wide, and she patted Deja on the arm. "So you and Skyler became a couple."

"A triple, actually. Though he never knew it," Deja said, looking upward, thinking of Skyler and Saint.

"Skyler must have been something special," Jill said.

"He was, he was. So kind. I even still remember how Skyler described how I looked when he first met me. He was so sweet. But you don't want to be bored with that."

"Please go on," Jill said, nodding encouragingly.

"I remember it vividly because I was pretty shocked—embarrassed really—by his description. But I loved it!" Deja said, her eyes lighting up. "But OK. He said, 'I was mesmerized by you.' Mesmerized! I love that word!" Deja said, blushing. "Then he said something like: 'Your honey-blond hair is cut shorter than most—seems stylish, but what do I know?'"

Deja looked unsure if she should continue, but Jill smiled and nodded encouragingly.

"Then he talked about my eyes. Said he loved their green color but loved the intelligence he saw in them even more. Can you believe that!"

Jill nodded her head.

"Lastly, he mentioned my body." Deja blushed even deeper as she looked at Jack, who just looked away. "He said it was on the slight side." Deja raised her eyebrows as her eyes widened. Then used a phrase "I'll always remember: 'just enough to be sexy, in how should I say, an unobtrusive way.'" Deja laughed. "I'm not quite slight now; kids will do that to you. But it was nice!"

"How sweet!" Jill said. "And I'm sure you pretty much look the same."

"Well, thank you. And needless to say, I was hooked!"

"And you met Dirk then too?" Jack asked, breaking the spell.

"Unfortunately." Deja frowned. "Evil man. He did *lots* of bad things. Importantly, you should know I've even had suspicions about him and Skyler's death. Lots of suspicions. Dirk had driven him away, stupid fraternity hazing stunt gone wrong—*supposedly*. Dirk came back." Deja looked away. "But Skyler didn't... Then Dirk disappeared... and I was so out of it."

"Thanks for filling us in; I know it's hard. And that's consistent with what we've learned about him. Believe me, we're going to track him down, find him, if it's the last thing we do," Jack said. "Do you have any idea at all where he might have gone? Anyone else from back then that we should talk to?"

"Dirk had fraternity brothers at that college," Deja said. "If you can track them down, maybe they'd have some clues as to where he could be—and what really happened to Skyler that night."

"We'll definitely check that out; any tidbit could be a key," Jill said.

"Do it quickly, please! I'm scared to death he'll go after Saint now. He's a very sick man!"

87

E lizabeth was naked.

Her prim and proper dress lay on the floor; her lacy underwear hung off the edge of the bed. She was sweaty and moaning loudly, imploring him to continue to explore. He was enjoying himself, clearly in command. He found her breasts hidden amidst her long hair, peeking in and out, as she bounced about. She began quivering. Her climax came with a shuddering shiver.

He looked at her, satisfied. But he was even more interested in the news she had provided. Heilbach turned over, his fully tattooed back disappearing from view.

"So he thinks you'll help him? What a laugh!"

"I know. The poor boy is so naïve."

"Well, I'm not. The Exterminator went down, which by itself ain't such a bad thing. I hated that pompous prick. But the way it happened—that could only have happened for one reason."

"What... ... what do you mean?"

Heilbach looked at her as if he were looking at a child. "An informant."

Elizabeth stared at him, a slim, painted fingernail placed on her smudged lip. "Saint?"

"Bingo. I never trusted that guy. 'El Diablo' my ass."

"Well, then, he needs to go to hell!"

"Exactly."

Unbeknownst to him, Saint was seen.

He was panicked that the authorities wanted to talk to him and decided to run. He left his home as quietly and quickly as he could, not taking much: just a protein bar, and a condom, stuffed in his pocket. He was unaware his mother saw him leaving. Deja didn't trust him anymore; she trusted her instincts instead. She followed him.

88

It was clear he was dead.

He was being crucified in the media when the news of the third killing got out. Hard to keep bar talk quiet. He was being called the "Duke of Do Nothing." Sheriff Earl "Duke" Klamp must have known his re-election chances were dead unless he showed the townspeople that he took the killings seriously.

Klamp finally spoke with county law enforcement and they agreed to bring in state help, so Jack and Jill were official. Tracy Dixon looked at him approvingly and set the plan in motion.

"That's good, Earl, that's real good. But..."

"Damn you, woman, what's it now?"

Tracy looked at him, her eyes squinting. She took a deep breath and thought about how to best answer him. She usually knew how to play him. Tracy changed her scowl to a smile—or at least her best facsimile of one.

"Earl, bringing in the SBI is a great move! But some people may think it's an expected move. A normal move. But you are no normal sheriff. You are Sheriff Earl Klamp. You need to make the unexpected move, the bigger move. There was another killing just over the state line. Call in the FBI; show the voters you will pull out all stops for the safety of your community."

"Well, ah do appreciate that, but, ugh, won't that show ahm weak, that ah can't git the job done?"

"Not at all. It shows you are smart! Smart enough to call in the specialists. You can say the safety and security of everyone in your town is your number-one mission. Because of that, you determined it's time NCAVC was called in, that real help is on its way. You'll be showing them real initiative and true leadership!"

"The N what?"

"National Center for the Analysis of Violent Crime. In Quantico."

"Oh. Right. They still operate outta that basement?"

"Well, what I recall is their operations center was built originally as a bomb shelter. For post-nuclear intelligence operations, I believe. I'm sure it's just fine now."

"Harrumph. The FBI. Ugh... I hear they're arrogant bastards. But maybe, just maybe, you're right... I guess we really have nothin' to lose."

"And maybe a lot to gain."

"OK, OK, I'll talk to the others an' see if I kin convince 'em. Course, I'll tell them it's my idea, so they're more likely to go along with it."

Tracy gave him a look, but decided not to say anything since she'd played him into agreement.

"But I'll do it on one condition."

"What's that?" Tracy asked.

"Well, given the media has gone nuts, and the town too, I need ta calm everything down. Specially with a 'leckshin comin' up. I'm a gonna hold a press conference about the guy I, uh, you, took down at the college. He likely did all three shootins. I'll say I'm a-goin' tha extra inch to bring in the FBI cause I care for this here community so much, but they can rest easy just the same. We got the guy."

"I'd love for it to have been him, but we just haven't got the evidence!" Tracy exclaimed.

"He did it. I knows he did it. You don't have ta attend the press conference."

"You know, Earl, I think I will skip it."

"Good. In the meantime, why don't ya find out the correct channels ta go through ta contact that FBI."

Tracy smiled, knowing she certainly had the contacts in Jack and his buddy Doug Russler of Behavioral Science. Klamp probably just thought she was smiling at him.

89

J ack and Jill got him.

They got the name and address of one of Dirk's former frat brothers and quickly set up a meeting. Once there, the frat brother spilled his coffee when Jack brusquely started asking questions. As Jack rapid-fired them, standing over him, he then spilled his guts pretty readily.

The frat brother said, "OK, OK. Here's everything I know. I knew him from the fraternity—not before, not after. And in the fraternity, he was something else. To tell you the truth, the more pain in pledging, the more Dirk liked it." He glanced at Jack, then quickly looked away. "That's how he always was. I was actually in a pledge class with him, then watched, concerned—I was, believe me—when he was put in charge a couple of years later."

Jill gave Jack a side glance.

"Is that when Skyler pledged?" Jill asked.

"Well, yeah, it was. Sad, sad story. I mean, we had it rough—pledging—the things we had to do. And later, some mean shit, stuff I'm not proud about. But when Dirk was the pledge master, he took it to a whole other level."

"Tell us," Jack urged.

"At first Dirk, now pledge master, treated Skyler like all the other pledges. Apparently, he was saving the worst for the end."

"Ugh," Jill said.

"While there were a lot of physical punches thrown during that final night, the toughest punch landed was actually a last question from Dirk, who knew Skyler's background from their hometown. I'll always remember that moment, clear as day: 'Last question, Skyler. And it's not why someone who is a dirtbag has the word sky in his name,' Dirk said, with a mean laugh. The other brothers looked back at Dirk, shaking their heads. 'The question is, what Beta Theta pledge has a mother who is a jailbird?'"

"Mother?" Jill said, exchanging a look with Jack.

"That's what he said. I remember Skyler took a breath in and moved his fist back, looking like he was getting ready to throw a punch."

"'Now, now, it's not a good idea to hit the guy who determines your fate,' Dirk had said."

"That's when me and the other brothers stepped in front of Skyler."

"'Why don't you tell everyone how your mother Gloria got put in prison. Don't know if we should have a criminal element in this frat.'"

"All the brothers and the pledges were staring at Skyler, transfixed."

"'Fuck you!' Skyler had said. He tried to charge Dirk but was stopped again by the brothers. 'She may be doing time, but she's a better mother than you have; tell them about yours, Dirk!'"

"With that, Dirk rushed forward and tried to punch Skyler, but was stopped by the other brothers."

"'My mother's fucking fine,' Dirk shouted, 'but yours is a con, just like you—conning everyone about your true background.'"

"'My mother made a mistake,' Skyler slowly said. 'She's

paid for it. But I'm not my mother. End of story.' From the look on Skyler's face, no one dared, or was heartless enough, to pursue it further. Dirk looked satisfied enough to have made his point and left it there. That was temporary though, as he continued to toy with Skyler during the rest of the pledge process."

"What happened next?" Jill asked. "Was the rest similar to what you'd experienced?"

"Unfortunately, no, not at all. I wish I had spoken up more, done something. Biggest regret of my life. There was lots of stuff that went on through the pledging process, but it was that last night that was the worst."

"Oh Jesus, what happened that night?" asked Jill.

"Umm. That night went pretty much the way they always went, pretty much as expected. Dirk actually took it a bit easier on Skyler at the start. Perhaps he wanted to ensure he was at the top of the class at the end. Skyler, and a big freshman named Little Joe, were the two left standing. Dirk yelled something like, 'OK, boys, off with everything. Just keep your underwear on; I don't want to see your little dicks!'"

"I remember that the boys looked at each other. They took a moment, but both went with it. Then Dirk told them to put blindfolds on. I remember how Little Joe and Skylar looked at the black blindfolds; Little Joe's eyes got big and wild. But they had no choice and were helped on with the blindfolds."

"'What now?' Skylar then asked. 'I thought we were done.'"

"'What gave you that idea, asshole? We are done when I say so,' was Dirk's response. Very typical."

Jack and Jill looked at each other, Jack interjecting, "Here we go."

The frat brother took in a deep breath before continuing. "Yeah. Well, Dirk then said, 'Next up is the championship round. Just one last thing to do, then you can sleep soundly.

We'll take you outside, you'll be driven to different locations, and dropped off. All you then have to do is find your way back here. First one back is in the frat. Simple.'"

"'Can I have my coat?' Little Joe had asked."

"'Can I have my coat?' mimicked Dirk. 'Of course not. You need to show you're a man and can make it as you are.' Dirk then said something like, 'You need to show you can tough it out. Though, of course, either of you can quit right now, if you prefer.'"

"I could see Skyler didn't give it a second thought, though Little Joe hesitated a moment. But then he must have figured he was so close, he could finish it. They both said they'd go on."

"Dirk then said, 'Jerry, you take Little Joe in your car to the location we talked about. I'll take Skyler in my car. May the best man win.'"

"Then what happened? Don't leave it hanging there!" Jill said.

"That's all I know."

Jack and Jill looked at each other. "You sure?" Jack said.

"Well, we all know that Skyler never made it back. He ended up drowning. An accident, the local authorities decided." He paused. "Personally, I think it was a very perfunctory investigation. Maybe the fact that the guy in charge of the investigation was a Beta Theta alumnus had something to do with that... And Dirk immediately disappeared."

"And life went on?" Jack asked, somewhat sarcastically.

"We all had our suspicions, that's for sure. But what could we do? It was too late. To be honest though, in the deepest dark of night, lying awake, it's hard to live with the memory. Hard to live with myself."

"But you do," Jill said.

"But I do."

*

Jack and Jill left feeling disgusted and discussed it on the way back.

"How the hell could boys do that kind of stuff?" Jill asked.

"Somehow, I guess, they leave their moral compasses at home when they go off to college. From what I understand, most of these boys were good students in high school, hard workers, received great references. Before getting to campus, they'd never do shit like hazing."

"Yeah," Jill said. "I suppose when they want to belong to a fraternity so, so bad, and then there's peer pressure, things can get out of whack. It's amazing how some boys can lose their values, their self-identity, even their soul, just so they're not seen as losers."

"Well, aren't you the psychoanalyst," Jack said, though stopped short when he saw Jill's glare.

"There are dead kids because of hazing," she said, shaking her head.

"Now let's go back and fill in Tracy. We should also see Deja again—tell her what we found, let her know we're tracking Dirk down so that she can feel at least a little better."

"And let's see if she remembers anything else," Jack said. "But most of all, we gotta find Dirk before he causes any more trouble."

90

Elizabeth looked like a vision.

Saint had been afraid of what the authorities might do, and the only one he could think of who might help him escape was Elizabeth. Now, he gasped as he saw her. Her beauty was just beyond his grasp. Her long, brown hair flowed back in the breeze, her white dress offset by her bright-red lipstick and matching nail polish. She smiled at him, beckoning him toward her. *Thank God*, he thought. Framed by two trees within the dense forest, she almost brought him to his knees; she was all he could hope for.

Until Heilbach stepped out from behind one of the trees.

"What?" Saint stammered.

"Sorry, lover boy. She's all mine," Heilbach said with a grin, while Elizabeth put her slim arm around Heilbach's wide waist. Saint's heart sank, as if it had been chained to an anchor and thrown into the depths of the sea.

"But, but..."

"But, but," Heilbach mimicked. "That's right, I'm putting you on your butt." He shoved Saint, who promptly fell backwards, indeed landing on his butt. Saint scampered back.

"Hey, hey. You can have her. No problem, I'm going."

"Not so fast, rat! We know all about what went down with

The Exterminator. And the only way that could have happened is if you're an informant!"

If Heilbach wasn't completely sure of that before, he was now. Saint realized the look on his face was a dead giveaway.

Heilbach grabbed his Glock, which had been tucked in his belt behind his back.

He had no intention of killing him; he didn't need cops after him for that. But he wanted to scare him... and beat the crap out of him—beat him as close to death as he could without actually killing him. Heilbach was a big believer in punishment as a deterrent.

Saint's eyes grew very wide as Heilbach pointed the gun at him.

91

Deja didn't trust him.

After she saw Saint sneak out of their house, she knew something was wrong. She'd decided to follow him, to make sure he wouldn't make more mistakes. To make sure he'd be safe.

The sun sank beneath the horizon, casting eerie shadows across the patchy grass. The air turned chilly, the colors of the surrounding forest replaced by muted tones of gray that whispered of impending darkness.

Deja's heart raced with a mixture of worry and determination as she peered through the trees, her eyes fixated on Saint. Her footsteps, muffled by the soft ground, brought her closer to the unfolding scene. A gust of wind howled, a mournful sound that sent shivers down her spine.

She saw Saint engaged in a tense confrontation with another man. The air grew charged with tension, like electricity crackling before a storm. Deja's pulse quickened, and her breath caught in her chest as she witnessed the conflict before her. It was as if time stood still, and her senses sharpened, absorbing every detail.

She saw a gun!

Her heart ached with a mix of fear and protectiveness, like a mother bear guarding her cub from harm. The man drew near Saint. Tears welled up in Deja's eyes, blurring her vision but heightening her emotions. The love she felt for her son, like the love she'd felt for Skyler, surged within her, fierce and unwavering. In that moment, the world around her faded into the background, and her sole focus became ensuring her son's safety and well-being.

With determination in her heart, Deja stepped forward, yelled, "Saint!" and charged onto the scene.

Heilbach jerked back as he heard it: out of nowhere came a scream shriller than Janet Leigh being stabbed in the shower. A figure was swiftly running toward him, looking like a psycho.

In the crazed confusion of the moment, Heilbach couldn't figure out what the hell was going on and pointed his gun toward the insane person rapidly approaching.

Deja ran as fast as she could toward them, arms pumping, puffs of dirt clouds kicking up under her feet, determined to save her son. Her eyes were wild, on fire.

She was yelling, "Not this time!"

In the split second, there was no way to tell if the approaching person had a weapon or not. Heilbach looked at Elizabeth. Elizabeth looked terrified. "Hon!" she yelled.

Heilbach put pressure on the trigger.

The figure was just about on them, not stopping, not slowing, about to smash into them. Yelling.

Saint reached out toward Heilbach's gun hand.

Heilbach pulled the trigger.

It was all so fast. Elizabeth screamed.

The blood started gushing immediately, like water from a broken dam. Heilbach and Elizabeth stared at the body on the ground.

"Goddamn it!" Heilbach screamed. They appeared shocked

by what had happened. He grabbed Elizabeth roughly by the arm and pulled her away. She looked back, then they took off, running away together as fast as they could. There was no looking back for Heilbach anymore.

Saint stood frozen. He slowly realized what had happened and fell to his knees over the dying Deja. He cradled her in his arms, disbelieving, tears streaming down his face, falling upon her resting place.

He watched as her labored breaths struggled out, each one a painful reminder of the precious moments slipping away. The weight of impending loss hung heavily in the air, suffocating his spirit.

"Mom, please don't leave me!" he cried.

Time seemed to slow down as Deja gazed back. In that fleeting moment, lifetimes of love, sacrifice, and unspoken words passed between them. She had been his guiding light as well as she could; now her light was fading.

The realization of her upcoming departure tore at Saint's soul. With her last gasping breaths, tears also in her green eyes, came a halting, "Love, you... forever. Next time..."

And then her eyes closed. She was gone in an instant, like the setting sun's evanescent green flash disappearing into the watery horizon.

Saint lifted his arms and head skyward. Tears streamed down his face, mingling with his anguish. The fragile thread of his being was unraveled. A guttural cry erupted from the depths of his soul.

"Nooooooo!"

92

I have such mixed emotions.

So much has happened. So much progress has been made. But my individual hobby, well, it's been a bit dormant. Need to wake it up. Shake things up. The thrill of the kill.

Some may think me crazy, having suffocated my sanity. Ha!

Yes, I must confront the demons that reside deep inside of me.

No. I must confront the demons residing outside of me!

93

The water beckoned. It was just beyond an aging gate.
The gate was open, and Saint walked through.

The weight of his loss settled upon his shoulders like an unyielding burden. His mother was gone, leaving him to navigate the darkness alone. The void she left behind was immense, engulfing him in a sea of sorrow.

He stood at the edge of the lake, barefoot, a constant wind pushing the water toward him. The internal battle between Saint and Diablo raged on. He couldn't stop thinking of Deja, desperate to hold on to the essence of her presence. He blamed himself for her death. Oh how he wanted to be with her again!

The evening sky was ablaze with hues of orange and pink, a stark contrast to the anguish that consumed his heart. The gentle breeze carried whispers of memories, stirring the leaves in the trees.

He thought of his life growing up without a father. A father whose life ended in the water. He wondered what it would have been like to have had his dad around to guide him. The thought of meeting him, of being with Skyler, was intoxicating. The movement of the water mirrored the turbulence within his soul. He gazed into its depths, feeling the weight of his sorrow pulling him deeper, tempting him to surrender.

He thought of Elizabeth, the only woman in his pitiful love

life, who had betrayed him and left him feeling like a dart had landed a bullseye in the center of his heart. He knew he'd never find a woman to share his life with.

He thought of a life without friends. Never had them. Tried, but never could, never would.

He thought of the authorities after him.

He thought of his future prospects—or rather, his lack of future prospects, in anything, anywhere.

In the depth of his depression, he knew down deep inside that the bonds of love transcend the boundaries of life and death.

Saint walked on the water.

It felt cold on the soles of his feet as he moved deeper in, the muddy bottom squishing between his toes.

He'd always had a natural aversion to any form of water: pools, beaches, lakes, ponds. No, he *hated* the water. But he soldiered on.

Up to his ankles, he looked ahead, saw nothing.

Saint streamed on, his knees drowning in the deeper water, then his thighs.

On he walked, his belly button below water, then his shoulders submerged. His neck was next.

As his mouth went under, there was an inscrutable smile playing on his lips.

94

Jill couldn't believe it.

Saint was gone. She felt a huge amount of guilt over this. Then the shock of losing Deja too was almost too much to bear. The capture of The Exterminator and prevention of a major bombing did little to assuage her pain. At times, she felt like she almost couldn't go on. At other times, more like her, she knew she needed to find Dirk immediately, and whoever else may be involved, no matter what it took.

Jill stared out the window, thinking back to her days on patrol, then becoming a detective. Have I really accomplished what I thought I would? she wondered. She thought back to her dad, the finest patrolman, the finest man, she'd ever known. Would he be proud of me?

The early memories never left her. Well, Patrolman Frank Jarred wouldn't give up, and I'm not giving up. Somehow, I'm going to get this guy. Get all these guys. Stop this killing, this madness! It had been a long and winding road, she reflected, and she still didn't know where it would lead. But she'd be in the lead in making things right.

"Lots to do," Jack said, which had become his most used expression.

They'd filled in Tracy and were discussing their next move.

"You know, with Deja dead, we should probably make a call on Gloria. With her history, our history, who knows what she'll do. Deja gone, Saint gone, Skyler long gone. She's all alone now. Who knows what this will do to her," Jill said.

"That's a good point. I hadn't thought of that. We need to keep an eye on her. But first we need to get ready for the FBI."

"Believe me, I haven't forgotten your FBI buddy! While we are dealing with these deaths, there's also those three deaths. A would-be rapist on a lonely road where a woman broke down, a man at Ponderosa Steakhouse, and a carjacker at a Gulf station," Jill said. "If it's not the guy Tracy took down, I don't want another killing while on the case."

"You got that right! And we haven't forgotten that murdered fifteen-year-old girl! Lots to do. Now that Tracy's convinced Klamp to bring in the FBI, I've called Doug Russler. He's made the arrangements and is on his way. Maybe he can stop the madness."

95

The meeting was raucous from the start.

After Sheriff Klamp and the others had agreed to bring in the FBI, a meeting was immediately set up. The day had arrived, and Klamp was totally intimidated by the guy from the FBI, Doug Russler. He started to think maybe he shouldn't have let Tracy talk him into bringing them into it. Bad enough he'd agreed to bring in the state. Russler's size, his commanding attitude, and his obvious intelligence left Klamp flustered and trying to assert his authority. He certainly didn't want to look bad in front of his deputy, the county authorities, and the others milling about.

It also annoyed him that Russler seemed to know Jack Ludlum and Jill Jarred, the State Bureau agents brought in. They had all been hanging out in the back of the room, matching self-satisfied smiles on their faces. Tracy was with them too, and he watched as Tracy said something to Jill, who laughed and patted her arm. No, he didn't like what he was seeing at all. He took in a deep breath as he rocked slightly in the corner. He felt like a first-grader on his first day of school. And he didn't like it.

Tracy walked to the front and made the official introductions. Sheriff Earl then moved forward and started to talk about the investigation, but Russler waved him off.

"Before we get started, I'd just like to say a few things, if you don't mind, Sheriff." The sheriff was a bit taken aback, but moved his right hand in a circle, palm facing up, giving him the floor.

"First of all, I want to thank you for inviting us to consult. And I want to assure you that this is your investigation. We will not step on any toes; we're just here to help, to advise as needed. We know you're all fine officers."

The others in the room looked around approvingly. There were even a couple of smiles. Sheriff Earl breathed a little easier. Russler continued, "Our value is often in linkage. We help to overcome linkage blindness, which is what most local departments unfortunately suffer from through no fault of their own. We have access to information on murders throughout the country, and with our insights, it's easier for us to find linkages from one murder to another. It's kind of like if you are on the ground, you can only see so much, but if you are up in an airplane, you can see much more."

"Now, we look for linkages in terms of the MO—for example, in your case, shooting from a distance. We also study victimology: what were the victim's risk factors, are there similarities in the type of victims chosen..."

"Well, obviously they were all Black men," Klamp said. "You know we got that big guy in jail, a nazi, so ya job is probably done before ya even start." Klamp's chest was puffed up, and he stood as tall as he could.

"Yes. Thanks, Sheriff—noted. But let me go on, please."

Klamp smiled and nodded.

"In investigating linkages, we also look for similar physical or sexual interactions—"

Klamp interrupted again, stating, "None here." Tracy kicked him.

Russler continued, ignoring him this time. "We look at

similar use of weapons and ammunition, cause of death, geographic locations, timing, and forensic results. We look through all this for linkages."

"Pretty basic," the county chief, Gil Gulim, exclaimed.

Russler shot him a look but smiled. "Yes sir, basic but productive. But the first thing we need to do here, today, is also fundamental... or basic," Russler said, shooting Gil a tight smile, "We need to make sure we are organized right."

Earl Klamp cleared his throat. "We are. We're all here."

"Yes you are, but let's make sure we have the right roles assigned. And let's make sure it's a tight team. When it comes to a good working task force, it should be relatively lean; too many personnel is often counterproductive." Russler said this while looking around the crowded room; everyone looked away and tried to make themselves small.

"Now, a well-organized team needs one lead agency: one person to be the leader. Since you called us in, I assume that will be me." Russler looked around the room and saw everyone nodding, except for Klamp, who just stared. Jack surveyed the room too, noting Klamp's reaction. Russler went on: "Now, for this area's representation on the task force, besides our representative from the local FBI office, I suggest that it be Deputy Tracy Dixon." Russler stood tall, waiting for a reaction. It didn't take long.

With that, Klamp turned white, then red, and scowled. "Now just one minute here." Russler must have known this would be coming, having been briefed on Klamp and Dixon, and doing a little investigating himself. His look said he saw Klamp as a caricature.

"Hold on, Sheriff, hold on. I know what you're going to say, and I've given it a lot of thought. You are just too important to be bothered with the nitty-gritty of this investigation. We need you out in front of the people, reassuring them that everything is under control. I know you're an ideas man, so let's not waste a resource like you on details."

The sheriff puffed out his chest again, and now with a slightly red face said, "I was just gonna say ah understand, Agent Russler, I truly do. Smart move. Very smart."

"Thank you, Sheriff. Now I know you've all been looking at these folks in the back of the room," Russler said, motioning his hand toward them, "wondering why they are here. Well, those are our fine detectives from the state, who of course are part of the team. They'll help keep us kosher."

Klamp narrowed his eyes at the mention.

"So the gentleman is Mr. Jack Ludlum. You know he's from the State Bureau. I happen to know him quite well: tough, and smarter than he looks," Russler said with a wink, "and a terrific background: military, cop on the beat, then continued movement through the ranks; he'll be a big asset. And dare I say, an equal asset, or maybe better," Russler said with a smile, "is Detective Jill Jarred. Also from SBI. Great instincts, smart as a whip. They always work as a team, and far be it from me to split them up."

"Is that it?" the county chief asked, looking agitated. "That's the task force?"

"No, no, no," Russler answered. "We need a few more roles on the task force. We'll need someone to be the official liaison with the victim's families: keep them updated on our progress."

"Those dead guys? Huh. If they have families, they're probably darn happy they're dead," Klamp said.

"Shush," Tracy said. "Everyone deserves a little respect. The Ponderosa Steakhouse shooting girlfriend was not very happy. I spent plenty of time with her. The vic was a fine man. And God forbid there is another shooting of another innocent, we need a point person with the family."

"She's right," Russler added, nodding his head and looking

at Tracy approvingly. "We need to ensure the families know we're doing everything possible to find the killer. Everything. And we definitely need to make sure family members don't talk to the media. Last thing we need is to end up with talking heads on TV spewing their own thoughts and theories, giving out misinformation, and causing a damn ruckus."

"And speaking of media, someone needs to be assigned as the key media liaison, and prepare daily briefings: for the media, and for patrol officers too."

"I'll be doing that," Klamp said, thinking of the re-election PR.

Russler looked at him, looked about to say no, then glanced at Tracy and Jack, and apparently changed his mind. "Right. Thank you. Now it's best to do this with an associate, just in case you can't make it one day due to other priorities."

"I don't think…" Klamp saw Russler furrowing his brow and crossing his arms. "Yeah, sure, I can tag-team it," he said, thinking he could easily outmaneuver a partner.

"Great." They assigned people to the other roles, and those without a position on the task force left the room. Slowly, dragging their heels.

"OK, now we can start talking about the investigation," Russler said.

"Jesus be praised," Klamp said under his breath, though loud enough for everyone to hear.

96

Gloria held the gun lovingly.

She needed something to do. Her "son" Skyler, gone. Deja, gone. Her "grandson" Saint, gone.

She'd bought the rifle at a gun show in a hotel ballroom. She paid cash, no I.D. asked for—in fact, no questions at all asked. Of course, no receipt given.

She actually wasn't sure why she bought it, or what she would do with it. Gloria tried to convince herself it was for self-defense. But a rifle? Deep down, though, on the edge of her subconscious, she had a gnawing suspicion that somehow, she needed revenge for her losses. She'd learned more in prison than any official would have wanted her to, and her education could now come in handy.

She'd taken shooting lessons at a local range. The instructor enthusiastically agreed with her when she said it's a dangerous world and people need to be able to defend themselves.

While clearing out Deja's house, she came across bullets in the back of Saint's closet. *A sign?* She'd slipped them in her pocket, not noticing until later the number *88* etched into each. She wondered why but had other things occupying her mind. Her rage was building, and she needed to quench it. Either on someone involved... or perhaps anyone.

97

"When it comes to serial killers, nothing may be as it seems. But let's start with some basics," Russler said, as people shifted in their seats.

"Don't think of the unsub as a crazy, as a person easily identifiable as a misfit in society. Some are. For sure. But the majority of serial killers, if that is indeed what we have here, are not reclusive social misfits. They often don't appear strange at all. They frequently blend in effortlessly. Some go to church regularly. They are often married. Some are trained in the military. I even know of one serial killer who was a Boy Scout leader. Apparently, a damn good one, too."

"Military isn't such a bad thing," Jack declared, staring at Russler.

"No, no, it's not. But for some, who are a bit off to begin with, it can further desensitize them to taking a human life. And they learn marksmanship. They even get praised for being a great shot, for killing."

Jill defused that discussion. "And speaking of them not appearing to be social misfits," she said, "I remember reading that there was one serial killer who was actually a contestant on The Dating Game!"

"Oh, shit!" Deputy Tracy inadvertently exclaimed. "Hope he wasn't picked."

"Well," Jill said, "he actually was. Of all the men this sweet, beautiful girl could have picked, she chose him—and at a time when he was halfway through killing the eight women he eventually murdered. Not sure what happened to her, though."

Tracy shuddered. "Wow. Point made. Anyone can be a killer," she said, looking at Sheriff Klamp but then quickly looking away.

Klamp shouted out, "It's obvious this shooter is a member of the Klan! Three men killed, all Black. We got our man. If you want, just round up anyone else in the Klan."

"Well, it's not so much the Klan anymore," Russler countered. "Yes, they are around, but it's now more about these new versions of white supremacists. And not so much skinheads now: those scary-looking dudes with shaved heads and tattoos all over, though you'll find them too. But now you can find clean-shaven guys who look like they are straight out of a university class. But underneath, these guys are full of venom, jealousy, and a feeling they've been cut out of the American dream—and will resort to violence to take back what they feel is their birthright."

"Full of venom? Full of shit if you ask me," Jack said.

"Klamp, you're wrong!" Gil Gulim shouted. "It's clearly not a prejudiced guy we need to look for. We're talking about bad dudes committing crimes in our area that have been taken out! Sure, we have to get him, but our shooter is a straight-up guy. Like a Charles Bronson in Death Wish, or what's his name… Bernie Goetz, on the New York City subways years ago trying to do people a favor."

Jack and Jill looked at each other, wide-eyed, alarmed. Russler's eyes looked skyward, and you could almost feel him counting to ten.

"Again, I point you to the Ponderosa Steakhouse killing—doesn't quite fit," Tracy said sarcastically.

Gil exploded like a warm can of soda. "He had a record!" Tracy just shook her head. It seemed the louder he spoke, the less sense he made.

"Ladies and gentlemen, I appreciate that everyone has their theories," Russler said, raising his voice, but remaining calm. "But there is a process, and it starts with facts. And stop saying 'he.' We haven't established if the shooter is a man or woman."

"Of cuss it's a man," Klamp stubbornly said.

"And why is that?" Russler countered.

"Cause it just is."

"Jesus!" Russler composed himself, and gently said, "What we need to do first is to take a step back and fill out all the information that currently exists on the three shootings, so that we can run a VICAP."

"What's that?"

"Violent Criminal Apprehension Program. You fill out a questionnaire. That will take some time; there's 188 questions," Russler said. "It gets submitted to our Investigative Support Unit, to help churn out a profile of the assailant, among other things."

"A computer is gonna give us the answer? Gimme a break," Klamp said.

"Well, not exactly, but it sure helps a lot. There's a lot of data in there that can model serial killer behavior into identifiable patterns."

Jack interjected, "From what I know, VICAP provides a computer analysis that may identify patterns that could link to other crimes he—sorry, or she—may have committed and provide a profile of the killer. Most serial killers have their own signature. It's not perfect, but VICAP can often identify the killer's race, age, social status, employment, intelligence, dress, and even the type of car he may drive, to help narrow the field of suspects."

Russler was smiling, like a dad proud of his son.

"Jesus," Tracy exclaimed. "You're talking about profiling, just like on the TV shows." Klamp chuckled, but Tracy quickly went on, red blotches appearing on her neck. "Actually, I know profiling is something that's been around for quite some time, even before the FBI's Profiler computer and the criminal investigative analysis you're talking about."

Having now regained her dignity, she spoke with more authority. "In fact, I remember reading that back in World War II, the OSS—which, Earl, was the precursor to the CIA—profiled Adolf Hitler. They did it so they could anticipate what decisions he might make under certain circumstances. It turned out to be pretty accurate, even to the prediction that Hitler would commit suicide if he lost the war."

Jack whistled, impressed, but then a look from Jill shut him up.

"I just ain't buying it," Klamp said. "Computers. Hitler. The whole damn alphabet soup! Then what the hell do they need us for?"

"I can guarantee you," Russler responded, giving Earl a hard, long stare, and enunciating every word, "that it's just not the computer. Every output is analyzed in-depth by human profilers. The computer program is a tool. A damn good one. But human intelligence, experience, insight, and even hunch, is what rounds it all out and really gives us, gives you, direction."

"The killer is a racist. Over and out!" Klamp yelled. "KKK Killer!"

"No, he's a damn do-gooder," Gil shouted back. "Avenging Angel!"

Russler watched them yelling back and forth and it was obvious they might come to blows. He stepped in between them and was inadvertently pushed and stumbled. After a moment, he straightened himself up, staring at them both. The room went deathly quiet, like the moment after someone is slapped.

In a very quiet voice, almost a whisper, Russler said, "Gentleman. Let's use the resources you, ahem, asked for, to do the work before we come to any conclusions: half-assed or real."

Jack looked up and Russler continued. "There'll be plenty of time for lively discussions later. Understood?"

Russler stared from Gil Gulim to Earl Klamp until they lowered their eyes in acquiescence. Then he looked over at Tracy, adjusting his tie. "Tracy, you take the lead on filling out the questionnaire. Let's target twenty-four hours from now to review before submitting it to VICAP."

Russler started walking out. He stopped and turned back.

"Just remember what I said. Evil can have an ordinary face."

98

It was past time to check on Gloria. When they did, Jack and Jill immediately noticed the difference.

The Gloria they knew from the parole hearings was very different now. This wasn't the woman Jill recalled; it was a new woman. Or perhaps back to the woman she was all those years ago. Jill had always believed in second chances; now she wasn't so sure.

Now that Saint and Deja were gone, Gloria seemed gone as well. Gloria claimed she led a quiet life, was addicted to TV cop shows, which Jack and Jill thought strange, given her background. She said she watched *CSI, Dexter, The Mentalist, Criminal Minds*, and others. They caught her once doing so on a visit as they peered in through the windows before knocking. She seemed mesmerized, a strange look in her eyes. It was just about the only time the scowl on Gloria's face was replaced by something even more foul.

Jack and Jill began watching Gloria a little closer and started making unannounced visits. But Gloria, who had seemed to act like a recluse, recusing herself from life, suddenly wasn't home all the time. *Where the hell could she have gone in that big old boat of a car?* Jack wondered.

99

"I'm not sure this makes any sense. We spoke to her already. This is just a waste of time if you ask me," Jack said.

"Let's talk to Gloria one more time," Jill said. I just have a weird feeling that she knows more than she's letting on. Saint might have told her more about Dirk; any little thing might help us find him."

"Your weird feelings again! I just think with everyone gone, she's gone a little batty. She must feel more imprisoned now than when she actually was in prison. And so what if she watches a lot of crime TV? What else is she going to do?"

"Hmmm. I know. But…" Jill said.

"Come on, let's get back to hunting Dirk from more reliable sources."

"We can do both. There's two of us, you know. At least for now."

Jack looked up sharply, then nodded his head back and forth. Then he said, under his breath, "Like I have a choice."

He was fully cognizant that he could make any man bend to his will, but when it came to Jill, he knew it was a lost cause; she was as firm as an oak tree. And it wasn't about the sex. Or just about the sex. She was smart, had great intuition, and was stubborn. Smarts, stubborn, sex: insurmountable.

★

Gloria still wasn't home.

They'd headed over to Gloria's house in the dark. It was eerily quiet as they knocked on the door. No answer after increasingly loud raps. Just a few small animals sent scurrying about the yard with the noise. An owl hooted close by. Apparently, Gloria wasn't home. Surprising they thought, for this hour of the evening.

Jill went around the back and gasped as a black bat swooped by. She exhaled as it headed back into the blackness. She stood before a ripped screen door, a shoddy sentinel to a thin, wooden door adorned with peeling paint and cracked windowpanes. The screen door screeched on its rusty hinge. Jill tried the rickety second door, and the painted-over brass knob turned slowly in her hand. She called Jack. "Should we have a look inside? I know that's not quite by the book."

"Hey, wouldn't be the first time detectives got an important lead in, how should I say, an unusual fashion."

Jill glanced around and shifted her weight from one foot to the other. "All right. Just this once."

They did a swift but thorough search, moving as silently as parents putting out presents on Christmas Eve. At one point, they heard a sound and were afraid Gloria was back. It was just the wind knocking a shutter around. They walked softly, wincing every time one of the old floorboards creaked. Every moan and groan of her home stopped them.

They found nothing out of the ordinary.

They were about to leave when Jill looked up at the mantelpiece. She saw a framed picture of Saint, taken with Gloria, most likely by Deja. It was leaning on a light-blue ceramic jar with a cork top.

"You don't think Saint's ashes are in there, do you?" Jack asked. "Never did find his body. Who knows with her."

"Let's take a look," Jill said, gingerly picking it up.

Uncorking the top, they both looked inside, almost butting heads.

"What the hell?"

There were no ashes. Just a dust-covered bullet.

"Don't touch," Jack whispered urgently. He grabbed a pencil and tried to get a better look as Jill pointed the flashlight beam into the jar. As Jack pushed the bullet around with the tip of the pencil, they both saw it.

"An 88! I think that's a nazi thing. Jesus."

100

The Exterminator couldn't stand being locked up.

His cell was small, the room mostly taken up by a hard, metal bed with a paper-thin mattress. He looked around at the gray paint peeling off the cinder-block walls, and the spider web in the top corner. He felt just like the insect caught in that web, the spider greedily eyeing it. He smelled the scent of stale body odor permeating the cell block from bodies that knew real life was over.

The one thing he was proud of was that he'd kept his mouth shut. He was interrogated numerous times in numerous places but didn't give a thing up. *I'm no rat*, he thought. He simply pleaded the fifth when given the third degree.

It was bad enough he didn't get to blow up that church, he thought, but now behind bars, he had no way to make the world a better place. *What a waste.*

He hadn't heard from any of his Very Fine Men. He knew they wouldn't have a clue what to do without him. They'd just be like cockroaches running in all directions when the lights go on.

He spent much of his time thinking of Heilbach, and the more he thought of him, the hotter his hatred grew. Heilbach, who tried to take over, who made fun of him in front of others. He's the one who should have been punished in his stead. He did, though, begrudgingly think that perhaps Heilbach was right. *Maybe they should have just sown terror by shooting the invaders one at a time, randomly, from a distance.*

He had to fulfill his mission, had to break out. *But how?* He slumped on his bunk, hands behind his head, eyes looking upward.

He spied the ventilation grate, loosely secured to the ceiling.

101

Heilbach couldn't get him out of his mind.

"Can't believe what a fuck-up that Exterminator was," he shouted to Elizabeth. "I told him not to do that damn church bombing. Now it's hotter than ever for me and my men. And that Dirk is just as bad. A killing right in the middle of our march—dumb!"

Elizabeth backed up; she didn't know what to say.

"Why the hell couldn't they just listen to me—shoot 'em from a distance? That's the way it ought to be!"

"Well, no one is as smart as you, Spencer," Elizabeth cooed.

"Damn right. Wish that Exterminator was dead. You know what they say about too many chefs!"

"Well," Elizabeth replied, "at least he's in prison."

The Exterminator stopped eating.

Actually ate less, but no one noticed. And certainly, no one cared. The guards had no clue he was losing weight. He knew he had to be skinnier to fit through the grate.

He was hungry all the time. His stomach growled. Roared. He began believing the shit they served in prison was the best food he'd ever had. He longed for it, dreamed about it, felt the pang of hunger pain like fangs of a snake digging in. But he believed the ends justified the means.

He trusted nothing.

Doug Russler had everything from the three killings re-examined, starting with the scenes of the crimes themselves. The day was chilly, with a gray sky above and a mist snaking around their ankles, as if trying to trip them up. Jack and Jill were among the team that relooked the sites, using a grid-search method: after searching in one direction, the searcher proceeds in a perpendicular direction. Doug had said at the onset, "Go find something. Make Locard proud."

Jack looked puzzled, while Jill had a slight smirk. Doug laughed.

"That's Edmond Locard, who espoused what is called Locard's Exchange Principle. It states that there is always an exchange of physical evidence, however minute or difficult to detect. So go find some."

"Thanks, Professor," Jack said with a smile.

It didn't take long before they happened upon a shot-up tree stump and called in the technician to dig out bullet fragments from it. Back in the lab, they soon matched the bullets to the bullet found inside the "pastor" rapist. Russler surmised that this meant the kill was probably the work of someone who was in the area practicing his shooting, as opposed to a premeditated murderer waiting to pick someone off along the road.

"Are you sure?" Jack asked.

"No. But I will tell you shooters can generally be divided into organized and disorganized killers," Russler told Jack and Jill. "In its simplest form, organized are premeditated and carefully planned, with little evidence usually found. Disorganized are not planned, just spur of the moment, often by psychopaths. If it ends up we are dealing with a serial killer here, or someone who got a taste of killing and wanted more, that would likely be a disorganized killer. But it's early days. We have a lot to learn."

"Come on, Doug, we know that stuff already," Jack said. Jill's eyes narrowed as she looked back at Jack.

"Yeah, but we have to remember to be real sure on each shooting to determine if they are connected," Doug said. "It's not just one or two situations; we now have three." He held up three fingers.

"Well, thanks again, Doug, but probably enough lessons for one day," Jack said.

"Hey, I'm happy to learn whatever I can from you, Doug. Just keep it coming," Jill said, smiling at him.

Jack shot her a look, while saying to Doug, "You can probably put your fingers down now."

The Exterminator felt confident.

He believed everything was in place, everything was thought through. He knew he'd be successful; his mission demanded it. He was thin and wiry to start with, but it took some time, and he'd finally lost just enough weight to feel he could squeeze through the grate.

Late that night, he put his plan in motion.

Just as he began, the metal legs of the bed screeched as he pushed it in place, the sound reverberating down the hall. *Shit!* he thought. He heard a guard start to get up from his desk at the security station. It was a ways away, so The Exterminator just had time to put things back to normal and feign sleep.

Well, tomorrow's another day. Fate has to go my way. Tomorrow, he thought.

102

*S*trange.

The bullets from all three shootings were re-examined. Russler had the resources of true professionals take another look, and what the forensic ballistic examiners came back with was perplexing.

He met with Jack and Jill in the parking lot of a diner, and the three sat on the tailgate of a pickup, drinking coffee. He wanted to get their reaction to his findings before he reviewed them with the rest of the team. The steam from the coffee spiraled upwards, like a little spirit heading to heaven.

Jill took a sip from her cardboard cup and almost spat it out. She made a face, saying, "Starbucks this ain't!" Jack, who always took his coffee black, and prided himself on having drunk some of the worst coffee in existence, said, "Thank God."

"First of all," Russler said, "the guy who tried to kill the judge—no match at all. No prints, but the gun, bullets, method of attack, everything we looked at and analyzed—I highly doubt he had anything to do with the other three killings. As to those three, it turns out we have a match, but not a full match."

Jack and Jill looked at each other.

"The first killing, of the fake pastor/real rapist, and the

third one—the one at the gas station attempted carjacking—are a match. What's strange though is the second shooting: the shooting of that poor guy at Ponderosa. Well, we couldn't tell for sure if it was a match. I like to think it's one hundred percent science, but sometimes it's not fully clear."

Jack blew on his coffee and looked away, before turning back. "So could there be different killers?"

A group of four locals came out of the diner, looked over their way, and rushed to their cars, like a gang running in different directions when the police showed up.

"Or a killer with multiple guns and ammunition?" Jill questioned. She looked like she thought her suggestion was better. She stared directly in Russler's eyes, apparently seeking approval.

Russler looked back and forth between the two of them, and said, "Yes."

"Yes?" they both asked in unison.

"Yes. We'll keep all hypotheses open for now. Still more to learn. Could still be all three were the same shooter. But could be two people working together. That's happened before."

"I know, early days," Jack said, shaking his head.

Russler looked at him, disappointed. "This ain't Special Ops anymore, Jack. There's no mission to carry out swiftly and get the hell out. We need to take our time and execute properly."

"Not while people are being executed," Jack said.

Full of dust, The Exterminator squeezed through on his hands and knees, barely making it. He followed the dark duct, stopping once when he sneezed. He held his breath, heard nothing, and continued on, sweat dripping into his eyes. He came upon an opening and peered in. It wasn't another cell, and the room appeared empty. He waited an extra moment to be sure, then came down into what must have been one of the jailer's apartments. Once there, he quickly put on civilian clothes, grabbed a pack of Drake's Devil Dogs left on the counter, stuffed it in his pocket, and escaped into the night.

The guard rattled the bars, yelling it was time to get up. He was a human alarm clock that took no prisoners; everyone would get up immediately or suffer the consequences. When The Exterminator wouldn't move, the guard pushed into the cell, his heavy-duty flashlight thrust above his head. He pulled the covers down and saw pillows and clothing arranged in lumps like a body. But the body was gone. Gone guy. Escape 101. He frantically rang the alarm, dropping his flashlight as he fumbled for it, his face red and beads of sweat running down the sides of his head, but it was too late.

The guard looked up at the open ceiling grate and knew somehow, he'd gotten through. "Just like in the movies," he'd commented afterwards.

The Exterminator had no plan. No one helping him. No money. Nothing. But he was free. And he felt invincible. Taking back leadership and fulfilling the mission was now his life's work.

He ran straight to the mountains. Mountains where he felt most at home. Mountains where he could think, where he could plan his next move. Mountains where his rifles and special ammunition lay buried.

103

"Goddamn it, Earl!"

Russler had met with Tracy and Klamp to review the results of the judge's shooting. There was nothing to connect that one to the other shootings, he'd said, not without regret.

"Totally different MO. Close range versus far away, pistol versus rifle, nothing to connect the bullets, out in the open versus hidden. Nothing. I'm sure this was a totally different thing," Doug said.

"Goddamn it, Earl! I told you not to have that press conference," Tracy said. "You just gave a false impression and now the department looks dumb!"

"Oh, pshaw."

"I'm just glad I didn't participate in it!"

"Listen, Russler," Earl said, pointing his finger and raising his voice. "I'm told ya said it's not one hundred percent science!"

"The science isn't one hundred percent sure one hundred percent of the time," Russler said, staring him in the eye. "But it's pretty clear-cut in this case."

"I jus' don't believe it."

"Look," Doug said. "It's probably a copycat killing. Happens more than you'd think. We know this guy was a white supremacist. He saw the headlines of Black men being killed, and given his personal vendetta, probably thought he could get away with it, maybe blame it on someone else."

"I know copycat crimes have been around a long time," Tracy said.

"Oh yeah," Russler said. "And these days, we see a lot of copycat murders based on movies and videos. They kind of teach some crazies what to do."

"Well, ahm sure there ain't no serial killa copycats!"

"There sure have been," Russler said, moving into the professorial role he loved. "You've heard of the Zodiac killer, out in California? Well, years later, in New York City, there was another serial killer. While he was only a kid when the Zodiac was active, he left the same type of signs and cryptic notes for the cops."

"Well, we ain't in New York City, thank God," Klamp said.

"But why copycat a murder style?" Tracy asked.

"There are lots of theories. I believe they mimic a prior killer to reduce their inhibitions, create some psychological distance from what they are about to do," Russler said, speaking clearly and confidently.

Tracy bit her lower lip while looking sideways, then said, "I bet the killer thrives on the attention and publicity the original crime got. Thinks doing the same thing will get more attention."

"That's exactly right in many cases," Russler said, standing tall.

"Ah still don't believe it," Klamp said.

"Well, that guy is in custody. If you're right, Earl, there sure as hell better not be another killing," Tracy said.

Typical male, Jill thought, sighing. *Actually*, stereotypical.

Jack's dirty clothes were strewn on the floor. Near, but none actually in the hamper, like a last-place team that missed all its shots. She knew he hurried to get his clothes off last night, though missing the hamper was nothing new.

As she picked up his pants, something came tumbling out of the pockets. She heard a clink and thought it was some change. It wasn't.

Bullets.

"Jack? What's up with this?"

He reached for the bullets, but she grabbed them first. Jill took a closer look and saw *88* etched onto each.

"What the hell?"

"I picked those up at Gloria's, remember? Taking them to a better place for safekeeping."

Jill paused. She handed them to Jack, almost throwing them as they felt as hot as a firebrand in her hand.

She remembered one bullet. Not multiple.

104

The moon hung high in the ink-black sky, casting its ethereal glow upon the solitary figure standing below.

A gust of wind rustled through his hair, carrying with it a sense of anticipation and purpose. The Exterminator felt he'd been away for too long. But now, as he stood alone on the hill, his foolish mind ablaze with determination, he knew he had been destined to reclaim his position of leadership and guide his men toward the completion of their mission. *I'm the one to get it done*, he thought.

While he wasn't away that long, to him, it had felt like an eternity. And it was enough time for many of his men to disperse, lost in a sea of uncertainty. Some just disappeared, like smoke in the wind, while some turncoats went to Heilbach's group. His hatred for Heilbach heightened; he vowed to get his men back. He felt himself a phoenix, rising from the ashes, and like the phoenix, he felt he had the power to return to his former glory, to ignite the flames of their shared purpose and complete the story.

He put the word out that he was back in business, ready to lead.

"Destiny calls," he murmured to himself, his voice resolute, carried away by the night breeze. "I am the one to lead them, to finish it. By the blood and soil of my brethren, I swear I will get it done."

105

A task-force meeting was called; slow but steady progress was being made. One hoped the shooter wasn't moving any faster.

Russler reviewed the results of the re-examination of the shooting sites, updated status and next steps, and handed out numerous assignments. Then he gave them some information about serial killers. "If it ends up we do have a serial killer here," Russler said, "you should know that most serial killers are white men, in their twenties or thirties, though if not captured, it's possible that they continue to kill into their sixties before they tire of it. Or die. Women actually make up only sixteen percent of all killers."

Jack and Jill looked at each other, likely thinking of Gloria.

"What turns human beings into killers to begin with?" Tracy asked.

"Well, that's a long story," Russler said. "What I would say is that a killing gene hasn't been identified. But there certainly are some factors that could push a person in that direction. For instance, the absence of human bonding. Infants deprived of human attention and touch can actually begin developing psychopathic tendencies by two years of age. Two years! They find it hard to develop the span of human emotions, such as empathy, sympathy, remorse, or love. Especially love."

Jack thought about himself, abandoned at the doorstep of a firehouse as a baby, years shuttling through foster care before ending up with an abusive father and mother with mental health issues. His face remained impassive; he said nothing.

Russler, looking over his captivated audience, continued. "Another common factor is that as children, they usually had few or often no friends. This isolation leaves them with plenty of time on their hands, plenty of time to develop a fantasy world. As they get older, their fantasies grow increasingly violent, increasingly about revenge and a desire to have power over others."

"Yikes. How violent do they get early on?" Tracy asked.

"Well, often around ten, they start with killing animals."

"OK, so no bonding as an infant, no friends growing up," Sheriff Klamp said. "Poor me. Come on, lots of people grow up like that! But almost no one growing up like that becomes a serial killer. That's just BS." Klamp crushed his paper coffee cup in his hand and threw it toward the wastebasket. He missed the mark.

"Well actually, unofficial estimates conclude there are as many as two thousand people walking around who are, were, or will become serial killers. Could be in anyone's neighborhood right now. Could even be in this room."

Jill and Tracy exchanged a nervous glance.

106

The moon cast a dull, ghostly radiance over my darkened room, just like I like it.

I must admit, I smiled as I looked back at the newspaper open on the desk. A big smile.

I *love* being back in the news!

FBI brought in! Yes! I knew I was hot shit. It's just been too long. But now I'm happy. Starting now, the hunter will become the hunted.

That FBI head—that Black man—seems so sure of himself. A chill thrill coursed through my veins. What a target! Perhaps a game of cat and mouse first.

I love games.

I know that in order to truly complete my masterpiece, I have to strike at the heart of the investigation, at *all* those who might impede me. That FBI man leading the investigation, the emblem of authority and self-righteousness, will be my prime target, of course. He's the embodiment of the opposition I so vehemently despise. Some may pretend to like him; I know the truth. And if others get in the way and need to be killed, so be it. We're at war.

Of course, there will be those special ones; the thrill of the kill stands before me.

I threw down my half-eaten burger from White Castle. The scene has been set, the battle lines drawn.

Time for my dance with destiny.

107

The Exterminator was pissed.

He couldn't find Saint but was able to get a few of his crew back: the ones who hadn't moved to Heilbach. He was happy he got many key men to return—Slayer, Viktor, and Sarge—but pissed off that they hadn't progressed his cause at all while he was away.

A wicked smile played on his lips as he stood in the dimly lit room and addressed his small group of men, like a cult leader directing his dimwitted disciples.

"There's a group of illegal immigrants passing through here, stuffed inside a big old truck. I say we grab it."

"What are we going to do with them?" Slayer asked.

"We can drive that truck right back where it came from. Or maybe hold on to them, put them in the old body shop next door."

"Great name," Sarge said, clapping his hands. "And that place has been abandoned for a long time."

"You bet," The Exterminator said.

"Why would we keep them? We can't do anything with them," one man asked.

"Who knows? Drive them back, keep them. Whatever. We'll figure it out," The Exterminator said.

Some of the men looked uncertain, as if their GPS had stopped working. But they all acquiesced, as no one possessed the fortitude to fight The Exterminator.

108

"Incompetent jerks! I can't believe The Exterminator is loose again. Goddamn it!" Jack yelled.

"I know, I know. But never give up," Jill said. "Second time's a charm."

"How can you be so calm about it?" Jack thought for a moment. "That must be something Patrolman Frank Jarred would have said."

"That's now what I say. Let's put The Exterminator at the top of the list and go."

Jack felt his thigh, which still throbbed whenever he thought of a certain someone.

"It's crowded at the top."

Jill was first to figure it out.

She'd prowled around the dark web for supremacist activity, and clues to where The Exterminator might be. It took a while, but deep within the chatter, she uncovered some boasting and hints at plans being made that seemed like they could relate to The Exterminator. She put together a lot of bits and pieces, like an archaeologist with fragments at a tomb, then went to discuss it with Jack.

Before Jill could say anything, Jack could see the look on her face.

"Your instincts again?"

"My instincts again. I smell The Exterminator plotting something. A lot of code phrases being used, but it seems to involve a truck, and refugees."

Jill filled him in on all the information she'd gleaned from the web.

"Doug would be OK with us diverting our attention from the main search to get this guy, right?" Jack said.

"Of course, Jack, this could all be part of the same thing! This could be the main search! Hell, he tried to blow up a church; he's certainly capable of killing people with a rifle!"

"Yup. Let's go!"

From there, they worked the case relentlessly, like marathon runners refusing to stop even when barely able to put another foot forward. They went with little sleep, delving doggedly into dozens more deep, dark web chats and following up on a diverse set of leads. Jack leaned hard on the snitches. Finally, they got what seemed like a breakthrough: information about an abandoned body shop.

109

“This is it, Jack; I can feel it.”

The auto body shop stood as a decrepit fortress, its walls echoing with its dingy past. The clouded night sky made it hard to see. The scent of rancid motor oil, rust, and rat remains was revolting.

They hoped they were there in time. Cautiously, they moved beside a shed when they spotted three men in a dimly lit outer room of the shop. Shadows danced like demons from forgotten nightmares.

“That fucking Exterminator. There he is,” Jack hissed.
“Let’s call for back-up,” Jill whispered.

“You know there’s no time for that. And you know we are more than capable of dealing with just a few wingnuts.”

“I don’t know, Jack.”

They heard what sounded like a scream coming from within. They drew their guns. Jack used his fingers for a count of three. On three, they knocked the doors open.

The men were taken by surprise. But neither Jack nor Jill saw Slayer behind the door. He quickly got Jill in a choke hold, her gun falling away.

Jack pointed his own gun at Slayer.

“Choke holds kill. So drop your damn gun or she’s a goner.”

Jack knew those words to be true. He looked back at Jill,

who was shaking her head no. He looked at the other three men, knowing he was outnumbered. Jack dropped his gun.

The moment he dropped his gun, Slayer pushed Jill to the floor and reached for her gun. Mistake. Jack, with a look of determination in his eyes, wheeled around and kicked him in the head, sending him down like a bowling pin hit with a strike. He was knocked out.

Jack's movements were fluid and precise, his body a symphony of controlled aggression. His next target, Viktor, charged him, lunging forward with lightning speed, throwing a barrage of rapid punches. Jack evaded most, ducking and weaving, like a matador deftly avoiding the horns of a raging bull. With a sudden burst of power, Jack countered, rearing back his fist, striking with calculated precision, using Viktor's size and momentum against him. The strike landed with thunderous effect, breaking Viktor's nose, sending shockwaves through the room as the crunch sounded. Jack's punch sent Viktor reeling back, and he fell to the ground. The fight then completely left him, like a marionette whose strings were severed.

Jill was already on Sarge, who was trying to escape and slipped on Slayer in the midst of the mayhem. Jill got handcuffs on him, while Jack reared back, about to slam him, when he saw the look in Jill's eyes, which stopped him. He nodded and turned back.

Meanwhile, The Exterminator was running toward the gun that Jack had dropped.

Jack's senses sharpened; his focus intensified.

He summoned a reserve of strength and determination, and rushed at him. The Exterminator picked up the gun. Jack jumped toward him, flying through the air in a single bound like Superman. But he wasn't as fast as the speeding bullet. While the bullet just missed him, it hit Jill.

The Exterminator or Jill?

It was hardly a choice. Jack watched The Exterminator bolt out while Jill lay bleeding. Jack listened to the trailing scream of, "You haven't heard the last of me," as he listened to his heart and raced over to Jill.

He ripped Sarge's shirt off and used it to staunch the bleeding, while he got his cell phone out. The screen was cracked, but the phone was working as he called for backup and an ambulance.

"I love you," he said, tears in his eyes.

"Forever," Jill said.

"Forever," Jack said.

110

Heilbach cleaned his Bushmaster XM-15.

He applied solvent to the chamber, then gently inserted the brush. He turned it a few times, then took it out, reapplied solvent, and went again. He then used wet patches to flush the chamber and finished with a dry patch. Heilbach then inserted the rod guide to start cleaning the bore. He wet the bore, then soaked a bronze brush, gave the bore another two passes, and let it sit. Heilbach then cleaned and lubricated the bolt carrier group. He finished cleaning the bore, inspected everything, and assembled the rifle.

He buffed his bullets: the special ones. He'd loved the idea of 88 etched in, borrowed it for his bullets, the singular slugs sublime.

There, ready, he thought.

III

"It felt like a red-hot poker pierced my flesh."

That was Jill describing the bullet piercing her arm.

"Sounds a lot worse than all those years ago when you got hit," Jack said.

"Hell, that was a simple flesh wound. This time, it really got my arm; why do you think it was hanging limp like that? And every movement, even the slightest twitch, simply ignited fresh waves of pain."

"I know, honey, I know. Had that knife in my thigh not so long ago."

"Well, mine felt like shards of glass grinding against the nerve. How about yours?"

Jack looked back at her, thinking hell yes, it felt that way too, but simply said, "You're one tough cookie," and kissed her on the shoulder. "At least you'll get some rest. Have that arm in a sling for some time."

"Rest? With everything going on? No way! And hey, it's not my shooting arm that bullet pierced. With one arm, I can still take down the bad guys."

Jack looked down at her, a knowing smile on his face. "I have no doubt."

"Hey, I'm just a girl," Jill said, with a mischievous grin. "But seriously, I'm thrilled those assholes, Slayer, Viktor, and Sarge will be in prison for a long, long time. But I can't believe that Exterminator got away again!"

"Well, I have no doubt I'll get him. Ultimately, he can't hide. And I know I've been restraining myself..." Jill gave him an eye. "A bit better. But what he wanted to do to those poor people. Goddamn Exterminator! And he shot you, Jill. *He shot you*. When I catch up with him, I'll shoot him. I swear, Jill, I'll kill him."

112

Killed.
The Exterminator executed. Extinguished, an extreme surprise to him. After his extraordinary escape from jail, the authorities had had few leads. Similarly, his exit from the body shop left no tracks, no trace: yet another great escape. He seemed to simply vanish, as if abducted by aliens and exported to another planet.

But someone had kept track of him.

They found his body beside a trash dumpster in a White Castle hamburger joint parking lot. Earlier, he had been seen inside, gesturing madly, shouting about illegal aliens not bothering to change the oil in the fryers. Now, his blood mixed with oil stains on the pitch-black asphalt surface. A rat rummaged nearby, smelling its own kind, wondering whether to approach the strange new arrival, its whiskers twitching wildly.

There was only one wound in his body, so it was thought to be a close-range shooting by someone who had finally had enough of his rabid rantings. Even though he was killed in the general geography of the shootings the FBI task force was investigating, this one appeared different. The first cops on the scene looked at the dead man's clothing—old, worn and torn—the filth on his face and open cuts on his heinous hands, and it was obvious they didn't think he was someone who would be missed.

But Sheriff's Deputy Tracy Dixon appeared on site and made them hold off on anything besides securing the crime scene until she could make some phone calls. Soon enough, they began a proper investigation. When they ultimately checked his fingerprints and found out he was a wanted man—James Dylan, aka The Exterminator, who had escaped from prison, and shot Jill—Tracy felt gratified her instincts hadn't let her down.

When the investigation further found that the wound was caused by a single bullet entering the lung from quite a distance away, the authorities became electrified, thinking that it was connected to the other serial-killer shootings.

Tracy apprised Sheriff Klamp on the latest information, and his reaction was swift.

"A white guy got himself killt? Now that's different. Proves I's right!"

"How so? With this curveball, we now know less about the shooter than before."

"I told ya the guy that tried to do the judge did tha others. He wouldn't kill a white guy. This must be unrelated. We got our killer in jail. Let's see what this fancy FBI man and his computer have to say now." Klamp had a self-satisfied smile on his face, like he'd aced his final exam.

"Well, the one thing I agree with is let's see what the FBI does come up with."

Klamp gave Tracy a look as if she must have a low IQ. "We should've never called them in. They've just put the whole town on edge. I don't know why I listen to you, woman."

"Earl?"

"What?"

"Shut up."

113

*G*od, *I'm good*, the killer thought.

   Just needed one shot to take him down. Wow. Guess the old saying is right: practice makes perfect.

The shooter got his things together.

All right, who's next?

Lots to do.

114

"Makes no sense," Jill said, scratching her head.

She was seated around a small table with Jack and Doug. They were in Doug's hotel room, which had little price tags affixed to the "art" on the walls, a bathroom sink faucet that continually dripped onto a water stain, and a view of a brick wall two feet outside the window. Jill sniffled at the musty odor. But the room was neat as could be. Jack knew Doug was extremely organized and tidy; he probably cleaned up the room right after the cleaning crew left.

Russler said he was surprised they found only one bullet: the one lodged in The Exterminator. Apparently, the shooter was getting more skilled. And there were similarities in the bullets with this killing and the others, he said, without going into any detail.

"The mystery, of course, is why for the first time was a white guy killed?"

Jill said it made no sense. "Especially that this specific white guy—The Exterminator—should be the last one who should be killed in a similar manner, a manner used to kill Black men before, given he was so big in the white supremacist movement." She gave Jack a piercing look.

"That's what we need to figure out," Russler responded. He looked over at the painting on the wall, depicting Native

Americans doing a circular dance. He hoped the investigation would not be going in circles too.

"Maybe an internal war among them—battle for leadership?" Jack offered.

Doug nodded his head. "That could be. But we have some more information coming in soon, and I'll need to brief the entire task force, and then we will need to brief the press. But let's make sure we keep our theories to ourselves. Let's be brief and keep to just the facts, especially with the press."

"Well, at least that one's dead," Jill said, looking at her sling. "I hope he comes back in his next life as the cockroach that he is."

"He sure as shit ain't a love bug," Jack muttered.

The media went nuts with the news of a fourth killing. They alarmed the people to no end, each new headline more inflammatory than the last. They insinuated that all the killings were connected and no one was safe. Some called for an initiative to recall Klamp, especially given his press conference that previously proclaimed the murder spree to be over.

Serial Killer on the Loose, screamed one headline. Stay Inside! shouted another. People were afraid. Schools canceled outdoor recess and outdoor sports activities for their students. Traffic to fast-food restaurants was down by sixty percent. Ponderosa Steakhouse was thinking of closing. And anyone pumping gas did so as quickly as possible, usually waiting in the car while the gas automatically pumped. Overall, people kept to themselves and stayed inside, as if they were living through a pandemic.

The police spent their full overtime budget with extra patrols and shifts. Everyone was looked upon with suspicion, and there were random checks on the roads, often stalling traffic for a long time. They received many tips on their hotline, but none were valid—and some seemed to be called in just to put suspicion on neighbors or associates that were not liked.

But they never saw the shooter.

I saw them.

115

The task force meeting didn't go well.

"VICAP, NIBIN, BSS, all your acronyms and we are nowhere!" Spittle spewed from County Chief Gil Gulim's mouth as he shouted at Russler. "NWH!"

They had assembled the task force in the briefing room, Doug at the podium. The gray walls mirrored the gray faces creased with worry, feet and fingers tapping unconsciously. Since the last murder, everyone felt as if an anvil were on their chests, the media hounding them hourly for answers that weren't coming. Each day passing meant another day of frustration—and potentially a day closer to yet another killing.

Unlike most of the attendees wearing shirts open at the collar, sleeves rolled up, Doug Russler looked pristine. A starched white shirt with tightly knotted tie, a pressed suit with deep creases, shoes shining almost as if they were patent leather; he looked as if he'd walked out of a Brooks Brothers ad. While he'd probably never admit it, he looked like he considered style a long suit.

"OK, OK, everyone, let's calm down. I know everyone is on edge, the media has been non-stop hysteria central, but we *are* making progress. We'll make more if we can keep this team together."

"Well, what do we have? Anything?" Gil asked, his arms folded over his chest.

"Of course we do. OK, let's review. From the beginning."

Jack rolled his eyes.

"There are signs pointing to the very high likelihood we are in fact dealing with a serial killer," Doug began. "So you were right to call us in." Tracy looked at Sheriff Klamp, who looked back with a curled lip and crossed arms. "This one is a little different, though. The most common driving force of serial murder is sexual control and dominance. Obviously not the case here."

"Obviously," Klamp said. People turned their heads toward him, but quickly looked back to Russler, who ignored the remark and continued on.

Klamp stuck out his chin, still not giving in. Russler stared directly at Klamp. "But besides sexual dominance, there are other reasons for the behavior, in fact, other factors that could have been at play back in the development of the serial killer. For example, many had traumatic childhoods. Psychological abuse, physical abuse, even sexual abuse. Some constantly bore witness to violence. Grow up with that, and maybe it seems normal. Then it's right around puberty when this conditioning manifests itself into fantasies. Fantasies against other living things, to be precise."

"How about physical trauma causing the brain to go haywire?" Jack asked, then unconsciously put his hands in his pockets.

"Well, head injuries—brain injuries, have been evident in many serial killers. But it's probably more the other factors, especially the psychological. Even simple things could make a difference, like parents punishing their kids by hitting, while saying things like, 'It hurts me more than you.' It can give the wrong impression about proper social behavior."

"Or, 'It's for your own good,'" Tracy volunteered, before turning red and looking down.

"True," Russler said. "And then from there, it's a matter of facilitators, and the big trigger."

"Facilitators?" Jill asked.

"They are the lubricants, the things that ease the killer on his way to the first kill."

"You mean, like alcohol? Drugs, perhaps?" Jill ventured, looking a bit uncertain.

"Exactly. Anything that lowers inhibitions. Facilitators can also be things that fuel or reinforce existing fantasies or provide a bogus reason to take action. People will seek things online that support their feelings and beliefs: hateful things. Offline too—some even pick phrases or scenes out of the Bible as a justification for their actions against others."

Most in the group were nodding their heads affirmatively.

"Pornography?" Jack asked.

Sheriff Klamp looked away, his ears turning red. Tracy stared at him with a knowing look.

"That's controversial. Could be a facilitator according to some; other studies say not so much."

"And how about triggers; you mentioned that earlier. What's the difference between a facilitator and a trigger?" Tracy asked.

"Right. Well, the facilitators ease him into it. They get him closer to realizing his fantasies, opening him up to it, like some grease on a squeaky sliding door. But often there is a trigger that finally pushes the killer over the edge. It's frequently a key event, or combination of stressors in daily life. A lost job. A relationship breakup. Major indebtedness, a foreclosure on a home. That sort of stuff. Things that make him feel sorry for himself, make him want to take revenge on the world that treated him, in his mind, unfairly."

"Jesus. I don't think it's all that complicated. They're just evil," Jack said.

"Well, maybe. Maybe for some, that's it. And the truth is, overall, there isn't one formula that ends up making a serial killer. It's a complex concoction. Biological, environmental, and social elements are all mashed up in a blended brew to create a monster. And when they kill, it's no different for them than stepping on a bug is for you."

Tracy shuddered. "Maybe we should take a break, get some fresh air," she suggested.

"Maybe we should finally get to the point!" Chief Gulim said.

"Hear, hear," Klamp agreed, raising a fist in the air.

"Fair enough," Russler responded. "Let's do both: take a very quick break, then let's get to it. I think you have enough background now for what needs to be done."

Half the group headed to the bathroom, the rest outside: some to smoke, others to just complain about Klamp. One or two muttered negative things about Russler wasting their time.

116

I was stopped by the cops!

    I was heading out to do more work when I saw the police car in my rearview mirror. *Shit, it looks like it's following my Mercury Marauder.* My eyes darted between looking at the road ahead to the car behind, eventually keeping one eye on the rearview mirror all the time. Maybe I was being paranoid. I clung on to a faint hope that I wasn't being followed. I checked the speedometer frequently, keeping below the speed limit. But when the sound of the patrol car's siren blasted, I had to make a decision.

I made my decision.

I slowly and carefully stopped my car and played it cool. The patrol car drifted to a stop close behind. After a few interminable minutes, the officer came out of his car and walked unhurriedly to my side.

"Afternoon, Officer."

"Do you know why I stopped you?"

I thought about the gun hidden in the car.

"I don't believe I was speeding, sir."

"You weren't."

The police officer stared at me. I felt my leg moving up and down in a rhythm, as if working a drum set. It appeared that the police officer noticed as well. Said nothing.

"Did I miss a stop sign? I'm usually very careful."

"No, no you didn't."

I looked back at the police officer, trying to smile, wearing an expectant look. I moved my hand closer to where the gun was hidden. Thankfully, the officer didn't notice this.

"Looks like your tail light is out."

I moved my hand away from where the gun was hidden. *Jesus*! I exhaled just a bit, and my whole body relaxed some, relieved that such a trite situation had caused the stop—though I was not fully at ease yet.

"Oh my God, thank you, Officer. It's always something with this old clunker. Wish I could afford something new, but for now, it's all I can do to keep it running."

"I get it, I get it. Just make sure it's fixed this week. Probably just needs a new bulb. No big deal. But the next officer who stops you might give you a bit of trouble. Not everyone is as nice as me," the officer said with a chuckle.

With that, the officer got back in his car, slammed the door with a thud, and took off, waving as he passed me.

As the officer drove by, he noticed a hole by the car's trunk. Damn, *that is an old clunker*! he thought. *Hope that hole doesn't cause any further problems.*

117

B ack in the task force room, the natives were restless.
When they got back after the brief break, Jill said, "Hey,
just one more thing. Can these monsters be rehabilitated?"

Klamp slapped his hand to the side of his head. Russler
looked around the room. Jack shrugged his shoulders.

"OK," Doug said, "but just that. All the evidence says no.
I'll give you an example. Peter Woodcock."

"Keep it short," a lieutenant named Greg said.

"In his childhood, Woodcock was moved through many
foster homes and was often bullied. Later, his reaction was to
molest and kill children. He was caught, found not guilty by
reason of insanity, and sent to a psychiatric facility."

"Well, thirty-four years of treatment passed, and he was
declared rehabilitated. He was given a pass for a few hours to
become acclimated to the outside world. Within his first hour
of release, he got a pipe wrench and smashed it on a guy's
head, striking him until dead. Afterwards, he simply walked to
the local police station and turned himself in."

Tracy spilled her coffee all over and rushed to grab some
paper towels. "Shit!"

"Jesus, one hour," Jack said. "That's why, sometimes, you
can't show any mercy at all with these guys." He clenched then
opened his fists several times. Jill gave him a look.

"That's all very interesting," Gil said. "But can we get back to our specific guy: what the thinking is here."

Russler looked at Gil, nodding his head yes, happy to be moving on. "Well, again, we think it's a male: a white guy in his twenties or thirties. And as I said, sex is not a motivator. And he's also not a 'visionary killer,' which is what we call someone suffering psychotic breaks from reality."

"You mean like Son of Sam, who claimed to be commanded by his neighbor's dog?" Tracy asked as she threw the wet paper towels away.

"That's right. A lot of visionary killers will say the Devil, or God, made them do it. But we're not dealing with that here."

"Then what the hell are we dealing with?" Gil interrupted.

Russler stared him down, this time unsmiling, and continued in a deep voice. "He's not a 'thrill killer,' or what we call a 'hedonistic killer.' I won't bore you with those definitions."

"Praise the Lord," Klamp said.

"Wouldn't bore me at all," Jill countered.

Klamp and Gil eyed her as if they wanted to kill her.

"We really have to move on, but I'll give you a quick example. A thrill killer gets real excited by inflicting pain and terror. There was this one guy who got a real adrenaline rush from abducting his victims and taking them to secluded woods. To their surprise, he would then let them go. But only so that he could then hunt them down and kill them."

"Shit," Klamp said, a little more interested. He was a hunter himself.

"Ouch. I think I've learned enough," Tracy said softly.

"Anyway, to get back to our situation…"

"Yeah!" Gil exclaimed, in a mock cheer.

"The shooter is likely a 'mission-oriented' killer. After our analysis, we don't think 'Avenging Angel,' as the media call it, is the motivation. We think anger coupled with ideology is the motivator. Anger as the unsub displays his hostility to a certain group of people, with—"

"Shit, I told ya so. He's killing Black people. He's the 'KKK Killer!'" Klamp yelled, then spat into his dirty handkerchief.

"With the ideology of furthering the goals and ideas of a specific group," Russler continued. "The members of that group are united in their failure to accept personal responsibility for where they are in life. They just blame others."

"Or they're just plain evil," Jack put in.

"White supremacists certainly fit the bill of what you are talking about, Agent Russler," Jill said.

"Yes," Russler went on. "Mission-oriented killers justify their acts by, in their minds, ridding the world of certain types of people they consider undesirable. For example, here they may see the killing of immigrants, actually probably all minorities, as curing society's ills. The idiots see it as getting rid of murderers and rapists, and people who they believe will unfairly take away their jobs, live off their tax dollars."

"Such stupid jerks!" Tracy said, with just about everyone in the room shaking their heads. "So we need to focus our efforts on finding white supremacists in this area?"

Jack and Jill looked at each other. Jack unconsciously put his hand over the wound area on his leg where he had been knifed. As they were about to speak up, Gil Gulim stood up.

"This is such bullshit!" His voice was as loud as it'd ever been. "After all this time, that is all you came up with? Don't you know a white guy was just killed? Are you stupid?"

Russler spoke slowly and quietly. "Sit down."

Gulim held his ground. He looked around and saw the disapproving glances, then slowly sat down, shaking his head from side to side.

"We believe there's a leadership battle going on among the supremacist groups. We believe the white man was likely shot as part of that battle. As you know, his name was James Dylan, otherwise known as 'The Exterminator.' We knew him well; his gang was associating with several other similar groups. Some extremely bad ones."

Jack and Jill exchanged a further knowing glance.

"The fact that only Black people had been killed previously gave the murderer some cover for shooting a white guy. And then he could take control of the movement," Russler explained.

"Like the Mafia wars, sounds like," Jack offered up.

"That's right—just like that."

"OK, at least now we have our focus to the investigation," Deputy Tracy said.

"Right," Russler answered, becoming energized. "So for now, let's all think about this, review our evidence with a fresh eye, and then regroup this evening. We can at that point discuss any new findings or theories you all may have." Russler then slapped his hands up and down, making a little clapping sound, signifying the meeting was over.

"Roger that," Tracy said, and everyone nodded their heads as they left the room, a bounce in their step for the first time since they began meeting.

Jill turned to Jack as they were walking out. "Well, at least that eliminates Gloria as a suspect. She's certainly not a white supremacist. She's not the shooter."

Jack nodded. "The FBI has spoken. I'm sure my good friend Doug Russler is right."

118

They started connecting the dots.

Russler met with Jack and Jill back in his small hotel room. He was standing by the window, looking at the dreary evening, while Jill sat on the bed and Jack sat on the desk chair, barely fitting in it. Rain began to fall, pebbling on the window, looking like tears before they rolled down a cheek. Russler told them that with The Exterminator's death, and their theory of a white supremacist as the shooter, they were re-examining all of James Dylan's connections. Apparently, The Exterminator had many; he'd been a very busy man.

"We all know about his connection to Saint," Russler said, "and thankfully he provided you with that intel before the attempted bombing of the church. Wish he was still around, though—would love to question him myself, go deeper into everyone Saint met."

"May he rest in peace," Jill said quietly, looking out the now-obscured window as the rain fell more heavily.

"And we certainly know this guy, Dirk," Jack said, patting his leg where he still had a scar from the stabbing at the United We Stand rally. He and Jill had filled Doug in on how that all went down.

"Yes, but there's another guy we are very interested in," Doug said. "We've learned he was always squabbling with The

Exterminator. The guy's name is Heilbach. Spencer Heilbach. Doesn't look like your standard supremacist; dresses more like he's from Greenwich, Connecticut. But he's a leader, a smart and fierce one it seems. I'm going to tell the rest of the team. You know, he was actually at that same rally where you got hurt."

Jack and Jill looked at each other. Thunder pounded the room; a bolt of lightning cracked through the sky. The storm intensified. It would become a huge deluge.

"Where is he now?" Jack asked.

"Don't know. After that rally, he disappeared. After that girl was killed at her quinceañera party, it looks like everyone took off for parts unknown and they're still lying low. But we'll find him."

"If he's the shooter, I'd love to be the one to find him first," Jack said. Doug and Jill looked at each other, knowing what that meant. Jill shook her head.

"We need to do things by the book, Jack," Russler said. "We are the FBI!"

Jack looked him in the eyes defiantly. "Thought you were with the justice department." He then stood up, his full six-foot-six height looming over them, muscles straining against his tight shirt.

"I can certainly mete out some justice."

119

Heilbach was planning his next move.

He was on the run. Word was out that people were asking about him. Lots of people. Feds and others. He was sick of hearing all the chatter and knew he had to move on. He shook Elizabeth in the middle of the night.

"Not again, honey. We just finished."

"Put some clothes on. Pack your bag. We need to go."

Elizabeth looked at the clock: 3:08 a.m. "Go? Go where? Why?"

"There's been too much chatter lately. My sixth sense tells me they are getting closer. I almost feel like I'm being watched right now."

"Come on, Spencer, honey, please. All we've done is be on the move. Can't we at least wait a couple of days?" She saw the flash of anger in his eyes. "Or at least wait until morning?" She saw him steaming and put a hand on his thigh. "Please?"

He pulled his hand off her, and in one swift motion, hit her across the face with the back of his hand.

The movement and the shock made her slide off the bed. She lay in a heap, a trickle of blood coming down one nostril. She cowered at the side of the bed.

"Don't fuckin' defy me! When I command, you follow! Or you can stay here by yourself, for all I care, you stupid bitch!"

She looked at him with fright and dismay, her body trembling. Her eyes got as puffy as her swelling nose. He could see she was about to whisper something and lifted his hand in the air.

I looked through the scope of my Bushmaster rifle.

The cabin was mostly dark, but there was a full moon providing enough light to make out the figures pretty clearly: definitely Heilbach—no mistaking that body profile—and a woman. As usual, the sight made it easy to target.

The red dot moved from figure to figure. I chuckled as I experimented with putting the dot on different body parts, wondering what would provide me with the most pleasure—and the most pain for Heilbach at the same time. The red dot landed on Heilbach's nuts. I saw Heilbach rear back and hit the woman across the face. I watched as she slipped off the bed. Then saw Heilbach raise his hand again to her.

The woman squeezed her eyes shut.

I squeezed the trigger.

The woman was immediately covered in blood, like a victim of a shark attack. Heilbach's body was falling onto her. I watched as she looked around wildly and then rolled to one side. Heilbach's lifeless body fell on the spot she had just vacated, blood pouring out of his head. She frantically moved her hands all over her own body, apparently trying to see if she was hit. The woman then managed to get up off the floor—after first sliding on a slimy, gray substance. She looked all around and obviously knew she needed to get away from the shattered window. She sprinted out the back door, streaked in blood.

120

There was enough craziness for a year's worth of crazies.

The media went nuts with yet another murder. The public went crazy with both fear and fury against all in charge. The city council met to discuss if Sheriff Klamp was the right person to be in charge of protecting them. And the task force went through its own form of craziness.

"What the fuck!" Klamp yelled. "I thought Heilbach was the killer! Now he's dead?"

"Hey, we were looking for Heilbach; at least we found him," Gil Gulim said cynically.

Earlier, when Doug had first arrived at the shooting, he'd found Heilbach lying face down, with bloody footprints on the hardwood floor leading out the back door. At first, he thought someone must have killed him at close range and then fled.

He spoke with the first officer on the scene, who had immediately called for backup, as well as a search of the area when he saw the footprints heading out. The young officer had viewed the scene, his first visit with death, as if he had entered a house of horrors, and screamed into his radio for the backup, before throwing up his Life cereal.

Unfortunately, when responding to the call for backup, they violated the first rule of a crime scene: arrive safely!

Two of the police cars responding to the call went screaming through town, thrilled for the activity, and hoping to be the savior. Instead, they hit each other at an intersection. One car T-boned the other, sending it spinning out of control, littering the road with assorted, sordid car parts, fluids flowing, the engines steaming and hissing in protest. One car spun toward the side of the road, smashing into the window of a Starbucks, which shattered, littering café lattes and chocolate croissants with shards of glass. Both patrol cars ended up out of commission for weeks—the coffee, just a day.

All this happened unbeknownst to that first officer on the scene, who after emptying his stomach, did the right things. He'd confirmed the victim was dead, scanned the surrounding area for hazards, and secured the crime scene; he knew before long there could be a media frenzy that would have to be contained, and he guarded against contamination.

Soon afterwards, the ME arrived, and the scene was crawling with crime-scene investigators, taking pictures and video, collecting evidence and bagging it, following chain of custody procedures to a tee. There were plenty of fluids to collect: not only blood, sweat, and tears, but what would turn out to be semen, as well as brain matter. Swabbed, bagged, collected in vials, all were carefully preserved.

They searched for hairs, skin particles, and fingernails. Of course, the bloody footprints were of utmost, and most urgent, interest. They looked to be female, or of an older child, and they knew the unique set of ridges would make up a print unmatched by any other person. Of course, fingerprints were also key; adhesive powders were used, the prints photographed and later printed, and specialized lifting tape utilized.

Dawn provided some more light, but they'd brought in extra overhead lights to not miss anything. They even brought in a drone to take some aerial shots of the scene and help search for the person who got away, though dogs—blood-hounds—were fast on the scent.

After Doug got his report from the first officer on scene (with the lousy-smelling breath), he stared at the shattered window, transfixed by the bullet hole surrounded by spidery cracks. He frowned and shook his head, knowing this would be more complicated than initially thought. And crazier.

It wasn't very hard to find Elizabeth.

Didn't need the dogs, didn't need the choppers. Tim was getting his small luncheonette on the side of the road ready to open for the breakfast crowd when a bloody woman burst through the door, running toward him, crying out like she'd escaped from Bellevue. He took a quick step back and reached for his phone. He kept her at bay while connecting to the police, and almost before he could hang up, they were at his door. It was as if they were just down the road when he called. Which they were.

Elizabeth was whisked away and given a shot of diazepam to calm her down. Later, she was cleaned up, given a jump-suit to wear, and the questioning began. Some suggested she be given some time to rest, to further pull herself together, but the counterargument prevailed: that there was no time to lose given this may have been another serial killing. She was Mirandized, then Russler headed up the inquiry.

Elizabeth sat on the hard steel chair, staring down at the cracked red nail polish she wore, which she thought clashed with her orange jumpsuit. It wasn't long before she herself cracked. She told them what happened, though couldn't explain how or why it happened. They continually asked her why she killed him, but she continually denied that she had, clashing with the investigators. All she kept repeating was: "I just wanted to be a good wife. A good, traditional wife." It was like a mantra. Now, she wished she could sleep, crash.

They knew she didn't do it, but pressed on to see what information they could shake loose. Amid the questioning, there was a knock on the door. Russler spoke to someone in the hallway, who whispered in his ear that the ballistic report confirmed the bullets found seemed similar to those used in other killings. Shortly thereafter he learned the key similarity was that 88 was etched into them. Russler knew what it meant and guarded the finding carefully. Preserving the integrity of that unique piece of evidence was paramount to ensuring the apprehension of the right person. Any potential leaks, even accidental ones, posed an unacceptable risk to the investigation.

He decided then to take a break, and left Elizabeth alone to stew, to possibly provoke a breakthrough.

After some time, Russler asked Jack and Jill to join the questioning, to take a different tack to elicit more information on who the shooter could be. Jack was quite the imposing presence, and his venom was more than evident to Elizabeth. She pushed herself back as he got closer.

"We know these killings are all connected, and you know who did it!"

"No way, I have no clue," she stammered.

"Clueless, fucking clueless. Maybe about life. Not about this, missy!"

Elizabeth looked shocked and scared, but just shook her head no, looking down at her toes.

"Who was Heilbach fighting with? Who wanted to take over your shithole group?"

"Well, he did hate The Exterminator."

"He's dead. Who else could it be?" He knew who it could be but wanted to hear it from her.

"I don't know! I swear I don't know!" Elizabeth screamed out with a sob.

Jill stepped in, actually sliding between Jack and Elizabeth after giving him a subtle shove. "OK, easy now, honey. I know you've been through a hell of a lot. The thing is, your life could be in danger from this shooter. We just want to help. You don't want to end up like your man Heilbach."

Elizabeth looked at her, thinking, then starting to nod her head.

Jill continued, "I know you were only doing what you thought was right. So think, honey, just try and think who would want him dead."

They all stared at her without blinking, and could see how hard Elizabeth was trying, could see the wheels slowly turning, like a freight train starting up a hill. She then haltingly mentioned a few names of supremacists she'd met, but clearly wasn't believing they had anything to do with it. Russler took down the names, then gently asked for more.

"That's all I can remember. I'm sorry. That's it," she said, trembling.

Jill held her hand, while Jack stood back over her. "It's for your own good, really it is. Please keep thinking."

"You gotta tell us more," Russler said.

"I just want to go home!" she said.

"You ain't going home, lady. Nobody's going home," Russler said.

121

It was a very strange feeling.

The bar, Morrie's, was raucous. While Jill's core case was the serial-killer search, she'd previously been working on a drug case. That case was finally resolved, and she'd been invited to the bar to celebrate. Jill felt she needed a break, especially after the grueling interrogation of Elizabeth, after yet another killing. She felt something calling to her—perhaps a glass of whiskey if nothing else. She sat at the bar, where the bartender had poured her their favorite: Old Soul Bourbon Whiskey. "It's small batch—just eighty-eight barrels, distilled in Mississippi," he'd said. "It's the real deal. You know, others, they don't make them the way they used to."

Jill took a quick sip, and then a second slower one, savoring the sweet notes of vanilla and muted brown sugar. Its aroma reminded her of her childhood. She then sat staring down at her drink, a wistful expression on her face.

"Hey," the cop sitting next to her said. "This is supposed to be a party. Smile." He was a patrolman who was involved in the takedown, now grinning from ear to ear at having been part of upturning a group of major fentanyl drug dealers. She looked at his name strip—Patrolman Nefesh—then at his smiling face. Couldn't tell his age, probably five to ten years younger than her.

"Can you believe it? We got them! We did it!"

Jill smiled weakly, taking another sip. "Yeah, it's great news," she said, though her voice lacked conviction. Her thoughts were heavy and gray; they were hard to keep at bay. She felt the weight of the world on her shoulders as she sat hunched over. She kept thinking of the darkness of humanity, which just made her heart ache.

Patrolman Nefesh's smile faltered. "What's wrong?" he asked, leaning in, his eyebrows drawing together.

Jill took a deep breath. "I don't know," she said. "I guess sometimes, it just feels like no matter how many of these scumbags we take down, there are always more waiting to take their place. One replacing another, in an endless circle. A circle of death. Are we really making a difference?"

"Wow," he said, blinking, his smile now a frown. He put a comforting hand on her shoulder. "Listen, you can't think like that. You make a difference every day. Every time you put a bad guy away, you make the world a little bit safer. You're one of the good ones. Don't you forget it."

"It's just so hard," she said, her voice barely above a whisper.

"Life *is* hard," he said, placing a hand on hers. "But what counts is the fight. We won this case. Too often, the bad guys win. But what matters, what really matters, is you keep striving, keep fighting. It's the quest that counts."

Jill's eyes were wet. "I'll keep fighting," she said, squeezing his hand.

The patrolman smiled, and said, "That's the spirit! Remember, even when a win seems small, what you do adds up and endures. Things endure."

"You're right, I guess. But I just wish the bad ones would learn their lessons. Not just end up back on the street, same as always."

"They will. Eventually. Not sure how long that takes, but eventually, most everyone learns their lessons."

Jill smiled slightly, feeling a little better. She looked away, suddenly lost in thought. She thought of her dad, who she knew would have said the same type of thing. Jill thought back to that last day, the fun she had as they went through their morning ritual as he dressed.

Jill turned back to the patrolman. His words did seem to carry weight—a weight she couldn't quite comprehend. She looked into his eyes, deeper than would normally feel comfortable, and she felt very close, felt at peace.

"Well, I guess enough celebrating for me," he said. "Got to get home to my wife; she's been feeling a bit down lately. I guess you're not the only one who needs some cheering up," he said with a smile.

He stood up. In a hoarse voice, Jill said, "Let me adjust your tie." She gently fixed it.

"Thanks," he said, and turned to go.

"Don't forget to take out the garbage," Jill said softly.

He turned, a bewildered half-smile on his face. "Right," he said, and then turned back around.

"Your hat," she said, "don't forget that; where would a cop be without his cap!" She grabbed it off the bar. As she was handing it over, she saw a name written inside.

"Wait, you actually put your name in your hat?"

"Indelible ink, baby!"

She looked at the name.

"Here you go, Frank."

122

E lizabeth didn't know what to feel.

Spencer Heilbach dead. She thought of Saint, the other man, a boy really, who'd been in her life of late. Elizabeth hated the fact that Saint had actually squealed, that he'd informed the FBI of their activities; Spencer had been right. *As usual, he was right*, she thought. Yes, she knew she had certainly used Saint. But at the same time, she remembered the anguished look on his face when his mother lay dying. And she certainly remembered the ecstatic look on his face the first time they had sex: his first time ever. The agony and the ecstasy. But in the end, she was happy he was gone, a traitor to her true love, to Spencer.

They hadn't questioned Elizabeth any more that day; apparently, Jack, Doug, and Jill could see she'd more than had it. They figured a night in the jail cell might refresh her memory, that perhaps she'd come up with something better than the small fry on the short list of names she'd provided.

And they'd figured right.

Early the next morning, they were back in the gray shadowed room to start the day of questioning anew. No windows, no sunlight, just gray, steel chairs, gray walls, gray table, and a gray outlook. Elizabeth was still groggy from all that transpired the prior day and hadn't been able to get much sleep.

Her eyes were red, and she could barely keep her heavy lids open. Those around her must have thought her beauty was now very hard to detect.

The detectives went to work; they had brought in breakfast sandwiches, bacon, hash browns and coffee, and the smell made Elizabeth's stomach rumble. She had eaten little yesterday, and suddenly felt ravenous. It perked her up, and she reached out to the bodacious buffet. But by being a bit audacious, she was immediately pushed back, almost taking a tumble.

"Let's talk first," Russler said.

Elizabeth looked longingly at the food, then with a distressed voice, said, "I told you what I knew yesterday."

"That's just not good enough," Jack said.

Jill stepped in. "You did good yesterday, real good, giving us some names."

Elizabeth nodded, her eyes widening with hope.

"But think about it another way. Think about it in terms of who were the leaders of other groups, besides James Dylan, that Spencer communicated with?"

Elizabeth whispered, "Well, there were a bunch of other groups. I can't really remember." She eyed the bacon, and her stomach made another noise.

"Was there someone who Spencer talked about with disdain? I mean, someone he didn't really like, maybe burned some bridges?"

"That coffee might help waken my brain," she said, pointing to the white Styrofoam cup with a plastic lid on it. "Though I don't remember any bridges getting burned. Fire wasn't his thing."

Jack looked at Doug, rolling his eyes.

"OK, honey, you can have that." Jill passed it to her and ignored the dirty look from Jack. "Take a few sips, honey.

Careful not to burn your tongue." Elizabeth blew on it and took a sip; she looked like she was in heaven.

"Oh, the simple pleasures in life," Russler said. "My kingdom for a coffee."

Elizabeth was perplexed.

Jill said, "Now let's try again. Think about someone Spencer met, maybe planning a rally, maybe at a rally. Someone perhaps who was rising in the ranks."

Elizabeth abruptly rose, spilling some of her coffee. "Maybe... maybe... there was this one guy. He was a real jerk. Spencer thought he was bad for the movement. Did stupid stuff. Bad stuff. He had a group with a crazy name. Ugh... wait, I know! 'The Boogaloos.'"

"It's the 'Boogaloo Boys.' Thanks," Jill said.

"And was the guy's name Dirk?" Doug asked.

"Yes, that's right. Dirk."

"Son of a bitch!" Jack roared. "Of course. I knew it!"

123

"Goddamn it!"

Jack and Jill were back in their motel room, needing a break, and pissed off—more at themselves than anything else.

Their motel was a step up from Doug's but felt more like a misstep. If Doug's was a Motel 6, theirs might be a Motel 6½. At least they provided free breakfast, in which the motel certainly lost money feeding Jack—though Jill didn't touch anything. The room had twin beds—not ideal for intertwining. Jack had pushed them together, toppling the plastic lamp over in the process, the bulb shattering—not that it mattered since it didn't work anyway. Jack barely fit in the combined beds. But that was the least of their concerns.

"Dirk, the fucking dirtbag—he is the one!" Jack spat out.

"Well, at least we were on the track. We've been after him and we learned a lot about him."

"Yeah, way more than the FBI! We told Doug about Dirk and he basically ignored us. He was so fixated on Heilbach!" Jack said, grabbing the Gideon Bible and throwing it at the wall, where it left a black mark.

Jill was shaking her head. "Well, he did say to keep all options open. It's our own fault. We should have forced the issue. I guess we figured the FBI knew what they were doing, with all their fancy analysis and vast resources. Dumb! And now yet another dead man!"

"Well, with that guy, with Heilbach, I guess it's not the worst outcome."

"Come on, Jack. You know that's not right."

Jack didn't look convinced.

"And besides, we need to get this killer before he gets someone else."

"That's been the plan," Jack said, spitting the words out.

"Listen, while it looks like Dirk is the one, just like we've been thinking, let's not make the same mistake again assuming that's it, that the mystery is done."

Jack looked at her as if he thought she was crazy. He kicked the nightstand, which rocked, sending Jill's copy of *Life After Life* falling to the floor.

Jill saw Jack was getting revved up, like a rubber band being twisted one time too many. She rubbed his shoulders before going on. "I know how you feel, Jack. And I'm as much to blame for not pushing it further with Russler. In fact, Russler's talk of killing animals made me think of Dirk. Damn guy started by slaying cats as a teen—probably graduated to murdering Saint's dad Skyler in college. And now he's killing those he hates, and whoever's in his way!"

Jack nodded briskly, his face red. "But how stupid was I? He stabbed me at the United We Stand rally! Not only that, but I'd seen Dirk, with his goddamn smirk, through binoculars getting ready for that rally earlier. Armed to the teeth! In fact, The Exterminator was there too—damn truck with a confederate flag emblem being filled up with sharpened flagpoles and all sorts of shit. Tons of ammunition. Boxes and boxes of bullets. Dirk's got to be our man."

"Well," Jill said, "at least with a full team focused now, his days are surely numbered. He's been a thorn in our side for too long."

"Time to get the tweezers," Jack said. "Or better yet, a machete."

124

Dirk wasn't going to be found.

    Ever since the killing of the girl at her quinceañera party, he'd been the master of evasion. He knew where and how to lie low, knew how to bide his time and be patient before eventually taking over leadership of the movement. Dirk considered it his movement and would not let those he thought of as bungling idiots stand in his way.

He'd gone underground, like a mole in its hole, but stayed close. He was around, but hidden, like a snake whose coloring provides camouflage.

He sat in his hole, petting the barrel of his Bushmaster XM-15 automatic rifle as if it were a favored pet.

"Tunnel vision can kill you."

Those were the concluding words from Russler as the task force meeting broke up. Everyone at the meeting thought they were in the last seconds of the game, about to end the killer's streak, take the win, and head home. Obviously, Russler too thought they were close. They'd used their profiling to characterize the type of killer they were likely dealing with, and now they'd identified him, Dirk, after a false start going after Spencer Heilbach.

There was a good feeling about where they were now in the chase: the home stretch. And apparently, that's exactly why Russler warned them to continue to pursue any other leads, not to get complacent, not to focus only on Dirk, because tunnel vision could kill you—and lead to others becoming victims.

Jill looked like she was listening with rapt attention. Jack listened with no attention. Or rather he heard but didn't listen. All he could think of was Dirk and prior encounters, images swirling through his mind, on an endless loop that he couldn't stop. For Jack, it had become way too personal. He knew Dirk was evil, was a devil, and was behind all of this. Dirk Devil. Jack would make it his job to end the evil.

Jill now wasn't as sure. She had hope, high hopes, that it was nearing an end. She thought about all that had transpired, even back to when she was first on patrol, then spending her own off-hours investigating, eventually teaming up with Jack. In the beginning, she'd been optimistic, full of energy and enthusiasm, thinking she could help rid her community of a few bad apples and all would be good. She'd had her father Frank as an example of a dedicated hero, which kept her going.

While the years had worn on her, her sense of wariness was intact. She knew Dirk was evil, but her instincts told her he may not be the only evil lurking about.

The shooter closed in on the prey.

125

They were on his trail.

They'd figured out Dirk was likely hiding somewhere in the surrounding woods, where some of the shots were fired from, or hiding within the anonymity of the city. They'd uncovered some information that narrowed it down a bit, and decided to separate. The air was thick with anticipation as they planned for Jack to search the labyrinthine streets of a small section of the city; Jill, an area of woods off the hillside.

Jack vanished into the urban darkness. The city's heartbeat pulsed through its streets, a rhythm that echoed with the energy of a thousand lives.

Jill headed out, determination coursing through her veins, adrenaline fueling every step. She followed the trail of breadcrumbs, her senses attuned to the smallest details. She was right on his tail, one arm in a sling, gun at the ready in the other.

She ascended a hill, drawn by an invisible force that urged her forward. As she reached the summit, her heart skipped a beat. There, standing in solitude against the vast expanse, was Dirk himself. Jill's pulse quickened. Victory seemed within her grasp. She approached, her footsteps barely audible on the grass. But just as she closed in on Dirk, the tranquility of the night shattered into chaos.

*

No one expected it.

Dirk had had his semi-automatic rifle in hand, rifling through his pack for just the right bullets. He was set to go; his time was at hand.

He was not expecting the hail of bullets that surrounded him like a raging blizzard the minute he stood up. Jill stared wide-eyed, shocked, her gun hanging loosely by her side as the bullets sprayed all around him. Dirk couldn't tell where they were coming from. It was like a whiteout. And then he was wiped out.

In under a minute, over thirty bullets spit out around him, most hitting him. His body jumped and spun in the air, cartwheeled, and went tumbling down the hillside. The bullet holes made much of Dirk's body end up looking like a wasp nest when the season was over, devoid of anything living within.

The police on the scene had not been expecting what they found.

Doug Russler had not been expecting Dirk to have been on the wrong side of the scope.

The entire task force was not expecting this, and now had lost all faith in Russler.

Jill had not been expecting this result. She wondered where Jack was.

And now no one expected this to end anytime soon.

126

Russler disclosed a new piece of information that only caused more confusion, consternation, and chaos.

"Ballistics confirmed that some of these bullets had the numbers *88* etched on them."

"What the hell does that mean?" Klamp shouted out.

"The *88* stands for *Heil Hitler*. We found that etched in bullets from past shootings."

Jack and Jill looked at each other. Everyone else went ballistic.

"What the fuck? You never told us that!" Gil cried out. He started moving forward toward Russler, his face a frightening fury. Jack stepped in, almost having to tackle him.

"Keepin' shit from us? What in hell happened to all yer fancy talk 'bout bein' a team?" Klamp yelled out, heading over to where Gil was being held back.

"What does that *88* mean? That the killer is definitely a white supremacist. That we were on the right path, just the wrong men?" Tracy called out, trying to be heard above the din.

Russler's booming voice rose up above the uproar, quieting the crowd for a moment, though they didn't sit down. "OK, I know you're all pissed. But everyone has to calm down. We still have a killer on the loose that we have to find—and yes, find as a team."

"What are you, Russler, the reincarnation of Nixon, keeping secrets?" someone yelled.

"There are reasons we couldn't divulge the 88 etching, not the least because we couldn't afford leaks, and we couldn't afford more copycat killers. We need to know we have the actual killer."

"You mean like The Exterminator? Or you mean like Heilbach? Oh no, you must mean Dirk!" Gil said, his voice dripping in sarcasm. Some in the room snickered; others waited for Doug to blow up.

Klamp added, "Nah, he must think the killa is Ted Bundy, come back to life, hah!"

"Listen, now that our prime suspect, Dirk, is dead, we need to regroup and figure it out. The key is to remain calm and remain a team," Russler said, looking pained. Many of the others looked disgusted. Some looked hopeless, as if they'd spent their last dollar on a losing lottery ticket. Russler straightened himself up. "And remember, I'd said to keep your eyes open, and not to one hundred percent assume it was him."

Jill stood up. "We need to tell you something." She looked to Jack for reassurance, who nodded. Everyone stared at her. It became as quiet as a library reading room. "We've seen bullets with 88 etched on them."

The quiet was immediately shattered, like a crystal vase hitting a marble floor. Some sat with their mouths agape, others just shouting "What?!" in a shocked tone.

Klamp yelled angrily to her. "What da fuck! Is everyone hidin' somethin'? So much for a fuckin' team. Who else is holding back on us? Huh?"

Russler's jaw was tight, and he looked back and forth between Jack and Jill, and curtly said, "Go on."

Jack stood up alongside Jill. "We meant to. It's just every

time we were about to, something else became the priority and got in the way."

"This is such bullshit!" Gil interjected.

Jack continued, "And based on where we found the bullets, we didn't really know that it mattered. But, Doug, if you had been square with us and told us from the start about the *88*, we could've avoided all this."

"Where the hell did you come across bullets with *88* on them?" Russler demanded.

Jill looked at Jack, then around the room, then stared into Russler's eyes.

"At Gloria's house."

The task force erupted.

"Gloria!" yelled Tracy Dixon. "What the hell?"

All Jack and Jill could do was look down and shake their heads.

Russler immediately called for investigation, and the hordes went flying out, like reporters rushing out to get the story when vital news came in. Most of them headed to Gloria's place.

But Gloria wasn't home.

127

It didn't take long to figure out what was going on.

The news was all over, though the shooter knew it wasn't over; the chase was on. Knew what house was being targeted, and where the search would go from there.

Gloria had left in a hurry, heading out to the woods, a refuge she'd come to know quite well. As always, she had her gun, knowing that trouble lay ahead.

Ahead of the pack out of the police station were Jack and Jill, as they'd known exactly where to go. In the car on the way there, Jack said, "At least we're *finally* gonna end this thing."

"Jesus," Jill said, "it's taking longer to find the true killer than the search for the Dalai Lama."

"Huh?"

"You know, whenever the Dalai Lama dies, a search begins for his reincarnation; they look for signs among the children, test them. Then the child that passes the tests becomes the new Dalai Lama."

"Fine time to be showing off. But… hey, how do you know so much about that?"

"Loved the Dalai Lama's book, *The Art of Happiness*. Read up a little about the beliefs."

"Happiness? Thought you found it with me."

"That's life, my man. It's all about the pursuit."

They continued their pursuit. Jack pushed down hard on the accelerator, and their conversation switched gears. They talked about the bullets with 88 scratched into them.

"We tried to tell Doug about them before, dammit!" Jack said.

Jill took a deep breath. "That's not the only time 88 bullets have been a secret," she replied, giving him a side glance. "How about those bullets that fell out of your pants? You said they were all from Gloria's. I know one was. Not the rest."

Jack looked like a baseball player picked off of first base. He then turned a cold eye to her.

"OK, Jill, I confess."

128

"Confess?" Jill said, holding her breath.

"Yes."

Jack slowed the car. Jill's body stiffened; her eyes blinked rapidly as she looked back at him.

"Keep going! We don't have time!"

"This is important."

Jill's breath quickened. Jack leaned over to her. Jill's mind raced with thoughts of what she might have to do next.

"Confess. That's right. I should have been open with you. I found those bullets in Saint's closet. I held on to them because I wanted to figure out the connection, what it meant. Provide the answer. I hadn't told you right away, because... well, because, I guess, I wanted to be the super sleuth, the hero."

Jill let out a huge breath. But then her eyes lit with fire. "A hero? Give me a break! You and your ego. You really still need to look like a hero to everyone, big man?!" She'd spat out those last few words.

"Not a hero to everyone. A hero to you."

Jill looked back at him, knitting her eyebrows, her head canted to one side.

"I wanted to tell you about the bullets. So many times. But I so wanted to figure it out. I so wanted to show you what I still could do."

"Huh?"

Jack stopped the car. He faced her and looked into her eyes. He grabbed her, shook her slightly, while he himself was trembling.

"I wanted to impress you! To be your hero! To figure it out, so you'd be proud of me." Jack let her arms go, his shoulders slumped. "I guess my desire to… to make you love me more… clouded my judgment."

"You darling dummy! You don't need to do that for me to love you. I love you with all my soul already. Goddamn."

"I'm sorry."

Jill hugged him. "Just don't ever withhold anything from me again."

"I won't. I guess I'm not perfect, no matter how much I thought I was!"

"That's for damn sure," Jill said. She smiled at him. "Well, I guess not too many of us are perfect."

Jack turned the ignition. "At least I've learned a big lesson. I guess that's what life's all about."

"Let's go! And I do hope you've learned it now; there may not be another chance."

"Yeah, gotta learn my lessons before I'm dead and gone."

"Certainly before I kill you," Jill said.

Their stop at Gloria's house was short; it was immediately evident she wasn't home. The rain the night before left tire tracks in the mud, which they quickly followed. The tracks stopped at the edge of the deeper woods, where they saw her car.

Jack and Jill slowly approached it, concerned they would be the next to get shot.

The driver's side door was ajar. They looked around, not

knowing if someone was behind it, or ahead watching from the woods.

They each headed to opposite sides of the car. They looked at each other with frightened eyes—not for themselves, but for their other half.

On an almost telepathic count of three, leading with their guns, they charged forward. Jack pulled the door fully open with a screech, mimicking the birds up above.

Gloria wasn't there.

But now they were even more concerned, knowing they were an open target, easily marked with a sight from an automatic weapon.

At the same time that they looked around for shelter, a van containing search dogs pulled up. They directed the dogs to the car, where they took up the scent, and took off. Jack and Jill decided to take a chance and go out into the open, and started chasing as well. The image of when she got shot back at the auto body shop flashed through Jill's mind: the instant jolt of agony, the shockwaves it had sent through her body. Filled with determination, she thought to herself, I'm not going to be the one to get shot this time!

It didn't take long for the dogs to find Gloria. She was terrified of their bellicose barking, snarling, and long, sharp canines. She'd never liked dogs, and now feared the bites that were coming; she could foresee her skin being torn apart, mangled by the mongrels.

Gloria at first was frozen. But then, petrified at what would occur, she hesitantly pointed her gun at the approaching German shepherds.

The K9 officer must have had an itchy trigger finger. He apparently didn't want to take any chances that his beloved dogs, animals he probably loved more than anything in his life, would get hurt.

As Gloria aimed at the dogs for her own protection, the officer shot her.

Shots rang out from another place!

The officer was nicked and ran to take cover. Gloria was still down. Jack and Jill returned fire to the direction the shots were coming from.

The shooter came out of hiding, sprinting toward Gloria. Bullets sprayed about, pockets of earth flying up. As the shooter was about to reach Gloria, one of Jill's bullets found its mark, striking the shooter in the heart. He fell atop Gloria.

Suddenly, all was quiet, like the silence on a battlefield after the combat concluded, emptied of all except its dead.

Both of them lay dying, Gloria and the shooter. Gloria, with her last ounce of strength, cradled him by her side, so tight against each other, becoming as one, curled in a position like an embryo in the womb.

Jack and Jill rushed over to see if they could help, knowing they were no longer in danger. The dying man seemed to softly mouth "*Momma?*"

The terminal death rattle occurred simultaneously for the two on the earth, the finale of killing concluded. Their final breaths expelled outwards and upwards, like the embers from a campfire, elevating to parts unknown.

Jack slowly and carefully turned the body fully over to see who the red-haired shooter was, knowing now that Gloria wasn't the killer. Jack looked at the face of the shooter, and he saw the most serene smile he'd ever seen on anyone.

Jill gasped, as if she'd seen a ghost.

It was Saint!

129

Without a sole survivor, it took a while before all the sordid details were sorted out. Almost all.

Obviously, Saint hadn't died before, just disappeared—and that's why his body had never been found. Through the ensuing investigation, including diary notes, it appeared that he had backed out of the idea of drowning himself, backing out of the water. Instead, still a wreck, he went to Gloria, seeking advice. He'd realized he wanted to live, to do some good in the world to honor his dead parents, not join them. He'd learned a lot and desperately desired a chance to start over again.

Still afraid of the FBI, he often met with Gloria in the secluded woods. To protect him, she monitored police communications on a police scanner, just in case. She'd learned a lot in prison. On that last day, she knew the police were coming, then heard the sirens in the distance. She'd grabbed her gun just in case, and taken off to warn Saint, to help him escape. She'd almost succeeded.

Saint had known the woods quite well. It was there that he had often practiced his shooting, after first learning from the Very Fine Men. The Exterminator, in fact, had given him the rifle. He had a supply of bullets he'd stolen from Dirk and the Boogaloo Boys, bullets with 88 etched on them. But the truth was, he knew down deep inside that he really couldn't shoot anyone if it came down to it. He just didn't think he had it in him.

Saint was the most surprised of all when he shot Dirk to death.

Turns out, Jack and Jill were right about Dirk, who left behind a half-written manifesto. He'd shot Heilbach in a fight for leadership—and simply because he didn't like him. Pleasingly balancing, as if ordained by the gods, it was Heilbach who had shot The Exterminator, also in a battle for leadership. And simply because he didn't like him.

The FBI was able to trace the Ponderosa Steakhouse killing back to Dirk; apparently, he'd loved the headlines of a "KKK Killer" and thought he'd take advantage of them. The first killing, the "pastor" on that empty road, was a fluke. He'd been practicing his shooting at a tree stump when he heard a scream. Thought the man made for much better practice. Same thing happened at the Gulf station, taking out the carjacker. Dirk considered himself very lucky.

"Ironic," Jack said. "That those evil men were taken down by their own bullets, by their nazi 88 slugs."

"Well, I guess," Jill said, "what goes around…"

"Comes around," replied Jack, a half-smile forming.

"And of course, it's great the town took that Klamp out of his role," Jill said.

"For sure. I think Tracy will make an excellent sheriff. She'll definitely prove herself on the job, and keep the job with the next election," Jack said.

"Well, it's just about time to get on to the next case," Jill said. "As Patrolman Frank Jarred would say, 'Time to stop some more bad guys.'"

"Right, Jack and Jill, on the case. Jack and Jill, forever."

★

The puzzling thing was Dirk's death. Jack and Jill discussed it again once the full investigation had been concluded. It was difficult to unearth.

"I still don't get it—don't get Saint shooting Dirk," Jill said.

"What's so hard to get? Remember, he told us that when he first laid eyes on Dirk, it was hate at first sight."

"You don't shoot someone because of first impressions, Jack; otherwise you would have been dead that first day at the academy!"

"Very funny, Jill. But to tell you the truth, it *is* hard to understand. Saint knew nothing about the suspicions that Dirk killed his father Skyler way back in college. Didn't know about anything Dirk did to Deja. And we thought we knew Saint. Hell, he helped us, and took a lot of risks giving us the intel on those damn supremacists."

"Agree. And we probably had him take too many risks." Jill said. "Think we may want to learn from that, Jack."

"Right," Jack said. "But again, Saint didn't really seem like a bad guy: just confused and conflicted. Lonely."

"Innocent almost. But with a lot to learn," Jill said.

"But Saint shooting a man, ripping him to shreds with bullets the way he did, I don't think even I could do that. At least not anymore."

Jill looked away, a small smile on her face.

"Agree. We both knew Saint wasn't a bad guy at heart. Got involved with some hellish dudes while trying to feel like he belonged to something. Got pressured to go along with some terrible stuff, but that truly wasn't him. He was really a good kid."

"Yup. Saint *was* basically a good guy. What we learned from Deja about him really does support that. And while working with us, he sure helped a lot of people."

"That's right," Jill said, nodding her head. "He actually helped save a church full of people!"

"That he did."

"He was actually a gentle soul, when you think about it," Jill said, her eyes clouding.

"Then why did he kill another man? Why did he shoot Dirk? Proactively hunting him down, shooting him down. Sure, Dirk was evil, but there doesn't seem to be any good reason for Saint to have been the one to have gone after him, to have violently taken another life. That would've been for the courts to decide—for the ultimate judge to decide," Jack said.

Jill shook her head slowly side to side, lost in thought. "Way out of character... just doesn't make any sense."

"Well, maybe there was something else deep inside of him we couldn't detect," Jack said.

"Maybe. I guess we'll never know. Guess he's taken it to the grave with him."

FINALE

Perennial

The light was blinding.

At first, it was a prism of the most amazing colors. Colors that were both deep and delicate, with depth and dimension. Then Saint's eyes adjusted to it, or it adjusted to him, and it became the purest white light he had ever experienced. In fact, it was nothing like he'd ever experienced, at least during his lifetime. It surrounded him yet seemed to emanate from a distance. He headed toward it.

He felt a presence, warm and loving. There were people standing on both sides of him as he walked forward, like a bride or groom on the way to the altar, surrounded by friendly and welcoming well-wishers. They were patting him on the arms, on his shoulders, beatific smiles adorning their faces, encouraging him forward. He didn't know them, just knew they loved him. And he felt he loved them. His mind was being suffused with love, almost overcome with it.

Messages meandered through his mind, telling him he had been a good son, a good man: a man who had learned much, and had no reason to be afraid. Saint was confused, didn't understand how he could be assessed as good.

The light grew brighter, and he felt caressed by it.

He heard the sound of giggling.

"Momma?"

Ahead was Deja, ecstatic to see him. Saint's smile became so serene. They rushed to meet each other, as if floating on air. She couldn't stop kissing him, mussing up his red hair as he held her tight. He didn't want to ever let go.

"My son," she said, "I've been waiting."

She was reluctant to put any distance in their embrace, but finally held him in front of her so they could talk face to face. "There are others who have been waiting too. Longer than I. People who are a part of you, who came before you, made you what you are. Continue to make you."

Saint didn't understand but was entranced.

As she held him, she kissed him, and deeply breathing in, as if resuscitating an unconscious man, drew some energy from within him. She slowly exhaled, and the energy, a piece of his soul, danced in front of them, a twinkling speck that was soon an orb of brilliant light. Deja beamed in delight, like an astronaut in orbit seeing the Earth from space for the very first time. Saint stood transfixed in his space, as he watched the orb take on a physical shape.

"Father?" Saint whispered.

"My son," Skyler said, embracing him.

Saint had never seen him, only in pictures. Skyler looked the same as he had in college before Saint was born, a picture of health and vitality. Saint began to cry.

"No tears," Deja said, though tears were streaming down her cheeks as well. The three of them embraced, becoming the young family they had never gotten a chance to be.

"Deja's right—no time for tears. We should be happy with all we've learned, how we've evolved, and happy we are together now," Skyler said.

"Dad?"

"Yes, my son."

"I'm sorry. Sorry for all I've done. Sorry I couldn't make you proud."

"Don't be sorry, my son. You've made me proud... all the time."

Saint looked at him, tears in his eyes.

Deja had not seen Skyler since he was killed; his soul had immediately gone back to Earth.

His soul had reincarnated as Saint.

This was the first chance Deja and Skyler had to reunite after death.

Skyler and Deja turned to each other simultaneously. The love they shared, for too short a time, they now knew was there for eternity. They would be together, forever. They hugged, and cried, and kissed, and wished they could stay just like this, in eternal bliss.

Saint was so happy, yet so perplexed. "I'm so confused! You mean, I'm not just me? I was someone else before? I was reincarnated from my dad when he died? Huh?"

Deja giggled. Her girlish giggle was back.

"Yes, that's right," she said. "You got it! Your soul, Skyler's soul, came back to Earth in you. It does take some getting used to! And I guess that's why you always hated the water: Skyler drowning. But yes, you, Skyler: one soul, that will now be with the loving souls around you for eternity."

At that moment, a light brighter than all before surrounded them. It was intense, and they shielded their eyes at first. Saint had no clue what was happening. The others clearly knew and stepped back.

The light swirled in place, and soon a woman with a tiara on her head stood in the middle of them. Not really a woman. A fifteen-year-old girl. A fifteen-year-old with a puffy, red dress, dusty rose lipstick, and brown curls bouncing lightly on her bare shoulders. The tiara was for her quinceañera, and her name was Karmen.

She welcomed Saint, smiled at Deja. "Many of us stay for eternity, that is true," she said. "It's only recently that I received that honor myself, after living and learning through hundreds of lives. But some of us need to go back, to complete their mission."

The others nodded solemnly. Karmen went on. "This may be difficult. Let me try to explain," she said, looking at Saint. Karmen approached Saint, moved his hair aside, and kissed him on the side of his head. The brown birthmark on the side of his head was beneath her lips, the same spot where Dirk had slammed Skyler with the branch. The mark from the bark.

"Once back here," Karmen continued, "everyone thought Skyler would finally stay in heaven. He almost did too. But everyone was wrong. He still had more to learn."

"And so Skyler came back as Saint," Deja reiterated.

"That's right," Karmen said. "That's right."

Saint was still a little confused. "I guess I get it, but at the same time, I don't really. Is this some kind of crazy dream?!"

Karmen smiled and gazed into his eyes, the windows of the soul. She bored directly into them, as if shining a light of enlightenment. The light dazzled him; he felt dazed, as if he may fall, and was half crazed.

"You're not dreaming, and you're not crazy. You're just Saint, but more than just Saint. You contain the spirit of many before you."

"So I really was Skyler? Who then became... me?"

"Yes. And you were many more before that," answered Karmen. "You don't just die. You're not like an annual flower that blooms but once, and once it's gone, it's gone. No, you are a Perennial. You are a soul that doesn't die, but comes back again and again, learning and evolving."

All were looking on lovingly.

"I guess I get it. Maybe," Saint said.

"Saint, all of this is so new to you. You'll have time to adjust, to understand."

Everyone looked incredibly happy as Karmen said that. But their smiles changed when she added, "After some time back on Earth."

"No!" Deja screamed. "He's learned so much. He's done good."

"No," Saint said, "I'm not good. I killed a man."

Deja yelled out, "You saved people! Remember Jose and Rosa, and Juanito, in the small basement apartment. The smoke! You saved them!"

Deja looked back and forth between Karmen and Saint.

"And the church!" she exclaimed. "How many people you saved at the church! They would have been obliterated by that bomb! You're a savior!"

"I'm a killer," Saint said glumly.

"Please, please," Deja said, looking desperate.

Karmen looked back at Deja, shaking her head, gently saying, "You know it's wrong. You know we can't take a life."

"But he knows it was wrong! He regrets it. He regrets it! Can't he stay? Can't you see he's now learned his lesson?"?

"Lessons are for learning on Earth. He deliberately went after that man, that Dirk. It was no accident, no mistake."

Skyler jumped in. "That killing wasn't done by him. It was done by the part that was me: my revenge. Revenge for Dirk murdering me! Revenge for what he did to Deja! Yes, Saint hated him from the moment he saw him—indeed, hate at first sight. It was deep in his soul, where I reside, that Saint knew Dirk was evil. But that enmity was me. That killer was me. Not Saint!"

"I understand, my dear Skyler. But putting the blame that way does nothing," Karmen responded. "Skyler, you know you are all one soul, one soul that still needs reckoning," she continued. "Not punishing, but circling back to complete the learning, to grow and fulfill *all* of your soul's potential."

They still looked aggrieved. Deja tried one more time. "But Dirk was evil! And influenced many others to do evil! Can't Saint help rid the world of evil?" Deja wanted so badly for her soul mate to stay with her.

"Not his job, sorry. You know that."

"Karmen's right," Saint said. "I'll never be a saint. I've made a mockery of my name. Even if there was a reason for the murder because of a past life, I'm still a killer."

"No one is asking you to be a saint," Karmen said. "You do not have to be as good as the higher saints. You just have to be as good as you can be. Fulfill all of your potential."

Saint nodded, as did those around him. "I must go back," he said.

"Thank you for understanding," Karmen said. "That's the first step. You killed a man, so you need to go back to learn to become a better person before you can stay here. You seem clear now that what goes around comes around."

Deja slowly went over to Saint and hugged him one more time. She let out a nervous giggle through her tears as she touched his face.

"Then we'll see you again. Later."

The energy that had manifested itself as Skyler now changed. Its physical being faded, like an old picture left in the sun, or a memory of a forgotten one. The spirit slowly and silently slid back into Saint, fusing together, back as one soul. Complete, though incomplete in learning.

Saint headed out, following another path of light.

His last thought was that he'd remember this day, the day he died, for the rest of his life.

Epilogue

Jack and Jill leaned down in the dirt, on their knees, staring at the dead bodies of Gloria and Saint. Jill was crying; she just couldn't understand any of it. She felt they'd achieved their mission but failed in their mission at the same time.

"Gloria, Saint. The others. All these years. And now this ending. I can't make any sense out of it. All the death. I just don't get it," Jill lamented. Her shoulders slumped.

"Hey, we done good," Jack said. "We had our successes— hell, saved a church full of good people. And because of the pressure we put on, all the bad guys were on the run. So many of those bad guys, due to us, are now in prison or dead."

"I don't think Saint was a bad guy. Or Gloria, really," Jill said. "But you're right, there is some celebration in that those evil supremacist leaders—The Exterminator, Heilbach, and Dirk—are dead."

Jill then whispered, placing a hand on each body, "I just hope that at least now Saint and Gloria can find some peace."

"Well, I guess Saint must have had his reason to suddenly become a killer. Maybe an avenging angel? Who knows? Don't know that he'll make it to heaven, though. If there is such a place," Jack said, looking dubious.

"I do hope somehow, his soul is up there. Left this broken

body at death," Jill said, touching Saint's lifeless arm. "Left the body and soared up to meet his maker."

And if your soul can fly up to heaven after you die, who's to say it can't just do the same thing and come back down.

He saw the light and longed for it. He'd do anything to get back to it. Then he felt himself being pushed toward it.

With a sudden and surprising quickness, the blinding white light surrounded him, invaded his being, down to his soul.

The lights of the delivery room were way too bright for his little eyes as he popped out. He had a very slight birthmark on the side of his head, near where a small tuft of reddish hair was sprouting, and a somewhat darker birthmark on his chest, mimicking a scar from a bullet to the heart. As he was put in his mother's arms, it appeared as if a smile as sweet and content as a yogi in the midst of meditation was on his baby face.

His mother giggled in delight.

"Nice to see you again," she said.

Acknowledgements

THANKS TO the pros who helped me: FBI agent George Burttram and his valiant wife Jan, Detective and Chief of Police Lew Perry, and Detective Courtney Zak. These are the genuine heroes who protect us every day. Any errors in the text are mine exclusively.

Thanks to my early readers, including Stephen Hinkle, Debbie Simmons and Stacy Kerrigan. Without your wise words and encouragement, this would never be. And of course, my earliest readers, my family, whose insights were incredible.

Thanks to my super agent, Danny Baror. The ties that bind will last forever.

Thanks so much to my initial editor, Lou Aronica, who set me on the path, and to my editors at Head of Zeus: editors, assistant editors, copy editors, proofers. Thank God for good editors! And of course, to my publisher, Nic Cheetham, who made the dream come true.

Finally, thanks so much to my entire family—close in and extended—forever with me.

I thank you all. As you know, what goes around comes around!

About the Author

MICHAEL WENDROFF is a global marketing consultant, and now, an author.

Michael comes from a bit of a publishing background. While now deceased, his mother was an editor at Dell Publishing and President of Belmont Books—one of the first female senior executives in the publishing industry. His stepfather, Henry Morrison, also deceased, was a literary agent to many best-selling authors, and a true force of nature. A stay in Robert Ludlum's house was an inspiration to Michael, as he watched Bob write every morning for three hours on yellow legal pads. Thankfully, Michael has a PC to type on.

Michael received his MBA degree from New York University. He also received his undergraduate degree from NYU, where he was inducted into their Hall of Fame. Besides writing, he enjoys tennis, boating, and traveling. He is married with three children.

Fun fact: his great-grandfather was brought over from the University of Copenhagen, Denmark, to work with Thomas Edison in his New Jersey labs. He obtained a number of patents, including for the invention of plastic buttons—in fact, newspapers called him "The Button King." Michael proudly wears button-down shirts whenever he can.